Piers Anthony was born in Oxford in 1934, moved with his family to Spain in 1939 and then to the USA in 1940, after his father was expelled from Spain by the Franco regime. He became a citizen of the US in 1958, and before devoting himself to full-time writing, worked as a technical writer for a communications company and taught English. He started publishing short stories with *Possible to Rue* for *Fantastic* in 1963, and published in SF magazines for the next decade. He has, however, concentrated more and more on writing novels.

Author of the brilliant, widely acclaimed *Cluster* series, and the superb *Incarnations of Immortality* series, he has made a name for himself as a writer of original, inventive stories whose imaginative, mind-twisting style is full of extraordinary, often poetic images and flights of cosmic fancy.

D0727064

By the same author

Chthon
Omnivore
The Ring (with Robert E. Margroff)
Sos the Rope
Var the Stick
Neq the Sword
Macroscope
The E.S.P. Worm (with Robert E. Margroff)
Orn
Prostho Plus
Race Against Time
Rings of Ice
Triple Detente
Phthor
Ox
Steppe
Hasan
A Spell for Chameleon
Vicinity Cluster
Chaining the Lady
Kirlian Quest
Thousandstar
God of Tarot
Vision of Tarot
Faith of Tarot
Split Infinity
Blue Adept
Juxtaposition
Bio of a Space Tyrant Volume 1: Refugee
Bio of a Space Tyrant Volume 2: Mercenary
Bio of a Space Tyrant Volume 3: Politician
Bio of a Space Tyrant Volume 4: Executive
Bio of a Space Tyrant Volume 5: Statesman
Incarnations of Immortality 1: On a Pale Horse
Incarnations of Immortality 2: Bearing an Hourglass
Incarnations of Immortality 3: With a Tangled Skein
Incarnations of Immortality 4: Wielding a Red Sword
Incarnations of Immortality 5: Being a Green Mother
Incarnations of Immortality 6: For Love of Evil
Anthonology
Shade of the Tree
Ghost

PIERS ANTHONY

Viscous Circle

GRAFTON BOOKS

A Division of the Collins Publishing Group

LONDON GLASGOW
TORONTO SYDNEY AUCKLAND

Grafton Books
A Division of the Collins Publishing Group
8 Grafton Street, London W1X 3LA

Published by Grafton Books 1984
Reprinted 1986, 1990

ISBN 0-586-05981-4

Printed and bound in Great Britain by
Collins, Glasgow

Set in Times

Contents

Prologue

Three million years ago a galaxy-spanning civilization vanished, leaving only scattered evidences of its operations, in the form of derelict Ancient Sites and a strange pattern of surviving species. Some Sites are merely huge earthworks, long eroded and overrun by vegetation and development; others contain valuable artefacts of intense interest to scholars and technicians; and some few are 'live' with operative equipment, sometimes self-animating. All contemporary cultures of the known universe eagerly seek such Sites within their spheres of influence, as the technology of the Ancients was beyond anything known today.

For example, all cultures now suffer from Spherical Regression, being unable to maintain an advanced level of civilization at their perimeters. This represents an inherent limit on their expansion, and is thus a considerable annoyance. The Ancients seem not to have suffered this regression; they had some secret that enabled them to maintain their civilization at its optimum level throughout its entire region. Thus the discovery of a functioning Ancient Site is generally the signal for a mad intercultural scramble, in which the usual restraints of civilization hardly apply. Yet often the effects of such discoveries are other than anticipated, and have galaxy- or cluster-spanning ramifications.

Many of the technological innovations that have transformed contemporary interspecies society derive from the knowledge of the Ancients as discovered in their Sites. Two of the three major systems of transport and communication are examples: Mattermission and Transfer. Mattermission is the virtually instantaneous transmission of objects and creatures across interplanetary and interstellar distances. However, this mode is so expensive in energy that it can only be used on special occasions. Unrestricted use would result in the deterioration of the substance of the galaxy in that vicinity, as the binding atomic forces weaken. That is not healthy.

Transfer is the artificial shifting of the aura, or soul – which includes personal identity, consciousness, and memory – from one person to the body, or 'host', of another. This system uses approximately one millionth the energy of Mattermission and automatically equips the Transferee with the language and background of the host, even when that host is a completely alien creature. With Transfer, interspecies commerce is feasible, and larger Spheres of Influence are practical. Empires can be formed and maintained.

An entire framework of Transfer has been developed, with many specialists. The Society of Hosts assumes responsibility for the welfare of hosts temporarily deprived of their auras. Its motto derives from Kipling: 'Lord God of Hosts, be with us yet,/Lest we forget – lest we forget!' The Transferee who forgets his origin will fade into nonexistence. The military has trained people with intense auras to be transfer agents, who transfer to hosts among the cultures being spied on. The work is dangerous, since if the alien host dies before the mission is concluded, the visiting aura dies with it. But this is a notorious, dashing sort of employment with unique rewards. Many seek it; few achieve it.

This is the story of one such agent.

CHAPTER 1

Mission

Ronald Snowden launched himself into the tube with his customary verve and plunged like a cannonball through the rocky heart of the planetoid. Some termed these orbiting chunks of material asteroids, he thought, but that was wrong; they were not small stars, but small planets. As such they had become quite useful to man, serving as way stations and isolated training camps and mines for assorted substances. Why, even gravel for concrete would be prohibitively expensive if lifted by the ton from the surface of a full planet! In a planetoid belt, gravel was cheap; one had only to seine it from space and float it to the construction site.

Ronald was a grown Solarian male verging on the nether side of prime, but at the moment he was like a boy, com- plete with the tousling brown hair and self-satisfied grin. He narrowed his gaze to make the details of the travel tube blur, and thought of himself as a zooming rocket.

When he came to the residential region, he caught hold of a bar and swung himself into the crosstube with the neatness of fine muscle tone and experience. He enjoyed token gravity and hated to return to full weight. But that was a necessary evil; if he ever allowed his system to atrophy in null-G, he would be unable to set foot on a full-mass planet without horrendous and possibly lethal complications.

Ronald popped into the residential cylinder. The volume of it spun about him, since the entrance was in the axis. This, too, he liked; he drifted, as it were, in the centre of this miniature world. What self-centred philosophies he might evolve to explain this phenomenon! *I, Lord of all I survey* . . .

But he had business. He could not dally in idle indulgence, however tempting it was. He was not lord of anything. He had no rank even among the personnel of this station; he was just an employee. A rather special employee, to be sure, but no more than that.

He drew the fins out from his sleeves and trouser legs, locked them in place with practiced shakes of his limbs, then stroked through the warm, damp air for the rim. Soon he was moving swiftly down, as the atmosphere helped him along and centrifugal force bore him outward. He guided himself toward his sector and his lot, banking sharply and running in the air to take the abrupt one-gravity landing. In his exuberance he overshot, and knocked down a cornstalk.

His wife shot out of the house as if jet propelled. She was a handsome red-tressed woman whose aesthetic countenance was marred at the moment by anger. 'You clumsy oaf!' she cried. 'You trampled my garden again!'

Ronald was obviously at fault, yet he wished she had not been so quick to take issue. She seemed not to be concerned whether *he* had suffered any injury. She cared more at the moment for a cornstalk than for him.

They were four and a half years through their term marriage. In half a year they would either renew for another five, or let it lapse. Their actual decision would have to come before then, to enable the changeover, if it came, to be smooth. Traditionally, promiscuous affairs were tolerated in the final three months of a term, as people compared each other to the remaining options. Generally the reality was considerably more staid than the tradition, and serious couples never experimented at all. Still, the matter bore consideration. Ronald had been conscious of the approaching deadlines, but not thought seriously about them. Perhaps it was time to do that thinking. Perhaps, in fact, Helen had already done so, and her attitude was showing it.

Yet he had to be fair. He *had* landed carelessly. He would have been just as annoyed if she had broken any of his puzzle-sculptures or his three-headed dog statuette memento. Their marriage should not be allowed to founder on trifles; it should be settled rationally.

'I admit fault,' he said. 'Name my penance.'

'Penance!' she snapped. 'How can you fix a broken stalk? That corn is done for! Besides, you haven't stowed your fins.'

Ronald quickly snapped his arm fins back into his sleeves. The leg fins closed automatically when he came in for landing; otherwise the procedure would have been almost impossible. The designers of station clothing had profited from decades and centuries of trial-and-error experience.

'If you knew how hard it is to grow corn out here in space . . .' Helen resumed.

She would not let go of the trivial. Well, if that was the way it was, that was the way it was. He would have to meditate on what kind of woman he would prefer next time. Certainly not one who nagged a man about stalks! 'I'm sorry,' he said, and stalked inside, conscious of an inappropriate pun. Stalk – stalked. It wasn't funny.

Then, in the inexplicable way of the sex, she changed attitude. 'You must have an assignment. Of course you were distracted. Let me make you some tea.'

Ronald used no mind- or body-affecting drugs idly, tannic acid among them. But it didn't matter; this wasn't real tea. Nothing available here on the planetoid research station was non-nutritive or habit forming in any physiological manner. Some people took coffee, cocoa, cola or

11

wine as purely social devices, since caffeine and alcohol and cocaine did not exist here. Helen liked the associations of tea, so she brewed dainty cups of it on special occasions. Sometimes, on cues known only to herself, she made demi-tasse instead. It was her way of apologizing for a display of anger.

Ronald indulged her in the ritual, accepting tea, sanitized sugar, and genuine reconstituted imitation cream in a pseudo-china cup on a decorated saucer. Helen had a flair for serving that he had always appreciated; it was her special indulgence, similar to his zooming through the low-gee tunnels, and she was at her best when honouring these forms. He realized that tea had historically been used as a social mechanism, giving form to encounters that might otherwise become awkward. He recalled a joke: 'I'm sorry I had to put poison in your tea, dear.' 'That's all right; it was delicious.' Then he glanced at Helen with a muted flash of uncertainty. Poison? But of course that was a foolish thought; she would never poison anyone, and in any event there was no such chemical on the planetoid or in it. If she did not wish to stay with him, she had only to wait six months.

She proffered him a little plate of delicate cookies. Ronald took one and nipped at its rim. He knew it was thoroughly fortified with all manner of nutrition, but it tasted just like vanilla wafer. She was really pulling out the stops!

Helen looked a query at him, and Ronald had to tell about his mission. 'There's an unincorporated region about a hundred and fifty parsecs out, not halfway to Mintaka. Of no interest to anyone except obscurity scholars, until this moment. We picked up a galactic rumour that there is an Ancient Site there.'

'An Ancient Site!' she exclaimed, almost spilling her tea. Only the grossest amazement could cause her to forget herself to that extent. 'The whole Galaxy will be charging into the area!'

'No, it's only a rumour. Been around for centuries, never verified. Mirzam's checked it out more than once in the past couple hundred years, and Mintaka ran a survey there last millennium, and even Sador in its heyday sent a crew there. Now Bellatrix, the closest Sphere, has a station there, but if they found any Ancient Site they never developed it. No one has been able to find the thing, so the other sapients have concluded it's a false lead.'

'All those other Spheres have existed longer than Sphere Sol,' she said. 'How do we know better than they do?'

'Solarian snooping. There's a local species, sub-Spherical. They're sort of spinning circles. All different colours. Like hollow-centred Frisbees. No society; they just float about magnetically, somehow. We call them Ringers. Seems someone transferred to a Ringer host, maybe a research nut, just to see if it could be done, and there in this thing's quaint mind was the memory of its visit to a kind of shrine where its ancestors learned to fly – and when that Transfer traveller came back, he realized that shrine must have been an Ancient Site in excellent repair. So now we're pretty sure it's true; there *is* a Site there. We don't know exactly where; that wasn't clear from the secondhand memory. But it almost definitely exists. So now all we have to do is find it, before any alien Spheres catch on to our hot new lead.'

'Why didn't you put that Transfer traveller on a total readout and get the specific data? There's always a lot more in the mind than can be consciously recalled, especially when Transfer is involved.'

'You're telling me? I'm in the business!' But Ronald was happy now, telling his secret. 'Couldn't. He wrote out his report, then went back to his Ringer host on a scrambled setting; couldn't recall him. Guy must have been addled, but his report seemed straight. So if it can be verified – '

'An Ancient Site!' she repeated, awed. 'All the key technological breakthroughs of Galactic history have derived from Ancient Sites. Matter transmission, Transfer of auras – '

Ronald set down his cup. 'I see you still remember your school lessons of so long ago.' When she did not dignify the slur on her age by reacting to it, he continued. 'So I'm to transfer to one of these Frisbee animals and search for the site. If its location is in the creature's memory, I'll bring the information back. Or someone else will; there are a dozen of us, male and female, transferring in. Shouldn't take long to do it. Funny no other Sphere ever thought of this simple expedient: ask the local animals.'

Helen considered gravely. 'Transfer is your thing; you're like a child with a zap-gun when you get a chance to transfer.'

'Naturally. That's why I signed.' Though there had been some bad moments during his breaking-in period. That three-headed dog . . .

'Each time you go, I wonder whether you'll make it back.'

'You knew my business when you took the term marriage. Five years, or till nonreturn do us part. I live for Transfer, and I can't think of a better way to die, if die I must.'

'So naturally you aren't swayed by the obvious risks. But I am.'

'What risks? As missions go, this is routine.'

'No mission involving an Ancient Site is routine!'

'Apart from that, of course. But we aren't supposed to go to the Site itself, just ascertain where it is. So in that sense this is an ordinary venture, with an ordinary alien element of challenge.'

14

'Except that several alien Spheres with a lot more experience than ours have failed to crack this riddle. You can bet they did not give up easily – not with a preserved Ancient Site dangling as the prize. It *can't* be easy to find.'

'I told you: we're using Transfer to explore not space but the memories of the natives.'

'And you think the other Spheres didn't?'

Ronald paused. 'It does seem odd. They really should have thought of that.'

'I submit that they did – and lost their Transfer agents.'

'Lost them? Even if that were so, we did have a Solarian who made it back, so – '

'And stayed only long enough to make a note, maybe to explain things to his relatives, then went back into Transfer covering his trail. He made sure he would not be recovered. Does that suggest anything to you?'

'You think that was part of a pattern?' His wife had a disturbing propensity to reason things out in ways he had not. This was one of the things that made her worthwhile. 'That all those aliens either died in Transfer or chose to stay there, so no information ever got back?'

'You know no aura can be recalled from Transfer if it doesn't want to go. In the old days they needed to build Transfer stations in alien territory to ship agents back. Now they can recall specially trained and adapted agents by using special equipment – but only if those agents are ready and willing, and trying to return. Sounds to me as if that first Solarian Transferee was afraid they'd trace his location, mattermit a unit out there, and force him back to his human host. So he made sure they couldn't. That's no ordinary matter. Coupled with the failures of the other Spheres – '

'I see you don't have much confidence in my desire to return to you.' There was a bitter edge to his voice; that matter of the cornstalk still rankled.

'Touché. But I'd hate to have you want to return and be too befuddled by something in the Ringer nature to make the attempt. I really am worried that I won't see you again.'

'And you with half a year remaining in the marital term,' he said mockingly. 'I'll give you a release now, if you want to avoid the inconvenience of – '

'That is not necessary,' she said sharply. Then she smoothed herself visibly and took another tack. 'Suppose the creature doesn't know where the Site is? Suppose none of them do?'

'Then we'll simply have to look for it. We've got to locate that Site. Sol's dominance of the Segment is at stake. System Etamin, with its Polarian-Solarian cadre and its circle-thrust logic, is coalescing as the real nucleus of human-oriented space. Sol will never regain her position unless she has the power of the Ancients. We have to have that Site.'

'For politics?' she enquired. 'That's all it means? A game of one-upmanship with Etamin to see which System shall carry the sceptre?'

'The power of the Ancients means more than politics. But yes, that's the essence.'

She shook her head so that her hair flung out in a way he had always liked. A woman was supposed to choose a man by his intellect, and a man to choose a woman by her appearance. Ronald doubted that was always the case, but Helen's appearance had certainly attracted him. 'What's going to happen to the creatures?'

'The Ringers? They don't matter.'

'Don't matter! If someone transferred to one of them, the creature had to be sapient. They must have rights – '

'No they don't. The Ringers aren't listed in the Galactic Index. They have no Sphere, no organization, no physical artefacts like spaceships. Legally they're animals.'

'How many species are in the same political vacuum? What about the Magnets we use on the big sublight ships? You really believe they're animals too?'

Ronald sighed inwardly. Helen was a creature of causes, and she had been on the case of the Magnets for as long as he had known her. The Magnets resembled nothing so much as self-motivated cannonballs, and were useful as watchdogs aboard ships where real dogs would have trouble getting around. He didn't want to work into another argument. 'Helen, I don't set Spherical policy. I can't be concerned about every stray creature that gets in Sol's way. That Ancient Site is important!'

'And sapient lives aren't?' she inquired dangerously.

'We're not out to kill them, for God's sake! The Ringers have no use for that Site; they don't even know what it is. We'll just ignore them, once we know where the Site is.'

'The way you ignore corn?'

Now she was back on the broken cornstalk. If there was anything downtrodden, figuratively or literally, she was on the case. She was a natural antagonist to human efficiency.

Maybe it would be better to let the marriage lapse. Ronald did not like this sort of complication, this incessant quest for objections to progress.

'Maybe we should let it go,' he said.

'The Ancient Site?'

'The marriage.'

She set her teacup down carefully, no tremor in her hand. That, in the peculiar manner of her type, meant trouble. Suddenly, now that the possibility of separating from her had been broached, it struck him how lovely she was. That made it twice as difficult. 'That is what you wish?'

Actually it wasn't, but he ploughed ahead. 'We don't seem to be getting along. It's not too early to think about dissolution. Give us time to line up new partners. You know the route.' He was making it sound a lot more casual than it was, testing her for reaction. *Was* this what she wanted?

'It is possible to disagree within marriage,' she said. Either she was not strongly concerned or she had excellent control. He couldn't tell which, and that disturbed him. He had thought he knew her better. Maybe it was both unconcern and control.

'Of course it is. But what is the overall balance? Four years, and we never could agree to have a child.' He had wanted one; she had not, and it did take two to do it, since both had to take the null-contraceptives in order to be fertile. 'Are we tired of each other? If we renew, will it just be further difference, getting worse? Five years is a long time out of a pair of lives if the match is wrong.'

'Is that what you wish?' she repeated.

'I really hadn't thought about it until this moment. I don't have any other partner lined up, if that's what you mean. I thought maybe you did.'

'No.' No histrionic frills.

'Well, it bears consideration. You don't like my work – '

'I did not say that.'

'And I frankly don't understand your causes. So maybe we're not well matched.'

She collected the cups and walked into the kitchen. Ronald watched her go. He had always liked the way she walked. There was general male humour about a woman's centre of gravity; it was not funny to him. Helen's centre of gravity did compelling things to him. Had that been the real basis of their marriage? Sex appeal unencumbered by thought? If so, four and a half years ago he had not used his brain much. But in what manner had she used *her* brain? She could readily have turned him down; why hadn't she?

'Promise me one thing,' she called from the bedroom. She must have set the cup down and gone right on in, figuratively shutting him out. She was angry, of course; she just had a variety of ways to sublimate it.

'Depends,' he called back. He felt as if he were in a morass, wishing he had never stumbled in, trying to slog out. What was on her mind?

'Do not harm any Ringers. Try to see their view when you transfer.'

He shrugged. 'For what it's worth, okay. I usually do see the alien side when I'm in Transfer.'

She emerged from the bedroom. She had changed to a stunning négligé and brushed out her hair. Had he thought himself obsessed with her centre of gravity? There was a lot more to interest him than that! She was a fine, fine figure of a woman, when she wanted to be; all the necessary attributes were there in reserve.

Ronald's conjectures of incompatibility, of thoughtful bases for marriage, dissipated. Who cared about such notions, in the presence of such a vision?

'You have something in mind,' he told her, as though this was not obvious. It was a little game of theirs.

'Or thereabouts,' she agreed, opening her arms.

It was blatant seduction. Maybe she just wanted to prove she could still work her magic on him. She could. If this was his reward for agreeing to consider the alien viewpoint more carefully, he was highly amenable.

CHAPTER 2

Rondl

Rondl became aware of himself with a certain timeless velocity. He was hungry, therefore he moved, and sustenance flowed in. He was ignorant, therefore he looked about. There was light, bathing the region, fragmenting across the reflective crystals of the nearest planetary ring and rebounding from the planetary surface below, radiating out in pretty beams, curving in rainbows –

In what?

Rainbow: colour patterning of light refracted through moisture in atmosphere; a natural prism effect. Yes, it was a suitable image; why had it surprised him?

Something loomed, then shot past. It was a flattened flying torus, bright blue, sliding along a loop of magnetism, changing its orientation as it moved. Now Rondl perceived the lines of force in the ultravisual range, a phenomenal intersection, interacting network surrounding him. Other little rings, of all colours and shades, swooped along these lines, catching the bright sunlight from two suns and flashing it about. This was beautiful.

Two suns? Yes, of course there were two suns; how could it be otherwise?

Rondl moved forward – and drifted off the magnetic line, losing input. He gyrated wildly, suffocating, floundering, his perception careening without control.

'Orient!' something flashed. But Rondl could not; his flailing only spun him worse. All his reactions seemed wrong. Now he was falling towards the hard planetary surface, and he knew that was disaster. His substance was brittle; it would –

A torus loomed close. It was large, this close, and bright red, and it frightened him. Rondl tried to avoid it, but could not. The thing matched his tumble, then jumped in close and fastened onto him, ring against ring. Rondl struggled, but he was caught. The red thing was hauling him away.

Now a second torus floated close. This one was off-white, like a miniature planetary ring seen from a distance. 'Relax, green Band; we have secured you,' it flashed. 'Do not offbalance the rescuer.'

Oh. This was help, not predation. Rondl relaxed.

'Can you maintain equilibrium alone?' the white ring flashed.

They were now on a strong, wide magnetic line. Rondl absorbed its ready power and felt better. 'Yes.'

The red torus released him. Rondl held his orientation. They were down near the surface of the planet, hovering between two massive, reflective walls. The second torus was in fact bouncing his sunbeam off one of these surfaces, and Rondl was receiving the reflection. This was the way communication occurred. Rondl's own speech was bouncing off the opposite wall to reach his rescuers.

'I am Malr,' the red one said in a formal flash.

'And I am Polg,' the white one said.

Which was as gentle a way of inquiring a person's identity as could be imagined. 'I am Rondl.'

'What was the cause of your disorientation?' Polg inquired. 'Are you malfunctioning?'

'I seem to be intact,' Rondl responded. Why did his own visual mode of expression surprise him? It was the only way to talk. 'I panicked, then I could not regain control.'

'It happens. That is why we patrol the lines near the planet,' Polg said. 'If you are now stable, we must return to our duty.'

21

'Yes. My appreciation. You saved me.'

The two patrollers glided away along convenient lines, the white and red fitting harmoniously into the scene made by the sky and vertical rocks. Rondl was left to ponder his situation. What was he doing here? What, in fact, was he? Somehow all this ordinary space terrain seemed horrendously unfamiliar.

He oriented on the nearest wall and looked at his reflection. He was a handsome green torus, the same size as the two who had helped him. His form was flattened, as was theirs, so that edge-on he would appear much less substantial than he did flat-on. Fine green fibres radiated from his rim, giving him a slightly furry aspect, but actually he was covered with protective oil that sealed off his inner functioning from the rigours of space; he needed no atmosphere. The oil also prevented the corrosion that could occur in certain gases. His hollow centre was actually his most important attribute: it was a magnetic lens that modified the light passing through it, enabling him to communicate. He could at the same time assimilate the nuances of flux, intensity, and pattern that constituted meaning, so that he had instant comprehension of all light-messages that touched his lens. This was independent of the more physical magnetism he exerted around his rim, which enabled him to travel the lines by attracting and repelling the metallic dust of his environment.

Rondl explored his memory – and discovered he had none. He knew his name and the language and the manner of his physical functioning, but little else. He was amnesiac.

So he was a green, magnetic individual of the species of Band, here near the planet of Band. There were thousands like him. Was there any reason for this situation to surprise him? What had happened to his memory?

Another Band swooped down, rotating in the sunlight,

22

not turning on an axis, but flipping over and over so that its black rim seemed to form a hollow sphere. It caught the light of both suns, causing rays to flash across the region and reflect from the nearer wall. 'Are you in difficulty?' it inquired. 'May I assist?'

'I seem to have mislaid my memory,' Rondl admitted. 'I have no notion of my employment or even where I reside.'

'I am Sunt,' the black Band flashed after a pause.

'I am Rondl. That's most of what I remember.'

'Now that we are acquainted, may I express confusion?'

'You cannot be more confused than I am!'

'Your employment is of course as you choose, but your reference to "reside" is a blank flash.'

'Where I live, my home – ' But as he spoke, even as the flash left his lens, Rondl realized that the concept was meaningless. Bands did not locate anywhere; they travelled perpetually along the lines. He was really mixed up! 'I think I mean I don't recall my associations. My friends, my favoured lines, the regions I most enjoy frequenting.'

'All Bands are friends,' the other assured him. 'Perhaps you were pursued by a Kratch and passed too close to a magnetic origin and suffered a wipeout. In that case your memories will return in time.'

'I hope so,' Rondl replied. What was a Kratch? He decided he didn't want to know, yet. Not until his position was better defined.

Sunt drifted off after assuring himself that Rondl was well. Why did it seem odd that strangers should so eagerly help one in trouble? It wasn't odd at all; it was natural to Bands.

Rondl experimented, watching himself as well as he could in the reflections, mastering the feasible mechanisms of motion and flashing. They came naturally, once he paid attention; his body obviously was versed in this. Then he lifted himself out of the canyon and up into the main flow of traffic. He kept himself stable and accelerated along the line, enjoying the motion and velocity. There was something about flying that he liked – though he knew that all Bands flew all the time. Perhaps his amnesia lent novelty to an otherwise most familiar experience.

The line was a beautiful thing. Somehow it did not honour the laws of physics he associated with magnetism, yet he could not identify what he thought those laws should be. The line was just a Band-sized strand of concentrated magnetic energy that could be tapped merely by moving his substance through it, cutting across it. The lines were the source of power to all Bands, and a Band could go almost anywhere a line could go. Since there was, properly, no end to any line, that was far indeed. There were many other lines nearby, so that Bands did not have to collect too thickly on any one. When a given line got too crowded, he remembered now, it began to lose potency, for it could not replenish itself at an infinite rate. But any line travelled moderately would endure indefinitely. So Bands tended to give each other room.

The other Bands were sailing along, rotating end over end, figuratively; being round they had no ends. Rondl caught flashes of speech: '. . . a most reflecting personality . . .' '. . . tired, not recharging properly . . .' '. . . the great soul-spirit . . .' '. . . in difficulty, Green?'

Rondl realized that the last fragment was directed at him. He knew what it was: he was not rotating. He remedied that quickly. 'No difficulty, thank you,' he flashed to the cosmos in general.

'Excellent,' the response came. Rondl realized that this rotating mode enabled Bands to hold dialogues without the intercession of a reflecting surface. A fragment of light-speech would be transmitted to one; then both would turn so that a fragment of response could be sent. The staccato mode obviously worked well enough for most Bands.

Now Rondl experimented with this, discovering the optimum rotation rate so that communication was orderly instead of ragged. If he was oriented the wrong way when a flash came, he missed it. Also, he had to address the light-source correctly; he could refract light through his magnetic lens at varying angles, but not more than about an eighth of a circle. Thus it was impossible to send a message to someone uplight from him unless he was near a reflector. He had to have another source of light. This explained why many lines ran down near the planet, with its ubiquitous reflecting walls: they provided diverse sources of light and direction, greatly facilitating social intercourse. It was not necessary to go right next to them; a number of walls were tilted from the vertical, reflecting rays upward and across so that the travelling Bands on this line had no trouble flashing any direction or in all directions. But farther out in space it would be a different matter; light was limited to two major sources.

Two sources? Of course; he kept forgetting. The twin suns Eclat and Dazzle provided the vital light energy. Why had he been surprised at their number? Double stars were common enough in the galaxy. There had always been two here; it equated with the basic number needed to hold convenient dialogue, and with the very structure of Band society: its system of rights and wrongs, perhaps even its separation into two sexes. Yet he had somehow reacted as though this were unusual. What had he expected – three suns, three sexes? Four? There was definitely something odd about his association! What kind of a Band had he been before losing his memory? A far traveller? A criminal?

Oops. Bands did not travel beyond their region of space, since they could not leave the lines; that was another irrelevant thought. Some lines extended to other stars, but none to systems with three or four suns clumped. He could not have been to any such region. And criminals did not exist among Bands. There was not even a term for criminality; he had postulated a concept of general wrongness that he could not effectively describe to any other Band. So even in analyzing his oddities, he was encountering more oddities.

He almost collided with a purple Band travelling the opposite direction on this line. Rondl wrenched himself out of the line, and immediately began to feel suffocated in the absence of its life-sustaining power. But he managed to retain equilibrium this time; he did have some reserve power to draw himself back into place.

'Are you well?' the purple Band inquired solicitously.

Strangers certainly were kind! 'Thank you; I am well,' he returned. 'Merely indulging in concentrated thought.'

'I am glad to know it. Perhaps you should seek a secluded region for your cogitation.' There was no irony; it was just friendly advice.

'Appreciation,' Rondl said.

The other Band moved on, reassured, and Rondl paid closer attention to his manoeuvring. He realized now that there were conventions for passing each other on lines; each Band turned edgewise to make room. He had failed to do so, interfering with the other. When he distracted himself too much, he wavered physically, attracting concerned attention.

Now he was sure there was, or had been, something extraordinary about him. There had been too consistent a flow of peculiarities. He needed to penetrate the veil of his own amnesia and discover what his secret was. That meant he needed a private place, where he could evince physical symptoms without alarming others – exactly as the purple Band had suggested. Where could he go?

To the tempest region, he realized. The planet was large and had many facets. There were wild mountains in some regions, unshaped to reflective purpose. Atmosphere tended to compress and rarify, to heat and cool and change the burden of particles it suspended; therefore it was generally in motion. When mountains interrupted the normal flow, severe disturbances could result, and these were called tempests. One area was prone to magnetic storms that disrupted the lines on which Bands travelled, and therefore was shunned by all but the adventurous. If he veered about there, his erratic course would seem to be the result of a magnetic flux. There would be some danger – but Rondl weighed that against the dangers inherent in not knowing his own nature. And of course he did not have to go far into the tempest region; just far enough to have privacy.

Were there safer places to achieve his objective? Rondl wasn't sure; his memory of the planetary surface was spotty, like a discontinuous line. That was part of what he had to explore: the pattern of his own ignorance, if that was possible.

Rondl accelerated. He had purpose now. He followed the line across the surface of the Planet of Band, zooming over walls, hills, valleys, forests, rivers, and intermediate, indeterminate terrain. He knew where the tempest region was; it was the part of his background information that survived.

He no longer bothered to exchange flashes with others. He oriented his body directly on the line, taking in power, propelling himself forward magnetically, leaving a trail of ionized particles behind. He realized that it was possible to detect the recent presence of other Bands by sensing the trace magnetic flux of the particles they had left, before such particles mixed again with the background environment. Particles were everywhere, though much thinner in space than near a planet. His velocity was limited only by his ability to process the abundant energy of the line and the friction of the local atmosphere. The speed was exhilarating!

In due course he came to the tempest region. There was no tempest at the moment, but few Bands were in evidence. Rondl proceeded cautiously, not wishing to be foolhardy. If he could fade into a cul-de-sac and be unobserved for a period –

He checked around. There turned out to be more Bands than he had supposed, evidently with the same notion. No, they could not all be amnesiacs; they must merely wish privacy for other reasons. He would have to penetrate deeper until he found a suitable and vacant spot.

The lines distorted here, and crossed each other randomly. Some were strong but narrow, others broad but weak. Tricky flying! Lines convoluted around outcroppings of charged rock and even dipped under the surface of the planet in places, forcing him to backtrack to search out other lines. No wonder there were few Bands here! It was a puzzle just to make progress.

Rondl wended his way about, enjoying this exploration. He discovered that he liked searching out new regions, even though his whole present situation was new to him. Soon he found a valley-nook, rich in lines, but shielded from the view of others. Here he could finally relax and think and gyrate without concern. If it was in him to remember his origin and history, he would do it now.

He concentrated – and came up against blankness. There was, simply, nothing. He could not even start.

All this trouble to get a private place for deep thinking – gone to waste. Apparently the rich lodes of strange notions had to be evoked randomly by events and spot thoughts; they could not be commanded per se. Disgusted, Rondl left the valley.

Now the puzzle aspect of this place became more challenging. He had, literally, lost himself here. He remembered the nearby terrain – but the pattern of lines did not seem to go there. He should have memorized the lines, not the landscape!

Soon he was in an unfamiliar valley, unable to cross to the one he wanted. Dull brown rocks littered the valley floor, with enough metallic content to fragment the weaker lines near them, and green plants twined about these rocks and climbed the steep sides of the hills, interfering with the closest lines there. Unfortunately, no lines extended from this region upward into space; maybe the tempests had somehow wiped them out. Yes – there was electricity in weather disturbances, and that related indirectly to magnetism. He was stuck in a two-dimensional maze.

Well, he would simply continue until he found another way back. There were many small lines, and one of them should lead to escape. If he could not find where he had entered this region, he might at least find some other line leading to space. Since lines did not end, they had to get him out eventually.

Rondl travelled along, admiring the scenery as it unfolded from valley to valley. The land was so irregular it was hard to know what was slope and what was pause. On the ledges, coloured things clung; when his line took him there, Rondl saw that they were flowering plants. They were anchored to the land, unable to fly the lines. They ate light instead of using it for vision and communication, with the single exception that the flowers arranged their hues to be aesthetic, to attract creatures that could fly. It was an interesting mode. But the plants also utilized substance. Some of it they took up through their roots, but some plants sought other sources. Their tendrils reached toward Rondl as he floated close. He quickly moved clear. It was amazing how much he knew, when the information was triggered by experience. Probably if he could only return to his most familiar haunts, much of his memory would return – but he needed his memory to find those haunts. Vicious circle.

He skirted a dull natural wall and entered yet another valley. This one was filled with water – a large lake or small sea. Rondl swooped over it. This was a new experience! The lines crisscrossed sportively above the water, and when they dipped into it, it didn't matter. Rondl dived, following one past the surface; progress was much slower underwater and the light diminished, but he could manage nicely. The Band body was largely immune to moisture, as well as to extremes of heat and cold; he belonged to one of the most stable living forms in the Galaxy.

There – he had intercepted some more information! He must know about other creatures of the Galaxy too – if only he could evoke the proper data. But he could not. Not voluntarily.

He pursued the line for some distance, following it down toward the bottom; the light had dimmed almost to nothingness. It didn't matter, since there was no one to communicate with and he did not need light to sense the line itself. This slow-motion, liquid-medium travel was pleasant, as contrast, and perhaps it would help evoke some of the information so tantalizingly locked in his mind. Interesting that this conductive medium did not dissipate the energy of the line. But magnetism was very special stuff, obviously.

Then something loomed. Instantly Rondl's danger-awareness flared. The sea creatures consumed anything they could catch! Why hadn't he remembered *that* before? He had so blithely flown right down into their region of power. This one was behind him; he saw its dim bulk by the refractions in the water, and by its crude magnetic component. Its frontal orifice was open, and the interior glowed slightly. The creature was straddling his line; Rondl had to flee forward. But the line continued down, with no crossing lines; this could mean trouble.

The water creature pursued, propelling itself swiftly through the water by threshing its flukes. In this medium, it could move faster than Rondl could. Trouble, indeed!

Was this a Kratch? No, it was a Trugd. Now his capricious memory yielded him such a detail – now that he had been trapped. Why couldn't his memory have had the simple courtesy to warn him before he descended to the point of dubious return?

Rondl moved on down – and found an intersection whose other line led upward. But the Trugd was too close; it would catch him long before he reached the surface. He had to continue on down, seeking cover, some place the monster could not follow. Some place too small for it to pass.

Now he was near the bottom of the lake/sea. There was almost no light; the contour of the land was obscure. The murk did not interfere with his perception of magnetism, but still he felt increasingly uneasy. He detected the minor metallic components of some plants or rooted animals; fortunately, they were not predators. He brushed past them, and so did the Trugd.

Suddenly the monster caught up to him. Its huge glowing frontal orifice was set with sharp bits of bone: teeth. These teeth slammed together as Rondl hurled himself out of the way.

Now he was off the line. No power was coming in. He had saved himself from immediate consumption, but he

31

was fading. He became uncomfortably aware that too great a drain of bodily energy would cause him to disband, to die. Magnetic energy held his physical substance together; there had to be sufficient charge to keep, as the expression went, body and aura together.

Yet the monster had control of the line. To return there was to be crunched. That would represent forced disbanding; in fact, that was what the monster sought. The sudden release of the metals and energy of Rondl's body would be an excellent source of sustenance for a creature who could neither harvest energy from a magnetic line nor draw matter from the ground.

Rondl realized he had only one chance: find another line. Normally the lines occurred in patterns, generated from positive-negative terminals elsewhere on the planet. In that sense, the lines did have ends – but all ends were at the centre of the Band universe. Why the lines meandered individually he was not sure; his background understanding of the phenomenon suggested they should spread evenly. Obviously they did not. Perhaps the metallic components of features of the land masses distorted the line-pattern until it became an unchartable confusion. So he had to search randomly, hoping to find a new line before he suffered energy suffocation.

He sensed one. He had not been aware that he could tune in on these lines underwater from a distance; he was still learning his own capabilities. But this line was below the water, within the land. Frantically he slid across the bottom, propelling himself by pushing against the low background magnetism, searching for an access. But progress was painfully slow, and any attempt at greater velocity only drained him further.

The Trugd, realizing the prey was not returning to the original line, came after him. Again Rondl scooted away, using his scant and dwindling reserves of energy, as the awful teeth bit into the nether soil. Then the monster, realizing it had missed its prey, drew back and spat out the unwanted dirt. No reprieve there!

Rondl had an inspiration born of desperation. He flung himself into the just-excavated hole. There at the bottom was the line he had sought. He straddled it as well as he could, drinking in its power, heedless of the sediment filling in above him. He could not travel, for the muck was too solid for his feeble propulsive force, but he was safe for the moment. The monster could not get him without also getting a lot of bottom-gook that it would have to spit out. In that event, Rondl would get spit out also. It was not the best kind of security, but it sufficed for the moment.

The Trugd snuffled about, then realized what had happened. It reversed its orientation and threshed its flukes at the ground. Silt wafted up and away. Soon a broad, shallow cavity was being excavated. Rondl was exposed – but so was a larger portion of the line.

The monster reversed again and nosed in to find its meal. Rondl shot to the end of the exposed line and buried himself in silt. The monster concluded that it had not excavated far enough, and reversed itself again. Its flukes wafted away more silt. Again Rondl was exposed – and again he shot himself into the soft extremity.

The third time the monster excavated, the line came to the surface of the ground. Rondl burst from the muck and cruised up and away while the Trugd still threshed, unaware for the moment of the prey's departure.

Now he was able to travel. Liquid was slow, but not nearly as slow as muck. Rondl soon found a line intersection – the lines never actually touched each other, but often passed close enough so that a Band could conveniently shift from one to the other – and moved up toward the surface of the water.

The Trugd finally realized what had happened and came forging in pursuit. It was horribly swift in this medium. Rondl felt the vibrations of its progress before it came into view; currents were forming in the water, churned by its huge flukes. Rondl drew all the energy he could from the line and strained forward, holding nothing back – and knew it wasn't enough. The monster would overtake him before he broke the surface.

The turbulence increased. Bubbles appeared in the water. Currents switched this way and that. For a moment Rondl lost his hold on the line and started to suffocate. But he clung to equilibrium and heaved himself back – and realized that the Trugd had hung back. It should have caught him by this time, but was instead diving for deep water. Why?

Rondl forged on up and into the air. What a relief! Then he discovered what had dissuaded the Trugd.

A tempest had formed during Rondl's descent. Wind and airborne moisture buffeted him. The entire surface of the sea was being whipped into froth. The monster evidently preferred the quiet depths, and was afraid of violence of greater scope than its own threshings. Perhaps there were even larger monsters, who generated even greater turbulence, so that this was a warning to hide. Maybe some such creatures were airborne and a frothy surface was the danger signal. Rondl had been lucky!

But not altogether lucky. It was difficult to cling to his line in this turbulence. Worse, the magnetic lines were twisting, because of the electrical components of the storm. The magnetism surged and abated, making Rondl feel ill. He could be disbanded by this natural phenomenon, too!

He struggled to rise above the disturbance, but the lines were comparatively feeble and, in any event, did not go very high. The turbulence got worse with even a slight increase in elevation. A gust of wind caught him and flung him off the line. He fell, tumbling, dreading another encounter in the deep water – but caught another line – and was blown off it also. He fought to recover, but the storm and confusion were too much, and in moments he was back near the ground.

He was afraid to enter the water again, though it was certainly calmer under the surface. The Trugd could be lurking. He flung himself across to a scanty beach, and landed jarringly. In this tempest, this was the best he could do; neither air nor water was safe.

Yet how long could he endure without an energy source? The answer was: until the tempest abated. He had no choice. Or until he ran so low on energy that he had to risk the water rather than expire outright. His experience-memory informed him that these storms were generally of short duration, and a Band who lay still and conserved his energy could last that time. The odds of survival were in his favour.

CHAPTER 3

Cirl

Rondl discovered that Bands also slept, and dreamed, and that during such periods of comparative quiescence their energy needs diminished. He had a greater reserve than he had thought – or at least a longer period over which stored energy could sustain his survival. His dreams had offered him a period of comfort, for in them he had found a line extending straight up to the nearest planetoid belt, far from any atmospheric storm. In this system each planet had its rings of debris, and each sun had its planetoid belts; there was a great deal of fragmentary matter.

He woke when another Band approached. The tempest continued, and water and air lashed the beach, whipping the sea into monsterish animation. It was easy to imagine that this was the result of the submerged wrath of a super Trugd, though of course he knew better. At any rate, this was no weather to be aloft in. The other Band was trying to achieve elevation, and failing, as Rondl had failed. The light was poor, but the Band's flashing cry of despair came across clearly as the creature plunged at last into the sea.

Rondl launched himself into the air. The background magnetism was irregular here, making his flight erratic. But he found a line and followed it into the water where the other had fallen.

He was fortunate. The line passed beneath the region where the Band was floundering. Rondl placed himself in position, then caught the other in a magnetic clasp, exactly as red Malr had done for him. Then he used his small tendrils to maintain the hold while he shifted his magnetism to propulsion and rode the line back to the surface, bearing his burden.

The tempest was diminishing at last; it now seemed safe to remain airborne. Rondl released the Band, then rotated to flash to it. 'Are you well?'

'Why did you have to interfere?' the Band flashed angrily. Rondl realized with a start that it was female; there was a characteristic signature that showed the sex unmistakably. A bright yellow, youthful Band. 'I was about to disband!'

'You wanted to disband?' Rondl asked, amazed. 'To suicide?'

'Suicide?' she asked blankly. 'This storm interferes with communicatory light; I do not grasp your meaning.'

Indeed, he had not expressed it well. This was another concept largely foreign to the Band intellect. Plants and animals lacked sufficiently defined auras, so when their physical forms succumbed, they died. But Bands were not supposed to die, so could not suicide. Or so Bands believed. Rondl found he did not believe. So still the tantalizing oddities came, though he could not fathom their source. 'Disbanding,' he said. 'I cannot believe any person would choose to disband.'

'You are a male,' she retorted with a savage flash.

'Oh – a romantic entanglement? I apologize for whatever the oaf did.'

'Oaf?'

'Negative male.'

'You regret the action of another male?'

'He was surely a very misguided individual to wrong a female as attractive as you.' For she was indeed attractive; her personal magnetism had literally drawn him in. He was not clear on what qualities made a Band female pleasant to male perception, apart from raw attractive power, but she seemed to have these too.

She spun out a bright flash of mirth. 'You are a strange one!' Her colour seemed to intensify. 'Do you really like me?'

'Yes,' he replied, surprised. 'But this is not to be regarded seriously; I do not know you.'

'You like me without knowing me?' Now she seemed intrigued, rather than confused.

'Would I like you less if I knew you better?'

'Another did.'

'Did like you less – or know you better?'

'Yes.'

Yes to both, she seemed to mean. 'I am not the same as the other.' He paused. 'At least I do not think I am. I do not know him, and I do not remember me.'

'Do not remember *him*, you mean.'

'Do not remember *me*. Before I came here. I – '

'You don't remember! How can you come out here to the place of private thinking if you don't remember your problem?'

'That *is* my problem. I do not know who I am, other than my name. I seem to have amnesia.'

'You poor creature. Yet I think I would exchange my situation for yours. I don't *want* to remember.'

'Let's trade!' he flashed.

She radiated mirth again, her colour and light making her seem like a little sun. 'You want to obtain cause to disband? You must have been strange indeed before you lost your memory.'

'That's what I fear. I keep having inappropriate images, but I can't trace their derivation. I came out here and almost got consumed by a Trugd. Now I am lost; I don't know the way out of this region.'

'I will show you the way out,' she said. 'Let us introduce ourselves.'

'All I know is my name: Rondl.'

'I am Cirl. I am – you don't really want my history, do you? It's not very interesting.'

'It is bound to be more interesting than mine.'

'Let's just find our way out of here,' she decided. She led the way up the line, forging through the dissipating storm with confidence. Rondl followed, glad he had saved her. He would have done it anyway, but this was an excellent benefit: a quick route out.

Still, they needed to converse while travelling, because a noncommunicating Band was difficult to perceive accurately at any distance. The body of an individual became part of the background scenery; a ring visible but not obvious. A communicating Band, in contrast, compelled attention; all Bands were hypersensitive to incoming speech beams, and could receive them from a wider angle than they could transmit them. Rondl had seen Cirl when she flashed in despair as she plunged into the water. It was the difference between an inert object and an animated one. So now, in the diminishing but still-powerful tempest, they could lose track of each other if they did not each augment their visibilities by talking.

'I am interested in your history,' he flashed. 'Tell me how you came to the point of disbanding.'

'Well, I didn't really come to that point,' she replied. 'I thought I would fly through the dangerous region, and if the Viscous Circle wished to take me, it would. And it did – except you interfered.'

'I apologize,' Rondl said contritely. 'I just needed someone to lead me out. Otherwise I might have been disbanded myself, and I was not eager for that to happen.'

Again she evinced mirth, knowing he had had a more socially conscious motive than that. 'Maybe the Circle intended to have us meet, and this was how it happened. I no longer feel like putting the issue of disbanding to the test.'

'I don't really understand disbanding,' Rondl said. 'That seems to be part of my amnesia. Oh, I know it relates to death, but not exactly. What is the Viscous Circle, and why should it guide us?'

'You must have suffered extreme damage!' she exclaimed. 'Everyone knows about that!'

'Everyone but me. Cirl, I really need some information.'

'I suppose you do. But we are coming clear of the tempest region, so there won't be time.'

No time? She intended to depart, then. Rondl found he preferred a longer contact, since she was the first person he had had more than incidental contact with. And she was attractive; perhaps that influenced him more than it should have.

'Of course I would not want to occupy your time,' he flashed cautiously. 'Yet if you were willing to delay a little, to explain a few things to me – '

'Are you ridiculing me?' she demanded. She expressed the concept awkwardly, because the Bands had no convenient term. Bands did not ridicule each other or any other Being. So what she actually said was more like 'Are you generating a humorous conjecture or misunderstanding of which I might be the object?' But Rondl understood her meaning perfectly; his mind was evidently more at home with the concept than was hers.

'No such thing!' he protested. 'You are the first Band I have conversed with more than momentarily, and I enjoy your company, and I fear I sought to prevail on you more than I should have. I apologize – '

'For enjoying my company?'

'Not for that. But – '

'Rondl, I'm pleased. My former male friend, whom I thought to marry, informed me I was too communicative. He said I flashed so much his lens was getting hot. I thought you would have similar objection.'

'How can a magnetic lens get hot?' But actually he understood the image. It would take a great deal of intense light to heat a Band to discomfort; her male friend had been indulging in hyperbole, in humorous exaggeration. Only Cirl had found it unfunny. Apparently she did talk a lot – but for a person like himself, with gaps in memory that were sure to prove awkward, such a companion could be comfortable. Who would notice his lacunae, if he seldom had to fit in a flash?

'He said it,' she insisted. 'It was this sort of analogy that brought me to the region of tempests.'

No single facetious remark should have done that. This one must have been part of an intensifying pattern that had shaded from humour to rejection. That male friend had been practicing sarcasm – another obscure concept – on Cirl, making her suffer. Rondl didn't like that. For one thing, it showed that Bands could be less pleasant than they believed was possible for their kind. They were not, after all, perfect. Rondl's sympathy was with Cirl, the victim of un-Band behaviour. 'See if you can heat up my lens,' he suggested.

'You requested it,' she said, flashing brightly in the reflected light of a wall. They were now safely out of the dangerous area; she had certainly known the route out. 'But if you really want untrammelled reception, fly high and downlight from me, and I'll summarize it all. We'll use the light of Eclat.' Eclat was slightly brighter than Dazzle, so was the preferred origin.

Rondl flew high and downlight. Cirl placed herself in line, ceased her rotation, and focused her beam on him. Now there was no interruption at all to the flow of communication, and it came across rich with nuance and deep with feeling. Cirl had a lovely mode of expression; it was a delight to receive it. And the wealth of minor details she included, not really relevant to the main meaning, nevertheless provided him with an improving notion of Band culture and practice. Some concepts triggered little memories of his own, helping him flesh out his awareness of self. In fact, this was in certain respects the self-revelation he had sought when he entered the tempest region. He had just not known how to go about it.

'The physical form of the Band is merely a housing for the individual aura, or section of aura,' she said didactically. 'When a Band is created, part of the species spirit is taken to animate him for the time he exists apart. He gathers experience all his life, and when at last he disbands his aura-fragment returns to the great soulmass, the Viscous Circle, and he merges with it and contributes his amassed experience to it. For the species soul has no physical component; it cannot acquire experience directly. Only indirectly, by allowing portions of itself to break off – to animate separate hosts, existing apart from one another and the Circle during the gathering of experience – , and then to return with their burden of knowledge as an offering to the whole. Our entire physical existence is merely that process of assimilation, our mission for the group soul. We have no better purpose than to learn all we can, for that knowledge is all that we are capable of carrying with us to the Viscous Circle. Our only wrongness, our only error, is the failure to garner the best experience we are able: that which will enrich the soul.'

She paused to make sure Rondl was assimilating all this. He slid up the sunbeam to flash to her. 'I am receiving.'

'Did I heat up your lens?'

'You warmed it pleasantly.'

Her magnetism intensified momentarily with pleasure. 'Does it make sense to you, the Viscous Circle?'

'Seems like Nirvana,' he flashed.

'Like what?'

He seemed to have produced another alien concept. 'Like an ideal reunion after disbanding.'

'Oh, yes, that's it!' She resumed her broadcast position and he slid back downbeam. 'When I was rejected by the Band I loved, I no longer wanted to gain new experience, but wasn't sure I had amassed enough to be worthy of return to the Soul, the great Circle. So I did not disband, exactly; I flew into the region of tempests. If the Viscous Circle wanted me, it would let me disband then; if not, it would arrange to leave me in fragmentary state, doomed to live separately for some time longer. Yet when it seemed the Circle was indeed ready to take me, I suffered uncertainty and was afraid. Somehow I wanted to cling to substance, unpleasant as it was. I fell – and you are conversant with the rest.'

Somehow, as she flashed, Rondl absorbed the larger concept. There was a gigantic and beautiful imagery associated with the Nirvana soul. The Viscous Circle as Cirl envisioned it was a tremendous swirl of colour, perhaps as big as the universe, turning quickly at the centre, slowly at the fringe, so that its internal structure was constantly changing while its external torus shape remained constant. Of course it was shaped like a Band; the gods of all creatures resembled those who believed in them – except that this god was not rigid, but fluid, viscous – beautifully so. From it tiny sparks of consciousness radiated, as though flung out by centrifugal force: the individual flakes of aura, to animate living, solid Bands. To it other sparks, or embers, returned, gratefully: the tired lives of disbanded individuals, heavy with their burdens of experience and the rigours of separate existence.

She paused again. Rondl shifted around so that he could reestablish the dialogue, using the light from

Dazzle. 'No, my lens is not heating uncomfortably,' he informed her before she asked. 'I take pleasure in receiving your beam.'

'I take pleasure in your pleasure,' she returned. 'I do love to communicate.'

'And you do it well.'

She seemed almost to glow with her own light.

'So you believe there is no death,' he continued after a moment. 'Merely the release of individual auras to the Viscous Circle.'

'Of course. Don't you?'

Rondl considered. 'No, I don't. I don't know why, since I have no basis for belief or disbelief, but I find I can't believe in a nonphysical consciousness. It has to be a myth. But I admit it *is* a pretty concept.'

'It is reality!' she flashed, dismayed by his doubt. 'Everyone knows! How could you ever disband if you did not believe in the Viscous Circle?'

How indeed! Rondl certainly did not want to disband. 'How can consciousness exist without physical substance?' he flashed. 'There can be no organization, no mind. Death to the body must mean dissipation of the aura it houses, the soul. It cannot be otherwise.'

'You poor creature!' she returned. 'How horrible to be thus deluded!'

She felt sorry for his disbelief! 'I'm not sure which of us has the delusion – '

'I must labour ever so much to get you well again!' she flashed warmly.

Rondl realized that it was pointless to argue further. 'As you wish.'

'Of course I wish! How lonely your life must be! And no wonder you feared to let me disband. You thought I was erring!'

That was it exactly. 'At any rate, there is much to be

44

appreciated in the physical existence. We must live for the present – me because I know there is no other life, you because you believe you are amassing information for the eventual benefit of your Viscous Circle.'

'I must make you see the error of your nonbelief!' she insisted. 'It is mooted that those who disbelieve are not welcomed back to the Viscous Circle, and that is a fate too horrible to be contemplated. I must reason with you, show you – '

'You are welcome to try,' Rondl agreed, beginning to appreciate a quality in her that might have annoyed her former male friend. She had to have a concept her way. 'If you can spare the time.'

'You saved me from disbanding. Surely the Viscous Circle arranged this. My time is yours.'

Rondl was not sure of the logic, but was amenable. Cirl remained, after all, a very aesthetic figure of a torus. He still needed help figuring out this society and recovering his balky memory. So if she wanted to make a project of him, good enough. 'Our time is each other's.'

'And I didn't heat your lens?'

That remained a sensitive subject for her, understandably! 'You can't heat it enough to make me uncomfortable.'

She paused, and Rondl feared he had overdone his reassurance, making it possible to apply a negative interpretation. But in a moment she came around to the favourable aspect, and flashed an affirmative. It was all right – but he would have to be careful.

First she took him on a tour of the premises. Before, Rondl had only a vague notion where things were; now the picture became much more detailed. The Bands did not reside on land, but did need a number of planetary structures. There was the physical plant: a tube running through a volcanic mountain, where the internal heat

45

vaporized the metallic substances that made up the Band body. Each flying pass through this tunnel enabled a Band to concentrate a layer of alloy about himself. Many of the Bands flying through here were young ones who needed to flesh themselves out to adult mass. They were adult diameter, but not adult thickness. This acquisition had to be effected gradually, for each condensed layer was merely inert metal until properly assimilated by the magnetic forces of the Band. Many hundreds of passes, spaced across years, were required to complete the process. Other Bands attracted to the tunnel were gravid females, who needed extra matter to build up an entire extra ring segment. When it was substantial enough and imbued with the proper magnetic patterns, it would split off: a new Band. Still others were old individuals who had suffered demetalization and thus needed restoration. A few were injured Bands, concentrating on particular cracks or abrasions; one had lost a small segment of his torus and was labouring to re-form the missing link. For creation and maintenance of the physical host, this tunnel was essential.

Then there was the line generator. Some magnetic lines extended far from the planet, right on out to the moons and on to other planetary systems. The lines, Cirl happily explained in much detail, had originally been natural, emanating from the intensely metallic core of the home planet, but as the Bands achieved civilized status, they constructed line generators and organized the lines for greater convenience. There was no longer anything very natural about the lines; they extended from star to star, and even to the systems of other sapient species.

'Other Spheres?' Rondl flashed, surprised.

'Spheres?' She was perplexed.

He had run afoul of another confusing term. 'Aren't Galactic sapients organized into Spheres of influence and

46

colonization and trade, that are highly civilized at their centres and regress inevitably toward their edges?'

'I don't know. We Bands aren't. We just exist where we belong.'

'There is no Sphere Band?' But he was already aware there wasn't.

'Of course not. What would we want with something like that? We already have the Viscous Circle.'

Rondl rotated uncertainly. 'I'm not sure. I suppose I thought that since other species – '

'How do you even know of Spheres? Are you remembering?'

'No. There just seem to be these concepts that flash out. Strange ones that don't attach to much of anything we know. Like alien Spheres. I know they exist, and I think I know something more about them, but I can't evoke the information when I want to. Only by accident. I wish I could explain it.'

'You must have been to such Spheres in your former life, so they became part of your vocabulary.'

'That must be it,' he agreed dubiously.

'Do you know, your past identity becomes an intriguing riddle. I'd love to solve it.'

She was questing for reassurance of his interest again. Cirl needed a lot of that. He was happy to play the game. 'I would love to have it solved. It is my dominant concern. But are you certain you can spare the time? You have a separate life – '

'That would have ended this phase, except for your interference.'

'I apologize for – '

'Oh, stifle your flash! You know I didn't really want to go. Not yet. You just helped me make up my mind.'

Her belief in the Band afterlife was imperfect, evidently, despite her protestations. Maybe in trying to

47

convince him she was also shoring up her own belief, much as a Band shored up his physical substance by passing through the volcanic tunnel. 'Still, there is little hope of resolving this matter quickly. You would be obliged to spend a lot of time with me.'

'Does that disturb you?' Her yellow dimmed; she had been rebuffed before. 'I would not want to impose.'

Rondl had to think seriously and quickly. Cirl had volunteered to stay close to him indefinitely. Was this what he wanted? He really had very little basis to decide what he desired. He realized he might be making a mistake, but decided to go with his subjective impression. 'I would be delighted. I seem to have no purpose, alone, and I enjoy receiving your flashes.'

She was delighted upon reassurance as only uncertain individuals could be. 'Then I will help you. I think the Viscous Circle dictated this to be. It brought us together. You need someone with memory to assist you; I need someone who needs my help.'

That covered the situation succinctly. Rondl made a circular flash of agreement. And wondered, a trifle guiltily, whether he would have felt the same if Cirl had not been a physically aesthetic, magnetically attractive, socially winsome young female. After all, he had not been interested in further help from any of the males who had checked on him.

Did it matter? Maybe it was best to accept her explanation: the Viscous Circle had willed it.

CHAPTER 4

Quest

'First we must see if others have news of you, or notions how best to proceed,' Cirl decided. 'I will convoke a circle.'

'A circle?'

'Not a true viscous circle, for there is only one, and that exists only in the spirit life. But we do have a physical approximation. I will show you.' She set off on a high line, going out into space, and Rondl followed.

The surface of the planet fell away below. The network of mountains, valleys, plains, seas, and walls shifted in perspective, and the reflected beams of light spread farther apart, making communication less convenient. The atmosphere thinned, making travel easier; too great a velocity in thick air led to heating that at its extreme could begin to melt the body structure and cause discomfort. Bands had little use for air, other than as a medium for the support of vaporized metals in the condensation chamber. The resources of the planet were vital to certain stages of life, but awkward at other stages.

Space was exhilarating. Rondl was amazed that Bands could fly through it so readily, and again wondered why he should react that way. Bands had always flown through space, needing only the lines for energy and the ambient microscopic metallic dust particles or gas molecules for reaction mass.

Time passed, for interplanetary distances were great. This was a jaunt only out to near space, well within the orbit of the nearest moon, called Fair, but the thinning atmosphere kept progress slow. In deep space, Rondl realized, Bands could accelerate to half the velocity of light, provided they had good lines to ride.

Vision improved out here, too. Rondl could now see the more distant moons of Glow, Spare, and Dinge, though two were well around the planet. They reflected light like massed Bands, and were of pretty colours, though at this range he could not make out individual features of their surfaces. Moon Fair was bright and golden, a little like Cirl; Moon Glow was reddish, with a softer effulgence; Spare was a cold blue; Dinge, a drab brown.

There were planetoids too, particularly in sections of the orbits of the moons, helping define these orbits as rings. It was as though a given moon complete with its delineated orbit was a Band, monstrous but familiar, and Rondl liked that. There was a certain harmony to this form; the circle was obviously the fundamental shape of nature, manifesting in divers ways. And of course there was the real ring of smaller particles, prettifying the planetary environment within the orbit of the nearest moon. That ring was less evident now, because they were too close to it; they could see right through its flat surface.

Rondl caught the correct angle on the light of Sun Dazzle and flashed a message to Cirl: 'You are the colour of Moon Fair.'

He had sought to flatter her. He succeeded beyond expectation. She went into a continuous flash of gratification. Females, he recalled from his anonymous wellspring of odd information, liked to be foolishly praised. But he had better be careful, because if he flattered her any more than he had just done, she might fall off the line and spin out of control. He wondered again what kind of a male it had taken to cast her off. Rondl rather enjoyed this byplay, and he liked Cirl well.

But how could he afford to like her? He had no memory

of his past associations. Suppose he were married to another Band? This species, he realized now, was monogamous; individuals associated intimately with only one partner at a time. Other species in the Galaxy were different, some having several sexes, or group matings, or –

But, frustratingly, the moment he realized he was gaining information that might be relevant to his past associations, the memory faded out.

Cirl slowed, and Rondl positioned himself to take advantage of the two suns again for regular intercommunication. 'Now the summoning,' she announced. 'It will take a while for them to arrive, but if we made a circle closer to the planet it would disrupt traffic, and that would be unsocial.'

To be unsocial was unthinkable in Band culture. Cirl's comments were constantly evoking additional background knowledge from Rondl's mind. That was useful in itself, though more was needed.

Now Cirl broadcast a bright call: 'CIRCLE-CIRCLE-CIRCLE-CIRCLE!' the words flashed out in a sphere that expanded at lightspeed as she rotated and revolved. Apparently this was a general summons to anyone receiving. She continued it for some time.

Then responses came – 'Joining!' 'Joining!' – flashes from different directions, some from such distance that no Bands were visible. Rondl wondered just how far a meaningful flash could be read, and realized as he thought of it that there really was no limit. A tightly focused flash travelled as far as light could go; only the interference of dust and gas in space abated it, making it gradually less intelligible. There had been some instances of messages received between two stellar systems, though there the problem was one of alignment rather than clarity, since – but the memory faded. Still, he realized, communication was no problem at all inside a moon system; it was necessary only to intercept a number of Bands in the vicinity, and Cirl had evidently blanketed the region sufficiently to gain the desired responses.

'But what is to happen?' Rondl asked while they waited. He remained bothered by his seemingly wide background knowledge of things that was nevertheless rent by gaping gaps wherever his interest was most specific. Why should he know about alien Spheres and not about Band circles? But of course this was what they were trying to find out.

'A circle is best experienced,' Cirl told him. 'It can't really be explained.'

In due course the other Bands arrived. They were orange and grey and violet and all other colours, male and female, young and old: a complete assortment. But all were the same diameter, and very nearly the same thickness. The magnetic and optic properties of ring and lens required this particular size, so that all Bands could interact effectively. They were standardized in this respect; age and sex made no difference. They flashed greetings to the group at large; it was evident that most of them had not met the others before, but all found each other agreeable.

What would happen, Rondl wondered, if Cirl's former male friend should appear? Presumably nothing; their relationship had been sundered.

When Cirl deemed their number sufficient, she organized the circle. 'Rondl, take your place downlight from me, on a suitable line,' she directed, positioning herself flatface to Sun Eclat. 'The others will fall in.'

'But what will this accomplish?' he asked.

'You will discover.' For once she was not being overly communicative.

So Rondl took his place, stabilizing himself as Cirl did,

unrotating, so that his stationary lens received her full beam. She moved him out a certain distance, then had him hold position. It took a certain amount of coordination to align both beam and line, but they did it.

A grey Band fell in downlight from him, and others farther along, each taking pains to be the correct distance away. The communication was all one-way, with Cirl's flashes passing through a kind of tube formed in space by the growing sequence of stationary Bands. Some of them were unable to remain on a magnetic line and must have been in some discomfort, but they were governed by the necessary position in the formation and did not complain.

Now, under Cirl's direction, the line of Bands began to curve. As it curved, so did the magnetic line, which was distorted by the pull of the line of Bands. Rondl angled himself slightly, so that Cirl's focused beam angled to the side. The next Band moved over to continue intercepting the beam, and the following Bands moved over farther. The tube kept curving until at last it closed on Cirl, completing the circle. It resembled yet another Band: a living ring. Several magnetic lines intersected it, each bending through part of the arc, then breaking free to continue its natural route. The formation began spinning slowly, so that each Band had his turn taking in energy from a line, then hanging on between lines. As the circle spun faster, the interception of lines became more regular, so that all participants had a comfortably sufficient supply of energy.

Now, abruptly, the single-person stream of communication Rondl had been receiving from Cirl expanded in amount and intensity and quality and variety, becoming a group-communication circuit. Perhaps a hundred Bands were contributing their inputs – but it was no cacophonous jumble, but rather a supremely unified whole of many components. A hundred individual threads, as it were, had been fused into a single massive cable.

And almost as he thought of that, fashioning a mental image of a multithreaded twined cable, his thought came back to him, modified by the input of all the other Bands. Suddenly the cable brightened, becoming amazingly lifelike, and each thread was a separate colour, and the colours merged in the curving distance like flashes of light, making the whole wonderfully artistic.

But it was the extraordinarily enhanced meaning that almost overwhelmed Rondl. It was as though his thought was magnified a hundredfold in power, clarity, and depth. For his communicative flashes were assimilated and modified by those of each other Band in the circle. What was valid was multiply enhanced; what was suspect was reduced or eliminated. There was a constant flow, the result of many minor corrections. This was the true viscosity, the remarkable yet consistent motion of comprehension. It was a marvellous experience.

Now Cirl's thought circulated. 'I convoked this circle for my friend Rondl, who cannot remember himself, and who suffers strange images like this one of some physical connection of threads. Where does he come from? What is his history? How should we proceed to return his history to him? He has odd flashes of information, yet is ignorant of much of what we take for granted. Does anyone know of him, as he was before his amnesia?'

The massed thought concentrated on Rondl, who felt embarrassed by the cynosure. It was as if every level of his being was being scrutinized simultaneously, as if he were a cable that was being unravelled to its component threads. Many darts of query came at him, each tugging at a particular thread, suggesting identities that faded as the proposed match-ups failed. Very soon it was concluded: no one knew Rondl's nonamnesiac self.

Then came a rapid survey of his informational oddities and lapses. A hundred beam-thoughts pried at his situation. It was like being interrogated by computer.

Computer! For a moment the viscosity thickened and stalled. That was exactly the kind of oddity they were cataloguing! What was a computer?

'It is a big electronic machine with millions of informational bits that can be coded for rapid access, many circuits that respond to certain directives – '

Machine? The circle was having trouble with this concept also.

'A device that performs a task. A complex tool. Instead of – ' But Rondl found himself confused by their confusion. Suddenly it seemed preposterous that he should be describing a thing no other Band knew about. Where could such information have come from? How could it be valid? What did he know about such an alien construction?

Alien construction. Alien. The circle oriented on this. Had Rondl associated with alien creatures? Had he come from the farthest-reaching lines, the ones that extended all the way to the Spheres of other sapient creatures?

They pierced him with investigatory needles. The massed experience of this randomly assembled group was considerable; some of them had travelled to other Spheres. They clarified that such travel was no casual matter; it required many years, the significant fraction of a lifetime, to reach even the nearest alien Sphere. Rondl was not physically old enough to have made such a trip. Soon the circle concluded that Rondl had indeed had some experience with aliens, but had not actually travelled beyond System Band. That meant that the only aliens he could have encountered were those of the local enclave, the hoppers of Sphere Bellatrix.

They explored this in greater detail. The alien colony

maintained in System Band by the Bellatrixians interacted only minimally with the natives. The aliens were huge greenish things with leg projections that propelled them in leaps across the surface of a moon or planet. They were largely nonmagnetic, unable to endure in off-planet space in their natural state. They had to wear special suits to contain the atmosphere they constantly bathed in, the gases passing in and out of bodily orifices. It was understood that the aliens would disband if this process of ventilation was ever interrupted, so devoted to it were they. The Bellatrixians could not traverse lines alone. Apparently their gross physical features were necessary to enable them to host auras nonmagnetically. They functioned, in their fashion – but what a horror it would be to be captive in such a host!

Under the wealth of this information and feeling, Rondl responded. He *had* had experience with Bellatrixians! They maintained a moderate Sphere about halfway between Sphere Mintaka and Sphere Sador, both of which were huge. They resembled a creature he termed grasshoppers, which hopped from blade to blade –

He lost it. The circle tried to evoke his further memories, but could not. No Band knew of this species of Grasshopper; none of the animals of Planet Band propelled themselves quite like that. But at least this was progress. They resumed the exploration of the nature of Bellatrixians:

There was a certain compensation to this gross, limited form. The aliens were physically dextrous. They could support heavy objects and transport nonmagnetic things, and fashion impressive artefacts. Some few Bands had travelled the tenuous interstellar lines to visit Sphere Bellatrix, or had had friends who had done so in past generations, and reported that the aliens had constructed marvellous structures on their planets, like artificial

56

mountains, with many lights and all manner of vehicles hopping from one to the other. Each Bellatrixian had a nest-hole in a structure that was shared with a mate or family; in this manner they kept their species going. Their machine structures were formidable – in this limited context the circle was coming to understand the concept of machine – and the aliens possessed matter-affecting devices they termed 'weapons' that could cause their ships to disassemble like disbanding Bands, and planetoids to break apart as though smashed by meteorites. But these formidable creatures had not come to System Band to break apart planetoids but to 'trade'. They were eager to do this, for they could readily accomplish some things Bands could not, in exchange for some things the Bands could do more readily for them. As it turned out, this was a beneficial arrangement; the aliens removed some mountains that were inconveniently located, and hauled in some metallic planetoids that the Bands had not been able to handle. In return for these 'services' the aliens accepted some of the skills of the Bands, such as the internal adjustment of magnetic circuits within semiconductors. The aliens had had to utilize clumsy metal threads sewn through other substances to fashion their crude magnetic circuits; apparently they were unable to reach in magnetically to modify the field properties of objects directly. Bands could do this easily, and could duplicate the magnetic attributes of given artefacts in much smaller compass without changing the shape or mass of the objects. The aliens had been at first amazed by this: how could a tiny block of metal be made to perform the complex switching operations of one of their gross devices – when the Bands did not even touch or change the object physically? But they were quick to accept such transformed objects once they tested them.

At first the aliens had not even recognized the Band line

generators and modifiers as constructs of sapience; they had thought of them as unique natural objects the Bands had happened to discover and adapt. But again they were quick learners. Now Bellatrix represented a good 'market' for many magnetic artefacts of specified nature, and such artefacts were used in the alien space-travelling vessels and even for 'export'. That concept remained confusing; apparently 'export' items were neither retained nor used, but sent to other Spheres in return for some intangible statement of status.

Rondl found he understood the concepts of trade, services, market, and exports without difficulty. But this time he withheld his thoughts, preferring not to confuse the circle further. He merely absorbed the massed thoughts of the others, finding this process highly useful to his mental adjustment.

It did not matter what the artefacts were used for. As long as the Bellatrixians were willing to accept such easy work in exchange for such imposing labours as moving mountains, the Bands were satisfied. In fact, a fair subsidiary vocabulary was developing, used by those Bands who specialized in alien negotiations. Such Bands could hardly be understood by others; they flashed glibly of 'credit' and 'deficits' and 'investment', all things that seemed to relate to the mysterious alien system of 'economics'. They also flashed warning: it was their judgement that though the Bellatrixians were compatible despite their amazingly alien nature, they were typical of the species of the larger Galactic society. These species had concepts that were difficult to comprehend, even devastating. One that completely eluded the great majority of Bands was 'war'. It seemed to relate to the attempt by one species to degrade the welfare of another. Some few Bands had, by dint of deep study and prolonged concentration, managed to assimilate this concept. They had then disbanded. Thus other Bands had decided to leave that concept alone, and to remain generally clear of aliens.

'I know of these aliens,' Rondl flashed. 'Yet it seems to be part of a general, erratic background I have. I also know of Mintakans and Sadors, and perhaps others if some key concept were to invoke them from my secret memory. But until such invocation comes – '

The circle considered, and recommended in its viscous consensus that Rondl survey a wider range of Galactic species. Some one among them might have the associations suggested by his vocabulary. Then he could survey the particular Bands who had been in that region of space or who specialized in studies of that species. One of them might turn out to be himself, or at least an acquaintance of his former self. That would finally give him the information he was questing for: who was he?

At length the circle disbanded, breaking up into its component entities. This was the way the spirit circle was supposed to be: a special, superior entity, losing fragments of itself to the physical Bands, recovering them when their separateness terminated. He understood that myth better now. But it remained a myth: the greatest viscous circle of them all, a deific entity created in the likeness of the most moving of living-Band formations. A really charming fantasy he almost wished he could believe in.

Now they had a course of action: survey the alien contacts and look for a Band who had departed the association of the specialists in particular alien relations. A tedious, unpromising chore, but necessary – unless he preferred to travel out to the alien Spheres themselves, to see what matched his knowledge. If there were a Matter-mission unit –

A what? He lost it. Somehow he had had the notion he

could blithely jump to far places without the passage of time. Of course he could not do that! He could not go to any alien Sphere without consuming years, and he lacked the patience for that sort of thing. They would have to research in a library instead.

Except that the Bands had no libraries. This was yet another alien concept in his mind. A library was a place where references existed, open to all persons interested. Books, tapes, holo-recordings – all alien devices. There was nothing like that in this region of space.

Cirl, however, was not dismayed. 'We shall go to the Education Nexus and question the instructors. They have much broader experience, and will be able to help us.'

Of course. Young Bands, like the youth of all sapient species, needed to be trained. Animals inherited most of their vital patterns of behaviour, but sapients had to be taught. Naturally the individuals with the greatest stores of information were the ones to do the teaching. Maybe these instructors had taught Rondl himself, and would remember him as a student. Maybe they had records –

'Records?' Cirl asked blankly as they flew back toward the planet. 'What are they?'

Another anomalous concept! Aliens kept records; Bands did not. Material continuity was of little importance; what counted was the immaterial continuity of the Viscous Circle. Since all the Band information theoretically went to the group Soul eventually, no physical repository was needed. No wonder the Bands were not recognized as a Galactic Sphere. They simply did not organize themselves in conventional sapient fashion.

Yet as he considered this, Rondl was not at all sure that the other sapients of the Galaxy had the better system. They discriminated against the Bands because the Bands were different. Difference was not at all the same as inferiority.

Cirl was leading the way more slowly than she had on the way out, so that Rondl could use Dazzle as a beam source for communication and rotate for convenient converse. They travelled on roughly parallel lines and flashed back and forth. It was very pleasant, and Rondl found himself wondering whether it was possible to increase that pleasantness.

'I found another gap in my information,' he said. 'Perhaps an awkward one.'

'What is it?'

'I do not know how Bands develop romance.'

She was flashless for a moment, and Rondl feared he had committed some impropriety. 'Do you have a female in mind?' she finally inquired, guardedly.

Had there been any question? Rondl suddenly realized that there had been several quite attractive females in the recent circle. Cirl might think he wished to pursue one of those. 'I have – if it is permissible – you in mind.' Now he was afraid she would react negatively. Friendship was not the same as romance, and she had had a bad experience recently.

'I should hope so. I formed a circle for you.'

This was a response he had not anticipated. 'This is significant? I thought the circle was just for information.'

'It is, true. But when one Band organizes for another, it presupposes liaison.'

'But all the others were strangers. They couldn't know – '

'The very nature of it was suggestive. We invoked the circle; they merely participated. It was our circle. We put the questions.'

'Oh – they were like witnesses to a ceremony.'

'One does not convoke a circle for just anyone,' she flashed primly.

'I thought maybe – I feared you retained some attachment to the male Band you knew before me.'

'That matter is becoming less serious. In retrospect I perceive flaws in him I did not fathom before. You take up my attention now.'

So part of her interest in Rondl was as a diversion from that former liaison. He had an alien term for this: rebound. Yet that was not necessarily a bad thing. It merely accounted for a more rapid progress of interest than might otherwise occur.

'You are attractive to me,' he said. 'Perhaps I lack a proper basis for judgement, and I do not know how I myself am as a potential object of interest for the opposite sex – '

'Complementary sex,' she corrected him without breaking his pattern of communication. It was possible to receive a flash while sending one out; Bands did this all the time.

'But if you find me potentially worthwhile as a male, not merely as a riddle – '

'The riddle is a pretext,' she flashed. 'A reason to associate while we ascertain whether we like each other.' She could speak to the point with remarkable clarity; it was part of her love of communication. Perhaps that, as much as the amount of her flashing, had embarrassed her former associate. Directness could become indelicate.

'But I do want to find out who I really am,' Rondl persisted a trifle awkwardly.

'Of course. But you could indulge in that quest alone.'

Indeed he could. He had agreed to collaborate with Cirl because he liked her appearance and company. It was somewhat startling to learn how much more cynically she viewed their association than he did, but she was correct. The quest was real – but also a pretext for another kind of quest, which was perhaps as important. 'Then you are amenable to my serious attention?'

Now she was diffident. 'I did not say that.'

'My apology,' he flashed quickly, disappointed. 'I must have misunderstood. You prefer to keep it businesslike?'

'Businesslike?'

Yet another alien concept. 'Orderly, proper. Without emotional involvement.'

'I did not say that either.'

'Then I am confused. What sort of connection do you wish?'

'Oh, you really are ignorant about this, aren't you!' she flashed in cute exasperation. It was as close to a negative sentiment as she came.

'Yes. I am ignorant. Am I offending you? I don't know what to ask.'

'I suppose I just expected you to know the conventions, even though you obviously don't. I'm not supposed to tell you how to do it.'

Rondl began to catch on. A thing performed strictly by expressed agreement would lack that special element of mystery and romance that was the essence of male-female relations the Galaxy over. Cirl was amenable to his interest – but did not care to say so too openly, lest the admission have a negative effect on that interest or its application.

Well, he could proceed on trial and error. Compliments – that must be part of it; she had certainly reacted when he had praised her colour. 'I think your circle is marvellously round.'

Cirl's magnetic explosion of mirth almost flung her off the line. '*All* Bands are perfectly round!' she flashed. 'Males and females. That is no distinction.'

'Your surface is beautifully sleek,' he essayed.

This was no better. 'Every Band has an oil-sleek surface, to enhance travelling through atmosphere without suffering friction and heat damage.' Actually this was true only in atmosphere; out in space the fibres were extended, as stream-lining was not important. Either way, Cirl was not really distinct.

Why had he supposed physical descriptions were appropriate? They might have no relevance to Band romance!

But then, why had she been so flattered when he praised her colour? Colour did distinguish individuals . . .

'You have lovely colour,' he essayed.

'You used that before,' she flashed coldly.

Another error! Compliments could not be repeated, it seemed. Too bad he had wasted his most potent one before.

'You have a delightfully informative mode of flashing,' he offered.

She rewarded him with a brilliant splay of refracted light. 'Now you are scoring,' she admitted. 'Don't tell anyone I told you, though.'

'Never,' he agreed conspiratorially. Since her prior male friend had condemned her too ready communication, she was of course sensitive in this area, positively and negatively.

By the time they reached the planetary surface, they were well established as a courting couple. But two things inhibited Rondl. First, it had occurred to him that he might, in the course of the life concealed by his temporary amnesia, already have a liaison with some other Band female; that could be extremely awkward when he recovered his memory.

Second, he had no idea how Bands made love – and knew better than to ask Cirl for instruction.

They arrived at the education centre. Here were many polished walls, some curving so that the flashes of the instructors reached many students simultaneously, while the student responses were reflected from all around the site to a single spot for the instructor's assimilation. The massive trunk lines split into many lesser lines, so that all students could sustain themselves comfortably in class. Rondl found that he liked this place, both for its academic association and for its physical layout. Was that a natural Band reaction, or a clue to the nature of his prior life?

Cirl found the instructor she knew. This was an old Band she called Proft, a weathered green-brown in hue, who no longer flew the lines between planets but still had excellent mental facility. Proft, she claimed, knew almost everything.

This seemed to be true. The old Band conversed with Rondl casually, then flashed: 'You were educated at this planet; you have not been far from it.'

'You remember me?' Rondl asked, excited.

'I recognize your accent. A Band's mode of flashing varies with the region he frequents during his formative stage. Your accent is pure local.'

'But how do I know about strange things?'

'You must have done strange research. That would account for stray bits of information, without depth, and lacunae where you omitted your homework or skimped. Students are not what they used to be! I am sure your life has not been remarkable heretofore; there is no evident trauma. You have to have been one of hundreds of thousands who resided in this vicinity.'

'Then why should I suffer amnesia?'

'Several possibilities. You could have had an accident, such as passing through a random magnetic flux of burn-out intensity, or attack by a wild creature that frightened you away from your memories, such as a Kratch.'

'Or a Trugd,' Rondl agreed.

'Indeed. Such things occur routinely to careless individuals. It is of no special significance, since you retain your ability to function.'

'But suppose – ' Rondl hesitated, but realized he had to

express his concerns now or lose the opportunity. Proft had granted him an interview at Cirl's behest, and otherwise would surely be busy elsewhere. 'Suppose I have commitments in that prior life?'

'Disbanding ends all commitments in this incarnation,' Proft explained. 'You have evidently suffered partial disbanding. I doubt you have any commitments remaining now.'

'But if I were married – '

'Marriage is a voluntary association of male and female for the purpose of rebanding. It can be terminated at any time by either party. If you were married then, and no longer wish to be now, then it is finished.'

'But what about dissolution procedure, property settlement, legal reversion of status, adjustment of records, disposition of and provision for offspring?'

'You do have unusual notions!' Proft flashed, amused. 'Bands have no procedures, no reversions, no records, no dispositions, and do not even know the meaning of property.'

'Who does?' Cirl put in quickly.

'Property is an alien concept. It is the allocation of a particular segment of the surface of a planetary body for the use of a particular individual.'

'Why would anyone want that?' Cirl asked, perplexed.

'Land is valuable,' Rondl said. 'It can be used for many things. Some property, too, is portable. It can be a form of wealth.'

'Wealth?'

Proft flashed amusement. 'The true Band response. Wealth is a function of personal possession. Without a concept of possession, wealth does not exist.'

'But I know about it!' Rondl protested. 'If no Band knows – '

'Research, again,' Proft said. 'Any good course in alien

66

mores and management will acquaint students with such notions, and the more apt ones will actually comprehend them to some extent, as you seem to. The various Spherical aliens have many remarkable conventions, property among them. You must have been a specialist; you retained portions of this knowledge while losing your own identity.'

'That is my mystery.'

'I wonder – do you by any chance grasp the alien concept of War?'

'Certainly. It is a matter of – '

'No, no, do not define it! Someone would disband! I asked merely conjecturally. It is possible that you studied that concept, and mastered it, and suffered a near disbanding that damaged your memory without, ironically, eliminating the concept. Perhaps it was an intellectual crisis: that devastating concept could not cohabit with your personality, so one or the other had to go, and the concept prevailed. If so, you are unique among individuals. Others have not survived that concept.'

Rondl was not entirely satisfied, but could not refute this explanation. He did not see what was so mind-destroying about the concept of war. War occurred all over the Galaxy, and was a recognized manner of establishing empires. But he realized that it was not the motley collection of odd facts that set him apart so much as his unusual attitudes. He had not been repeating rote when he spoke of the problem of eliminating marriage; he had been expressing what he believed were genuine matters of concern. Yet of course Bands were not faced with any of these.

What kind of shock could have replaced his Band values with alien ones? If mental revulsion had wiped out his memory, surely the first thing to go would be the offending concepts, not the innocent detail of normal existence. He was now almost afraid to seek the answer.

Yet he inquired slightly further. 'Do you have any idea what alien culture might have concepts such as the ones I have expressed?'

'Which specific culture you researched?' Proft considered. 'There are many thousands of Spheres in the Galaxy, and most of their creatures have notions of property. I would not know where to begin.'

'Perhaps my name is in the past course rolls.'

'Course rolls,' Proft repeated. 'That would be a form of record, an alien concept you have already referred to. We have no records of anything; Bands don't need them. Why should we keep track?'

'To prevent students from falsifying their – ' But this didn't work. There was nothing to falsify, and falsification itself was an alien concept. Bands learned what they needed and what they wished, departing when satisfied. So there were no records.

'We thank you, Proft,' Cirl said. 'I agree that Rondl must have suffered some magnetic derangement that wiped out some of his real experience while leaving some of his education intact. So his responses are mixed.'

She led Rondl away. She was wrong, he was sure – but he decided not to pursue the matter further. He had a foreboding that disaster could come of too ardent a quest for knowledge of his past life, and he liked this life with her too well to place it in jeopardy.

CHAPTER 5

Invasion

The news flashed rapidly through the Band society: alien monsters were intruding into the Band region of space. They were utterly horrible, possessing gross, fat limbs, liquid-filled eyeballs, and teeth like those of a Trugd. They had no magnetism; they tramped on planetary surfaces vaguely like Bellatrixians, except that they could not even jump far. Their ponderous nether appendages hauled forward one at a time, leaving indentations in the ground. The creature could not fly; they employed tremendous devices to convey them from planet to planet and even from place to place aboard a particular planet.

Why were they coming? No one knew. One Band had been in the vicinity when a huge alien vessel materialized near a neighbour star. He and a friend had recognized the alien nature of it and concluded that the creatures were lost, and the friend had gone to that ship to proffer assistance, flashing back spot reports. The aliens had grasped that Band physically and hauled him into their vessel. In a moment had come the magnetic ripple of his disbanding. The aliens had destroyed him without even bothering to communicate, or had so horrified him that he had felt compelled to vacate this existence immediately. Now the surviving Band had travelled in all haste back to the home planet to give warning.

Other reports came in; other Bands had disbanded. The survivors did not take this too seriously, for they considered disbanding to be but an act of transformation, of return with news to the Viscous Circle. They were alarmed, however, because of the unsocial nature of the intrusion. Was something important causing the aliens to rampage? Or had they merely lost their way?

Rondl experienced a cold, grim fear. Somehow he knew it was more serious than that. The reports were garbled, of course; the first encounter could not have been at another star, for the Band would have required many years to return with the news. But certainly an alien ship or ships had entered System Band, perhaps out beyond Moon Dinge. Large-scale movement of equipment by Mattermission was expensive; it consumed a significant value of property and was unlikely to occur by accident. Spaceships did not readily become lost. These aliens had come here on purpose, and they wanted something – and it was best to fathom what that thing was as soon as possible.

More aliens came. They overran the outer reaches. Bands disbanded in droves, unable to adapt to this rough intrusion. Only those who peeked and fled survived with news. They reported that the aliens were setting their gross ships down on moons and small planets, disgorging metal vehicles, and racing across the surfaces of those worlds. It was a mystery what they were doing.

'I know what they're doing,' Rondl said grimly. 'They are searching for something.'

'Why don't they ask us where it is?' Cirl asked. 'That is the sensible thing to do.'

Indeed it was. Rondl had no satisfactory answer. Yet he knew that terrible trouble was in the making. 'We must do something,' he said.

'Maybe they will go away,' she replied with innocent hope.

'I don't think so,' he said. 'There's something – '

'What is it?'

But he could not evoke the substance of his concern. 'All I know is that something has to be done.'

70

'But what?' Cirl persisted. She did not approve of unclarity. But Rondl still didn't know.

Gradually the reports achieved a semblance of organization. There were a dozen or more planets in the double System of Eclat-Dazzle, together with considerable lesser matter, and the aliens were taking over the outermost ring of substance, piece by piece. They remained far from Planet Band, but were slowly approaching it and its moons. There seemed to be no way to stop them, and it did not occur to other Bands even to make the attempt. What would be, would be.

'Let's fly about the planet,' Cirl suggested. Rondl realized she sought to distract him from his impotent concern about the alien intrusion. Perhaps she had romance in mind. He was amenable – if only he could find out *how*.

They flew on a line through a richly fertile region. The lines curved through gently sloping valleys and around mountain peaks. Partially magnetic animals grazed in the fields, consuming the short vegetation, using the lines for orientation instead of for energy. They were harmless. This was certainly a romantic setting. But how was he to proceed? This was a riddle as bewildering as that of the alien intrusion!

Cirl floated blithely along, awaiting his move. He had to do something. If only he had retained this portion of his memory!

Well, he would simply have to try, and hope nature guided him correctly. He might get lucky, as he had with the 'yellow' compliment. If not, she would let him know – probably with devastating clarity.

Rondl slid close on the line. 'I love you,' he flashed. And he did. Only – what next?

Cirl did not reply, and realized he had already made a mistake. She was still rebounding from her prior love; she

71

was not yet interested in total commitment. She needed a kiss, not –

Not what? And what in the System was a kiss? As he tried to interpret the concept into Band reality he garnered only a vague feeling of obscenity. Whatever a kiss was, it was not fit for Bands.

'That is, I think you're – ' But physical compliments were useless, generally. He had used up all the good ones. 'Extremely pleasant.'

'Of course,' she agreed without emotion.

'A beautiful shade of – ' But he couldn't repeat a given compliment. 'Of delight.'

'Are you well?'

Well, yes; adequate, no. He was destroying himself with inanities. But what else was there?

Then Rondl spied another pair of Bands coasting along farther down the valley. Maybe they were on a similar excursion. Maybe they would say what needed to be said and do whatever was supposed to be done and he could find out by observation. All he needed to do was keep them in sight long enough.

'Let's explore this mountain,' Cirl flashed, detouring toward it on a new line. But the other couple continued on down the valley. The two were drawing closer together; perhaps any moment –

Cirl zoomed away, and Rondl had to go after her. The other couple disappeared behind an outcropping of rock.

He caught up to her, then led her. 'Let's loop the peak!' he flashed, hoping to come back into sight of the others.

They looped it – but the other pair was not in sight. The two must have paused for a private matter. Maybe right now they were engaged in –

Rondl moved on down the slope, trying to find them. 'Where are you going?' Cirl flashed.

He had to desist, not daring to admit his object. They

72

slid slowly down the line. At the base of the mountain they almost collided with the other couple, who were just separating, spinning. Both were sending out flashes of satisfaction. He had missed it!

Still, now he knew – assuming the others had done what he assumed they had done – that whatever it was did not take long. Maybe it was merely physical contact. Many species made love by some form of touching, didn't they? His unreliable memory indicated so. Too bad he knew that, without knowing what Bands did. What good was it to know about aliens, and not about his own species?

Cirl continued to drift amicably along, as if innocent of any complicity. She was not even flashing her usual ultrablue streak of comment. She knew he wanted to do – whatever – and also knew he didn't know how, yet she would not enlighten him. Yet this was the way of females the Galaxy over; the fundamental frustrations of the sex were constant regardless of species.

Other species – did he really remember in detail how they did it? If so, he might extrapolate, to arrive at a viable technique here.

Rondl concentrated, but could come up with only vague concepts of overlapping, interpenetration, and substance exchange. Not only were these probably inapplicable, they were repulsive. He was beginning to feel nauseated – which itself was alien. No help there.

So it had to be trial and error. He angled close to her and exerted his attraction, the way he had in order to rescue her from the water at their first meeting. The fibres about his fringe could twine with her fibres to hold them together without constant magnetic exertion.

'What are you doing?' Cirl protested irately.

Rondl hastily let go, embarrassed. He had flubbed it!

'I never expected you to try something like that,' she

73

continued, her flashed tinged with maidenly abhorrence of the obscene.

Rondl was too mortified even to attempt an excuse.

They flew up a convenient line away from the planet. Their romance had been stifled for the nonce. He simply had to find out elsewhere how to do it without mishap. How he wished he could have remembered!

The alien invasion continued. The gross creatures overran another System planet and its moons and rings, causing horrendous waves of disbandings. More information came in, and now the educated individuals were able to identify the species.

The invaders were Solarians, from a Sphere several hundred light years distant. They were one of the more quarrelsome, less responsible species. They had an extraordinary affinity for material things, being largely material themselves; their concept of property was overwhelming and their concept of spirit insignificant. They were certainly the type to expend resources in quest of something material. Yet they required special atmosphere to breathe, like the Bellatrixians, and constantly imbibed liquid – surely to fill their fluid eyeball sacs – and consumed and excreted in rapid intermittence all manner of solids. They were messy creatures, depositing refuse wherever they went. It was hard to imagine a more grotesque manifestation of encroachment; it was an aesthetic as well as physical horror.

Now the monsters progressed to the outermost planetoids of Planet Band. Thousands of Bands disbanded at the very notion. 'We must do something!' Rondl exclaimed as though he personally were responsible.

'What?' Cirl asked. She was always uncomfortably practical.

Rondl still didn't know. But he tried to find out. He

74

flew towards Moon Dinge, where the aliens were cluster-ing. Cirl was terrified, but went with him. Death in the form of disbanding did not much alarm her, but the presence of grotesque monsters did.

The moons were scattered around the home planet, so that Rondl and Cirl did not pass close to Moons Fair, Glow, or Spare on the way out. But in the orbit of each was its thin collection of stones, and between Glow and Spare was a disadvantaged comet, caught at last in orbit about the planet instead of the suns, and reduced to a diffuse cluster of metallic fragments and a few wisps of worn-out gas. It seemed like a nice place to visit.

'Threat! Threat!' Cirl flashed abruptly. 'Flee, Rondl, flee!'

Rondl drew close to her, trying to discover what she saw. It was soon apparent. A shape was hurtling towards them. He had seen it before, but taken it to be a rock fragment. It was roughly cylindrical, with a tapering spike in front and a flat or hollowed rear, from which occasional gusts of dust emerged. It was black-brown, streaked with red, like stratified rock, unpretty though symmetrical. The very sight of it made him react unpleasantly.

'What is it?' Rondl asked.

'Monster! Monster!' she flashed wildly. 'Flee! Flee!'

She was obviously too frightened to make much sense. The approaching object was no Solarian, unless all that he had recently learned was wrong. This was something else. Yet Cirl's fear was contagious; he felt fright himself, and kept himself under control only with difficulty.

If this thing really was a serious threat, it was better to tackle it sensibly. If it was not, then there was no need to flee. Rondl flew towards it.

'No!' Cirl flashed, horrified, halting her flight as she saw what he was doing. 'It will consume you!'

Oh – like the toothed water creature. Now he had

proper caution. Yet this was space, with good magnetic lines; he was free to manœuvre to fly at full speed. Surely this squat thing could not catch a Band!

'It's the Kratch!' she flashed. 'Don't you know?'

The dread monster! Despite his decision to be objective, Rondl yielded to apprehension and reversed course as Cirl came near.

Rondl, Cirl, and the Kratch were now in a roughly equilateral triangle. The monster veered, going after Cirl, who was obviously the more delectable creature. She fled, accelerating desperately – and now Rondl saw that the thing was faster than she was. It had a kind of circular scoop at the base of its forward spike; he could see how a circular object like a Band could be caught on that spike and set down firmly against that scoop. The mechanism of this predator was becoming apparent. No doubt it consumed the substance of Bands the way the water monster did, assimilating the disbanded substance into itself while utilizing the magnetic reserves to enhance its own energy.

Why hadn't the Bands organized to rid the System of this nemesis? It was evident that the Kratch had evolved as a predator of Bands; its whole design oriented on them. For millennia it had culled at will. Yet obviously it could capture only one Band at a time, and if a number of Bands attacked simultaneously – no, that was no good. Bands had no offensive capability. Still, they might make a machine – no, they did not even understand the term. Maybe they could have the Bellatrixians build one to destroy the Kratch. Surely there were ways, if they were to decide to do it.

And there was the real problem. The Bands would never adopt methods of violence and destruction, albeit of an enemy or predator on their kind, for they were completely pacifistic. They would simply continue to tolerate this vile predation . . .

There was another blast of dust or gas from the monster's rear. The Kratch moved forward faster. Action and reaction – evidently this was a magnetic creature, touching the lines, but it could also boost its velocity by jetting out bursts of substance at key moments.

Cirl's line curved, and she curved with it, as she had to. Now the Kratch jetted itself off the line, cutting across the curve, gaining distance. It wasn't really faster than a Band, Rondl saw now, but because it was not limited to the lines, it could manœuvre better. That gave it its edge on Cirl. It would soon catch her.

Rondl was already accelerating towards them, cutting across on the most available lines. Because the gap between Cirl and the predator was closing slowly, he had time to manœuvre closer at a tangent. Then, acting on what impulse he did not know, he cut in between the two.

The monster, confused, veered to follow Rondl, who was closer. Apparently it was, after all, not smart enough to distinguish between one morsel and another. But it lost relative velocity in the manœuvre, for it had substantial mass, and Rondl drew ahead.

Cirl, relieved, slowed, falling behind. Then she realized that her gain was Rondl's loss. Flashing misgivings, she came towards them.

'Stay clear!' Rondl flashed. 'I'll handle this!' But now that he was committed, he didn't know how. He was sure the Kratch had the means to destroy him; it was too solid, too certain of itself, and had survived too long as a predator to be incompetent in this respect. He had to escape it – and now the thing was gaining on him as it cut across stray shortcuts between lines.

Rondl dodged to a diverging line, and the monster dodged after him. He reversed, and it reversed too, not being led astray. He accelerated, but it accelerated at the same rate. It was locked on him, holding even or gaining.

Only if he found a perfectly straight line that went directly to Planet Band and the safety of atmosphere and great numbers of his kind, could he hope to escape this predator. The Kratch never went into atmosphere or too close to a massive planetary body or into a crowd of Bands, Rondl remembered now. Atmosphere fouled its system; gravity tired it rapidly; multiple targets confused it.

But the lines were not straight, and the planet was not close, and every curve would allow the monster to shortcut across and creep up. This chase could have only one end.

Could he somehow fight it? No, not without a weapon.

Weapon? What did any Band know about weapons?

Well, *he* knew something. A weapon was a tool for combat – something to enhance the individual's powers of destruction; something like an explosive object that could damage or disband the pursuing monster. Maybe his obscure research in his prior existence could benefit him now.

What was available? Nothing physical; this was space. The only substantial matter in range was that of the derelict comet, and he could hardly throw that at the monster.

Or could he? There was more than one way to use a tool. A small readjustment of outlook and definition, and he might have his weapon.

He surveyed the nearest lines, found the proper configuration, and threw himself into a tight turn. The Kratch, more massive, was unable to change course so abruptly; its turn swung outside Rondl's arc, and for once it lost distance. But this was temporary; as it slowed, it regained manœuvrability.

Rondl completed his turn and shot forward towards the debris. The Kratch accelerated after him. Rondl followed a line that went straight in among the moving rocks; at this

78

velocity they seemed close together. He threaded between two big ones, but the Kratch threaded also. This was, after all, where the Kratch had been hiding; it knew how to avoid rubble. Rondl let a little rock pass through his lens; it made no difference to him, since the lens was not solid. It made no difference to the Kratch either; it caromed off the metallic slanted surface harmlessly. The monster got its metal from consuming Bands; its surface ought to be of good quality.

Rondl found a huge chunk with a lot of metal, enough to cause several nearby lines to bend. He swung around it as tightly as he could, hoping the Kratch would have to swing wide again. Here, inside the comet, the rocks would interfere with such a swing. But Rondl's pursuer slowed, jetted more dust, and swung almost as tightly as Rondl had. The creature was stupid, but it did learn from immediate experience. The gap between them narrowed again. Soon the monster would catch up, regardless of any manœuvres Rondl might essay . . .

Unless he found what he needed in time, and was able to make it work. It seemed to him that it should be here, somewhere – if only he could locate it.

The Kratch was nosing very close now. The dread horn was almost near enough to touch Rondl. If he didn't soon find –

There it was: A cloud of metallic dust interspersed with diffuse gas, thick enough to obscure the rocks beyond. It was what remained of the heart of the comet – something resembling atmosphere! Rondl swooped into it.

The Kratch followed, intent on the incipient capture. Rondl's hope dissipated; the creature was not at all put off by the gas. Eliminate one illusion! Perhaps the stuff was too thin, here in space, to have much effect. Maybe it lacked whatever corrosive component damaged the Kratch, or acted too slowly to be of much help at the moment.

But there was another possibility. Rondl exerted his magnetism, collecting a large mass of crude material. It coalesced about him, furring his circle, turning the green to grey, fuzzing his lens, interfering with his perception and his motion. But he kept on, adding to it as if he were going through the tunnel of formation, making himself a dust-encased travesty of a Band. Soon he had increased his apparent mass by half. The sensation was awful.

The Kratch caught him. Its cruel snout poked through his lens, disrupting the magnetism – but Rondl had already blinded himself by the cluster of dust and fragments. He felt himself sliding up on the spike, toward the consuming orifice –

Just as he touched that dread circular aperture that (his mind's lens suggested) gaped to take him in, Rondl reversed the charge on his surface, repelling the metallic debris instead of holding it to him.

The Kratch drew it all in, assuming this was Rondl himself disbanding. The monster's lack of intelligence was now paying off for Rondl. While the dust disappeared into the orifice, Rondl himself slipped off the spike and away.

Almost immediately there was trouble for the Kratch. Debris might superficially resemble the material of a Band, but it was unrefined, with gross impurities. Had it been edible, the Kratch would have scooped it in instead of chasing Bands. This was space garbage – not that there was any Band concept of garbage.

The monster was suffering intense indigestion. It choked the stuff back out. Had Rondl not already freed himself, he would at this point have been flung off its spike and away. His strategy had, after all, been sound.

He caught a line and zoomed out of the comet, leaving the monster to its agony. Probably the Kratch would survive, but it should be some time before it had the gumption to chase another Band.

Cirl joined him, amazed. 'Oh, Rondl – you escaped the Kratch! I thought – '

'Relax,' he flashed. 'I told you I would handle it. I was fortunate.'

But inwardly he realized that it had been more than fortune. He had fought the monster in a way no other Band would have. He, Rondl, knew how to fight, and had the will for it. This was significant. He had not merely researched alien ways, he had mastered them.

He no longer needed to investigate the invading Solarians. They were obviously of the Kratch type: ruthless predators. Instead he needed to investigate the Bands' potential for resisting the invasion. If he could foil a monster, it should be possible for other Bands to do so too. The techniques of self-defence could be mastered by Bands – since he himself had done it.

They went to the education centre and flashed again with Proft. The educated Bands were already investigating the invasion; they had sent out individuals to neighbouring Spheres for advice. Or rather, they had made use of a Mattermitter borrowed from the Bellatrixians for the purpose, since actual star travel would have taken too long. The Bellatrixians were remaining neutral on this matter, but would always make advantageous trades.

But no one could make sense of the advice received. 'War – resistance – fight – destruction – retaliate.' What was the meaning of these alien terms? The experts were working on the matter, trying to come up with comprehensible definitions that would not cause Bands to disband . . .

War – an organized effort of mutual destruction, as if two groups of Bands encountered each other and, instead of conversing amicably or forming circles of mutual understanding, attempted to disband all its members first, or to cause the other group to disband first. The thing remained nonsensical; disbanding was always done voluntarily, except in those rare instances when a Band foolishly became trapped in a lethal situation, such as within range of a Trugd or Kratch.

Resistance – the effort of one person or party to oppose the will of another when that will was asocial. This, too, was almost incomprehensible; no Band would indulge in asocial will, so would need no opposition – and opposition itself was asocial. Avoidance was the appropriate course, not overt resistance.

Fight – active attempt to do harm to another person while the other person did the same. The one who hurt the other first or worst was deemed the better creature. How could any Band grasp this? The very notion was enough to cause some Bands to disband – as several had when presented with this appalling concept.

Destruction – the reduction of objects to nonuseful status. This was too silly on the face of it for further consideration.

Retaliate – to do similar harm to another, following the pattern of the harm that that other had done to the first person. This resembled half a Fight – and half of an intolerable concept remained intolerable. In the present case, this would be an attempt to 'destroy' the alien ships and force them to disband, so that none would be left to make mischief.

'Even if we were willing to perform such horror,' Cirl asked, her colour pale, 'how would we accomplish it? We have no – '

'Weapons,' Rondl provided when she paused, at loss for a term or concept.

'What?'

'Weapons. Devices that facilitate destruction and disbanding.'

Her magnetic field wavered so sharply that for a moment Rondl feared she would disband. But, with an effort, she stabilized. 'Your strange, horrible, alien knowledge,' she flashed weakly. 'I know you have odd attitudes, yet sometimes – '

'You do seem to have a certain tolerance for difficult concepts,' Proft remarked diplomatically.

'Yes. I now doubt my amnesia derives from contact with a Kratch. I just encountered one, and foiled it without further complications in my memory.'

'You foiled a Kratch?' Proft was astonished.

'He led it into a comet and stuffed it with dust,' Cirl said excitedly. 'He stopped it from eating me.' She made a demure spin. 'That is the second time he salvaged me from disbanding.'

'This is impressive,' Proft admitted. 'Your tolerance for violence far exceeds what I have seen in other Bands. What do you think is the proper course in the present crisis?'

'I suspect the advice of the other Spheres is correct. Aliens have opposed each other violently for millennia. Aliens are long hardened to asocial concepts. We Bands must harden ourselves, so that we can somehow abate this devastating thrust. Because if we do not, we may suffer colossal destruction ourselves.'

'Intellectually, I can appreciate your point,' Proft said. 'Yet I cannot support it. I have been long exposed to a variety of attitudes, so have more tolerance than most, but I could never indulge in – hardening. It is contrary to my nature.'

'And to that of the great majority of Bands,' Rondl agreed. 'I admit the notion makes me uneasy too. Yet not as uneasy as the notion of allowing ourselves to be dispossessed.'

Even as they conversed, more news flashed across the

region. The aliens had landed on the outermost major satellite of Planet Band, Moon Dinge, and were setting off explosions on its surface. The magnetic lines in that vicinity were being distorted, causing Bands to be stranded. There was another wave of disbanding.

'Will they never stop?' Cirl exclaimed, appalled.

'Not until they obtain what they want,' Proft replied grimly.

'Which may be the extirpation of the Band species,' Rondl added. 'How are the Bellatrixians reacting to this? Isn't their enclave near Moon Dinge?'

'They are watching, but remaining quiescent,' Proft said. 'In this System they abide by our conventions, and do not seek violence, though I believe they are capable of it.'

'They certainly are!' Rondl agreed vehemently, tagged by another stray memory. 'Once they had a war with Sphere Mirzam, at the area of intersection of their respective Spheres, and they destroyed fifty warships with a single – ' He broke off, seeing their confusion and horror, and the memory faded. It didn't seem to make much sense anyway: considering the difficulties of Spherical Regression, how could a major modern engagement take place at the fringes of the Spheres? 'Sorry. My recollection caught me by surprise. I think it was fiction, anyway. But I agree that the Bellatrixians are not bellicose here. If the Solarians do not attack their enclave – '

'The Solarians do not seem to know about the enclave,' Proft said. 'Certainly it is well concealed, in a planetoid in the Dinge orbit, and the Bellatrixians are keeping themselves hidden. They are following our policy of staying out of mischief.'

Something about that concept of an alien base concealed in a planetoid intrigued Rondl, but he could not place the notion. Had he been to that enclave in his prior

84

life? Some memories burst full-blown from minor triggers, while others remained below the threshold of recovery despite his best efforts, radiating only tantalizing suggestions of their nature. One impression came through, however; should the Solarians actually attack the Bellatrixian enclave, or even venture near it in their warships, another side of the Bellatrixian nature as Bands knew it would manifest itself. He was certain of this, without any definable reason for his certainty. Perhaps it was that aliens of any species could be extremely touchy about their operations.

Cirl fluctuated again. 'You are right, Rondl. We must must oppose this. Somehow.' For her, this reluctant acceptance of the notion of opposition was a considerable shift.

'Is there any – any authority in charge of – of defence?' Rondl asked.

'Authority?' Cirl asked blankly. 'Defence?' She had assimilated one alien concept; others remained beyond her.

'These are other Spherical matters,' Proft replied. 'Bands have no government in the Galactic sense. We are governed solely by convention and our nature.'

'Then how can I consult with the Band military – ' He broke off, realizing there was no such thing. How could he have thought there was? 'Or obtain appointment to whatever organization is supposed to preserve Bands from extinction?' he asked, frustrated.

'You must appoint yourself, and recruit anyone you can,' Proft said. 'That is how any cause is served. Whoever has the interest expresses it and seeks the support of others with similar interests.'

'But I have no authority! Not even memory!'

'These are irrelevant concepts.'

'But there has to be some – structure. Some organization. For example, who appointed you to your educational position?'

'I appointed myself,' Proft said.

Rondl assimilated this. No central administration at all? 'Do you mean that I can just go out and ask Bands to work with me – and they will?'

'Those who so choose. Those who have the will. It depends on how persuasive you are.'

'But there are so many things that just had to be organized! Who set up trade relations with the Bellatrixians?'

'Some time ago, when the Bellatrixians came to proffer their trade, a self-formed group laboured diligently to grasp the concept, and was so successful that it arranged all the benefits we have derived from that connection, including the construction of these convenient reflective walls for this institution. This was done by one Band who had strong motivation and perception; he is a hero to our memory now. Wonr the Trader.'

What would be Rondl's reputation, if he did something like this? Rondl the Warrior? Warmonger? Well, why not?

Yet that seemed foolish vanity, for one with no memory. 'I can hardly persuade myself. I seek to join an existing apparatus.'

'Apparatus?' Cirl asked.

'You perceive the problem,' Proft said. 'If you wish, I will invite you to address my classes. Perhaps some individuals will join you.'

Another general flash of news came: more Solarian ships had been spied, hurtling towards System Band at sublight velocity. In a few days they would arrive.

'They must have a major Mattermission station set up in this vicinity,' Rondl flashed. 'It would take hundreds of years for them to move from Sol to Band at sublight velocity.'

'You have an amazing knowledge of Spherical space,' Proft observed.

'I do, for an amnesiac.' But he could not take time to dwell on that at the moment. 'I think I had better accept your offer, and talk to your students. Give me time to organize my case, and I will see what can be done.'

Rondl and Cirl retired to consult. 'I must try to summarize the problem and offer a viable mode of action,' he said. 'But the problem of definitions seems overwhelming. If I start in defining combat, counterintelligence, and military discipline, I'll never get to the subject.'

'Combat? Counterintelligence?' she asked.

'You see? I can no more communicate such concepts to you than you can communicate the correct mode of lovemaking to me.'

She assimilated that. 'Perhaps I *could* – '

'You could?' Suddenly this was more interesting.

'If I could find a way to inform you, maybe you could find a way to inform others of your concepts.'

'I'm not sure that follows. Still – '

'Sometimes it is easier if others do it.'

'But *we* have to do it!' Suddenly he was not sure they were talking about the same thing. But assuming the subject was love, he did not want to commit himself to making love with some other female, while Cirl – no!

'Like a story of others. Others make war, whatever that is. And love.'

Oh. A story, rather than an actual – yes! Rondl realized that she was offering him something similar to what he had sought before: a look at another couple in action. 'A story of others,' he agreed, relieved. 'Call him One, call her Two. What is it they do?'

Cirl considered, still finding this difficult. 'One wished to – to express himself to Two, and she was willing to receive the expression. More than willing! So he – '

87

This was obviously extremely awkward for her to present. It occurred to him that in many Galactic cultures there were things that were socially acceptable in the doing, but not in the describing. Other things could be described, but not done. The gratuitous murder of a member of the same species was an example of the latter, while the detailed processes of procreation – yes. That was the barrier they encountered here. Perhaps he could assist her narration.

'I assume this happened a long time ago,' he said. 'Both parties have long since disbanded, so there can be no offence in the memory of their history.'

'Yes,' she agreed gratefully. 'A long time ago. They later disbanded after full lives. Maybe their auras merged in the Viscous Circle, and they were sublimely happy for an eternity, and after that, sections of those auras fragmented off to join new Bands, and parts of both are in our own auras – ' But that was getting too personal again, causing her to balk. Anything that made the analogy too plain was taboo.

'Parts of earlier auras are in all of us,' Rondl said, playing along with the mythology, which he found charming. 'But they are spread so thin, as the result of centuries of viscosity and dilution in others, that nothing is recognizable now. All we have is their story, not their spirits.'

This enabled Cirl to continue. 'It is flashed that when the time came, he – positioned himself so that – ' She paused again, her colour pulsing with embarrassment. It was amazing what magnetic fluctuations could do to surface hue! 'So that his communication beam intersected her – ' Yet again she paused, her flashes fuzzing with the supposed shame of the unutterable.

An alien concept came to Rondl now: *pornography*. What was natural and necessary in life became, through the alchemy of social perception, indescribable. To him, he discovered when he thought about it, the evil lay not so much in the act, or in the depiction of it, as in the twisted attitudes of others who perceived it as unclean. Yet his own attitude had undergone a gradual transformation with experience. There had been a time, on a backward fringe world – but what was he thinking of? The memory evanesced with a fleeting picture of some alien creature with a triple-head extremity. Absolutely meaningless! 'Some things are not to be expressed,' he flashed. 'I think I know of the phenomenon in other cultures.'

'True.'

'But many aliens are monsters.' Triple-headed monsters? 'We are not.'

'Yes,' she agreed. And tried again. 'So these two reversed their – '

She could not complete it, but Rondl had caught on. There were, after all, only so many positions two Bands could assume with respect to each other. Position was the key!

He positioned himself so that the output of his lens intersected the output of hers. This was no good for dialogue, as neither could assimilate the message of the other. The lenses placed backward did not communicate. Not intelligibly. But the mode turned out to be excellent for love.

Rondl experienced an exceptional thrill as her flash passed through his reversed lens, and he knew that she was having a similar experience. The lens was dual-purpose, he realized now: one way for intellectual communication, the other way for love.

'Love, love, love!' he broadcast, drawing nearer, orienting more perfectly to the light of Sun Dazzle while she oriented on Sun Eclat. And he felt her response, more wonderful than any intellectual thing could be: *Love,*

89

love, love! There was communication, but of a nonintellectual, nonobjective nature. Love was not intellect, but feeling. The other side of the lens.

Then Rondl stopped thinking and gave himself up entirely to feeling.

CHAPTER 6

War

Rondl floated before a class of twenty young Bands. All were attentive to his beam as it flashed across the enclosure and reflected from the curving wall. Could he get his message across?

'This is the story of the ugly Solarian and the three innocent species,' he said. He had the nagging feeling he had adapted the story from some other narration, but he could not think what that might be. There was nothing similar he knew of in Band lore. 'The Solarian is a gross physical creature with bone-filled extremities, flesh-filled torso, and liquid-filled eyeballs sliding within moist sockets – '

There was a shuddering flash of revulsion among the students. He was overdoing the horror! Rondl cut short the description, not wanting to disturb them too violently. 'And an asocial nature. He comes upon a creature of a different species who is bathing in a favourable light while contemplating an aesthetic notion. The Solarian desires this particular patch of light, though there is plenty of other light from this sun, so he shoves Creature One aside and takes the place for himself. Now how should Creature One proceed?'

The students were responsive. 'He should move to a new spot,' a blue one replied. 'Unsocial behaviour by one party does not justify the same by another party.'

There were affirmative flashes: this was the consensus. 'So Creature One moves to a new spot,' Rondl continued. 'But the Solarian concludes that the new spot must be

91

better than the old, so he shoves Creature One again. Now what should One do?'

There was a trace of doubt, but again the answer was to move.

'And the Solarian, determined that Creature One shall have no peace, pursues him there. It seems that Creature One cannot avoid mischief merely by moving, for the Solarian is jealous of any comfort he may possess. What should One do now?'

There was increased doubt. 'He is in an untenable situation,' a green student concluded. 'All he can do is disband.' The others, after due consideration, agreed.

'So Creature One is gone,' Rondl concluded. 'Now the Solarian casts about and comes upon Creature Two, of a different species. He seeks to move Creature Two out, but Two, having noted the futility of moving, refuses to budge. She is an extremely aesthetic member of her species, but she is in the way of the Solarian. So he destroys her.'

There was a muted flash of horror. Yet not of disbelief, for the current intrusion by the Solarians into Band space was in their awareness.

'What should Two have done?' Rondl inquired, forcing them to tackle this ugly question. When they could not answer, he prompted them: 'What could she have done to save herself from destruction?'

Now, reluctantly, they tackled the problem. 'She could after all have moved,' a white female student flashed.

'But the ugly Solarian would have followed until she had to disband,' a yellow one objected.

'So she would have gained nothing by passive resistance,' a black one concluded.

'Except perhaps dignity,' a grey one put in.

'She needed another alternative,' a brown one said.

'Yet if to remain or to remove are both negative – '

92

They were getting into it, as Rondl had hoped they would. His hypothetical situation was forcing them to struggle with difficult alternatives. Time to give them some help. 'I fear Creature Two is finished; she had no viable alternatives, in the face of the Solarian's ugliness. Now the Solarian casts about again with his liquid-filled eyeballs, as his appetite for mischief seems to be insatiable. He spies Creature Three.'

'Oh, no!' the white female flashed, already horrified.

Rondl paused, letting them build up morbid curiosity. He was, he realized, a fairly good storyteller; he must have done some of it before. 'Now Creature Three has observed the prior two histories. He realizes that it is futile either to move or to remain. In fact, he knows he can do nothing to help himself – alone.' He paused again. The key concept was coming up, and it had to be presented properly.

'But two creatures would still have trouble,' a bright-red student objected. 'First the Solarian would move one, then the other.'

'Unless they act together,' Rondl suggested.

The class was blank. They did not understand. Bands did not work together, except to help each other briefly or to mate. The ad hoc formations were exceptional. Here was the delicate point.

Time for a separate theme. 'When I spun out of control, another Band helped me to recover. When my friend Cirl fell in the water, I brought her out. There is ample precedent for one Band helping another in need.'

'True, but those were special circumstances,' a silver student said. 'Those were positive acts. It would have been unsocial to allow another to suffer when it could readily be prevented.'

'If your friend is attacked by a monster, would it not be positive to help your friend?'

93

They were muted, pondering that. Some had picked up the flash about Rondl coming to Cirl's rescue when the Kratch attacked her.

'Now Creature Three has enlisted the aid of a friend. Together they are stronger than the single Solarian.' Again Rondl paused. He had been building up to this gradually, trying to keep them with him. Would he succeed? 'Now there does not have to be asocial behaviour. The two creatures simply say to the Solarian: 'If you push one of us, both of us will do the same to you.' Now what do you suppose the Solarian will do?'

They considered. 'He will depart,' a purple student suggested, a trifle uncertainly.

'Then no one has suffered,' Rondl concluded.

Immediately there were objections. 'But suppose he does push?' They were as yet unable to express the concept 'Attack'.

'Then has the Solarian not brought the counterpush upon himself? He knew that various actions would have certain consequences. If he lumbered on his gross bone-filled extremities into a wall, he would come to an abrupt and uncomfortable halt. If he drained the liquid from his eyeballs, he would lose his sight. If he pushed Creature Three, he would be pushed back by two creatures. He had been warned; the choice was his. Creature Three has merely helped set the scene.'

But they had trouble with this. 'Suppose the Solarian brings another monster, to destroy them both?'

'Then perhaps Creature Three needs to fetch more of his own friends.'

'But this would escalate! It would be – ' The students could not find the applicable concept.

Now was the time. 'It would be war,' Rondl said. Now they were ready to absorb the necessary definition. 'The organized effort of many creatures to safeguard their

94

interests against aggression by others.' Would any students disband, or had he brought them to it positively enough?

None disbanded. The discussion became animated. 'How could many creatures organize? Bands do not organize.'

'They must have a leader,' Rondl explained. 'One who guides the activity of all. Then they can act effectively.'

They considered and discussed and questioned. But they kept remembering the invading Solarians, and inevitably came to agree with his suggestion. In fact, several of them elected to accept his leadership in the effort to save the Bands from the ugly, liquid-eyeballed Solarians.

'But I was not recruiting!' Rondl protested. 'I was only presenting the case, to see if people could accept it.'

Proft had been present, but without flash. Now he entered the discussion. 'It is a good case, but you must be prepared to complete it. This, I suspect, is to be your project.'

Rondl realized that if he retreated now, it would seem that he did not believe in his own thesis. Someone had to stop the invading monsters, and it seemed he had to be the one to try. 'I will recruit,' he said. 'But I will insist that any person who wishes to join me check with his family and friends first, so as not to make a rash decision. The action I contemplate may be difficult for Bands to comprehend or accept, and certainly can be dangerous. People may be disbanded.'

'Disbanding is merely a return to the Viscous Circle,' the red student flashed. 'It is not an occurrence to be feared.'

Belief in Band Heaven seemed to be universal. Risks did not bother these people as much as they bothered Rondl, because they did not really believe in death. Was it fair to them to put their lives in jeopardy on the basis of that faith?

'I would not encourage any of you to disband merely because you don't mind doing it,' Rondl said carefully.

95

'There may be important things remaining for you to accomplish in this life.' He hoped that was both accurate and diplomatic. He had no call to disparage their faith, though he regarded it as myth or superstition. 'So consider carefully, before risking your physical lives. The task I offer – ' He let it lapse into implication.

'Let us disperse now and consider separately,' Proft suggested. 'Those who wish to enlist in Rondl's effort may do so tomorrow. He has other classes to address today.'

Other classes! This was rolling along much more swiftly than he had anticipated. Yet he had to complete what he had started.

As it turned out, Rondl spent many days addressing assorted groups. After the first day, and following each class, an increasing stream of recruits came. Not every Band who received his message decided to join, but one in ten did – and as time passed, the ratio improved. Soon Rondl had more than a hundred recruits.

It was time to start training. He wondered whether he had done something like this in his prior life. Certainly he had had some similar experience – if not physical, then through research. Strange, though, that there was no news of any project of this magnitude; if he had done it here on Planet Band, someone should have recognized him.

First he had to organize the volunteers he had, and categorize the associated abilities in his group with attention to the job they had to do, considering their general reluctance to act in an unsocial manner and their readiness to disband rather than oppose the onslaught of a monster. This was unlikely to be easy. First he had to toughen them, make them able to contemplate violent action and then to participate in it.

The technique came to him as he formulated the problem. He had to decivilize the opposition, make the enemy seem beneath consideration as a sapient species. It was easier to oppose a monster than a fellow sapient. The Solarians had to be monsterized. That should not be too hard to do, since they were most of the way there already.

Rondl set up a series of skits with assigned parts. A suitable planetoid represented a Monster spaceship. As a matter of policy, he no longer referred to Solarians; they were all Monsters. The planetoid was a cylindrical and partly polished chunk of rock with assorted fissures and outcroppings; it really was ideal for the purpose. It suggested the shape of both the Kratch and the Solarian spaceship, reinforcing the impression of monsterism without being too obvious.

Certain hardened Bands were stationed around the 'ship' and assigned to flash crude impulses of hate at all who approached. This took some practice, and one trainee disbanded, but in due course the mock cadre of Monsters was ready.

Rondl led the practice attack with a picked squad of his most promising recruits. One was Limn, a yellow-white male whose speciality was alien mechanics; he understood space vessels and thought he would be able to disable one if he could get inside it. So he was about to try to get inside the mock ship. Another was Tembl, a dark blue female of winsome magnetism who planned to study philosophy, but had a lot of emotion and felt impelled to rout the invader from Band space. A third was Blut, a grey student of Solarian languages; he knew Solarians were not asapient monsters, but he had had a friend disband prematurely because of the invasion, and wanted no more of that. Despite their mythology, Bands did have a certain objection to involuntary or untimely disbanding; for one thing, a prematurely disbanded individual brought less than the optimum amount of accumulated experience back to the Viscous Circle. Thus the harvest was unripe. It simply wasn't proper to undertake a physical life only to

97

return without full experience. This represented a certain waste of the loan of a Soul. So though Blut was incapable of conceiving it this way, he had a score to settle with the Solarians, and Rondl was glad to have his linguistic expertise in the party. He wanted to be able to talk with the Solarians, if only to warn them to withdraw. That was the civilized thing to do; it would make his effort legitimate if the Monsters then ignored the warning.

If they ignored it? *When!* Rondl somehow knew that nothing short of violence would cause them to reconsider. It would be as useless to reason with a Kratch as to expect the Solarians to desist merely because someone asked them to.

They flew towards the ship. Suddenly the hate flashed from it: 'HATE! HATE!' Though it was a setup, on a mock run at a pretend ship, and they all knew it, the scenario abruptly seemed to come to life. An actual message of hate – that had phenomenal impact! Most Bands had never experienced anything like this. The ship became metallically menacing, and the creatures associated with it became Monsters indeed. 'Hate!' Rondl flashed back, and the Bands with him picked it up, at first tentatively, then with more conviction. They were, after all, the objects of mindless hate; how could they fail to respond?

They flew closer, flashing their mutual animosity, getting into the terrible spirit of it. It was as if a cloud of malevolence encompassed them. Suddenly one of the mock Monsters exploded. Particles puffed outward in a dissipating cloud.

Oh, no! That person had disbanded. Rondl realized that this practice exercise had become too serious. He had concentrated all his efforts to make it realistic, to overcome the Bands' natural reluctance to indulge in violence, without realizing that success could be as mischievous as failure. The hate broadcasters had not been properly prepared to withstand the return of their hate. He would have to abort this session and prepare more carefully for the next. 'Desist! Desist!' he flashed in a spiral.

But the others, intent on the battle, swept up in it, did not receive his message. The position of the two suns was not right; he could not attract the attention of his associates. The charge continued.

The Monster flashes doubled in intensity and frequency: 'HATE! HATE! HATE!' They were angry about the loss of their companion. An emotion long suppressed in their species was being brought out; they were reverting to a primitive state.

One of Rondl's group disbanded. This was awful! They were all caught in the malign spirit of the battle, suffering emotional overload, and could not get free. Even if some received his message to desist, they were no longer capable of responding to it.

Rondl slowed, hoping to cause his companions to slow. Then he could lead them away from the Monster ship and allow them to cool. But it didn't work; they charged right on. His reticence only made it seem that he was losing courage. So he had to resume his place in the lead, hoping to think of something else before disaster ruined them.

Another Monster disbanded; then two more allies. Casualties were mounting, just as they would in a real battle. What horror had he loosed among these peaceful people? Was this any better than the havoc wreaked by the Solarians?

They arrived at the ship. Limn went near it, trying to get inside so he could disrupt its operation. The others surrounded the remaining Monsters, flashing savagely.

'That's enough!' Rondl flashed in a full sphere. 'Enough! Enough! We have achieved our objective.'

But still they fought, radiating hate at each other.

Another Band, overwhelmed, disbanded; and another. It was carnage! The destruction-fever was on the group, and they couldn't fight it, just each other.

At last the last Monster-ship defender disbanded, destroyed by the messages of hate bombarding him from all sides. Victory.

Then the Bands settled down, exhausted, finally paying attention to Rondl. But it was too late for nine of them.

Now that he had their attention, he hardly knew where to begin. They had got into the spirit of violence too well, and paid the penalty. Buried in the Band nature there was, after all, a remaining spark of aggression, of violence, and he had brought it to the surface with its consequent mischief. He had evoked another kind of monster – the one that lurked deep within the Bands themselves. Now he wished he had not.

At least they were educable. 'This is what a real battle might have been like,' he told them. 'War is hell. Hateful things occur. People have to be toughened to violence, or it overcomes them. We lost a number of us in this exercise because we were not toughened enough. Those of us who survive are the hardened ones. But the hate of the true Monsters will be worse. We must become more disciplined, and more resistive to negative flashes, if we are to have a chance against the real enemy.' As he said it, he realized its truth: discipline. That had been the major weakness. He had to have his troops responsive to leadership at all times.

Another Band disbanded.

'But the exercise is over!' Rondl protested.

'Now we are realizing what we have done,' Tembl said. She was the philosopher; she was working it out. 'We have, however briefly, become monsters ourselves.' And as the others picked up her flash, two more disbanded.

Rondl had hoped to conceal this fact from them, but perhaps it was best that they know. In the very process of opposing oppression, they were losing the values they lived for. This, too, was the nature of war.

CHAPTER 7

Dream

Rondl relived the mock battle in a dream. He experienced the flush of excitement as he and his troop charged, then the flashing 'HATE! HATE!' of the pseudoenemy. How powerful it was, like Cirl's 'LOVE! LOVE!' yet opposite, making him want to disband. And beside him others *were* disbanding, going to their mythical reward. They believed in the Viscous Circle, and so they threw away their lives for trifles. He knew better than to do this himself, yet now he felt an almost overpowering temptation. To leave this misfortune behind, and return in comfort to the Viscous Circle –

He woke radiating horror. Cirl was there to comfort him. 'A nightmare,' he told her. 'An unpleasant dream. All those needless deaths in that practice mission, some of our best personnel lost – '

'There is no death,' she reminded him. She had not participated in the mock battle, having been busy helping new recruits to orient. Rondl was now immensely grateful for her absence then. Gentle Cirl would have been the first to disband!

'Still, they should not have – '

'Disbanding is perfectly natural. You need feel no guilt about that.'

She, too, believed. She, especially, believed. It was one of the pleasant things about her. He loved her in part for that belief; it was her signal of faith and innocence, the qualities he lacked. 'I know you feel that way. You were considering disbanding when we met,' he reminded her

102

fondly. 'You were even annoyed with me when I interfered.'

'True,' she agreed guilelessly. 'I am no longer annoyed.'

'Yet if you had disbanded, wouldn't your grief have
accompanied you to the afterlife?' Rondl asked, intrigued
again by the notion of death as a mere transition between
forms. The notion was insidiously tempting. It certainly
would be a wonderful comfort to believe in such a thing –
but he was too objective for that. 'What then would you
have gained?'

'I would not have gained very much at first,' she
admitted. 'The disbanded aura remains discrete for a
time, until it orients and finds its way to the Viscous
Circle. But slowly the hurt would fade.'

'Wouldn't it fade similarly in life?'

'It has done so,' she admitted. 'I am glad I did not
disband at that time. I would never have met you.'

'You do not find me repulsive because of my alien
notions? Because I grasp the concepts of war and violence?'

She considered. 'I think, at this pass, it is necessary for
someone to grasp these horrors. You are the one who has
assumed the burden, for the good of the society.'

He had really been seeking reassurance that she loved
him. He had got a disturbingly relevant answer. Could
she also answer his doubts about the Viscous Circle?
'And if you had disbanded then, and if the hurt you
carried with you had been too intense to fade in the
afterlife, what then?' Now, in a perverse countercurrent,
he was trying to make her see that the mythology was
pointless – and hoping that it was not, that she would
have a sufficient answer. Wouldn't it be better to embrace such an illusion, to relieve himself of his morbid
fear of extinction?

'When the individual aura/soul rejoins the Viscous

103

Circle, all hurts spread out, diffuse, dilute in the viscosity of the totality, and affect the individual only slightly. A great hurt to one is insignificant when borne by the entire soul-mass.'

'But you, also, would be diluted! You would lose your individuality at the same rate, stirred into that enormous mass!'

'Yes, that is the beauty of viscosity,' she agreed. 'Maybe you should have let me go. I almost want to do it now. If you will come with me – '

Rondl concealed his sudden horror. 'We have other tasks first,' he said hastily. He certainly didn't want her disbanding now, or taking him with her! 'The burden I have assumed, for the good of society – '

'Yes, yes of course,' she agreed immediately. 'And you must rest, for there remains so much to do.'

Rondl returned to his interrupted sleep, reassured.

And dreamed again. This time it was more realistic than before. He really felt the stress of battle, and the hate seemed to come from genuine aliens. Such malignity! Yet now Rondl answered it with his own flashing hate and, fending off the alien animosity, led his people all the way up to the dread spaceship. It was a real ship now, with portholes and bulging turrets and grotesque projecting weapons that fired out bright light and physical projectiles. But Rondl let the light pass through his lens, ignoring its inanimate malignance, and avoided the slower projectiles. The Monster weapons could not hurt vigilant Bands! Yet his Band companions were not aware of this, and were disbanding in droves. He had to get them away from here so that he could instruct them how to handle this attack. He had not prepared them for reality, thinking this was only a mock run.

But he could not communicate with them. Everyone he flashed to, disbanded before comprehending. All his troops were exploding into gas and particles, until he alone remained.

A Solarian hatch opened. A grotesque Monster-head appendage protruded. Its liquid-turgid eyeballs swivelled gruesomely in their twin sockets to orient on Rondl. Its gross oral cavity writhed open, revealing Trugdlike rending teeth. Atmosphere issued from that appalling vent, charged with noise.

'And now, Ringer, you shall be one of us!' the Monster projected verbally. The most horrible aspect of this nightmare was that Rondl was able to assimilate that gross gaseous vibrational pattern that constituted sound, though he had no organ for it, and to comprehend the awful meaning embedded in that shaking atmosphere.

'No!' he cried, atmospherically, impossibly. But the thing reached forth a gruesome physical appendage, replete with ungainly long bone supports inside the taut flesh, and knobby joints, to grasp Rondl. At the end of this apparatus the flesh split into multiple tiny extensions, each of which had little bones and joints, and these extensions sought to close on Rondl's body. One of them poked through his lens, like the tip of the Kratch's spike. A more horrible contact could not be imagined; even a genuine Kratch was better than this, for it at least was comprehensible.

He woke radiating revulsion and fear, and again Cirl comforted him. She clasped him magnetically close, then withdrew enough to indulge in a rotating-mode dialogue. They discussed the dreams, and concluded that Rondl was experiencing the semialien emotion of guilt for the way he had led a dozen Bands into disbanding. 'It is a function of your disbelief,' Cirl said. 'You suppose they are dying, so you are concerned. If only you believed – '

'What Band ever disbanded and then returned to report on the Viscous Circle?' he demanded.

'Why none, of course. No Band returns without first rejoining the Circle – and thereafter he is completely mixed by the viscosity, and returns only as elements of new-formed Bands, as new hosts are generated.'

'Have any of these remixed fragments reported?' he asked.

'Fragment is an inapplicable concept. When a Band merges with the Circle, he loses his former identity, so there is no real memory.'

'Experience changes us day by day, yet we remember,' he reminded her. Her picture of the myth was so complete!

'Perhaps some do remember,' she agreed. 'That must be how we learned about the Afterlife.'

'How do you know some Band didn't simply make it all up, for the notoriety?'

'For the what?'

Another alien concept! 'To become widely known among Bands.'

'Who would want to be widely known?'

'Or for whatever reason. So he invented – '

She was incredulous. 'No Band would invent!'

He gave it up. Her faith was lovely, and was part of what made her lovely. Why should he seek to lessen it? 'At any rate, I want to send no more Bands to oblivion – ah, anonymity in the Viscous Circle before their time.'

'Yes, that would be proper,' she agreed. 'But still you need not dream about those already gone. Your dreams cannot affect them.'

Here she was more sensible than he! Of course his dreams were useless, even as apology. 'Yet still I feel remorse, for causing – '

'You did not cause,' she reminded him firmly. 'Disbanding, even in extraordinary circumstance, is always an individual decision. They decided to go.'

106

'What about when the Kratch – '

'It is better to disband than to suffer physical demolition by such a creature.'

So she considered even that case voluntary. To resign rather than to be fired – whatever that alien notion meant. Charming naïveté! Yet the presence and persistence of her faith made his unfaith easier to bear. They turned about and made love, and it was wonderful.

Yet even then Rondl wasn't satisfied. 'We have never married,' he said.

She flashed humour. 'You have used that term before. Alien creatures marry. Bands are able to associate amicably.'

'Proft understood it. He said – '

'Proft is familiar with alien concepts, and may even forget they are alien. He surely knew what you meant, and spoke to that point without quibbling about the details.' She was glowing more brightly now, enjoying herself.

'Yet there should be some social commitment, acceptance in the vision of the community, a family situation to raise offspring – ' Rondl paused, realizing. 'You know the concept! You were going to marry your prior male friend! You're teasing me!'

Her laughter radiated merrily. 'How long I have wished to catch you just once in your own alien mesh of concepts! Of course I grasp marriage!'

'Then marry me!' Rondl flashed, relieved.

She glowed. 'I will arrange this thing, if it pleases you.' She was still shining out her satisfaction at having confused him about an unalien concept. Rondl realized he surely deserved it; he had been confusing her all along with alien concepts.

She took him out into space and summoned another circle, and in that sublime viscosity of common thought

Rondl and Cirl agreed to love one another as long as it was convenient and mutually satisfying to do so, and to see that their little Band was properly treated when it arrived.

Afterward, individual Bands flashed to Rondl. 'That was a pleasant gesture,' an orange one said. 'How nice to make your love public for all to appreciate. I think I shall do the same, one day.'

Most Bands, Rondl realized belatedly, kept marriage private between the two parties concerned. Since there were no records, it really did not matter who else knew about such agreements. So he had, after all, brought an alien tinge to this. But he was not dismayed.

The training progressed. Rondl proceeded more carefully, with more gentle exercises and frequent dialogue to warn the recruits of the fierce emotions likely to be conjured from the depths of the Band nature. Gradually he built up some people and persuaded others to abandon the programme, until he had a nucleus of very fit, tough Bands. But could they actually engage the enemy and survive?

There was only one way to find out. The Solarians were advancing steadily, overrunning the outer satellites of Planet Band, and it was time to go to meet them.

He slept again, and dreamed again. This time his dream-troops, responsive to his instructions, took evasive action. A number survived the onslaught of the Solarian weapons. They ringed the enemy ship and tried to infiltrate it, to short out its electrical system. But again the hatch opened and the dread Solarian head-protuberance poked out. This time the detail was horrendously complete. The Monster had a translucent, lenslike, bubble-thing encircling the appendage, so that all its ghastly excrescences could be seen. Bits of living flesh projected on three sides, with the half-sunken, fluid-tumescent

108

eyeballs set near one of these projections. Below was the mobile orifice, a gash that opened and closed at irregular intervals, the tooth-bones showing only partially as if the wound was not quite complete. The opposite side was covered by long-sprouting fur, vaguely like Band tendrils but far more extensive.

The grotesque head swivelled on the flesh-clad neck and the orbs bore on Rondl. The orifice parted to show the animalistic teeth more fully. Each tooth erupted from moist pink tissue, like bleached bare rock from a slope of tinted clay. The creature exhaled in its obnoxious fashion, noisily pushing atmosphere out through the slit. And the noises said: 'Ringer, you are one of us!'

Somehow it seemed that Rondl was being drawn into the Monster, into its head: not past the emerging gas of its mouth-orifice, but directly into the solid lump above. This was a fate worse than disbanding! He fought and flashed desperately, as he had when caught on the spike of the Kratch – and woke again.

It was getting worse. How much more of this could he take without disbanding? The Viscous Circle, illusion and all, was becoming a more viable alternative.

'I think you will have to conquer the Monsters in the waking state,' Cirl said wisely and sadly. 'Then they will rest in your dreams.'

She had to be right. Rondl had many concepts of action and violence, but the prospect of encountering the Solarians directly horrified him. He was afraid – yet he had to do it. Otherwise they would destroy the entire Band society.

Now the occasion arrived. Rondl and his company took up positions near the moon next in the path of the invaders, Moon Spare. 'We shall wait for them to come close,' he flashed. 'Then we attack, as we have practiced.' They were now able to tolerate such direct language.

Yet his preparations seemed insufficient as the ship came close. Three Bands disbanded as the tension built. Rather than suffer further attrition before the action started, Rondl ordered his troops forward.

The ship proceeded without reaction. No weapons appeared, no hate was broadcast. Rondl realized with relief and dismay that the ship had not even noticed them; or perhaps it considered them to be of no account. They flew right up to it without event.

This was suspiciously easy. What about the projected 'Hate! Hate!' and the burning lasers? Where were all the threats they had braced against? He began to fear this was merely another dream, though he was sure it wasn't. What could they do, except proceed? 'Go on, Limn,' he flashed to the yellow-white specialist in alien mechanics. Limn was the key to their thrust. If he could disable this ship –

The ship was absolutely huge, many times the mass of the planetoid they had mock-attacked with such loss. Limn glided across its surface, following convenient lines. He found a vent where hot gases emerged – a stabilizing jet, Rondl knew without knowing how he knew – and slipped into it. Bands were not affected by heat of this level, though that could change if the ship started manœuvring more actively. At the moment the hulk was merely drifting, not wasting energy during its approach to the moon. Even Monsters had to be aware of energy consumption; they did not want to be stranded in deep space.

Could Limn really short out the control system? They had studied models of alien ships provided by the Bellatrixians, but nothing like this had been attempted before. They had simply to wait for Limn to nullify the critical electric circuits so that the ship could not function. Then Blut would try to communicate with the Monsters, using a crude ON/OFF flash code the Monsters were supposed to understand, to get them to surrender. At the moment the

110

whole thing seemed exceedingly doubtful. But very soon they would know.

Suddenly the ship accelerated. Tremendously hot gases shot from its vents as it shoved forward. There was no sign of Limn. 'I fear he was disbanded by the exhaust,' Blut flashed. Bands understood about exhaust, because it was an attribute of the Kratch, who fired out collected space dust along with its own waste products. That was another distinguishing trait of Monsters of any type: they had waste products. This ship was reacting exactly as the similarly shaped Kratch would have.

Then the moving ship looped about and came back. 'Scatter!' Rondl flashed. 'They have become aware of us!'

Indeed they had. An object lofted out of the ship. The Bands fled along all available lines as the object flew to the spot where they had congregated. There it exploded violently, sending fragments and radiation outward. The effect resembled disbanding, only much exaggerated.

The Bands were already distant from the detonation, but its power caught them anyway. Rondl was hurled off his line and through space.

He fought to recover equilibrium. He found a line and brought himself to a halt, dizzy. How had the others fared? 'Report presence,' he flashed in spiralling circles. forming a sphere of query.

Only a few responses came. Most of his party had been disbanded, not by the power of the explosion, but by the sheer malignance that alien attack evinced. In this respect the mock battle had been accurate; instead of 'Hate! Hate!' it had been a missile. Blut was gone, and the other specialists he had depended on. Only blue Tembl and a few others survived.

'I suspect we are not yet a match for the Monsters,' Tembl said. Something about the way she flashed made him more aware than he had been that she was female.

111

'Yet surely we disturbed them,' Rondl replied, as though that were justification for the disaster. 'Limn must have affected their system, alarming them so that they fought.'

'Yes, that does represent a certain progress,' she agreed, drawing near. 'Next time we must be able to stop such a detonation.'

Next time they would have to be much better prepared in every way, he realized. More than twenty Bands had been lost in this effort, accomplishing virtually nothing. All Rondl had succeeded in doing was to alert the Monsters that Bands were at least theoretically capable of attempting weakly to resist.

The succeeding nightmare was worse. He had many more lives on his conscience, and these new ones had not by any means been voluntary. He had tried to protect his troops from Monster hate, and had failed.

He and his companions charged the Solarian ship much as they had in reality; in fact for a while he confused the dream with reality. The ship looked more than ever like a tremendous Kratch, with a deadly spike and feeding aperture at the front, a filthy waste-products exhaust at the rear. They came up to it without difficulty, for it held them in contempt. This time they watched for the emergence of an explosive weapon. They had along a Band specialist in explosives; he thought he knew how to exert his magnetism to short out the electrical system of a bomb or shell to prevent it from activating.

But again the hatch opened and the hateful head appeared. The turgid eyeballs squished about in their confinements. 'You shall be ours!' the foul voice called.

And suddenly Rondl was drawn into that hideous head, settling on it though it had no spike, down onto its revolting hairy surface, merging with its blubbery flesh.

112

Rondl tried to disband, but was too late. He lacked the proper control in this dream state. His awareness penetrated the dreadful solid bone of it and expanded to embrace the grotesque organs, even the fluid-inflated eyeballs. Those orbs seemed almost to slosh as they slid about within the bony sockets of the skull. They were spheres with cubic housings, round pegs in square holes. About their only aspect of familiarity was the eyeball lens: it was small and physical and closed-in, but it did process light. Rondl oriented on that, striving to establish a bastion of sanity. Maybe he could still find a way to escape this horror.

The Monster drew its head back into the ship. It was a male, whose bone and flesh appendages enabled him to stand on a support and reach up to haul closed the hatch cover. Gas hissed into the chamber, pressurizing it. The Monster's fluid-lubricated flesh-tissue orifice opened, and breath/air/waste gas shoved out noisily. 'Ringers again,' he said. 'Blast 'em out of space.'

Machines functioned, hideously self-motivating. Radiation flared on vision screens. The group of pretty discs outside puffed into little clouds of dust. The Ringers were gone.

'Like shooting clay pigeons,' the Monster said, his bellows-body heaving in laughter.

Rondl's horror became so great his whole consciousness shattered. For he, in the jellybrain of the Monster, had in effect participated in this murder. He stopped trying to orient, to retain sanity or even consciousness. He flew apart, disbanding –

And woke. Cirl was hovering anxiously. 'The worst one yet,' Rondl flashed, almost afraid his communication would emerge as a blast of vibrating atmosphere. 'I entered the body of a Monster. I saw my companions destroyed.'

113

'But only some were destroyed,' Cirl reminded him, then quickly corrected herself. 'Some disbanded. Bands cannot be destroyed; they can only be hastened to the Viscous Circle.'

'And if all the physical Bands disband, what will happen to the Viscous Circle?' he demanded, fastening on that rather than on the fading nightmare.

'Why – there have to be *some* physical Bands, to provide hosts for pieces of the group aura,' she said. 'If all disbanded, the Circle would be without sources of new experience.'

'And so it would gradually stultify,' Rondl pointed out. He no longer tried to debate the existence of the unbodied aura; it was easier to assume its validity for the sake of harmony and dialogue with Cirl. 'So we must save the physical Bands from disbanding. Some of them, at least.'

'That's true,' she agreed, realizing the broader ramifications of the situation. She had supported Rondl because she loved him; she had stayed clear of the actual training and combat. Now she seemed to be joining him intellectually as well as emotionally.

'Only I keep failing, and these nightmares are threatening to finish me,' he said. 'I don't seem to be up to the job. I tried to disband myself. At least that finished the dream.'

'No Band is up to the job of battling Monsters,' she said. 'Maybe the dreams are a function of your uncertainty, which leads to errors in your actual attempts. If you could conquer obstacles in your sleep, maybe you could succeed better awake.'

'Maybe,' he agreed uncertainly. Cirl loved to conjecture reasons for his failures, excusing him from responsibility, and many of these reasons seemed plausible. But this one was the opposite of her last one, in which she had thought conquest in realism would help the dreams. 'I suspect both dreams and failures are merely reflections of my

114

incompetence, but since no one else is trying to save the Bands, I have to try whatever I can to become competent.'

'I will help you conquer your dreams,' she decided. 'I know you can succeed, if only you have the proper support.'

He was touched by her faith, but remained dubious. 'No one but me can enter my dreams.'

'That's not true. I can go with you.'

She seemed to be serious. 'How is that possible?'

Now she seemed diffident. 'There is a way.'

She had been like this when ready to make love. She was able to do but not to describe. 'Show me how,' he said, still not really believing.

She oriented with her beam steadily toward his beam, in the love position. She used Sun Eclat, he Sun Dazzle, as always. Surely it was not love she intended, though. Rondl held steady, waiting for her move.

'Sleep, Sleep, Sleep,' she sent. He received this emotionally, not intellectually, for it was arriving backward, to the subjective side of his lens. Love was blind; so was this message. But he needed no sight to feel sleepy.

He waited, and she drew closer, 'Sleep, Sleep.' He continued to respond, falling into the trance state verging on sleep; he could imagine no more pleasant mode for it. Cirl came all the way up to him and fastened her yellow circle to his green one. No wonder she had not been able to describe the action, for had this been love, it would have been prohibitively graphic. But it was instead sleep, of the most pleasant sort: embraced and enhanced by her.

Rondl slept and dreamed – and now Cirl was with him. 'You're here!' he flashed, astonished and gratified. 'You are in my dream!'

'Of course,' she replied, unconcerned. 'Two cannot make a viscous circle, but we can make a hint of it by

115

merging emotionally.' It was not the spirit circle she referred to this time, but the physical one. 'I will always be with you when you need me.'

But already the dream was carrying them on. They charged the Monster ship, and the hatch opened and the awful thing's head poked out. 'Now you will be ours!' the Monster blasted with its heated atmosphere, and Rondl was drawn in.

He tried to resist, and Cirl tried to hold him back, but the nightmare sequence was too strong for them both. Rondl and Cirl were drawn into the Monster.

'Hang on!' Rondl flashed foolishly, more worried about her than about himself. 'It is awful, but it can be survived!'

As it turned out, Cirl bounced off the male head and landed in a female head. This was reasonable; male auras could only occupy male hosts, and female auras female hosts. Did that hold true in the Viscous Circle? How could the auras of both sexes be merged therein? He would have to ask Cirl, when they woke.

Though he could no longer exchange flashes with Cirl, somehow Rondl remained in contact with her. In a dream this sort of thing could happen, fortunately.

The Monster Rondl occupied peered at the flat viewscreen. Rondl saw the image; even filtered through the unpleasant mechanism of watersac eyeballs, it was clear enough. 'Ringers! Blast 'em!' This was as it had been in the last dream; either Monsters or dreams were not bothering with originality.

'Ringers?' Cirl asked, perplexed. Since she could not flash in this form, communication between them did not make sense. But actually they were sleeping together, linked emotionally, and that translated into an intellectual linkage in the dream so that they could converse even when the dream suggested they could not. Dreams

116

did not follow the normal rules of life, which was the wonderful and horrifying thing about them.

'Ringers – that is the Monster name for Bands,' Rondl explained. 'I believe it evinces contempt.'

'Contempt?' This was another new concept for her.

'Low esteem. Dislike. Monsters do not respect Bands.'

She had to laugh, her pulsating flashes manifest to him by the magic of reality beneath the dream images. 'Non-respect – from Monsters! Yes, now I perceive this Monster's thought. There are personality currents forging through this jellybrain. She does not care for aliens.'

'Aliens!' Rondl flashed, finding further humour in this notion.

'To Monsters, we are the aliens!' She, too, found this funny.

'But this is our nightmare, not theirs. Maybe we can change their disesteem to respect.' Rondl concentrated, as the Monster's hand-appendage reached for the machine that caused explosions. Rondl willed the hand to draw back, extending his presence into the tubes and strings and fat deposits of it, causing the muscle tissue to convulse, and the thing did indeed go astray.

'Hey, my hand's not obeying me!' the Monster exclaimed with his huge exhalation of atmosphere.

'Let me see,' the female exhaled. She convulsed her own fat-encased leg appendages, balancing on the bones and joints, and moved across the room. She was grotesque, with ponderous masses of meat-flesh padding her limb-bones in places that distorted their outer configurations without enhancing their locomotive efficiency, and additional fat-stifled gland masses dangling from her torso, so that they had to be tied in place externally by a special band of material. Her glistening eyeball orbs slid about in their malformed sockets, showing white around the fringes, and an extraordinarily thick mass of fibres, completely dysfunctional, hung from her head. Incongruously, these superfluous fibres were yellow – the same colour as Cirl's own substance.

Rondl was amazed. He saw the female Monster as she was in all her horror – but the sodden tissue-brain of the male Monster perceived her entirely differently. The Monster perceived her as a lithe, slender, well-formed woman with excellent legs, an outstanding bosom, lovely green eyes, and beautiful golden tresses. The convolutions of her torso as she walked directed his mind immediately to reproductive matters. But he could only look, not act, because she had committed her reproductive capacity to the attentions of another male. Whatever faults they might have, Monsters had some brute sensitivities about interbreeding.

Cirl, too, was surprised. 'This female believes herself to be attractive to another of her species,' she commented. 'She thinks the orbs of your male are liquefying from their perusal of her meaty anatomy. Such illusion!'

'No illusion,' Rondl responded. 'The male Monster wants to – ' But he broke off his explanation, as he assimilated a more direct notion of the actual mechanics of what the male would like to do to facilitate reproduction, had he the opportunity. The actions were barely comprehensible, and completely disgusting.

As the female tried to touch the kill-machine, Cirl exerted her will and prevented her. 'Something's stopping me!' the female Monster exclaimed, alarmed.

The male's attention departed from the female's posterior and returned to the machine. He tried to reach it again, but Rondl made the muscles convulse all wrong. The female's liquid eyeballs seemed about to burst as she glared about in panic, her torso jerking in ways that were no longer quite so appealing to the male.

The Band nightmare was becoming the Monster night-

118

mare. 'We can control them!' Rondl flashed. 'We can make them do our will!'

Then he woke. Cirl remained with him, ring fastened to ring. He could no longer communicate with her objectively – strange how subjective expression turned objective in the dream state – but he could do so emotionally.

Exhilarated at their success in controlling the nightmare Monsters, Rondl proceeded to the other thing this position was good for. He did not choose to admit that the thoughts of the male nightmare Monster had given him the notion, but he did like the notion. 'Love! Love!' he flashed.

Cirl returned his signals. Soon they were deep in unmentionable bliss. Yet Rondl remained buoyed independently; together they had conquered the nightmares! They had prevented the Bands from being annihilated, this one time. He need no longer fear the Monsters of his dreams, thanks to Cirl's timely help.

CHAPTER 8
Campaign

Rondl and Cirl reorganized their group, which despite prior losses was now swelling enormously as increasing numbers of Bands became alarmed about the alien intrusion. Rondl set up a hierarchy of the trainers and staffers, so that each newcomer's skill could be integrated into the effort. He appointed a special corps of record-keepers who kept track of the others, since Bands had no written or computer records. When he needed a good geographer to chart the pattern of magnetic lines in a given region of space, the record-Bands identified one; when he needed a good circle-organizer for a conference, they located one.

The Bands were intrigued by what Rondl was doing. This was their first experience with government; they regarded it as a game or an emotional discipline, and once they mastered the fundamental principles, they cooperated well. A virtual nation of Bands was evolving and gaining in competence. Not again, Rondl hoped, would he lose half his party to disbanding without accomplishing anything.

Tembl, the blue philosopher, became more valuable. She was always near by, and willing to perform any minor task. It occurred to Rondl that she might be angling for – but no, he interrupted himself, that was his alien information putting unfortunate notions into his consciousness. Cirl was his love.

Now, how did things rest? He had, with Cirl's marvellous help, conquered his nightmares, but he had yet to conquer the actual Monsters. The liability of his effort was in the nature of the Bands: they disbanded too readily at the mere suggestion of violence, then lost discipline when finally worked up to some semblance of combat fervour. Clearly it was an unsane state for them, leading to awkward instability.

He needed to give them direct combat experience against a lesser foe than the Monsters, to sift out and toughen his most effective troops. He had to do this soon, because the Monsters would not sit back politely and wait for him to get ready.

What offered? He needed a real enemy, not another mock-up. A real challenge, but not too great to be overcome. Something like the water monster, or –

The Kratch! There was a suitable challenge! The Bands saw evil in very few things, but the evil of the Kratch they conceded. The spaceways would be well rid of such a monster.

Rondl put it to them fairly. 'We aren't ready to tackle the interstellar Monsters yet. But I will form my complement from those who prove they can handle the necessary rigours by performing satisfactorily in an interim mission. This will not be easy, but I think it is easier than dealing with the Solarians.'

'But what is it?' Tembl inquired eagerly.

'We are going to eliminate the Kratch from the zone of debris nearest the home planet, to make this region safe for Bands.'

Suddenly there was nervousness. This was real! Bands wavered and dimmed and spun erratically.

'This is volunteer,' Rondl clarified. 'I want only those who choose to join me, knowing the danger. Because I deem the Kratch to be a lesser threat than the Solarians, and anyone who is unable to face the Kratch will not be able to oppose the real Monsters. This is a selective process; I want no more Bands getting into situations beyond their endurance and disbanding at critical moments. Those who do not wish to tackle the Kratch do not have to give up the overall effort; there will be other tasks, such as marking the progress of the Monsters and conveying messages – tasks that are less stressful, but just as important. So consider carefully what type of participation you prefer. This particular mission is for the most aggressive of you.'

They considered carefully. The Kratch was not theoretical; the Kratch was dire and direct. No Band could approach a Kratch and be ignored. The Kratch was involuntary disbanding incarnate.

In the end about thirty Bands volunteered for the Kratch mission. Rondl had hoped for more, but was not about to force the issue; that would be counterproductive.

'I was pursued by a Kratch,' Rondl flashed to this more select group. 'It caught me, but I managed to collect a load of dust, and jettisoned the dust into the monster, giving it indigestion. I feel that way is too dangerous; we need safer alternatives. But it does indicate that the Kratch is not extremely intelligent, and can be balked by fairly obvious means. Do any of you have suggestions?'

Tentatively, they closed with the problem. 'We could lead it into a dangerous place,' a yellow Band suggested. 'One with many rocks.'

'I tried that before,' Rondl said. 'It gained on me, and caught me before I found a suitable place. Who would like to lead the Kratch that way?'

The Bands were daunted. None of them were eager to assume this type of chore.

'Actually, if we had a region of sure peril to the Kratch, and knew precisely where it was, we could safely lead the monster there, provided we had a sufficient lead,' Rondl said. 'It is a matter of margin. If it thinks it can catch one of us, and we know it cannot, the task becomes feasible. Preparation is the key.' Now more of the Bands became positive, but still no one had a suggestion.

After a pause, Rondl continued. 'I do have two notions relating to this problem, which you can consider and judge. First, we must thoroughly scout the region so we know exactly where to find the proper formation, so there need be no dangerous guesswork when the Kratch is roused. I repeat: planning is fundamental.'

'But suppose the Kratch comes upon us while we search?' a dark blue Band inquired.

'Now you're thinking ahead,' Rondl said approvingly. 'This is where my second notion comes in. I'm going to teach you the art of cross-tag.'

They spun uncertainly, not knowing what he meant. Small wonder; it was another alien notion. 'It is a game in which one person pursues another,' Rondl explained. 'Then a third party cuts in between them, and the pursuer must follow the new one until a fourth cuts between, and so on.'

'But wouldn't the pursuer grow tired?' a red Band asked. Bands did get tired when exerting themselves; it was difficult to process energy at maximum rate for very long. Some Bands worked hard to build up sustained high-energy processing so that they could travel between stars, but most were not in that condition.

'That should be the case,' Rondl agreed.

'Then the game could not go on,' the Band protested. 'The pursuer would not be able to compete.'

'It could not go on longer than the players wanted it to,' Rondl agreed.

'Then what is the reason?'

'The Kratch will in due course be the pursuer, in the game I contemplate.'

'But the Kratch will grow tired, and decline to play anymore!'

Rondl let them ponder that. In a moment the Bands began catching on. 'To the Kratch, it's no game!' one exclaimed. 'The Kratch could not catch – ' another began. Then all began shimmering with relieved mirth.

'If we are proficient in this game, we should not have to fear the Kratch,' Rondl concluded. 'We could escape it at will. If we have not yet located a suitable place to dispose of it, we can simply flee it when it becomes too tired to follow.'

'Then it will be easy!' a green Band flashed.

Overconfidence was dangerous! 'Not necessarily,' Rondl cautioned. 'There is always the unexpected.'

'Unexpected?' the green Band flashed blankly. 'What could happen?'

This was the naïveté of inexperience! 'Anything that can go wrong, will go wrong,' Rondl informed them. And wondered how he knew. Rondl himself had very little experience he could remember.

'How can we prepare for what is to go wrong when we don't know what to expect?' a white Band asked.

'That's difficult,' Rondl admitted. 'I think we should organize a plan of escape and develop an alternate way to destroy the Kratch. So we need a new set of notions.'

The Bands, being sociable and helpful, humoured him. They formed two circles and sought for new answers. Soon they had some good ones. One group worked out a way that a number of Bands could line up and so finely concentrate a ray of sun that a great deal of heat would be generated at its focus. If another line of Bands concentrated a beam similarly from the other sun and focused that beam on the same point, the combination might be strong enough to begin to vaporize the material of the Kratch.

'Let's try it!' Rondl flashed, pleased. They did, aligning and focusing on a fragment of rock. In moments it heated and cracked apart. Rondl encouraged them to practice this manoeuvre. One problem was that the magnetic lines on which the Bands had to congregate were not necessarily aligned with the light of the suns, so that the formations had to be carefully located. It could be difficult to focus on a moving target. So they needed to scout the positioning of magnetic lines as well as of rocks.

The other group wanted to locate metallic fragments that they could use to bombard the Kratch. The problem was that they needed time to locate and collect the stones and would be in danger from the Kratch while doing so. In addition, they were uncertain that the small chunks they could handle with individual magnetism would have mass enough to do the monster harm. Perhaps they could group in twos and threes to handle larger pieces. But they would be in danger from the Kratch while locating such items and manoeuvring them into place. The beam-focusers could practice out in clear space, but the fragment-hurlers would have to go into the zone of debris, where the Kratch lurked.

They agreed to rehearse the safer techniques first, then go for the stones. If at that point the Kratch should appear, the engagement would be on. If it did not appear, they would collect a huge arsenal of stones and locate several suitable trap sites, preparing for the time when the enemy did appear.

It occurred to Rondl that they might be able to employ magnetic circuitry to make a bomb: a rock that would fly violently apart when magnetically stimulated. But that would be complex, perhaps requiring a prolonged period of research; he would have to follow it up later.

They got to work. The Bands were naturally cautious in this vicinity, nervous about the cover the planetoid belt provided for the monster. They were not at all sure, despite their expressed confidence, that this exploration was feasible.

Promising locations showed up. Rondl checked each as the news was flashed to him of its discovery. One was a large irregular fragment of rock, partly split along a fault so that there was a notch that a Band might slide through, too small for the Kratch. But it was too shallow and slanting to be properly effective; the pursuing Kratch would probably glance off and be cautious thereafter. Another prospect consisted of two boulders joined by an isthmus, the whole slowly rotating. At the proper angle, there was a tight passage between the two masses. This might do. A brown Band was designated to be the final member of the tag team; he would lead the monster through the centre.

The brown Band began practicing immediately, timing his approach so that he seemed to be heading for a flat face of rock, arriving as the rotation brought the cleft into place. Since the gap was too narrow to pass the mass of the Kratch, this could be devastating. But if the monster saw it coming –

But where was the Kratch? Rondl had expected it to show up by this time. Was the monster chasing around the other side of the ring of rock, so that all their preparations would be wasted?

'Now let's collect metallic rocks,' Rondl flashed, concealing his misgiving. This exercise would not be much good unless they flushed the Kratch.

The cross-tag Bands had been practicing their game with much glee, augmented by a number of those who at first had been too timid to volunteer. It seemed that this positive approach had spread confidence, and now more of the Bands were ready to tackle the task. That was fine; Rondl was sure the ones who joined after due consideration would be at least as sturdy as those who joined without thinking. All these Bands were becoming skilful in the interception manœuvre; they enjoyed precision flying, and Rondl thought they were good enough to accomplish the mission. He made quite sure they knew where the terminus was, though they did not approach it; no point in giving their scheme away to the Kratch, who just might be lurking and watching. It was not that Rondl feared the monster might be more intelligent than estimated, but that the number of Bands in the area might make it cautious; that might indeed be the reason it had not appeared. The safety of numbers could be interfering with the project.

'Those who are not actively prospecting, withdraw some distance,' he directed. 'We want the group to seem small enough to be vulnerable.'

Now the stone-group discovered a rich lode of stones, and began moving them to a convenient deposit area, forming a small artificial meteor. The ring of debris was layered, with bands of larger rocks, fine sand, and metallic fragments. Rondl wondered how it had been formed, and an odd concept came to him. 'Roche's Limit'. A moon was unable to orbit a planet within a certain radius, because the tidal forces broke it up. But he was sure this was not generally known among Bands; why did *he* know it? That was the kind of question that had bothered him from the outset.

'You're internalizing again,' Cirl reproved him.

'A creature must be permitted some faults,' he grumbled, privately satisfied by her attention. He liked having her here with him, despite the danger to her. For one thing, Tembl tended to keep slightly more distance.

'Next time, internalize externally, so I can share,' she flashed.

It was of course a humour concept. But what might

127

have developed into a pleasant interchange was cut off by an alarm flash: 'Monster! Monster!'

Suddenly everything was serious. 'Tag team, you know what to do!' Rondl flashed, flying toward the action. 'Engage the monster, keep it moving, tire it!'

They had already engaged the Kratch, and it was moving. It was a great grey-metal hulk, gleaming in the light of the suns, and it was horribly fast. The Bands were cutting across, and the system was working; the Kratch swerved to pursue each new Band, because the new one seemed closer.

But Rondl worried. He knew, from the anonymous depths of experience, that things seldom worked out perfectly – and if anything went wrong, they would lose a Band. They could lose several to disbanding, even if successful. If unsuccessful, it could be horrible. Already some Bands were leaving the game, apprehension having conquered their prior enthusiasm. Some of these were the newest enlistees – but some were the original ones. So the stress of action turned out to be a different type of selection process than anticipation. Fortunately most of the group remained, so the Bands remained rested and fresh.

There was no sign of a problem. The Kratch was too stupid to realize what was happening. It followed each new Band that seemed so close, but by the time the monster achieved the new vector it was no closer than it had been to the old prey. Energy was required to change direction even slightly. If the monster finally caught on, and declined to be distracted from the original Band it was following –

It did not. Now it was visibly tiring as the constant course corrections demanded energy. It had a lot of mass, and had to use a lot of power to move itself about. In the short term it could outperform a Band, which was why it was so deadly, but on an extended chase the advantage went the other way. That was good to know; probably a chain of as few as three Bands could tire the thing, enabling them to escape it.

Even if the Kratch got belatedly smart and clung to one Band, now it would not be able to catch up. It had expended too much of its resource. 'Lead it into the trap!' Rondl flashed.

They led it toward the cracked rock. The brown Band hovered, ready to do his part on the final link.

There was a new flash of alarm. 'Another Kratch!'

Another Kratch? Rondl had not anticipated this! Yet of course there was more than one. Why hadn't he reasoned it out before? There had to be a breeding population. There could be hundreds. The mission had abruptly become considerably more complicated. Maybe the first Kratch had been late arriving because it was informing its friends of the rich harvest here.

'Tag team – lead the new monster!' Rondl flashed. 'Same way! You can do it.'

They could do it – but their confidence had been shaken by this development. They were no longer fresh, though they were hardly tired. Nervousness weakened them. Thus they fumbled the chain, and failed to make the connection with the brown Band at the trap. Some of the Bands led the first monster; others went after the second.

No Bands had disbanded, at least. But suppose more monsters appeared? How long could the cross-tag game continue if there was always another monster, a fresh one replacing the tired one? This could become another form of tag, with the Kratches making the rules.

'It's only one new challenge!' Rondl flashed, desperately trying to improve their resolve. Inaction was disaster! 'Lead it! Lead it!'

They led it. There was nothing else they could do, for

once a Kratch began pursuit, it never relinquished the chase. But now there was confusion: who should intercept which Kratch? Sometimes two Bands swooped together; sometimes there was a dangerously long pause between interceptions. There was bound to be trouble.

'Lead the second away from the first,' Rondl flashed. 'Separate the groups so there can be no confusion. There are enough of you to handle two monsters. Any Bands who are tired can join the group with the tired Kratch; as soon as we get reorganized, we'll feed it to the trap, as we were about to before we got confused.' He hoped his evinced confidence would encourage them. Hesitancy and disorganization were greater threats than the two Kratches.

They obliged, and the situation improved. Two tag teams were operating smoothly now: a fast one and a slow one.

'Conduct the first monster to the finale,' Rondl directed. 'After that has been handled, lead the second monster in.'

Then there was a third alarm. Another Kratch had appeared.

The Bands, already shaken, lost control entirely. Both tag teams flew apart, leaving two monsters pursuing two hapless Bands.

Disaster! Rondl spent one moment absorbed in horror, then reacted with the dispatch of desperation. Two Bands were near him: Cirl and Tembl. Both were fresh and competent. He flashed orders to them.

'Tembl, go intercept the first Kratch and lead it directly to the trap. Let the brown Band finish it. Cirl, find a Band you know well and make him join you in intercepting the second Kratch. I will handle the third.'

'But – ' both protested, concerned for him.

'Now!' he flashed imperatively. They departed.

130

When the other Bands saw the game continuing, he hoped, they would repent their foolishness and reorganize. Band pacifism was more than just a theory; these people lacked the stamina for sustained effort in adversity. They would respond to the proper example, surely. But if they did not, or if more monsters appeared –

He needed something more immediate than cross-tagging to deal with the Kratch. Something obvious and devastating, to rout the monsters and give the Bands instant courage. Something like the burning lens –

But that was impossible to organize in this disarray. He had to put together something simple, that required no fine-tuning in the midst of confusion.

He saw Tembl leading the first, tired Kratch into the zone of rocks. That would finish one. Cirl would lead the next the same way. Rondl found a mild irony in the fact that of all his bold Bands, two of the gentlest females were the ones he was depending on in this really dangerous pass.

Two Kratch accounted for, for the moment. But the third – and possibly fourth, fifth, sixth – what was fast and sure, even against infinite odds?

Suddenly it came to him. Defence – ideally suited to the Band temperament. Defence was the best offence. But this new tactic would take nerve, initially. Did these shaken Bands have enough?

'All free Bands orient on me!' he flashed in spirals. 'I have a new formation that should be secure from attack!'

That got their attention. Embracing that hope, they clustered about him. 'We shall make a tube,' he flashed. 'Dual purpose: it will focus the light to burn the monster – but it will also secure us from harm. This is to be a body-contact tube held together by our fibres, not by alignment from a distance. Just as one Band carries another during emergency – only in this case we shall have a dozen Bands

131

together. The Kratch cannot digest what it cannot take inside itself – and this formation will be far too large for it. All this requires is the courage to hold position – no matter what occurs.'

They hovered doubtfully. Rondl gave them no time to think about it. Thinking was hazardous to courage. 'You blue Band – adhere to me!' he flashed.

The blue Band took the course of least resistance and obeyed. Now there were two of them together. 'You, orange Band – adhere to the blue,' Rondl flashed through their doubled lens. In a moment there were three – a formation virtually unknown to the Bands.

They continued until they were twelve, and the resulting tube was as long as a Kratch. Obviously this mass could not be assimilated by the monster!

'Now form a second tube – and a third!' Rondl flashed down the length of it. Manœuvrability had suffered; this structure was clumsy. But it could be moved, with care. 'Practice focusing the beams of the suns, as you did before. Try to burn up stones. When the Kratch comes, burn it.' He wasn't sure how much of his message was getting through to the other tubes, or how feasible it would be to burn the Kratch, but at least this was a positive programme of action, and the members of his own tube would understand.

Rondl led his tube toward the Kratch that Cirl was leading. Though clumsy, the tube could generate considerable forward velocity, for the motive power of the Bands was accretive. They cruised up beside Cirl. 'Adhere to us!' Rondl flashed. 'You will be secure as long as you do not separate from the tube!'

Cirl could hardly have picked up much of that clumsy flash, but she saw the formation. She trusted him, and she was now tiring. She had to take what offered. With a final flair of effort, she angled forward and sidewise, and

132

fastened herself to the end of the tube. The monster was close behind.

Cirl could not flash to Rondl; the communication was one-way. But he knew how she was reacting, for he had been this close to a Kratch himself. He sent down a constant flash of reassurance. 'You are the end of the tube, Cirl; the Kratch will come up to you. But though its spike penetrates your lens, the creature cannot consume you, because you are part of a structure too large for it. And we are going to make things ever harder for it.'

For he had thought of a new approach. Under Rondl's direction, the tube oriented on Eclat, flying straight toward the sun on the most convenient line. With all thirteen Bands exerting themselves together, their forward velocity became greater than what the Kratch could maintain. 'We can outfly the monster now!' Rondl exulted. 'But we aren't going to! We're going to show off our captive to the other Bands, then dispose of it. Everyone must know that Bands have nothing further to fear from monsters!'

They made a slow loop, changing lines carefully, and the Kratch followed. They showed the other Bands how well this formation worked, and Rondl knew the encouragement was tremendous. It no longer mattered how many monsters there were; only one at a time could approach a tube. A dozen Bands could pass through a crowd of a thousand Kratches this way! Rondl had truly devised the perfect defence.

Then he remembered: he had forgotten the third Kratch, the one he himself had promised to handle. That one was chasing down a red Band, and getting close. The poor Band was on the verge of forced disbanding. Rondl had to help!

Keeping his tube intact, he shifted magnetic lines and cut across to parallel the red Band. Then he drew ahead.

'Form a tube! Form a tube!' he flashed. He oriented toward other Bands and sent the same message.

They understood. A purple Band flew up and adhered to the red Band. Then a yellow one joined them. Soon there were too many for that Kratch to handle; they were safe.

Now Rondl took his own tube back toward Eclat. 'Focus the beam on the Kratch,' he directed. Their Kratch had followed obligingly during their manoeuvres while communicating with the red Band; it was amazing what control was possible when proper advantage was taken of the monster's stupidity and determination. 'Burn its nose. The monster may not be able to approach us at all!'

But it was hard to focus from this tight a formation; the Bands had no experience in it. Rondl was sure they could accomplish it with practice – but right now the beam was diffuse, generating only slight heat. The Kratch was nudging up close.

'We can't burn it this time,' Rondl flashed regretfully. 'That technique remains to be mastered. But we can still resist it. Cling tightly, now. Cirl – trust me. Though the monster comes near, you are secure – if you only hold firm.'

The monster came near. Its spike shoved up into the tube. Rondl hoped Cirl's nerve would hold. To a Band, there was nothing more terrible than the approach of the Kratch's horn. It seemed the Kratch did not realize, even now, that it was dealing with an object impossible to consume. It thought it had a single Band.

As it would have, indeed, if Cirl lost nerve and de-tached. 'You're doing well, Cirl!' he flashed. 'Hold on, hold on!'

The dread spike came half the length of the tube. Rondl realized that the other Bands would be similarly appalled. 'Stay tight, all of you!' Rondl flashed continuously. 'Do not lose confidence. Hold the formation, and all is well! All is well!' If any of the Bands lost nerve and let go, the whole tube could break up, and Cirl was already on the horn of the monster. If any Band in the tube disbanded, the effect would be the same. 'We are beating the Kratch. We are nullifying its power; no matter how close it nudges, it cannot prevail. Have faith, have courage. There is victory in unity. This is a significant occasion!' How he hoped it was! What would he do, if the formation broke, and Cirl lost her life – when she had trusted him?

The tube stayed tight. They all trusted him. The Kratch shoved in close, burying its spike the entire length, trying to take in the morsel – and could not.

Meanwhile, the Bands of the tube continued to work on the focus of the beam, making it finer and hotter. There was nothing like the stimulus of menace to make the effort stronger! Rondl slowed down the column – and the Kratch shoved forward harder, not comprehending.

'We can tire it rapidly!' Rondl flashed, uncertain how much of his message reached the Bands in the latter portion of the tube, since their lenses were pierced by the spike. They were probably blind for the moment, proceeding on trust alone. 'We can make it carry us all!'

They slowed further, and the monster kept labouring to maintain velocity. But burdened with that intractable mass, it lost strength. Finally the Kratch fell away, exhausted, drifting, now too weak to maintain forward velocity.

'Now we can do with it as we wish,' Rondl flashed. 'We have conquered it. We have met it in battle and proven ourselves stronger.' He was reinforcing the mood: he wanted all these Bands to depart with confidence that Bands could defeat the worst enemies, if they only maintained the correct formation and discipline. 'Break formation; form a spread-out focusing tube.'

135

They spread out, and re-formed into a more normal line. Now it was easy to focus the sun. In moments a fine beam touched the drifting body of the Kratch, burning into its side.

The Kratch jumped, struggling to avoid the heat. It was hurting now! The Band formation followed, refocusing the beam, catching the same place. Again the monster moved, but with less vigour; it really had little energy to spare.

A third time the hotspot formed, this time refined to especially narrow dimension, hotter than before. The Kratch wiggled, but could no longer escape. A hole began to form in its metal hide.

There was an explosion of vapours as the creature's armoured flank was perforated. Its internal pressure had been released; it was mortally wounded.

And two Bands, appalled at what they had done, disbanded. They were so set against violence that even the destruction of a monster bent on killing them caused them to react with horror. But the rest had been sufficiently toughened; they survived. Which was, after all, the point of this exercise – to locate and prepare the survival types.

Even so, Rondl tried to ease the strain. 'Perhaps they go to carry news to the Viscous Circle,' he flashed – and then wondered whether he might be right. It was pretty good news, after all.

Now he checked on the other teams. The first had successfully trapped the first monster. Templ and the brown Band had done their jobs. The Kratch had smashed into the double rock, and remained wedged there, dented. Unfortunately that meant this site could not be used again: another thing he had not anticipated.

The second team, or rather the third team, had profited from Rondl's advice; the tube was still leading its monster. Rondl now flashed to them how to dispatch it, and it did

136

not take long to conclude that issue. This time only one Band disbanded.

They had met the enemy, Rondl thought again with relief, amazement, and joy, and conquered it. Only six Bands had disbanded – three from victory, three from the initial excitement at the notion of coping simultaneously with three Kratches. None from actual combat. Rondl now had his cadre of toughened troops.

And Cirl – she was safe. 'I knew you would not let me disband,' she flashed brightly. 'You don't believe in life after disbanding, so you would not let me go.' Rondl was weakly glad it had proved so.

Meanwhile, the Solarian Monsters progressed on toward Planet Band. They took over the two outer moons and most of the larger moonlets, neglecting only the one that was the base for the Bellatrixians. It was evident that the Solarians did not want trouble with Sphere Bellatrix. The Monsters' advance eliminated virtually all Bands in the outer reaches. Now they were closing on the inner moons.

Little time remained. Rondl did not feel adequately prepared, but he knew he had to make his move now. His battle-seasoned troops had to be up to the job!

He set an ambush on the second moon, Glow. He knew from observation that the Monsters typically approached a planetary body cautiously, fired several explosive shots into it, then landed their vessels on the surface and disgorged assorted vehicles to traverse the terrain. It was this traversing that took time, because they covered every part of each planet or moon, crisscrossing and pausing at any unusual formations. Obviously they were searching for something – and that was the whole mystery of their presence. What could they want? There was nothing but rock and sand and gas on those moons.

At any rate, the Monsters had to be discouraged,

because even if they never found the object of their search, they would destroy the Band society in the process of looking.

Destruction of the Solarians was not Rondl's strategy. Most Bands could never tolerate such an asocial concept, even to save their own society. So the objective was merely to thwart the Monster invasion, preferably without destruction of scenery or loss of life. At first this had seemed a hopeless task, but Rondl had consulted with his advisers and worked out a plan they thought might work.

More than a thousand Bands went to Moon Glow ahead of the Monsters. The great majority of these had not been seasoned by the campaign against the Kratch, but that campaign had had a salutary effect on Band morale, and many more volunteers had come. Since it was necessary to cover the entire surface, these inexperienced people had to be used. But Rondl took care to intersperse among them the seasoned ones, so that wherever the action occurred, there would be experienced people to handle it.

The Bands hid all around, in all manner of ways. Some buried themselves in sand, others in the scant snow and ice of the deep shadows, and others beneath rocks and boulders. They concealed themselves by coating their surfaces with clay or flakes of rock, so that they became filled discs or lumps, and lay scattered across the land all over the moon. Some hovered in the tenuous atmosphere, riding the twisted lines spawned by the odd magnetic patterns of this region. Others established physical orbits, becoming moonlets themselves, concealed among the chunks of rock already there. In short, Monsters were bound to encounter Bands, without knowing it.

There was a system of communication, with selected individuals positioned to receive and relay flashes from the surface. Rondl and Cirl waited well out from Glow with a reserve troop of Bands. This was the command

138

post. Such a concept no longer seemed alien; it was practical. Large-scale missions had to be organized hierarchically, and once he had got this concept across to his troops, they had cooperated.

The fleet of Monster ships arrived as projected. They blasted away at the moon, as though seeking to make it twitch with discomfort. Rondl hoped no Bands were at the sites of the explosions. Yet this was a necessary risk; they had known some could be disbanded randomly. Those would be the first to convey the report of this engagement to the Viscous Circle. Rondl felt guilty using that concept to encourage the Bands, but at this point he had to facilitate things in any fashion that offered. If they did not halt the Monsters, the entire species of Band could make that trip to the Viscous Circle!

After the usual nonreaction by the moon – what had the Solarians expected? – the Monster ships settled down on the surface. Actually there were several types and sizes of them. The larger ships remained in orbit, as they were unable to withstand the effect of surface gravity. The medium-sized ones went on down, and the smallest shuttled between, conveying specimens to the large ones. Rondl realized that, coincidentally, this operation was organized very much like his own; the alien command post was also in space.

Wheeled vehicles emerged from the landed ships and commenced their canvassing. They moved rapidly, as each had extensive territory to cover. Perception devices extended from them, emitting radiation. Now at last the rationale began to manifest: the Band communications system relayed news that the Monsters reacted to anything metallic. Were they short of metals? Surely not; their ships were mostly metal, suggesting that they had substantial quantities of it in their home system. Therefore it was likely that the metal merely signalled the possible presence of something else the Monsters wanted. What could that be?

Rondl thought he should know. But when he concentrated on that thought, it vanished as though deliberately hiding from him. He let it go, being by now well used to this frustration.

The Band body was to a large extent metallic, though evidently not the kind of metal the Monsters wanted. That was just as well; it would have been terrible if the Solarians had charged in to Planet Band and begun capturing Bands for their metal content, in the manner of the Kratch! Now some Bands were located and ignored; others were taken aboard the land-travelling vehicles. There seemed to be a preference for those Bands who had coated themselves with metallic dust and fragments, holding them in place magnetically. It seemed that this additional concentration of metal made them of interest. But not compellingly so; the Bands were merely dumped in hoppers with other objects and ignored. That was exactly what Rondl wanted.

A new hint came. There was a concavity in the surface of one of the large lava-flow plains, and several vehicles converged on this. Rondl's planetary geologist specialists had already advised him that this concavity was natural, the result of the long-ago collapse of a volcanic bubble of gas. At times some water had condensed in it, leaving concentric marks; now it was dry. It really was of very little interest to anyone except a geologist – and it turned out to be of no further interest to the Monsters, once they too had ascertained its nature. The vehicles went on. But this diversion indicated that it was not merely metal, but special shapes that they were searching out. Perhaps they collected the small bits of metal in the hope that these were fragments of the main mass, so that an increasing density of them would chart its presence.

140

In due course the vehicles reached rendezvous points and delivered their samples to the shuttle ships. The shuttles blasted off with much flame and smoke and wastage of energy – and with a few concealed Bands within.

Now it should get interesting. Each Band had been drilled in the procedure, and knew what to do. Rondl was not in contact with these captives, but did not need to be. The effects of his strategy should become apparent soon.

The first shuttle homed in on its command ship. A docking-hatch opened in the larger vessel. The shuttle flew neatly in – and misjudged slightly, colliding with the rim of the aperture. It seemed to be an accident of chance, a minor malfunction causing a small but awkward deviation in course.

There was a pause. Then the dented shuttle backed off, reoriented, and moved forward again – and banged into the other side of the hatch, staving in its nose-point.

'It's working!' Cirl flashed with almost unsocial glee. She was becoming hardened to violence by her association with Rondl, especially during the dreams and the Kratch hunt. 'Our plan is causing them trouble!'

So it seemed. There was a Band aboard that shuttle – and that Band had used its magnetism to distort the internal control signals of the shuttle, so that the craft moved slightly off the mark. The Monsters did not know the cause; they thought it was a real accident. Apparently Monsters were accustomed to equipment failure, and took it in course.

Other shuttles were arriving. Similar accidents occurred. The shuttles had to park in orbit, waiting for robots from the command ships to clear the debris and fix the crushed mechanisms. A spreading ripple of complication developed, as delayed shuttles missed their scheduled rendezvous back on the moon, and the collector vehicles had to wait to deliver their loads.

'Snafu,' Rondl flashed contentedly.

Cirl was not familiar with the concept. Rondl started to clarify it – and lost it himself. 'But it covers what is happening to the Monsters,' he said.

Finally space-suited Monsters emerged from the command ships and crossed clumsily to the shuttles that had been misbehaving. Rondl felt humour; he knew the Monsters would find few genuine malfunctions. The Bands would remain quiescent as long as any Monster was paying attention. So at last some shuttles were properly docked and their cargoes unloaded.

The troublemaker Bands were now inside the command ships, undiscovered. The arrogant ignorance of the Monsters, who took no note of Bands in their cargo, was about to cause them grief.

'Situation normal,' Rondl said.

The flow of shuttles resumed – until more accidents happened. One misjudgement was worse than most; the shuttle accelerated instead of decelerating as it entered the docking port. As a result, it collided violently with the interior mechanism of the larger ship.

'All fouled up,' Rondl continued.

There was a flash of an explosion. Smoke puffed out the port, dissipating into space about the ship. 'I think that Band interfered with the wrong circuit,' Cirl remarked. 'They weren't supposed to do that much damage.' But she did not seem unduly disturbed.

Rondl gave her a satisfied flash. His prior efforts to stop the Monsters had been failures; this abrupt success was highly gratifying. But he was not sure how long it would continue. The Monsters were gruesome, but not stupid; they would investigate, and eventually catch on. What would happen then?

As it turned out, the confusion caused by the series of accidents prevented the Monsters from concentrating on

142

the origin of those accidents. The Band connection remained undiscovered. Signals flashed from ship to ship, comparing sites and actions – and the orbiting Bands were able to intercept and modify some of these signals, causing further mischief. One command ship changed its orbit when it was not supposed to, disrupting the shuttle schedule again.

Rondl could not resist participating. He located the laser-signal lenses and positioned himself carefully between the lenses of two ships. This was the sort of manœuvre a Band was naturally equipped for. Laser beams were narrow and plainly visible to Bands; it was child's play to intercept a fixed beam, as though talking to a distant Band.

Sure enough, messages were crossing. Rondl expected to intercept gibberish, for the Monster language differed from that of the Bands, and even when translated into light it should not be intelligible. But to his amazement he understood it. Was this another dream? Surely not! But he refused to be concerned at the moment; he would exploit this anomaly to the utmost while he could. By rotating in place he could pick up both sides of their dialogue. The Monsters were very crude conversationalists; first one would transmit a complete thought, then the other would. That gave Rondl plenty of time to reorient.

'. . . thought that was the directive, sir. We have it on recording. "Correct orbit to Specification DL-11." We did not question – '

Here the signal was interrupted by an imperious override beam from the other ship. Quickly Rondl reoriented.

'. . . *should* have questioned, Major! You know we have not completed Stage Four of this assignment. Now get that tub back to the Stage Four rendezvous orbit!'

Rondl reacted with the ability of his kind, modifying the message as though he were participating in a circle-communication. He did not need time to reflect; the message he relayed became part of his thought, and his input was automatic. The tiniest, most precise flux in his magnetic lens modified the light passing through it very slightly. Thus the second 'four' became 'five', changing the directive a little bit.

'Return to what stage, sir?' the major queried, confused. Rondl did not know what the numbers of the stages signified, but he was sure that the wrong number would make further mischief.

'Are you deaf?' the senior officer retorted with typical Monster courtesy. 'I told you *four!*' Only Rondl changed it again to 'five'. It was so simple to add one light-bit to the relevant sequence.

'Yes, sir,' the major replied dubiously. This was all in laser, which was the machine-translated form of the Monster's verbal communication, but Rondl could almost see the creature's mobile, fleshy mouth-orifice rims rippling and his liquid-centred eyeballs squishing in confusion. 'Five.' And, of course, Rondl converted that back to 'four'.

That out-of-place ship shot out its voluminous gases in the clumsy way these machines had, looking like the System's messiest Kratch with indigestion (Rondl liked that image), and lurched toward the new position. This turned out to be the jump-off orbit for the return journey to the Monster base station set up near Moon Spare.

Rondl was not able to intercept the following communications between the two ships, as he had to pay attention to his own operations. But he could guess their nature. He saw the major's ship move out, then pause, then travel back to its proper orbit: Stage Four. By this time the shuttles had stacked up horrendously, and two had collided in space – surely an accident facilitated by the Bands aboard. There was an almost hopeless tangle to sort out.

Meanwhile the Monsters were having other problems. Rondl had other Bands monitor the laser communications; the Bands were unable to comprehend the meanings, but reported that messages were continuous and seemed increasingly irate. Many things were going wrong inside the ships, as the Bands in the cargoes exerted their mischievous influence. More shuttles went astray, causing more damage. Several ground vehicles got lost, some wrecking themselves on rough terrain, requiring special expeditions to extricate them. Some shuttles got confused and travelled on the wrong schedules, causing further obstructions.

By the time the mission was finished, it had taken three times as long as the one that surveyed Moon Spare, and the Monsters were evidently tired and irritable. An increasing number of their errors were now of their own making. A number of Bands had been lost, but most found their way back to Rondl's headquarters. The overall mood was one of satisfaction.

Rondl regarded this Band operation a success. They had disrupted the Monster schedule, giving themselves more time to organize for their next effort, and they had learned a great deal about the vulnerabilities of the enemy. Next time they should be able to do a more competent job of interference!

Cirl was especially pleased. She organized several circles, so that participants could exchange information and assimilate larger perspectives and plan superior future efforts. Now everyone knew that there was an alternative to mass disbanding as the Monsters advanced. It was possible to fight back – without actually doing brute violence.

CHAPTER 9

Monster

Rondl woke into another nightmare. He was back in the gruesome body of a Monster, complete with fleshy projections and orifices and those dreadful, paired, fluid-filled eyeball sacs. He had thought they had conquered these dreams, but evidently he had let his guard down and been caught again. Because this had happened unexpectedly, Cirl was not with him.

Yet this was different, and much worse. He was not merely a prisoner in the Monster's head, but now occupied the entire body. He was not observing the Monster's actions, he was actually experiencing the Monster's sensations and remembering the Monster's memories. He had been able to tap into some of these during the last nightmare, but now he was wholly immersed in them.

In fact, he had become the Monster. This was truly horrible! But at least he had the security of knowing that in due course he would wake, escaping this. Next time he slept, he would be sure to have Cirl with him to abate the effect.

This time he was not in a spaceship, but in a planetoid station. It seemed his nightmare had telescoped, eliminating the tedious buildup; it picked up somewhat beyond the situation of the last one. His jellybrain Monster memory filled in the details how the Solarians – they did not think of themselves as Monsters, any more than the Bands thought of themselves as Ringers – had suffered a population problem in the System of Sirius and had to colonize a number of planetoids, hollowing them out and pressurizing them and establishing extensive hydroponic gardens, mineral refining factories, and production facilities. Each planetoid was a self-contained city, with its own government and its own legal status. This one happened to be a military base, from which troops and supplies were mattermitted as necessary to regions elsewhere in space. It was not a bad place to live; there were extensive recreational facilities for off-duty personnel, including a torus-shaped pool in which Monsters could swim round and round without ever turning a corner, if they didn't get dizzy. Some nice effects were possible in free-fall space.

It was amazing how much he knew when he concentrated. All the oddments of information that Rondl had been unable to explain before, now fitted into a cohesive whole; there were no blanks when he concentrated. No wonder he had been good at organizing the Band resistance to invasion: he had been trained for exactly such things. To transfer to some alien host, organize the natives, foment a rebellion against the government that opposed the interests of Solarians –

Now, wait! *He* had not been trained! The Monster of this nightmare had been trained to these iniquities! Rondl could not have –

He stiffened in horror. Not unless –

He forced the unwelcome thought through reluctant flesh-nerve synapses. *Unless he was the Monster*.

His memory filled in relentlessly, as if a tap had been opened and was gushing fluid information into his chamber. He, Ronald Snowden, a Solarian, had been sent on a mission to the Band region of space, his memory blanked. He had become Rondl the Ringer. He was indeed the Monster.

Talk about nightmares!

Now he sat in a padded cell in the debriefing section of the Station, as was standard procedure for returning Transfer agents. It usually took a while to readjust, and

147

this could not be rushed. It was not easy to adapt to a new host, even for an experienced Transfer agent, and not easy to revert instantly to oneself. Whole new systems of organization had to be adapted to, such as the solid-state magnetic patterns of the Bands, and now stringflesh nerves of the Solarian form.

The imposition of amnesia compounded the complications. His present confusion authenticated that. He had retained the Ringer identity. That was a laugh.

'Okay, slobs, I'm back!' he called. 'Let me out of the can.'

Immediately the chair restraints released and the chamber door opened. Rondl got up somewhat unsteadily, stretching his limbs. The Society of Hosts took good care of the bodies of Transfer agents, but even so there was always some stiffness, and a few kinks. The debriefing officer had been through this before, and knew that regardless of his physical condition, once Ronald had collected himself enough to announce his ire, all was well.

He stepped out of the chamber into the debriefing room. The computer screen was on; the machine always handled this part. Once, centuries ago, a Transfer agent had returned criminally insane; the man had been clever enough to conceal his malady from the human debriefer, then had gone amok when free and killed several people in the name of the 'Ghost of Ganymede'. He hadn't even been to Ganymede, and did not believe in ghosts. Or so he had claimed before his ill-fated mission. Unfortunately he had fought recapture to the death, literally, so they had been unable to determine the specific nature of his malady. The SolSphere government disliked this sort of complication, so no one since had been permitted contact with human beings until cleared by the machine. The computer would wring Ronald dry before turning him loose. The best way to get through comfortably was to cooperate completely, harbouring no secret reservations. It really wasn't so bad, with the proper attitude. In fact, it was beginning to get perfunctory.

'Did you find the Ancient Site?' the computer asked. It spoke exactly like a human being, complete with idiom and occasional uncertain pauses at awkward places, though in fact any uncertainties it might have were rectified in microseconds. Traditionally, sapient machines were called 'Robbie'; this one tended to get nasty when so teased, and it had enormous capacity for subtle mischief, so smart Transfer agents avoided that particular ploy.

The Ancient Site. Ronald had forgotten about that. 'No. It would have helped if I had been allowed to keep my memory of my mission.' He became angry, remembering his confusion during Transfer. 'You robbed me of my chief asset.' He slurred the end of the word 'robbed' slightly, so that it made a small warning light blink on the computer. A foolish thing to do, he knew, but his anger made him reckless. 'I had no notion what I was looking for. In fact, I was not aware that I was looking for anything. I didn't even know what an Ancient Site was, for God's sake.'

The computer ignored that. It was not required to justify the policies of Sphere Sol to a mere Transfer agent. 'Did you learn anything that might indicate the possible location of the Ancient Site?'

Ronald considered, still smouldering. 'I really did not. I might as well have been looking for the Ghost of Ganymede. My whole attention was taken up by the Solarian advance into Band space. And that's another question: why the hell did Sol commence the occupation before acquiring the essential data? That messes up the whole search and wastes resources foolishly, not to mention imperilling our relationship with Sphere Bellatrix.'

Again the computer ignored the irrelevancy. 'Did you

149

identify any individuals of the Ringer species who might have this information?'

Ringer. Something about that term made Ronald grow still more irritated. 'The way to obtain the information is to query for it in a viscous circle.'

This time the machine, figuratively, blinked. It thought it was being mocked, but was not yet sure. 'What is the nature and proper pronunciation of this locale?'

'It is not a locale, it's an effect,' Ronald said with perfect honesty that he knew was registering on the machine's sensors. It was beginning to wonder about his sanity.

'This does not calculate. A query cannot be addressed to an effect.'

'How would you know?' Ronald was beginning to enjoy this. He had always liked to bait the machine, carefully, and felt he had legitimate motivation now. Computers were not the only creatures who could generate subtle mischief, and this computer was aware of this. The day was centuries past when a man could beat the machine at chess or any other two-dimensional game, but in the complex arena of Station influence-peddling a smart and unscrupulous man could give the machine a fair run. 'You yourself are an electronic effect.'

'Please address the question. What is the nature and proper pronunciation of this effect?'

Ronald realized that the machine thought he was mis-pronouncing the term 'vicious circle'. Since the computer knew that Ronald's vocabulary was competent here, the mispronunciation could be significant. It would of course be nonsensical to query a vicious circle for information. He was tempted to play with this confusion further, but knew it would only lead to trouble. He could not afford to anger the machine overtly. Games were games, but they had to be kept at inconsequential level.

'That's viscous, as in viscosity – the thickness of fluid. Except that it's not really fluid. A mock viscous circle is fashioned of light, so that Bands can better communicate, pooling their resources.'

'Please omit the mock effect and define the real one.'

This contraption was asking for it! Ronald considered again the sensors focused on his body, making telltales of his involuntary physical reactions. The computer knew when he was lying and when something made him nervous; that enabled it to zero in on the most relevant aspects in a hurry. Ronald doubted that ability was helping it now; most of what he felt was irritated humour. The machine did not care how a Transfer agent felt about alien things; it was merely supposed to elicit the key facts and form an opinion about the agent's emotional equilibrium. This was more of a limitation than the computer could be aware of, because sometimes the feelings that were in suitable balance were key facts. A hardened murderer might feel justified in assassinating an official of the Station, so would be in emotional balance, while a novice agent might feel strong guilt about his reaction to the sight of a humanoid female, and be in severe emotional imbalance. Ronald did not care to explore his feelings about the Bands at the moment; he would do that when he had suitable privacy.

'The real Viscous Circle, as defined by the Band society, is the swirling nebulalike soul-mists of the species. The combined auras of all the dead and unborn Bands. Uncreated Bands; they aren't born in the same fashion as Solarians are. All these auras mix together, like seasoning stirred into a vast pudding. So it really is viscous, but not of much use to the likes of you.'

'The aura does not survive the death of its natural host,' the computer said. 'There is no afterlife. This Viscous Circle appears to be a fallacious concept.'

151

'I agree. It's all one big myth.'

'Why, then, do you suggest it can be the source of the information we desire?'

'I did not suggest that. Check your circuits.'

'I quote your words: "The way to obtain the information is to query for it in a viscous circle."'

'Exactly. *A* viscous circle. A mock one. But you shunted me off to the *real* Viscous Circle, which we agree does not exist.'

Theoretically the machine had no temper to lose, but experienced agents knew better. Its screen clouded warningly. 'Correction noted. A mock viscous circle does exist. In what manner can this be the source of information we desire?'

'The mock viscous circle consists of a number of Band individuals pooling their thoughts. One or more among them may have relevant information, and the circle would bring it out.' He spoke with perfect sincerity; that was the way to locate the Ancient Site.

'This would necessitate another mission to the subject system,' the computer grumbled. 'We lack the personnel.'

'Lack the personnel!' Ronald exclaimed. 'A dozen agents were sent in!'

'Only two returned.'

'Only two!' Ronald was amazed, and didn't care how his physical reactions showed it. 'What happened to the rest? This was supposed to be a moderate-risk assignment, not a ninety-per cent casualty thing!'

'Eighty-three-per cent casualty.' The machine was a stickler for detail.

'Still more than adequate for bonus pay!'

The machine did not react to the half-facetious nature of the comment. 'The bonus has been credited to your account.'

'You deceived us? You knew that few of us would

return?' Incredulity was hardening rapidly into righteous anger.

'We did not deceive you. We anticipated nominal losses, such as occur routinely. Part of our investigation now is to determine the reason for the deviation from statistical expectation. Do you have a conjecture?'

Ronald considered, feeling shaky. What was statistical deviation to the computer meant in retrospect five chances in six that he should have been dead. His closest brush with oblivion, thus casually quantified! Of course there were always casualties; that was a grim part of the lure of this line of work; that element of risk. But accidents happened mostly to the careless and the stupid, and he was neither. He was a survival type. He had ascertained that the hard way when he faced the three-headed dog eight years ago. He would not have accepted this mission had he known the odds were worse than 75 per cent in his favour. Now it turned out that they had been a lot worse.

Of course the high rate of attrition would be a mystery to the authorities; they had not been there. With certain spectacular exceptions, the military mind had never been noted for its flexibility or imagination. Naturally the Transfer spies had been in trouble. Band society was completely *un*military. Rondl himself had been in severe difficulty, and had nearly perished. It had been his great good fortune to encounter Cirl, the lonely female Band.

Cirl. She was nothing, of course. Merely a tool to be used and set aside. Yet he felt a tug at his emotion. He had, in the period of his identification as a Band male, loved her. Now he felt a certain disgust at himself for that lapse of emotional discipline – yet not totally. She was nothing but a flying metal torus, but she had, in her peculiar fashion, been a nice girl. The nicest.

The computer supposed his emotional fluctuations were merely his horror at his close call with death. That was the

153

liability of lie-detector type interrogation instead of direct mind reading. How fortunate that no human being or human machine had true telepathy! 'What is your hypothesis for the rate of attrition?' Robbie prodded him.

'Bands, the hosts we were sent to, suicide easily. A simple act of will, and they're gone. Agents with no memory of their real nature, confused – of course they would disband.'

'Disband?'

'Suicide.' He snapped his fingers. 'Like that.'

'Suicide is not a survival trait. Explain the situation more cogently.'

'The Band society differs substantially from ours. Bands are not well suited to military discipline. I suspect our operatives simply were not able to adjust. Their Solarian urges would have made them seem unsociable, and to be unsocial – '

'No military action was taken against them? No counterintelligence measures?'

Ronald laughed. 'None. The Bands have no facilities, no faculties for such things. They don't even have concepts for them.'

'You do not believe direct action was taken against the Transfer agents? Such as by the Bellatrixians in that vicinity?'

'I'm sure of it. They simply disbanded.'

'We do not employ suicidal personnel.'

'They were no longer personnel. They were misfit Bands.'

'Clarify concept, please.'

'You took away their memories, you fool! You left them – us – nothing to relate to our real natures. We all became Bands, and tried to act in the Band manner. These agents were blank and confused. They had more than a little wrong with them – and an extremely easy

154

remedy at hand, for all that Bands don't have hands. I was lucky, and I suppose the other survivor was lucky too. Maybe I should talk with him and compare notes. I might then be able to come up with a better thesis why we survived. But I think chance accounts for it, mainly.'

'I shall refer you to a human operative.' The machine was throwing up its figurative hands. It did not understand suicide or alien confusion or luck, other than as statistical phenomena, and evidently it had decided that Ronald Snowden was neither crazy nor potentially violent.

The Solarian officer entered: Colonel Branst, a man Ronald had worked with before. 'I understand you're giving the calc a nervous fit!' Branst remarked cheerfully. Naturally he would have been tuning in to the entire interview and making notes for his own follow-up.

'Yes. It can't understand why I survived.' Ronald laughed, nervous again in retrospect. 'I'm not sure myself. One thing's certain: there'll be a breach-of-contract lawsuit if I ever get sent on another eighty-three-per cent mortality mission without being warned.'

'There will be a lawsuit anyway. We have ten angry families to account to as it is. Something blundered badly.'

The confession was some satisfaction. Ronald turned to a more positive approach. 'I'd like to consult with the other survivor. Is he anyone I know?'

Branst smiled. 'Her name is Tanya Coombs. She's from another Station.'

Ronald shook his head, disappointed. 'Never heard of her. Can you put her on vid for me?'

'Sorry, regs prevent. She is being separately interviewed. The computer will align the two interviews and establish the overlap. Then we'll have at it again. We'll have to get the location of that Ancient Site, and fast.'

'The machine wouldn't tell: why didn't you wait for our reports before sending in physical troops? You're tearing things to hell over there.'

'Coordination. We need to occupy the Site and commence research instantly. So we're investigating suitable bases in the vicinity.'

'Bases, hell! Think I don't know a search pattern when I see it? You're looking for the Ancient Site directly.'

Branst's brow furrowed. It was a broad brow, with wellworn ruts for this expression; he worried a lot. 'You saw the pattern in operation?'

'I was fighting it!' Rondl exclaimed.

'You *what?*'

'My memory of my origin was blanked by your superstrategy experts who hardly know their posteriors from Black Holes! I thought I was a Band. I was fighting to protect my System!'

'You were fighting our occupation!' Branst repeated, catching the irony of it. 'Now I see why you were so mad about the memory blank. Good thing you didn't do any harm.'

'No harm?'

'We've had a hell of a lot of fouling up out there, by the reports, but no technical resistance.'

So no one had caught on to the nature of that fouling up. Ronald decided to let that pass; he just might be charged with treason, if the truth were known. 'Well, we never really got it on,' he agreed. 'Bands aren't much for combat.'

'Fortunately. Look, there's good reason for the memory deletion. We did not know what kind of check system the Ringers might have. Sure, they're technically subsapient and socially backward, and they have no representation in the Galaxy's listing of Spheres. But lots of regressive cultures have pretty sharp ways of identifying

156

strangers among them. We couldn't risk tipping our hand – not with an Ancient Site the target. So we blanked out all information. That way none of you could betray us, either accidentally or because of torture. Failsafe.'

'Failsafe!' Ronald snorted. 'You're lucky I didn't find a way to destroy one of your ships!'

Branst smiled complacently. 'Small risk of that. We spotted no weapons in that system, apart from those in the possession of the Bellatrixian enclave – and we're honouring their neutrality scrupulously. They know what we're looking for; they have assured us that they checked out the Site rumours centuries ago, and found nothing anyone could use. They could be lying, but at least we have their guarantee to stay out of it. We have no reason to fear the Ringers themselves, with or without human memories.'

'But I had no Band memory either!' Ronald cried. 'I couldn't orient!'

'There was reason for that too. A normal Transfer would have been obvious to alien diagnostic equipment. So – '

'The Bands have no such equipment! They don't bother to check or classify auras at all! They figure every aura is only a fragment of the Viscous Circle, to which it will in due course return, so they don't worry about it. It's a completely open society.'

'Sounds like anarchy,' Branst remarked. 'At any rate, we didn't know that, and could not take a chance. Too many other species could be waiting to move in on this, if they ever got a notion that Ancient Site was more than a mirage. Their spies may be among the Ringers already.'

'There isn't even a term for spy there. No concept for it!'

'But there is such a concept in other Spheres. So we arranged to make our Transferees seem like natives. We worked an exchange of auras, shunting the Ringer auras

157

into human hosts, so that there was only one aura in each Ringer host. We figured that would fool all but the most sophisticated verification process.'

'Except that it militated severely against the agents' ability to survive, let alone function in the mission.'

'It does appear to be a blunder. We'll put the host auras back on the next mission.'

'The computer said we lacked the personnel for another mission.'

'There is no such thing as a lack of personnel when an Ancient Site is involved. We'll start a whole new bunch of agents if we have to. But for now we do have two.'

'Stick with the two. Even forewarned, new ones will not be competent. But if I go back, leave the host aura out. I don't want to be distracted by a whole set of memories and obligations.' Ronald marvelled at himself. Did he care what obligations the host Band might have? 'I worked things out myself; I want to finish them myself.'

Branst shrugged. 'It may be academic. With only two agents remaining – '

'And no news yet on the location of the Site – '

'Yes, I suppose we'll have to send you back. With memory intact. And hope the attrition problem has been solved. Even a single agent is enough, if he knows enough to survive and to do the job.' He made an expansive gesture. 'You'd better take a break, now; it'll be a day at least before we assimilate the two reports and plan our next move. You're anxious to see your wife, I'm sure.'

'I sure am,' Ronald agreed. Then wondered privately: *was* he?

Branst was quick to catch the doubt. 'You have a problem?'

Ronald spread his hands, embarrassed. 'We're near the end of our tenure. I'm not quite sure I want to extend.'

'No problem at all. If you figure you have little time left

with her, play it for all it's worth. If it doesn't work out, you've lost nothing.'

Moron! Ronald thought. But aloud he agreed: 'Maybe so. She's a good woman. We just don't seem to hit it off perfectly. She doesn't go for the Transfer duty.'

'The Service can arrange to have you debriefed elsewhere for an extended time,' Branst said. 'You don't have to see her at all. But what's the point? Go settle it.'

'Right you are,' Ronald said. It was pointless to discuss a complex emotional situation with a military man. They shook hands, and he left the debriefing premises.

CHAPTER 10

Woman

He entered the null-gravity system and hurled himself along. He had always enjoyed this aspect of life at the Station, but now it reminded him of the travelling mode of the Bands. Their light construction and use of magnetic lines made them essentially free-floating. He saw himself now not as a Solarian temporarily free of gravity, but as a Band in different form. At least that was his subjective impression of the moment. He knew he was no Band, of course; he was merely experiencing a temporary subjective reversion, as was common among recently returned Transferees. In a few hours his reorientation would be complete, and the entire Band experience would have no more force than a dream or distant memory. Yet right now the effect was potent and poignant.

How much force did a dream have? As a Band he had suffered what he took to be nightmares, actually unconscious enactments of his real nature. Cirl had helped him stave these off, and he had been grateful to her. What was Cirl doing now? Did she think him dead, and would she disband? He did not like the thought of that. He regretted having deceived her, though at the time he had not known it was deception. He had not realized he was a Monster.

The tunnel sent off sideshoots leading to the various subdivisions of the planetoid – hydroponics, recreation, personnel processing, training facilities, and so on. There was even a carefully cultivated wilderness area. But he was headed for home, not because he was really that eager to brace Helen, but to get into a private situation where he could unwind without embarrassment. There was no telling what the future held at a place like this, and he needed to be restored as quickly as possible.

This was a flying city, and also a military station. It was only partially self-sufficient. Should war come to this sector of space, the Station could become independent, but at the sacrifice of combat readiness and efficiency. So there was no point in becoming obsessed with self-sufficiency. The Station protected its sources of supply by protecting System Sirius – which was as it should be. Without such stations, the Solarian Sphere would be as vulnerable to alien encroachment as were the Bands.

There it was again – that lingering disquiet. It was likely to be harder to shake off this Band experience than it had been for prior Transfer missions. Had he spent too long in Transfer this time, running down his aura, or was there something else? That blanking of his memory had been troublesome, even damaging; unlike other missions, this one had got to him, causing him to believe he was really an alien. Maybe that accounted for it; his continuity of identity had been interrupted.

He entered the residential section, automatically drawing out his fins to make the glide down. Bands did not do this; they rode only on magnetic lines. It seemed to him the Band way was better.

Helen was waiting for him. Her hair was arranged in a billowy red cloud that enclosed face, neck, and shoulders artistically. She wore a translucent blue dress that complemented the hair, and elfin slippers. She was an extremely well-formed woman, even after four and a half years of marriage, and knew it, and knew exactly how to show her body off to advantage.

Why, then, did she look like a Monster?

Ronald landed imperfectly, just missing a cornstalk, but his wife seemed not to notice. She stepped toward him, arms spread, smiling brilliantly. 'Welcome home!'

161

Ronald arranged to stumble. He dropped to the ground, avoiding her embrace. Why had she dressed up for him – and why was he nonreceptive?

'Oh!' she exclaimed. 'Are you hurt?' She helped him up.

'Just a little out of phase from the Transfer,' he said. 'Takes a few hours to realign. You know that.'

'Yes, of course,' she agreed immediately. 'I understand it was a rough one. Come inside; I'll make you some tea.'

Tea. A beverage. A liquid that Monsters imbibed. Bands never imbibed. 'No thanks. I'll just stay out here a moment and get organized.'

Again she was agreeable. 'I'll set up chairs.'

'I fear I've scuffed your garden.'

'It doesn't matter.' She bustled about, setting up the chairs. Space was limited, here in space, so that most furniture was temporary. A garden would not grow well under a chair; it needed access to the scheduled rainfall and hours of admitted sunlight. *Sun*light; there was only one sun, here.

So now she cared for him more than for her garden. Did absence make her calculating heart grow so dramatically fonder? Ronald distrusted this. Helen wanted something, and planned to use attention and sex appeal to get it.

Best to tackle the matter forthrightly. 'What's on your mind?'

'Does there have to be something on my mind?' she asked archly.

'Always. I scuff your dirt, you smile. That means mischief.'

She dropped the pretence. 'Before you went on the last mission, our marriage was foundering on indifference. While you were gone, I thought about that.'

'Why?' He had appreciated her sendoff, but had not suffered illusion about the overall prospects.

She looked startled. 'To preserve the marriage, of course. Why else?'

There was the question she hadn't answered. *Why else?* 'If the marriage is going to founder, that is the best time for it to do so. We can simply let the term expire and go our separate ways. We don't need to go to heroic measures to extend an untenable relationship. That's the whole point of term marriage – to put a peaceful and expected sunset on mistakes. In prior centuries it was a much rougher situation.'

'Ronald, I thought you wanted to extend!'

He realized it was true. She had intelligence and sex appeal, and she kept house well. One need never realize that she had a laboratory job at which she was quite competent; she was content to play the housewife with him. Whenever he came home, she was there, though surely this complicated her own work schedule.

That was why he had married her, and why he had wanted to remain married to her. But her need for him had been less than his need for her, and she had done nothing to change that situation, and he saw now that that had gradually turned him off. He did not want to be vulnerable. Now she had inexplicably reversed – and he was being turned off more sharply.

'As far as I know, I have done nothing to merit any change of heart by you,' he said. 'I haven't even been here.'

'That's it,' she said. 'You were away, and I had a chance to think it out. Whether I'd prefer life with you, or without you, or with another man.' She had a precise way of expressing things, without hems and haws or stumbles or regretted misstatements, just as Cirl did.

He was still comparing Solarian to Band! Yet it was true: in this one respect, and perhaps in others, he had fallen in with similar females. Had Cirl in fact been a

163

surrogate for Helen: expressive, competent, but of a sweeter disposition? 'Such reevaluation is necessary at intervals,' he said noncommittally.

'Certainly. We don't agree on some things, but you're not a bad sort.'

'Thanks,' he said with irony. He had expected a more positive assessment. 'You're not bad yourself, for a Monster.'

'Monster?'

'Private image. To the species I transferred to, Solarians were Monsters.' Actually, he himself had foisted that image on them.

'Oh.' She reset her legs and her train of thought. His eyes necessarily fixed on the one while his mind fixed on the other. 'Then the returns started coming in,' she continued. 'Six agents in succession, wiped out. No returning auras. I realized I might not see you again, ever. That made me think much more deeply. Generally your missions are not matters of life-or-death. I knew then that I cared for you more intensely than I had thought. It was a kind of shock treatment, a vision of hell.'

'Hell does not exist,' Ronald said, feeling awkward.

'That depends on your philosophy. You are atheistic; I am religious. I won't claim to believe in a literal hell, the kind with brimstone, but I do believe in a final accounting and in the perfectibility of the spirit. Certainly there is hell-in-life, and that is what I sampled, briefly. Without you, I would be less than I am, and that I hardly care to contemplate. So let's not debate about literal hell, and just concede that visions of hell certainly exist.'

Just as the mock viscous circle existed. Again there was that similarity of outlook. Ronald found himself unable to respond directly to her implication. She was saying that she loved him, or at least that she wanted to renew their term marriage. Before this last mission, he would have been delighted to accept. Now he was in doubt.

'You know, the Bands have no vision of hell,' he said, deciding to make a more open test of his insight. 'But they do have one of heaven. They call it the Viscous Circle – a great soul-mass comprising all their auras mixing viscously together.'

'Ringer Heaven!' she exclaimed, smiling.

'Don't call them Ringers. They are Bands.'

'You kept your promise!' she cried. 'You tried to appreciate their viewpoint.'

'My memory was blanked; I remembered no promise.'

'Unconsciously, then. That was possible, wasn't it?'

Ronald was surprised. 'Yes, it was.'

'How do you feel about the Ringers – the Bands – now?'

He sighed. 'It's a utopian society. They don't fight, they don't war. Each person lives and lets live, and helps anyone who seems to need or want it.'

'That sounds wonderful! But suppose one attacks another?'

'None do. There are no Band criminals.'

'But if some alien species moved in – '

'As we are doing now?'

She chewed her lower lip, then her upper lip. Doing that, she looked very much like a Monster. 'You know, I don't like our alien policy. Of course I'm loyal to my own species, but sometimes the way we move in – but yes, what do the Bands do when faced with violence?'

'They disband in droves. Suicide. Go to their Viscous Circle heaven.'

'They're not fighting? Not even to protect their home?'

'Only one group fought – the one I organized. Now I understand why I alone possessed the ability to do that. I'm a Monster.'

She looked askance at him. 'Are you playing with me,

165

Ronald? That's the second time you've called members of our species monsters. I don't think it's funny.'

'I wish I were playing! It's coming back strongly now. A completely peaceful society, and we're destroying it. A year from now there won't be a Band left. Genocide! We'll get our Ancient Site – but at what a cost!'

'You sound like me!'

Ronald considered that. 'I suppose I do. I never really understood your view before. But now that I've been a Band – can you imagine how it grates to hear these fine, truly civilized creatures called Ringers?'

'I think that's wonderful, Ronald! You've seen the light. I think that was the main thing separating us before, though I always hoped, believed, that someday it would change. I sensed in you the capacity for that change. You were a warrior, treading down other species as though they were all monsters to be slain, while I sought to protect them. Now you want to protect them too.'

With a vengeance, he realized. He had been trained to overcome alien monsters, starting with that three-headed dog, and had continued to do it – until this mission. Now the passage of time was not realigning him with the Solarians; it was bringing him to greater identification with the Bands. He had suffered some sort of conversion. His fundamental orientation was changing; the essence of his longing now was alien. 'The harder they fall . . .' he murmured.

'It's your long-buried conscience emerging.'

'But I am a military man!' he protested. 'Or at least I'm associated with a paramilitary venture. I must follow my orders and complete my assigned mission. They'll be sending me back soon, along with the other surviving agent – this time with our memories intact. I will have no excuse not to locate the Ancient Site.'

'You could resign,' she said.

'They'd only send in new agents. It would be less efficient, and there would be many more losses, but new ones could do the job, now that I've prepared the way. My first report has already done the damage. I'd know I was responsible for what happened.'

'I suppose you'd better go, then, and warn the Bands –'

'Which would mean treason to my species.'

She frowned. 'I appreciate the problem, Ronald. Still, I'm proud of you for becoming aware of it. Other species do have rights, especially the right to exist. Maybe you could warn the Bands away, so we could take the Ancient Site without hurting them. That's not ideal, but maybe practical.'

'They won't move. Can't move. They travel on magnetic lines of force that are strung out around their home system. They'd rather disband than move over.'

'They prefer to die rather than compromise? That isn't reasonable.'

'Bands aren't reasonable by our lights. They don't understand our imperatives. And they don't mind dying, because of their foolish mythology of the afterlife. They regard disbanding as the proper way to counter aggression. You can't fight a creature who suicides first. They are the ultimate pacifists.'

'Yet it would be less drastic to move than to die, and pacifists should not object to that course.'

'I told you, they can't move. If Solarian ships do their usual survey on Planet Band, detonating shells on the surface and all that, the Band equipment that generates all the lines will be destroyed. All the lines will vanish. Without the lines, all Bands everywhere will perish, most within minutes, the rest within hours. There are no longer enough natural lines to support their population.'

'Like returning mankind to stone-age technology, stranding us out here on the planetoid,' she agreed. 'We'd soon perish without our technology. But I'm still pleased you appreciate their position.'

Ronald's growing frustration vented itself on her, Monster-fashion. 'Well, maybe you'll also be pleased to know I married a Band female there. How's *that* for appreciation?'

Helen paused, but managed to take this in stride. 'Fidelity was never a requisite of our marriage. When in Transfer, you are expected to do as the hosts do. It's essential to your missions. And of course you had lost your memory. It is virtually a contradiction in terms to be unfaithful to a faith that is not in your mind. Since it may have been politically or socially necessary to align yourself with one of the local – '

'You're thinking like a Monster. There are no politics and no social necessities, other than leaving others alone and helping those in need. I married Cirl because I loved her.'

'Yes, of course,' she said, her tone showing she did not believe it for a moment. 'It is always best to do these things for ethical reasons. But now your memory has returned – '

'And I'm still a Band at heart. A Band in Monster form. I didn't realize that at first, but I know it now. And you – you're a gross, fleshy, liquid-filled-eyeballed female Monster. I can't stand you!'

Then both were silent, shocked at what had come out. What a can of worms he had overturned! For he had spoken the truth, though he had not realized it was truth until it pressured its way out. He really did remain a Band in outlook, rather than a Solarian. And that meant –

What did it mean? What *could* it mean? Objectively, he knew he was a Solarian. He had been born and raised Solarian, in this Solarian System of Sirius, in the heart of Sphere Sol. He had spent a short time, relatively, in

Transfer as an alien, and then reverted back to his proper host. The computer had passed him as normal, and the computer did not make mistakes of that nature. Unless the computer happened to have a grudge against some other responsible party, so was messing up the Transfer approvals – no, ridiculous! Rondl – *Ronald* was Solarian! He had to be.

'Helen, I apologize,' he said quietly. 'I must be overtired, or not properly acclimatized. Funny things happen when a person's aura is out of phase. No fault of yours.'

She recovered her composure in the efficient way she had. 'I understand. And I'm interested. Do you really love this alien creature?'

'I don't want to discuss that. I don't even want to think about it.'

'And that expletive – liquid-filled-eyeballed? – That's beautiful!'

'You're being very polite. Bands have no eyeballs, no liquid in their bodies. No soft flesh. They're just hard rings, metallic, with no moving parts except a fringe of tendrils that hardly count. Their nervous systems are wholly magnetic – like printed circuitry, transistor diodes, semiconductors. Only they're a good deal more sophisticated than that. They can alter currents by applying magnetism, without changing the physical structure of a thing. Some kind of finely attuned system of impedances – I'm no physicist, I don't know what it is, or even if such a thing exists as magnetic impedance, but it works. They are the original magic rings. So to them, a purely physical living form, with soft flesh and moving parts and leveraged limbs and liquid in flows and sacs – a Solarian is an assemblage of repulsively odd anatomy. They react much as we would to a maggot-ridden barrel of rotten eggs poured into our bathwater.'

Helen let out a peep of stifled laughter. 'An egg shampoo – a real live shampoo!'

'But if you don't mind dropping the subject – '

'Rotten eggs,' she repeated. 'Eyeballs made of rotten eggs, with yolk-pupils and – ' She stifled some more mirth. 'I look like that?'

'Of course not! You're – ' But he could not think of a suitable refutation, because her eyes *did* somewhat resemble – ridiculous!

'Let's put it to the test,' she decided. 'If I can't turn you on, then I must be a monster.' She inhaled deeply, making her breasts accentuate, and recrossed her legs to show more flesh.

'Why does everything have to turn sexual with you?' he demanded. 'I don't want this. I just want to relax and think, to work things out in my own mind before I make a worse fool of myself.'

'Because this has been my only real hold on you,' she answered seriously. 'I'm not really a sexual creature, you are. I can take sex or leave it, but you've always needed it, so I have perfected it for you. We never saw eye to eye – liquid-filled or not – on any really important thing except this. Sex is the one thing that always pleases you. I am willing to bet that your Band female caught on to that early enough, too! So if it ever fails to move you, then I've lost you. The hook will have slipped.'

She took another deep breath and leaned forward, and her torso-mounted flesh masses shifted form in a manner that ordinarily would have had a profound effect on him. 'I thought you were a good man despite your flaws, which is why I married you,' she continued. 'I had about given up hope, after four years, that your worst flaw would ameliorate. But I think my original estimate has abruptly been confirmed. I am a creature of causes, as you know, and the redemption of you has been a prime cause.'

170

'*I* was one of your causes? Along with the cornstalks and downtrodden aliens?'

'Of course. I felt you had the capacity to understand all the rest, and I was right. Only now you have turned entirely over, and not only sympathize with the plight of an alien species, but identify with that species. You think you may love an alien female. That's somewhat farther than I would have had you go, but not a disaster. If you really love her, I can't compete. But if I *can* compete, then it's not true. That is, what you think is love for her is merely newfound empathy. I know you have never separated love and sex; if you don't love, you can't – '

'I mated with her.'

'Yes, I thought that was the case. Any worthwhile female of any species finds out how to hold her male. So I want to find out now, while you think you love elsewhere, whether you really do, or whether you're fooling yourself. It's important for me to know, for one thing, because – '

She was amazing! And despite his intensifying alien perspective, she remained desirable to him. True, her flesh was ponderously puffed by liquid and gel, eyeballs and all – but that was the mode of Monsters. And her reaction impressed him. He had insulted her in more than one way, and she had risen immediately to the challenge. He called her undesirable, so she proposed to make proof of that by seducing him. It was probably a valid test.

Yet there was something missing. She really should not be that interested in him. There were other men in the Station, and she was an attractive Monster, and some of the other men had indicated, in the approved manner of such things, that they would be interested in Helen if she were ever free. For that matter, there were other women who had indicated similar interest in Ronald. In a Station like this the regular personnel got to know each other pretty well, and there was a standard system of private

171

communication that everyone understood perfectly. Only within marriage itself did the communication seem to break down; whether that was nature or irony he wasn't sure. Maybe emotion got in the way of objectivity. Or perhaps the culprit was commitment, since plenty of emotion could precede the formal alliance. 'Why is this important to you?' he asked, becoming aware that she had broken off as though expecting his challenge.

'Because I want your baby.'

She had hit him hard that time! He had wanted a baby at first, and she had not. Since it was necessary for both parties to take fertility pills in order to make conception possible – countering the universal contraceptive medication of the Station – that had meant they had been childless. As their marriage term wore on, his interest in that aspect had diminished. He might have been thinking, unconsciously, of contracting his next term marriage with a woman who also wanted a baby.

'But with less than six months to go in the term, we'd have to renew. They won't give us the null-pills otherwise. Children have to be born to marriage with at least three years remaining.'

'Did you ever wonder what I saw in you?' she asked. 'We know what you saw in me: the natural padding on my chest and bottom.'

'Oh, there was more to it than that,' he corrected her, smiling. 'Others have similar padding, but you moved it about more aptly.'

'That took practice,' she admitted. 'But you don't have much padding in those places, and you hardly move it about at all.'

'Well, I thought you liked my character. My sunny disposition – '

'Others have that. You're not remarkable in that respect.'

172

'I admit I came to doubt my remarkability, but as long as you were satisfied I did not see fit to question too closely. Something about not eyeballing gift horses in the teeth.'

'Gift horse,' she muttered darkly. 'I would have preferred another analogy.'

'I didn't really look at your teeth.'

'I *know* what you looked at!' She ran her gaze over him speculatively as she reverted to her thesis. 'It was your mind I liked. Largely frittered away in nonessentials, but beneath the garbage of your indolence you had a first-class intellect.'

'But we have always disagreed intellectually!' he protested, surprised.

'And your aura. You're no 200, but you *are* a 55, and that's one hell of an intensity. Fifty-five times as intense as the sapient norm.'

'The minimum aura for a Transfer agent is 50, so that's not special. And your own aura is equivalent. You could be a Transfer agent too, if you wanted to.'

'For posterity,' she said. 'I wanted a child with a mind and an aura. Aura does not seem to pass from generation to generation; still, it seemed better not to settle for a low-aura father. At any rate, intelligence is largely hereditary, and so that part seemed like a good investment.'

'But you could have had my baby three and a half years ago, if that was all you wanted!'

'True. That was not all I wanted. I needed to be sure the marriage would be renewed at least one term, because I don't like an unstable family situation. Not for a child. I know they claim that the Station nursery can raise a three-year-old child better than the parents can, but I don't believe it.'

'*I* was raised in a nursery!'

173

'That's part of your problem. You oriented on the Station instead of on humanity. You lack empathy – or did, until this past experience.'

Ronald hadn't thought of it that way. 'Could be. I don't orient on Monsters at all now. I prefer the Band society.'

'Yes. You lacked really strong human roots, perhaps, and have now found stronger ones. It does sound like a nice society.' She readjusted herself, downplaying the sex appeal for the moment. 'Environment does play an important part, and a stable family is *the* most important part of the environment. We differed so persistently that I could not be sure it would last, so I had to wait.'

Ronald shook his head. 'You are a calculating female!'

'Indeed I am. Now my calculations indicate that it can work out, because your attitude about minority aliens has suffered a promising change, and I want that baby.'

'Right when I tell you I love elsewhere – that turns you on?'

'An alien is no threat to me, Ronald. This mission will finish and you'll never see her again. I owe her a debt for doing what I could not: evoking your fundamental empathy, making you suitable to be the father of the kind of child I want to raise. In a unified family. Personally. You are, despite your momentary present confusion, definitely human. Which I am about to prove.'

'I'm less certain than you are,' he muttered. 'I don't necessarily follow your logic. Extension of our marriage tenure is at this moment in greater question than ever before, yet you suddenly decide all is well.'

'No. Now that you've seen the light about aliens, I've decided we could be philosophically compatible for a longer period. You're more human.'

'Did it occur to you that if my love for my alien wife passes, so could my understanding of alien causes?'

'Emotion passes. Understanding remains. You will

174

continue to realize that we can't just ride roughshod over creatures like the Bands. Not even when an Ancient Site is involved.'

'That much is true,' he agreed. 'I've got to help the Bands some way. But I don't know how.'

'I know where to look,' she said. 'I'll tell you, after we make love.'

He drew back. 'You're setting a price on it?'

She laughed. 'Touché! That's prostitution, isn't it, and we women aren't supposed to be too obvious about that sort of thing. On top of that, I'm the one who's paying. All right, I'll let you know now. You'll have to talk privately with the other survivor of the mission, Tanya Coombs. I know where to find her.'

'Good idea!' he agreed. 'She's the only other person who has been there. But why would you be reticent about suggesting that?'

'I understand she is a remarkably attractive woman.'

Now Ronald laughed. Trust a woman to think of that first! He knew he had a certain reputation for a wandering eye, so she would prefer to keep temptation out of his way.

Helen moved in to him. Flesh was all over her, wrapped around bones and shifting under tendons, and her eyeballs were indeed liquid-filled and glistening moistly as though they had sprung leaks, and the red fibres of her head were all over. Yet despite his sharpening memories of the Bands, he found himself reacting positively to the Solarian female.

He was, indeed, a Monster.

CHAPTER 11

Tangent

It was not easy to arrange his talk with Tanya Coombs. Her Station was in a planetoid on the far side of the System; it would take hours to travel there by shuttle. He could do it instantaneously by Mattermission – except that the prohibitive expense meant the authorities would never authorize it. They would throw away horrendous amounts of energy mattermitting a whole fleet of warships to a distant Sphere, but none for one person within the System. And Transfer to a host at that other Station was out; the Society of Hosts kept too close track of all such transactions.

No, a physical meeting with her was not feasible, and perhaps not desirable. What did she know of him, or he of her? Only that each had survived. Did she share his new concern for the Band society? Did she care whether a species was about to be incidentally exterminated? If not, it would be foolish of him to make known to her his own questions. The very fact of his sneaking out to meet her privately would betray him; he might blurt out his treason to the universe. For treason was really what was in his mind: he wanted to help an alien species at the expense of his own.

He would have to call her. But here too were problems. All calls to and from military Stations were monitored. There would be no privacy. In fact he could not even place the call without clearance from the Transfer authorities. It might be possible to have Helen place a call to a friend of hers at that Station, who could then contact Tanya Coombs – but this would be tedious and uncertain, would not enable him to learn what he needed to about her private attitudes, and might not escape the notice of the authorities anyway, even if Tanya did not turn him in. And if she *did* share his concern for the Bands, how could she trust him? She could take him for an administration agent testing her loyalty. She would tell him nothing of her true sentiment. Not by vid. So he was effectively blocked off; he had to keep his concerns to himself.

Meanwhile, there was Helen to think about. Would it be smart to renew his term marriage to her? How little he had known her, these years of the first term!

He had thought there had been no connection between his professional life and his personal one, when all the time she had been trying to reconcile the two. She wanted to align their philosophies so as to fashion a harmonic situation for their child. He had thought she had simply lost interest. She had proved that she had not – and had also proved *he* had not. He now saw himself and her as Monsters – but just as a person could adapt to changed circumstances, he could adapt to an alien host – or to his own host body experienced as alien. Monsters, too, could love.

Helen was right: after this mission was over, and the Ancient Site was in Solarian possession, he would remain a Monster, and have to deal with Monster things. Band Heaven was merely a tantalizing interlude, impossible for a Monster to join permanently. A devil could only gaze upon an angel in envy; he could not change his own nature. So if Ronald did not arrange to procreate by Helen, he would have to do so with some other Monster female. Was there really a better one on his horizon?

Yet could he conclude he still loved her? His emotion remained with Cirl, the alien female. Why was that? It really did not seem to make much sense. He had to resolve the question before he recommitted himself to

177

Helen. And perhaps before he saw Cirl again. He could not be fair to either if he did not know his own mind.

What did a military man with an emotional problem do? Standard Operating Procedure had the answer: he went to see the chaplain. Anything discussed with a chaplain was confidential. In fact the chaplain might help him contact Tanya Coombs privately. It was certainly worth a try.

Ronald walked out to the residential launch platform and set himself in place. When he touched the proper button, the platform moved forward and upward, accelerating him in the direction opposite the great cylinder's spin. Thus he found himself in midair, seemingly rushing across the landscape, but actually hanging without momentum while the cylinder spun around him. He extended his fins and stroked towards the central exit, aiming sidewise just enough to counter the drag of air that sought to carry him along with the spin. The air was viscous, moving with the cylinder at the edge and remaining almost stationary at the centre. He was far more conscious of viscosity than he used to be!

Around him the cylinder-world came clearer as he rose. Ronald had lost his sense of elevation when he became weightless; now he was more or less the centre of a world that rotated around him. He always noticed this effect, and always enjoyed it. Perhaps this did suggest his basic narcissism, his tendency to see himself and his species as the centre of the universe. His experience with the Bands had shown him that there were other centres, perhaps more valid than his own. Yet his delight remained.

The colours of the yards and roofs of the houses made an irregular pattern; when he narrowed his vision, so that his eyes did not automatically track, those colours blurred by like animated pictures. This was a huge kaleidoscope: the roofs like bits of glass, the river like a blue-grey wash of paint. The amount of fall of the water was not great,

178

only a few metres, but it held to its channel faithfully and clung to its little lake at the base, from where the water was filtered and pumped to its 'mountain' origin for recirculation. Small children were swimming in the lake; he heard their faint glad cries and saw their splashing. Ah, yes – this was as close to paradise as Monsters could get. The Monster version of the Viscous Circle.

Ronald reached the centre and had to take the exit, lest he obstruct the traffic. Feeling a gentle nostalgia for this imitation Heaven, and for the real one the Bands believed in, he caught the rim bars and launched himself through the tube. Now he thought of himself as a flying shuttle rocket, zooming through locks and buoyed channels that marked the only safe route through a planetoid belt. It was childish fancy – but one he could afford to indulge within the sanctity of his own mind. System Band had many more planetoid belts, around their suns and around their planets and perhaps even around their larger moons; there one could really play dodge-the-chunks. Maybe that, too, attracted him there. Perhaps hindsight was making his assorted motives come clearer.

He swung abruptly around a corner and zoomed toward the chaplains' quarters. Everything had its place, here in the Station; one had only to know where these places were. There were no signposts, no guidelines; this was part of the security system of the base. No stranger could readily find his way around it, and certainly no alien creature would be able to move with facility. Only natives developed the necessary expertise, knowing where every handhold was, and knowing which handholds were rigged as alarms. Natives became unconscious of all the deliberate little pitfalls while avoiding them, and that was the way it was supposed to be.

Now he reached the smaller, faster-spinning Neutrals, Aliens, and Chaplains cylinder. There was no great panoply here; the chambers opened directly off the free-fall chute, unmarked. The first was Polarian, the second Nath, and so on down the line of Spherical allies of Sol. Any alien detachment, no matter how small, had its right to its own chaplain or equivalent. It was part of being a Registered Alien. Humans did not interact much with alien allies, because of differing atmosphere and gravity preferences – the notion of alien planetary conquest was ludicrous, because who would try to conquer at great expense a planet the species could not use? – but many different species were stationed together here in space. Space was equally inhospitable to all creatures – except, he remembered with a renewed pang, the Bands, who lived in space. Here among the Monsters it was never possible to predict what particular skills would be required in a war emergency, so most available creatures were represented. The military spared no expense for its preparedness!

He paused by the aperture for Magnet, which was next to the one for Sol. The Magnets were a spherical metallic species using magnetism to propel themselves. They were not really sapient, as he understood it; they served as guards or watchdogs, and were excellent at that. A Magnet in attack flight most resembled a fired cannonball, smashing all before it. It occurred to him that the Magnets also resembled the Bands, because of their mode of propulsion and ability to survive in deep space.

But there was much more to a creature than the propulsion! The Magnets were really floating engines, consuming coal or other combustibles to generate their magnetism, but the Bands drew their power from the magnetic lines. The Magnets had to be near metal; Bands could travel best in deep space. In an analogy of machines: the Magnets were like ancient Earth-planet steam locomotives, while the Bands were like modern electric-ion spaceships. Maybe there was a kinship between the species, but it was no closer than that of bipedal dinosaurs to man.

Ronald drifted back, finding himself at the Polarian entrance before he realized where he was going. Surely he did not want an alien chaplain!

No? If he contemplated treason against his own species, what could be more objective than a third species, neither Solarian nor Band? The Polarians were renowned for their circular reasoning, incomprehensible to many Solarians, yet often productive of positive results. Polarians had spread into Sphere Sol as a result of the enormously waxing power of System Etamin, on the border between the Solarian and Polarian Spheres. In fact the present thrust for the Ancient Site was a ploy to stave off the shifting of power within the empire from System Sol to System Etamin. The logic of men could not, it seemed, compete with the logic of men and dinos – the contemptuous slang term for Polarians, based on their supposed resemblance to the droppings of the dinosaurs on the Etamin planet of Outworld.

What about approaching the matter at a tangent? Talk with the Polarian chaplain. Maybe nothing would come of it – but who could say?

Ronald nudged himself down the Polarians' hole. Soon weight manifested itself as he reached the outer portion of this spinning cylinder, and he had to catch hold of the bars set for this purpose so that he would not fall too swiftly. He reached the bottom and stood on the smooth walk there, his head feeling a trifle light. This was because, in this small cylinder, his physical height made a difference; his head was moving more slowly than his feet, so really was lighter. Some people could develop nausea from this effect.

He walked along the passage until he came to the

chaplain's door. It opened as he stood before it. There was the Polarian, shaped like a man-sized teardrop, a massive spherical wheel below, a tiny ball at the end of his trunk above.

The little ball touched the nearest wall, causing vibrations that sounded like human speech. The adaptation was so precise that Ronald glanced at the wall, almost expecting to discover an intercom unit there, though he knew better. 'It is possible to lose one's way in a Station of this complexity,' the creature said diplomatically. Polarians were seldom direct; they preferred to be circular, and their speech reflected this.

'In this case, sir, no accident,' Ronald responded. One addressed officers 'sir' regardless of their species, though Ronald, as a semicivilian agent, did not have to honour this convention.

'Then you may wish to enter. I am Smly of Polaris Sphere, counsellor to those in need.' The alien did not inquire whether Ronald had a need; that would have been uncircular.

Ronald did not introduce himself, as he preferred to keep this interview anonymous. The Polarian could readily run down his identity; Ronald's reticence was merely a signal. 'I want to commit treason against my species,' he said, without preamble. Ronald wondered idly whether Solarians normally pronounced this Polarian's name 'Smiley' or 'Smelly'. Polarians' names generally were easily lent to parody, and the creatures seemed not to object. Presumably they reserved their emotion for things of greater significance.

'This might be considered a natural urge, if there were justification for it,' Smly remarked obliquely.

Ronald explained the circumstances. The Polarian rolled about his small chamber, listening thoughtfully, his wheel making a faint track of moisture. His motion was

182

graceful, in contrast to the jerky movements of the Solarian form.

'So that's it,' Ronald concluded his discourse. 'I think I love the alien female more than I do the wife of my own kind, and my ultimate loyalty seems to be with that alien species. I fear this is treason.'

'Our definitions may differ from yours,' the chaplain said, this time buzzing his ball against the ceiling. Had Ronald's eyes been closed, he would not have been able to tell it was not a human being speaking, albeit one who seemed to flit about from floor to wall to ceiling. 'To us the welfare of the individual is paramount. In a conflict of interest with the apparent welfare of society, the individual governs.'

'What's good for one is good for all,' Ronald said, putting it into perspective.

'There may therefore be no treason.'

'But I'm not a Polarian!'

'Polarian custom is now a legal option for military personnel. This relates to the composition of, and balance of interests in, the larger sphere of interest of our empire. Should your kind bring you to trial or court-martial for treason, you might invoke our law and be exonerated.'

'I suppose I should be relieved to hear that,' Ronald said. 'But somehow I'm not. I'm more concerned with the moral aspect than the technical. I do not want to betray my species or my society, yet I feel the need to protect the Bands from exploitation or destruction. My private, personal welfare is of little account. What, then, is my correct course?'

'It is to honour your fundamental imperatives. If your loyalty to the Band female and the Band society is strongest, these are what you must support. You have only to be sure these are your loyalties.'

'I'm *not* sure! That's why I'm in quandary.'

'Why would a person love a Band more than his wife?' Again the Polarian was phrasing a direct question indirectly. A Polarian who lacked extensive contact with Solarians would not have phrased such a question at all.

'Do I?' Ronald asked, translating the indirect into the direct, as was typical of his kind. Sol was known as a 'thrust' culture, driving relentlessly forward. 'Yes, I suppose I do. I think it is because Cirl really needs me, and I need her. She was going to suicide, until I rescued her and gave her reason to live. I was floundering myself, until she showed me the ways of Band society. Helen and I don't really need each other. Not as much. At least, I thought we didn't.'

'One could be curious how Band society differs from Solarian society.'

'That's the whole essay in itself, a whole library! But I guess you mean how does it differ *to me?*' Ronald considered. 'In essence, it's a pacifist society, very much like the Solarian ideal, utopia – you know, the kind that would bore the hell out of real people in practice. Because we Solarians are a warlike lot; it shows in every aspect of our lives, in our constant competition, in our "free enterprise" system that really represents every man's right to claw one's way as high as he can go. But with the Bands this pacifism really works, and their vision of heaven – their Viscous Circle – is correspondingly remote. It's a myth, of course, but – well, I confess it appeals to me increasingly. I wish I could go to the Viscous Circle when I die.' He laughed ironically. 'I don't believe in it, but I long for it! Maybe it's not treason so much as insanity that beckons me!'

'Then one's love for an alien might be a function of one's longing for her framework or belief.'

'It must be! It's such a wonderful belief, better than ours. Solarians are so damned pushy, so infernally corruptible, so much like monsters. I was never much for philosophical notions, before, but somehow – I don't know. I never believed in pacifism, either, until I saw it work in the Band society – and of course then I had to teach them to fight, so they would not be destroyed. I guess I'm doing as much to destroy their philosophy as the rest of my kind is to destroy their bodies. So I'm really being a traitor to the Bands, too; perhaps a worse one. But – well, that's why I'm here. I'm an agent of incalculable mischief, like a germ cell. What can I do?'

'There may be times when one must consider whether it is ethical to advise parties of the truth.'

'Tell the Bands about my being a Monster spy? Do you think I'm crazy? They'd – ' He paused. 'No, they wouldn't. They don't react with anger. They just accept facts.'

'Is it possible that the truth would enable them to save themselves from possible destruction?'

'I'm not sure. I doubt it. They'd rather disband than cause considerable inconvenience to other creatures. That's the irony of their situation; the aggressive, grasping species like Solarians drive out the civilized, gentle species like Bands. Even knowing everything, they would not fight – unless they had an uncivilized Monster like me to lead them.'

'Yet if they were informed that all the Solarians desire is the Ancient Site – would they move away from it?'

'Yes, I suppose they would. And that might solve the problem. Assuming the Site is well away from Planet Band. Only – ' Ronald paused, trying to pin down his reservation. Then he had it. 'Only I don't want to solve it that way. That Ancient Site is in their space; they have the most proper title to it. If anyone gets to benefit from Ancient science, it should be the Bands, not the Monsters. The Bands, at least, would not abuse it.'

185

'Then it may be that the problem is not amenable to solution.'

'Not that way. I don't want the bad creatures to win.' Helen would be gratified to hear him now!

'Perhaps it is fitting to continue as you have been doing, enabling the good creatures to resist the onslaught of the bad. You may deceive the Bands about your nature and motive, for were they to learn of it, they might themselves convey to the Solarians' command the desired information, turning over the Ancient Site. Does this accord with your principles?'

'You make it sound terrible! But yes, I am a Monster, with Monster values. I can do the right thing in the wrong way. I can lie and cheat and steal and kill to achieve my objectives. I don't like it; I wish I were more like Cirl, pretty inside as well as outside. But I'm not, and I certainly don't want Cirl to become like me. If there is lying and cheating to be done, I'd rather take it on myself to do it, since I'm a Monster anyway, and spare them from any such thought. I don't want to corrupt the angels of Heaven. I have to do what my conscience dictates, however much it may violate my conscience – ludicrous as that sounds.'

'It accords with Polarian principles. The needs of the individual are paramount. Society is not permitted to judge the motives of the individual.'

'Maybe that's why I came to talk with you. I must have realized you'd endorse my selfishness.'

'That is possible,' the creature agreed without rancour. Polarians were like that; they really did have an alien viewpoint. 'Yet it seems you are making the ultimate sacrifice, casting down your own morals and scruples in order to ensure that theirs remain pure.'

And how many bigots had done exactly that, throughout human history, savagely protecting the morals of others despite the will of those others? Ronald felt unclean. 'Well, thanks, Chaplain,' he said. 'Thanks to your counsel, I am now resolved to betray both sides, in order that my will alone will be done, right or wrong.'

'That is the nature of Monsters,' the Polarian agreed equably.

Ronald reported to the interviewing room on schedule. 'We have decided to send both survivors back, this time, with memories intact,' Branst announced. 'We doubt there will be any aural check made there. That way, one of you should be able to locate the Ancient Site and report back to us. We can take it from there.'

'And the physical invasion – will you abate that until our report?'

'No. That will proceed, in case neither of you is able to locate the Site promptly.'

In other words, they did not fully trust these two agents, who had failed once to get the information. Ronald could not stall them. If he did not produce, they would locate that Site the hard way.

He had an idea. It was a long shot, but worth a try. 'I could coordinate better if I could get to know the other Transfer agent.'

'Of course. Here she is now.'

They were going to let him meet her! After all his own conjectures had come to nothing, the authorities were doing it for him.

The wall screen flicked into a picture that showed a chamber similar to this one. It was as if the room had abruptly doubled in size. Ronald had experienced this phenomenon many times before, but as with the tunnel-flying, it always intrigued him.

In the other half stood a comely young woman in military uniform, without visible insignia of rank, as was

187

the custom with Transfer agents. She might be military or civilian; it hardly mattered. 'Ronald Snowden, I presume?' she inquired.

'The same. Tanya Coombs?'

She nodded in confirmation, her hair rippling. It was black, falling to just below her ears, leaving her neck visible. She was slender and full and fit, her figure striving to express itself despite the restrictions of the uniform, and succeeding reasonably well. In feminine apparel she would be a knockout. 'You wished to compare notes?'

'Yes, and plan strategy. Privately.'

Branst and the officer with Tanya exited, leaving the two alone together. This was of course illusion; not only were they really not together, they were not private. The officers would be tapping the interview on separate screens, and the whole thing would be recorded by the computer and analyzed interminably for any special information that might be gleaned. Still, it seemed private, and that was what he wanted. By the time the analysis of the recording produced anything, Ronald would be safely gone.

'I discover certain complications,' Ronald said. 'My memory was blanked, so I did not remember I was married. So I married a Band female.'

Tanya smiled, in a quirky way that enhanced her prettiness. 'Me too,' she said ruefully. 'I now have two husbands. I did not care to advise my human husband of this.'

'I told my wife, and she was very understanding. In fact she was more concerned about my reaction to you than to the alien. But what will I tell my Band wife when I return?'

'Tell her nothing. My Band husband would disband if he knew.'

There was that. 'I think you and I should meet, as

188

Bands, to coordinate our search for the Ancient Site. There has been such attrition in the complement that I believe it is too risky to operate independently anymore. Do I have your agreement to say nothing inappropriate to my Band wife?'

Tanya nodded understandingly. 'And you say nothing to my Band husband. He's a good creature. I would not have survived without him, and don't want to hurt him. However, we can avoid any such complication simply by staying clear of each other. I think independent investigations will suffice.'

'But I thought – '

'I agreed to say nothing to your Band wife should I encounter her. I did not agree to meet you.'

Their dialogue had sounded promising until she revealed her preference not to meet him in Band form. He could not speak freely here; for true privacy, he had to meet her there.

Tanya, like himself, had been drawn into the Band philosophy, at least to the extent of marrying. She cared about her alien mate. But had her conversion gone as far as his own had? He could not ask her directly, but might glean some hints if he tested her. 'Did you like the Band society?'

'Isn't that immaterial to our mission?'

Avoidance. That was promising. 'Perhaps. Yet we have to understand it, to survive within it. Ten agents didn't. I almost didn't. Perhaps we had something in common. We don't know whether any of the others married, but it may be a reasonable conjecture that they did not, and so had no help.'

She arched a black eyebrow at him, attractively. What was a creature like this doing in Transfer? She should never want to leave her Solarian host body! 'We both did survive,' she said, 'perhaps because of our acceptance of

189

Band society to the point of marrying natives. I think the worst is over.'

'Yet we shall have to question Bands carefully, to get the information we require without tipping our hands – or rings, as the case may be.'

'I don't think that matters – '

'Because if they caught on, their military arm would get involved and set up an effective guard on the Site, making acquisition much more difficult for us.'

'Their military arm?' she asked blankly. She knew the Bands had no such thing. And this was his verification that he was in fact talking to the other Transfer agent, not a ringer (no Ringer; no Band!), a fake whose job it was to interrogate him. If by chance this Tanya were not the one, this would throw her. The computer and certain key officers would be aware of the nature of the Bands, but that information would be classified secret, not because it really needed to be, but because that was the way the military worked.

'Military people can get pretty ugly when aroused,' Ronald said. 'If the Bands' president called up the guard, our chances of success would suffer.'

'Oh, yes, their president,' she agreed faintly. The Bands had no president. Was she catching on to his meaning? He did not know how intelligent Tanya was, and his nuances might be bypassing her. But he could not speak more plainly without alerting the eavesdropping officers.

'So I don't want to alert their administration,' he continued. It was the Solarian administration he meant: his own government. He ran a double risk here: she might not catch on; or, if she did, she might not agree to the ruse. She could ruin him by giving the lie to his comments if she chose to do so.

'Yes, it would not be good to alert their military,'

190

Tanya agreed finally. 'That could lead to lethal complications.'

It seemed she had it, and was going along. Solarian traitors were mindwiped or executed, depending on the situation. 'So probably we should meet there and coordinate. We can't risk using their public communications system; we have to talk privately. Because if they catch on to our true nature – '

Tanya nodded. 'Yes, I believe you are correct. We can't afford to have the Band military listening in to our plans. That wouldn't be safe at all.'

'They'd interrogate us and disband us in prompt order,' Ronald said. *If she betrayed him now . . .*

'They would indeed. How shall I locate you there? What colour is your wife? My husband is blue. I'm orange.'

'I'm green. My wife is yellow. So we can't conveniently match colours. Could we meet at some known planetary landmark? Where some privacy exists? So that the military cannot intercept – '

'Maze Mountain,' she said.

'I don't know where – '

'You can inquire. I'll meet you beside the orange spire.' Convenient enough, since orange was her colour. 'Agreed.' But he wondered whether there really was such a place as Maze Mountain. Was she putting him off? Because if –

What choice did he have? He had taken the plunge, and hinted to her his true attitude. She seemed to agree, but if this were a ruse on her part, it hardly mattered whether she betrayed him in System Sirius or in System Band. He would simply have to proceed on hope and faith. If he did not get arrested for treason here, and if there was a Maze Mountain there, she was probably with him.

Unless she turned him in privately, and still met him there, giving him further rope to hang himself . . .

Well, he had approached this problem at a tangent, obliquely. He hadn't found any better way. He had to try, to take the risks. The alternative was to participate in the destruction of the finest society he had known.

CHAPTER 12
Double Circle

Rondl found himself in Cirl's embrace. 'Hey, I'm not drifting!' he flashed.

She released him immediately, then moved down the line far enough to obtain a suitable angle on Eclat for flashing back at him. 'Rondl! You have recovered!'

Suddenly he realized his Band host had been left unattended. That must have been a horror for Cirl! 'I have recovered,' he agreed. 'But I have been in nightmare. Tell me what happened here.'

'We were sleeping when you drifted off the line,' she said. 'I tried to wake you, but you would not revive. I brought you back to the line, but still you were blank. I was horrified. I realized that the strain of this unsocial campaign has been very great, and that you bore up under it without disbanding, as no other Band could do, but that it had finally been too much for you and your aura had taken leave of your body. But you had not disbanded. I remembered how strange some of your memories had been – so there was hope that you were away in that strangeness, and that you would return when your aura recovered. So I held your body, keeping it on the line, waiting for that recovery, refusing to believe you were gone forever even though – oh, I was so afraid!'

'That I can appreciate!' Should he tell her the truth, or pretend this had been an aberration? Her explanation was close enough to stand.

'Oh, Rondl – if you should disband, I don't know what would become of me or of our species! I think we would all have to join you.'

Join him in oblivion? For they could not transfer to Monster hosts the way he could. That decided him. He had to be honest with Cirl, whatever it cost him personally; she was the one he loved. 'Cirl, had you not helped me, I would have perished.' At least his Band host would have, making it impossible for him to return, which amounted to the same thing. 'I must tell you the whole story, though you may find much of it painful.'

'You have always been fair with me,' she flashed gladly.

'Cirl, I have recovered my memory.'

That dimmed her colour. 'You know whom you are? You have other commitments?'

Yes, this was going to be difficult. 'I do, and I do. But I also have commitments to you and to the species of Band. I now have two lives to reconcile. I fear you will not like what I have learned about myself.'

'You have to leave me?' she flashed tragically.

'No! I am not leaving you!' *Yet*, he added mentally, feeling guilty.

'Then the rest I can tolerate.'

He hoped she was right. Actually, she was not prone to disband lightly, for she had not done so when rejected by her former male friend, or when chased by the Kratch. But this might be a sterner test. 'I must go to a rendezvous.' But that had not been what he intended to say; he was evading the issue.

'I will go with you! Where is it?'

Go with him? Meet the other Monster in Band guise? Yet how could he prevent this? 'The Maze Mountain.' Would she know it? Did it even exist? Perhaps he had no problem, in that sense.

'I can guide you there!' she flashed. 'Whom must you meet?'

Her questions were making it easier; they provided form for his confession. 'A female – a married female –

who has had similar nightmares. I met her in this last nightmare, and must discuss it with her.'

'You share your dreams with another Band?'

Treacherous domain! 'Not as I shared them with you, Cirl! It just happened our nightmares overlapped – and now we must straighten them out in the waking state, to avoid further trouble.' He flew along the line for a moment, considering. 'Worse trouble.' Like genocide.

'I could not enter your dream this time. Your aura was absent. How could she be in it?'

'This is the worst part of it,' he said. 'Cirl, I fear this will hurt you, and I would spare you if I could. I don't have to tell you – '

'Tell me. Anything is better than having you disband, or half-disband, dis-aura like that again!'

Why hadn't the original Band aura been returned to the host body for the interval? This body certainly would have died, had not Cirl acted so devotedly to save it, and Tanya's host might now be dead for the same neglect. That was criminal carelessness!

No, not carelessness, he realized as he thought it through. There were prohibitive risks associated with returning the native Band to his body. The Band, having experienced Monsterdom, could have second thoughts about this arrangement, and decide not to cooperate further. He might be appalled at what had happened and disband immediately, depriving Rondl of the available host. In a mission of this importance, it was pointless to risk this. It was also possible that they had done some damage to the original Band in the process of the exchange, not understanding the nature of Bands. He might have tried to disband in the Monster host. What would be the result? The Solarian body would not disintegrate, of course, but might well die. So perhaps they had no aura to return to this host anyway.

195

At any rate, they had had to let the Band host be blank for the brief time Rondl was back in System Sirius, not realizing how risky this was. That was just as well for Rondl; he preferred to keep the Monsters ignorant. And suppose the original Band had returned here, to find himself in Cirl's embrace? What would he have said to her? That could have been yet another kind of disaster.

'I will tell you in a moment. What have the Monsters been up to while I was out?'

'They remain between moons. I think our interference has made them pause. We have a respite.'

'Good.' Rondl gathered his thoughts and courage as they slanted toward the planet. Cirl was guiding him from one line to another, taking him towards a region on the planet's equator. He trusted her guidance. 'This last nightmare was of the Monsters, as before, but more complete. I was not absorbed by a Monster host, I was the Monster himself. I interacted with other Monsters. One of them was called Tanya, and we agreed to meet in our Band form when the nightmare ended. We could not afford to have the other Monsters overhear our discussion, you see.'

'But I still don't see how she shared your dream, when I could not.'

'Because it wasn't really a dream. My aura really was in a Monster host, and hers was in another.'

'But you did not disband! I could understand your aura retreating to deep inside you, or becoming extremely weak so that I could not detect it for a time – but how could it travel while your body remained?'

'In the alien Spheres there are devices that can move an aura intact from one host to another. Such a device was used on us.'

She assimilated this. 'So you were not really dreaming. You became a Monster, for a while.'

196

'True. I really was a Monster.'

'Your nightmares foresaw this. But how could your dreams know what was about to happen to you?'

'Because my unconscious mind, my deeper aura, knew. Consciously I did not know, for my memory had been blanked, but the information leaked out when my consciousness slept. This has to do with the nature of memory repression; it is not an erasure so much as a blockage. Complete removal of any part of a given segment of experience cannot be accomplished without enormous damage to the personality. Memory is like a holographic image, imprinted on every part and aspect of – '

'Holographic?'

'A visual concept. Maybe I should use another analogy. Memory is like a lens: you cannot remove a part of an image by eliminating part of the lens – '

'Of course you can't! The lens is a totality!'

'Yes. So is memory. So they really blocked my conscious awareness of my Monster status. Much of my vocabulary tied in with that status, which led to the many little mysteries of my communications, but I could not directly pass that block. Deep in my mind was the knowledge that I would – in due course – become a Monster. My nightmares were excerpts from that awareness, like refuse fished up from the deep ocean.'

She ignored the alien concepts of refuse and ocean. 'But no one can foresee the future!'

Rondl saw that she was not absorbing enough of his meaning. Perhaps she was resisting it on her own subconscious level. He tried again. 'It was not necessarily my future. It may have been my past nightmares reflected, in distorted fashion.'

She flew for some time in silence, flashless. This was a critical point. He had been trying to guide her to the realization carefully, in much the way he had learned to

197

train his Band recruits, so that she brought herself to the fundamental concept. That way she would fashion her own emotional supports along the way, and safeguard herself against being shocked into disbanding; her mind should balk before accepting too devastating a concept. He had not managed this perfectly, saying too much and too little, but perhaps it would work out. 'Before we met – in the time of your amnesia – you were a Monster?'

There it was; she had navigated it. 'I was a Monster. A Solarian. That was why I kept remembering odd bits of alien concepts, which leaked out around the memory block and vanished the moment I sought further detail. My Monster aura was sent to a Band host.'

'Your odd information!' she repeated.

'From my Solarian background.' He was beginning to relax, seeing her accept it.

'Now you remember everything?'

'I do.'

'All your Monster education, friends – do Monsters have friends?'

'They have friends. I remember it all. I share the Monster outlook. In that life I was a Transfer agent – one who had his aura moved to alien hosts, to gain information about their situation. Sometimes to foment trouble. I was sent here to find something important.'

'And when you have found it – you will return to your Monster host?'

She had not taken long to get the essence. 'When the mission is finished, they will recall me to my Monster host. I will have little choice in the matter. I might resist or avoid re-Transfer, but since my aura is alien to this Band host, it would inevitably fade as time passed. I can only visit this form; I cannot remain. That is my final nightmare.'

'Then I will disband!' she flashed.

198

'Don't disband!' he flashed back instantly. 'I don't *want* to go back. I want to stay with you!'

'I did not mean right now. I will disband when you leave me forever, since this life will have no brightness for me without you.' She seemed quite matter-of-fact about it, and that chilled him. She had considered disbanding when jilted by her former male friend; this time she was certain.

'But there is no need for you to die just because I am not what you thought I was. Not what *I* thought I was! How could I live with my conscience, knowing you had perished because of me?'

'Do Monsters have consciences?'

'Some do. I do. Now.'

'No Band perishes,' she reminded him. 'There is no guilt or sadness in the Viscous Circle.'

So she believed. He did not want to disabuse her of this touching faith. 'But I am not a Band; I'm a Monster. My kind does not believe in the Viscous Circle. I would be alive, knowing I could never join you.'

She was instantly solicitous. 'I had not thought of that! We must get you into the Viscous Circle!'

What harm was there in agreeing? It was such a nice concept. 'I'd like very much to join you there. But I doubt it is open to me, to my kind.' And he found that this was indeed very sad. What a fine thing it would be if the myth were true, and he could join. Better than any of the mythical human heavens!

'I must ask Proft,' she flashed. 'Maybe there is a way to get an alien, even a Monster, into the Viscous Circle. He will surely know.'

At least there was no immediate threat of her suiciding. She now had a positive aspect to focus on. He did care for her, a great deal; his emotion was every bit as strong and pervading as human love. Ultimately he would be wrenched from her, but he wanted to spare her any hurt he could. 'By all means, ask him.'

'Do Monsters marry?' she inquired after a bit.

Trouble again! 'They do. You must be aware of that; you teased me about my supposedly alien concept of marriage.'

But this time she did not respond with a flash of mirth. 'Did you marry?'

'Yes. Before I met you.'

'So you have a Monster wife?' This seemed to bother her more than the notion of death, perhaps because love was more real to her than death.

'I do have a Monster wife. On a five-year term marriage, almost over.' He was sure he knew what was coming, and he dreaded it. Females were females, the Galaxy over.

'You love her too?'

That was what he had feared. Yet the answer turned out to be easy. 'I don't know. I thought I did, once. Then I met you.'

Cirl was not swayed by the implied flattery. 'What does she think of me?'

'Competitive, I think. But she knows it can't last between us. She knows about fading auras. So after you, there will be her – if we should choose to renew the marriage for another term, which is in doubt. That is the reality of my condition.'

'Poor thing,' Cirl said sympathetically.

'I'm so glad you can accept it,' Rondl flashed. 'I was really worried – '

'I don't accept it,' she corrected him. 'I merely defined the problem.'

'But I thought – '

'Now we must convoke a circle and explore the matter properly.'

'But I have to meet – '

'Another female?'

'That's not – '

She was flashless, and he realized that he had better agree to her circle. The Maze would simply have to wait. 'Take me to your circle,' he flashed with resignation. He should have known this would not be simple!

She sent out the spiralling summons. In due course other Bands arrived – many of them, and soon, for they were now close to the planet, where many congregated.

This time Cirl directed them into a double circle, one flowing one way, the other flowing the other way. The Bands were carefully interspersed, so that every alternate one faced opposite. Cirl herself was in the other ring, on Rondl's subjective side. What was this leading to? He had not known this variation of the formation existed, and didn't trust it. But he trusted Cirl, so he cooperated.

Participation was strange. There was the massed, viscous current of light, as before – but also a similarly massed surge of feeling. Rondl knew this was merely the inversion of the communication flow of the reversed Bands, Cirl among them, but the quality was potent. It was not love, for that was unique to two Bands, but it was akin to it – a deep moving of the fundamental emotion. He had experienced nothing like this before, in either Band or Solarian existences. Well, perhaps when the Monsters had put him through hallucinogenic therapy – no, not even then. It seemed the full power and quality of his mind and emotion had been merged and amplified and rendered wonderful in a way his solitary self was incapable of appreciating, because it was simply too small. Even as the individual fragments of aura could hardly compass the majesty of the Viscous Circle –

Give. The urge transfixed him, and Rondl realized Cirl was sending to him from the other consciousness. The

201

requirement was nonspecific, yet impossible to misunderstand. What inner, suppressed secrets of his being was she picking up, reading his unconscious? She would comprehend his nature, surely, even those aspects he much preferred to conceal. Solarians were a secretive species, in contrast to the Bands; the sensation of exposure, of nakedness, was part of being Monster. He had to cooperate, as one might when joining a nudist colony, lest his failure to do so expose him even less prettily.

He gave. And the torus about him faded into the swirling thickening currents of its intellectual viscosity, and he became – an infant Monster. He had fat fleshy appendages extended by bone, and –

And was drifting through space, following a gentle line, watching the planetoids pass in their hundreds before the stars in their myriads. He was questing for something, but did not know what.

Wrong. This was a concept almost alien to Band nature, but it came through now. He was not, somehow, doing what he was supposed to. But he was locked in.

A current on this side came to his rescue. 'You have slipped through to the other side, and are picking up the unconscious theme consciously. You must not; that is the mirror of your conscious, and must be made conscious only after your conscious theme is complete.'

Rondl did not quite understand, but accepted the judgement of those who were experienced in this mode of exploration. He formulated his thoughts, concentrating on the Solarian aspect. In a moment he had it.

He took in fluids, digesting them internally, assimilating them into his system from the inside out. It was really the same as the Band mode of coalescing from the outside.

He stood on his two base appendages and looked up at the night sky. He hovered near the planet and looked down at its nocturnal mystery. What was he searching for?

Wrong. He had slipped back into the countermode. This was tricky! In the double circle, as in life, the separation of conscious and unconscious was imperfect. But this time it was easier to find his place.

He became adult and went to space – went to ground. And shied away from the Wrong. No ground, not in the Band sense. Space, in the Solarian sense. The great frontier of the unknown, space. To Bands, the unknown was the planetary surface.

He was uncertain he was equipped to cope with the type of mission he craved; eagerness warred with trepidation. Suppose he found himself in some totally alien situation, trapped on a planet amid creatures he could not relate to? As man or Band, he was daunted by this. Correction: as man only. He was exploring only his Monster side at the moment, consciously.

So he went on a training mission. He was transferred to a human host in a system near the fringe of the enlarged Sphere Sol, to Planet Hurri. This was a primitive world, at about the level of the ancient Sumerians of Earth; the colonists fancied they resembled the Hurrians of that space-time, a Mesopotamian tribe. It hardly mattered whether their level represented the year 2000 BC or the year 1000 AD on the confused Terran scale. It was pre-Transfer, pre-Atomic, pre-Machine, somewhere in the Metals age.

Ah, metals! the Bands of this circle agreed, finding an aspect of identification amid the confusion of alien concepts. They were following Rondl's thoughts, enhancing and clarifying them, giving him special powers of recall and comprehension, but they themselves were disoriented. Now they began to grasp his frame of reference.

The tribe leader Ronald was to meet for this practice assignment was called Speed Steelthew. Ronald found it easy to suppress his smile, for the man was tall, broad, and muscular, and he carried slung on his hip a gleaming two-edged sword, and in his left hand a three-metre spear. He was a formidable figure of a man, still strong though going slightly to pot.

Ronald himself occupied a host of this type: physically robust, scarred in numerous places, possessed of assorted minor discomforts and inhibitions where scar tissue was heavy, yet rather handsome of feature. His hair was fair, and it flowed down about his shoulders without tangles, and his beard was shorter but similarly fine. He was as pretty as a woman, in his fashion. He had reviewed himself in the imperfect mirror surface of a shield.

Pretty as a woman? Well, almost – for now Speed summoned forth two girls whose attributes were about as pronounced as Ronald had seen. Perhaps it was the style of their dress, cut away in front to expose provocative portions of their healthy breasts and cut away behind to show similarly firm buttocks. Yet the exposure was not complete; key areas remained concealed, and to these his eye was drawn almost magnetically. Primitive these people might be, but the art of sex appeal was well advanced long before science came on the scene. Did a nipple show in front? Did a stretch of cloth conceal the deepest crevices behind? He could not quite tell. That mystery was infuriatingly compelling, especially since his mission was not to ogle girls.

'Here are two of my concubines, Purrfurr and Wagtail,' Speed said. 'Will they be enough?'

Ronald had been advised that customs differed on regressed planets; the fact had just been brought home to him with abrupt immediacy. These young women were being offered to him for his sexual use during his stay here. He could not with grace refuse them.

'Uh, yes, surely,' he said, embarrassed. He would have to use them, too, lest he give offence to his host. To his

204

guest host, who was Chief Speed, and to his Transfer host, whose body he occupied and whose mind was discretely anonymous. Professional Transfer hosts, like well-trained beasts of burden, obeyed the will of the master so dependably that their presence was soon taken for granted. The good host did not intrude. As for Ronald, who hoped to be a good guest: when on Hurri, do as the Hurrians do.

But at the moment the girls were only decorations. They took the chief's spear and relieved Ronald of his, which was just as well, as he lacked any notion how to use it. They proceeded to the banquet, served, by assorted girls, on a blanket of glossy green leaves on the ground. The girls did not eat; they lacked the status to join the men in so meaningful an occupation. Ronald found it dismayingly easy to settle into this double standard. He believed in the equality of the sexes, but it certainly was nice being catered to by this bevy of shapely creatures.

First the men feasted on spitted boarhound and pickled platypus eggs; they guzzled voluminous quantities of mead ale, which was a thin, sour, but mildly alcoholic beverage. After the first gulp Ronald became acclimatized to the peculiar taste of it and, as the evening advanced and they became dependent on the light of the bonfirelike cooking flame, he even found himself liking it. The stuff was dilute enough so that it never put him out of commission, though it did take his head and parts of his body on a dizzy ride. At first he had questioned whether this culture had any real affinity for the historical Hurrians, who surely had been more civilized than this, with walled cities and cuneiform writing and irrigated gardens; but as the mead took effect, he concluded that there was nothing strange about this culture. Why shouldn't the Hurrians eat hunt-gathered items on the ground outdoors, before an open blaze?

Then they fell to with the concubines, who were so obliging there was no challenge. Ronald was not accustomed to public sexual display, but Chief Speed was doing it with abandon and conviction and considerable expertise, to the polite applause of the watching girls, and Ronald had to follow his host's lead. The mead helped him get into the spirit of the thing; there was probably an aphrodisiac in it. He was able in due course to acquit himself creditably with Purrfurr, unless the maidenly applause was purely polite. This was thanks in large part to Purrfurr's willing expertise and his own slowness in culmination, which permitted a longer and more varied display than would normally have been possible. The mead, again: not only did it reduce inhibitions, it dulled the edge of sexual response. Had he imbibed much more of it, he would have been able to put on the planet's most marvellous display, without climax.

When at last all human imperatives of hunger, sex, notoriety, competition, and expression had been sated, though not the need for recuperation, they proceeded to the business meeting. Ronald fought to keep his eyes open and his mouth closed, and to look properly attentive though his skull seemed out of phase with his brain by half a head and parts of his gut seemed to have been pumped dry. What an orgy it had been!

'. . . the monster,' Speed was expounding.

Monster! Again the Bands identified with this strange memory. Was he going to challenge a Monster?

Was he? Ronald was having trouble remembering, as it were, ahead. He also wondered why this particular episode of his past, by no means his proudest, was here unveiling itself. Now the Bands, too, had assimilated his uncivilized indulgence in the grossest fashion.

'. . . sends fear and nightmares among our people,' Speed was saying. Nightmares – a connection was beginning to show! 'Sours wives' milk, makes brats bawl. Annoying.'

Ronald nodded wisely, preventing himself from pitching forward into the dirt. The remaining leaves had been taken up when the meal finished; too useful to be wasted, they would be used to wipe knives clean and to serve as toilet tissue. 'Annoying,' he agreed.

'. . . destroy Cerberus . . . where you come in.'

'Of course,' Ronald agreed equably. Now at last he was getting a handle on his mission, the sample task he was to perform to benefit these primitive people. 'Let me draw a suitable laser rifle from Supply – '

Speed smiled, enjoying a private humour. 'No laser, Imp.'

Ronald wrestled groggily with this. 'Imp?'

'That is you. Polite address for an Imperial Sol Representative.'

Polite? Ronald doubted it. But at the moment he lacked the mental acuity to debate the issue. 'No laser?'

'There are very few operative modern weapons here in the hinterworlds.'

Oh. Of course. It required technology to maintain lasers, which needed to be periodically recharged. 'A solid-projectile handgun, then. With a carton of bullets, and a selection of exploding shells. Clumsy but adequate.'

'All the bullets were used up a century ago.'

'But new supplies can be shipped by sublight freighter. There should be a continuous stream of such supplies.' His head was clearing slightly. The sensation was not pleasant.

'Next ship to arrive in six Sol-years. Been on the way for two hundred years. Due care will be exercised, but bullets are precious. Supplies will vanish within weeks.'

'But it's not supposed to be that way! Ammunition should be issued to imperial troops only – '

Idly, Speed fished in the coals of the dying fire with a stick, watching the wood char. 'Mister Ronald – Imp – sir, how long would you retain your bullets if Purrfurr wanted them?' And the sensual woman reappeared, twining her luscious body against Ronald's. So lithe and full and cuddlesome was she that he started to suffer arousal again despite the thorough depletion of his resources. 'She will give you anything you desire, anything at all – in exchange for a bullet. How long will you tell her no?'

With difficulty Ronald refrained from responding to the woman's expert allure. He doubted he would have been able to hold firm had he been fresh and sober. A bullet? He would have given his soul for further pleasure with this creature! 'Point made. No bullets,' he said, his head clearing somewhat as Purrfurr pouted prettily and withdrew. He wished he had had a bullet to give her. 'But that puts us back to the – the crossbow.' He was a little weak on his knowledge of ancient weapons, but thought that was about right.

'Even that technology is beyond us,' Speed said with a certain satisfaction. 'We are simply not that far advanced. We can forge flat steel – when luck provides the proper alloys in our crudely refined iron – and make good swords, spears and primitive armour. But this exhausts our limited resources. The crossbow requires gearing to crank up the tension, and gears are devious things.'

'Yet it would be easy for Sol to send a factory ship, set it in orbit beyond the reach of native women, and produce and maintain the most modern weapons.'

'For centuries?' the chief inquired rhetorically. 'That orbiting ship would regress farther than the planet! But even at the outset, whether a ship in orbit would be truly out of reach is moot. Spacemen are notorious for rampages on leave; they are seldom satisfied with shipboard fare of whatever nature. I think one would soon encounter

Purrfurr or her like, and the rest would follow. Girls always filter into military posts.' Speed shrugged. 'But there is another aspect. Generally, offensive and defensive weapons parallel each other, armour defending against spear and arrow, the bazooka defending against the tank, the laser against the ballistic missile, the matter disruptor against the stellar dreadnought. To place advanced offensive weapons in the hands of iron-age primitives who lack the resources or philosophy to mitigate their impact – this would lead to internecine warfare, perhaps wiping out whole colonies. It is better to let the weapons match the culture. No mustard gas without gas masks.'

'You are amazingly conversant, for a primitive,' Ronald observed. Or was the intoxication of the mead just making it seem that way?

'I'm practical, not ignorant. You would be wise to be the same. Spherical Regression is a force that dominates every culture of the Galaxy. Of all known species, only the Ancients were free of it, which is perhaps the most tantalizing thing about them. The farther from the centre of civilization a given planet is, the further regressed it is. This serves as a natural limit to the size of empires; the fringe of one culture cannot preempt the centre of an alien one, because the aliens will at that position be more technologically advanced than the first culture. Oh, I know massive matter transmission is possible – but that is so hideously expensive that any species who tried to build and maintain an inter-Sphere empire using that would soon bankrupt itself and collapse. I for one am satisfied to have it that way. We face no threat of alien invasion here; the closest alien Sphere, Antares, is also at fringe level in this region of space. We trade peacefully with the few Jellyfish we encounter; anything else is pointless.'

So Antarians, who were sapient and technological aliens, were called Jellyfish here, just as CentreSphere agents were Imps. Good-natured contempt for outsiders. 'But I assumed you intended to – that you needed a civilized man to handle civilized weapons that you primitives do not understand.'

Speed choked on a mouthful of mead. 'Oh, that's rich!' he gasped. 'Civilized weapons!'

'What, then, do you need me for?' Ronald inquired, nettled. 'I'm certainly not going after your monster with a hammered iron handsword!'

'That's the best we have to offer,' Speed said, sobering. 'Much superior to a gun without bullets. I think it will do the job.'

'But any of you can do that! I'm not trained to use such a weapon. I would be worse than nothing.'

'Not so, Imp. Only you or your ilk can accomplish this mission. That is why we petitioned for a genuine civilized CentreSphere Transferee. Your host can handle the sword; he is well versed therein.'

That much was true, Ronald remembered. The Transferee assumed the capabilities of the host, if the host was cooperative. This one would certainly cooperate to save his body from the ravages of a beast-thing, not to mention ensuring for himself lagniappe like the goodwill of Purr-furr. Yet it was not enough. 'Somewhere, O primitive Chief, you have lost me. My host body may be competent with the weapon, but still this draws nothing from my civilized training. I also happen to be ignorant of the terrain, the nature of the monster – '

'Cerberus sends fear and nightmares – '

'Souring the milk,' Ronald agreed. 'That isn't much to go on.'

'We primitives are affected by superstition and magic,' Speed said earnestly. 'It's part of our culture, deeply rooted. You, as a truly civilized man, have no concern about such nonsense. You *know* magic is merely the ignorant explanation for illusion and natural phenomena, exaggerated for the credulous by medicine men and other charlatans. You do not let such concepts deceive you for an instant.'

'Naturally not.' Evidently the chief delighted in calling himself primitive the way some complex people liked to call themselves simple. He was nobody's fool, and Ronald distrusted whatever this was leading to. 'But that doesn't help in a sword-versus-monster situation.'

'Ah but it does, Imp! Because you will not be afraid. Supernaturally inspired terror will not stay your hand. The deceits of magic will not affect you.'

Ronald squinted at the Chief, uncertain whether he was being openly mocked. This man obviously had no special respect for representatives of the civilized Sphere; why was he being so effusive about their objectivity? Was this the result of some tribal political schism, which forced the Chief to call in help that he believed was not needed? 'You are afraid to tackle this monster? Magic will stop you?'

'Not exactly. But fear prevents me from dispatching Cerbcrus myself.'

'Isn't that the same thing? You implied it uses magic to make credulous people afraid. You yourself are not credulous.'

'Not at all. I said the monster projects fear.'

'That's nonsense! Fear can't be projected. There has to be something for a person to be afraid of, whether real or imaginary.'

'Exactly what I hoped you would say. You are truly civilized. You will not be vulnerable.'

'I think the mead has inhibited my comprehension. Why should I not be vulnerable to something you are vulnerable to?'

'You are civilized,' Speed repeated patiently. 'I am primitive. I'm hopelessly caught up in superstition.'

'The very fact that you can talk as rationally as you have been doing gives the lie to that. You have been circling me intellectually like the tortoise round the hare. What are you up to, Speed?'

'The tortoise round the hare,' the Chief repeated, smiling. 'I do like that, Imp. I suspect you have more wit about you than I had credited. As I recall, there is a point to that particular legend.'

'You know what I mean! The hare round the – ' Ronald paused. The tortoise had won that race. Yet the analogy seemed inverted. The mead was still irrationalizing his thought processes. The hare should represent the civilized person, which meant – '

'I can discourse rationally, by your definition,' Speed said seriously, 'because I am familiar with the litany of civilization. I know how you advanced people think. But it is not the way *I* think. I am a creature of my culture, and I could not throw that off if I wanted to.'

Ronald mulled that over carefully, driving back the mead-fog to the far recesses of his worn brain. 'You really do believe in magic?'

'Indubitably.'

'But you know it's nothing! Magic doesn't exist!'

'*You* know that. I know otherwise. I have been touched by the power of magic.'

'But you have done such a good job of being rational. You know how science works. How can you speak so sensibly, and not believe?'

'I believe in science because I have seen it work. I also believe in magic because I have seen it work. You assume the two are mutually exclusive. They are not. They are in fact merely different names for the same thing, as is shown in the Tarot pack of concepts. What we primitives call magic, you civilized people call science.'

'But – '

212

'How can you perform public fornication with a girl you never saw before today, whom you know to be the wife of your host, in the presence of that man, when your entire culture has contrary values?'

Ronald was taken aback. Concubine – wife. Much the same thing. He was guilty as charged. 'Well, when in Rome – '

'Were I in CentreSphere Sol, in the ambience of that culture I might afford the luxury of dispensing with the beliefs and prejudices of my cultural background. But I am not.'

Ronald was not sure it was a fair parallel, but was not inclined to argue the case. The forces of cultural conformance were strong. 'Very well. Magic affects only those who believe in it, for whatever reason. I don't believe in it, so the monster cannot cast a fear-spell on me. But still, if the creature is horrendous, like a griffin or a dragon, I could be afraid, and for quite adequate cause. I make no claim to being a courageous man. How do I know I can beat this thing with a mere sword?'

'You exaggerate the case. Cerberus is neither griffin nor dragon. He is merely canine. He will hiss and snap, but any man could cut him in pieces without difficulty.'

'Any man who isn't afraid.'

'You've got it, Imp.'

He had got it. But Ronald hardly believed it. It simply could not be that simple! There had to be something he had not been told.

The Bands considered, too. Some of the nether narrative began to leak through. Ronald squelched that, like a qualm, but in the process lost a little of his human narrative. He picked it up a few hours later, in its terms, passing over what he presumed in retrospect was a comfortable sleep in the arms of the pneumatic Purrfurr.

CHAPTER 13

Cerberus

The next day, after Ronald had made some progress at shaking off a primitive hangover, he set out to slay the magic monster. He carried a great, heavy sword that his own body could hardly have managed. Fortunately his host body was a muscular brute whose reflexes were attuned to this weapon. He could handle it for a short time – and that, Speed had assured him, was all that would be necessary. Three good strikes would finish the monster.

The march commenced with primitive pomp. The Hurrians did not employ animals for transportation, so they went afoot. It was no far distance, Speed assured him – a quarter day's trek. Plenty of time to do the deed and return by nightfall for another feast and some attention to the other loaned concubine, Wagtail, whose posterior was out of joint from last night's neglect.

A great drum sounded a cadence that forced every foot to land in time with every other. Several natives played crude twisted-tube horns to help the march along. Cloth and wicker banners flew at the tips of elevated pikes. It was quite impressive, in its primitive fashion.

Ronald, like the other warriors, wore armour lovingly fashioned to the contours of his body. Metal greaves attached to his legs and arms, and a doublet of overlapping metal plates covered his body. He wore surprisingly well articulated gauntlets and armoured boots, and a helmet straight out of Earth's history. It was a good thing his host-body was husky; the weight of all this metal was substantial.

They marched across a plain, carefully following set

214

channels so as not to tread down the cereal grain growing there. Ronald noted in passing that this region was, after all, irrigated. This society had not regressed beyond the neolithic level; the crops were important for survival. Perhaps the society of the historical Hurrians was the objective, not the present state; in a century or so this world might look much more like the historical model.

At the edge of the plain, rolling hills commenced, with flowering weeds and occasional trees. At this point a third of the escort party halted. 'First line of fear,' Speed explained. 'The monster knows we are coming, and sends forth his hostile magic with his baying.'

'I hear no baying,' Ronald said.

'Ah, but *they* do!' Speed gestured to the retreating people. 'The magic touches them insidiously, and the ears of fear are sharp indeed.'

Oh. As with the ancient Earth voodoo and other religious oddities, belief compelled the fact. Some among Ronald's escort were more sensitive than others – and would have reacted at this checkpoint even if no monster existed. It was really geography-magic, limiting them to certain regions. Taboo. The chief did not even try to fight it.

Maybe the monster didn't exist. If no one except the chief had the courage to approach it, that lent power to the office. An excellent way to keep the peons in line.

'Cerberus exists,' Speed reassured him. 'I have seen him. And we all have suffered the depredations of the fear he sends. At night, especially, he reaches farther, all the way into our village, tainting our sleep, making the babies wake and cry.'

'From the sour milk,' Ronald agreed again, wryly. Probably the nursing mothers heard a howl in the forest, and became tense, and the babes at their breasts reacted. 'Proof enough. You saw the monster – but could not slay

215

it yourself?' Ronald could see why the chief would want to affirm the existence of the monster no one else could see, and keep it alive to cow the tribespeople – but why would he bring in an outsider to eliminate this source of his benefit?

'Cerberus cannot be slain from bow range or spear range. His heads must be cut off.'

'His *heads?* How many does he have?'

'Three, of course.'

'Of course,' Ronald agreed, suffering a foolish siege of uncertainty. Cerberus, he now remembered, was the three-headed dog who guarded the gates to Hell. Naturally the local monster had been appropriately named. Earth's ancient mythology was common to all Solarian colonies. He did not relish the notion of trying to cut off three heads with one sword. What would the other two heads be doing while he chopped at the first?

They crested a hill and travelled down to a stream that was setting about forming its valley, as though this world was as young as its culture; a great deal of developing remained to be done. The bed of the stream was filled with rounded boulders around which the clear water coursed and bubbled merrily. The joy of youth! There would be no problem about crossing; there was more rock than water. But another sizeable contingent of Hurrians balked, including the drum-and-horn band.

'Fear strikes again,' Ronald murmured.

'Astute observation,' Speed agreed. 'Cerberus's power grows as we approach him, and his bellow is louder.'

Also, Ronald thought, the troops were getting tired. Marching any distance in iron was no fun, even for brawny warriors. He himself was uncomfortably sweaty inside his metal casing.

They navigated the stream and proceeded with the reduced forces. 'If he has three heads,' Ronald inquired with a casualness he did not feel, 'how is it possible to cut off one without getting bitten by another?'

'Oh, your armour is proof against that.'

His armour! The very thing he had been privately cursing! How could he chafe at his housing of iron without appreciating the purpose it served? Of course that would help; no canine could bite at a limb without doing more damage to its own teeth than to Ronald.

He was secure. Why, then, was he, a civilized man, experiencing a growing unease?

Ronald was not much given to worry about nonessentials. If something bothered him, it was something real. He had only to identify it. So he concentrated, and soon it came.

There was a rationale for all this nonsense. Chief Speed had a good thing going in this mythical magic monster; the tribe rallied to its chief in the continuing crisis of fear. He had no real reason to eliminate Cerberus – but he had to seem to want to, for the benefit of the tribe. So periodically he had to try – and fail. Now he had called in outside help – and it would be to Speed's advantage to have the outsider, too, try and fail. That would prove anew how awful the monster was.

Ronald was civilized, not vulnerable to superstitious fear. It would take a real monster to scare him off. So if Cerberus were more formidable physically than represented, and Ronald retreated from the beast, describing it as it was, that would be evidence that he, too, had been struck by the fear. Or if he fought it and lost: better yet. Who cared about an Imp? Speed's hold over the tribe would be painlessly reinforced.

But Ronald was here to eliminate that monster. He was trapped in the commitment. He would have to proceed, and hope that his sword and armour really did give him a fair chance. He was no hero, but he generally finished what he started. He did have pride, and to a certain extent that substituted for courage.

Now the landscape thickened into a forest. The trees had red-brown bark and rather pretty hexagonal leaves that were on top green, yellow below. But as the forest became dense, inhibiting the light, Ronald felt a constriction about his awareness. Probably it was the diminution of vision; that tended to bring out the nervousness in people. Yes, surely that was it.

They went on and the Hurrians continued to fade away, as each man reached his personal point of balk. Indeed, the intensifying fear was almost palpable.

'Impossible,' Ronald muttered. 'A spell can't make people afraid!'

'Especially not a civilized person,' Speed agreed. But the chief himself looked wan. He was breathing more rapidly than could be accounted for by the exertion, his eyes darted all about, and his cheeks seemed to sag under some private gravity. He was evidently feeling the magic. There were only six remaining in the party now, and all looked greenish.

Ronald realized what was doing it. All those people, so visibly afraid, making an inadvertent production of it: contributing to the mood, reinforcing each other in fear. No wonder tension was affecting him, too!

Now that he understood that, Ronald no longer needed to be affected by it. He walked on with renewed confidence.

There was a strange, ugly, many-throated howl.

Four remaining warriors retreated stiffly, trying to preserve their dignity despite their evident cowardice. 'We are drawing nigh,' Speed said unnecessarily. 'This time *I* heard it.' Under the partial cover of the chief's helmet, sweat beaded his face, and now Ronald caught the actual odour of fear.

218

So this was the first time the chief had heard the monster! But if the point of hearing was the point of retreat, how was it that Ronald himself had heard it? 'This is as far as you go?'

'I am chief because I can approach the beast closer than any tribesman,' Speed admitted. 'Sometimes I can come within sight of him. But I can go very little farther. You, a civilized man, are not in a position to understand.'

No? Ronald was holding his face calm and his body firmly erect by extraordinary exertion of willpower. That howl had petrified him. There really was a three-headed dog up ahead!

'I can take it from here, Chief,' Ronald said, surprised at how well modulated his voice was. He had more nerve under pressure than he had known! 'No problem about locating Cerberus now; if you can hear him, he must be very close.'

The man accepted the implication along with the flattery: the civilized visitor had not heard the howl of the monster. 'Yes.' Speed looked relieved. 'Right ahead, no more than a hundred paces, beside the cleft of Hell he guards. You can't miss him.'

'I'm sure I can't.'

'Three chops, that's all. One for each head.'

'Elementary.' Ronald wished the man would yield to his fear and go.

'One cut for each head,' Speed repeated, as though convincing himself. 'The necks are narrow. No trouble at all, for you.'

'No trouble at all,' Ronald agreed. 'I'll rejoin you shortly.' He faced forward and walked resolutely. It had become obvious that Speed's pride would not permit him to retreat; he was holding at his limit.

When Ronald was out of sight of the chief, with trees

and a boulder between them, he paused, sick with fear. He had acted to prevent Speed from seeing. The armour helped, since it concealed most of his body and caused him to walk somewhat awkwardly anyway. Pride had provided the backbone. He had not wanted it known that he, a supposedly civilized man, was also affected by the magic of the monster.

But it would be known anyway, if he did not slay Cerberus: the nightmares would still be curdling the mothers' milk. Ronald could vindicate himself only by performing.

The beast made his triple howl again. Ronald froze. It did indeed feel as if the blood were congealing in his ossifying veins.

How could he slay the monster, when the very sound of it terrified him?

Ronald fought to get himself in equilibrium. Dammit, he was *civilized;* magic could not affect him! That was why he was here.

Yet Spherical Regression had already deprived him of modern weapons, and put him in this crude iron suit, and brought him alone to this pass. Regression was a subtle but potent force. Was it possible that magic could, after all, affect him? Because he had strayed into its region of power, far from the realm of authority of science in the centre of the Sphere?

No. Magic was not powerless against him because he was civilized; it was powerless because it was fraudulent. Magic had never had validity; it had always been an explanation for misunderstood natural forces. Chief Speed had said as much. The Hurrians had accepted magic as valid because they were primitives; the Imperial Authority had assumed this was entirely psychological.

Now he was on the spot. The honour of civilization depended on Ronald's performance – and he had no advantage over the primitives. Because the magic was indeed affecting him.

Yet he did retain his rational mind. He did know more than the primitives did. He knew that the fear that paralysed him had no rational basis. He was afraid, almost literally, of nothing. Knowing that, perhaps he could devise an approach that would nullify the fear, just as Perseus had devised the mirror-shield with which to view the gorgon, avoiding petrification.

There he was, thinking in terms of magic again!

No – the scientific method was applicable anywhere. The border between science and magic lay within his human mind, not in any geographical frame. Perseus had used his intellect to figure out a way to divert the onus of the gorgon; Ronald should do the same here.

He was afraid – but what was he really afraid of? A mythical monster, or something else? He had already concluded that Chief Speed would benefit if Ronald failed to slay Cerberus – yet the rationale offered was that Ronald, as a civilized man, should be able to accomplish the slaying. Why, then, had Speed cooperated so well? That did not quite make sense. A sensible man would not leave his personal welfare to chance – the chance that a stranger just might succeed in his mission.

It burst upon him then: maybe there was no monster at all! The chief might have invented Cerberus, taking advantage of the eerie howl of some innocuous wilderness denizen to build a myth of terror that governed all the tribe. No one but the chief had seen the monster, after all!

But surely there had been some brave sceptics in the tribe. Why hadn't they betrayed the secret, after searching out Cerberus and finding him false?

Because any who approached the secret region had died. Not of fright, not by the triple heads of the monster, but by ambush. Speed had simply assassinated them,

221

contributing to the power of the myth. And if Ronald marched blithely there –

Probably the assassin was already there, having circled around while Ronald gathered his courage. To forge onward now would be to invite a shaft through the eye or a fall into a concealed trap. The Imp would disappear, and it would be known that the monster had prevailed even over a civilized man. Thus Speed would have even more power, and it would be long before it became necessary to make further proof of the reality of the monster. The nightmares would worsen, and more babies would bawl.

But it was best to make sure his theory was right. Ronald left his boulder and circled quietly around towards the spot where the chief was supposedly waiting for him. Naturally Speed would be gone.

The chief stood where he had been, unmoved. His entire aspect was of fear. Why should he maintain that attitude when he thought no one was watching?

Ronald moved away. Now his conjectures about Speed seemed ludicrous. In addition, he still felt the fear. Why should that be, if he had figured out a valid nonsupernatural origin of his concern?

Cerberus howled again – and again dread overwhelmed Ronald. He fell to the ground and cowered amid the crackling-dry leaves of the forest floor. No, he had to believe it now: there was indeed a spell of fear.

He sat up as the howl faded and his terror eased. He was afraid, but he had not given up. First he had to understand this phenomenon. The creature could project fear; there was now no doubt of that. But that did not necessarily mean the power of Cerberus was magic. What scientific explanation could there be?

Ronald's mind began clicking over as it came to grips with this specific problem. What about sonic waves? Sound, extended above and below the range of human auditory perception. Very low notes could instil fear; that had been demonstrated. Perhaps they could also curdle milk, or at least make nursing mothers tense.

But this monster's sounds were audible. Possibly it possessed another mechanism, a second set of throats; but this seemed unlikely. Why should it bother with audible sound at all?

What about telepathy? Some Galactic species had it; the phenomenon was hardly unknown. Could that account for the known effects?

Nightmares – certainly! Bad thoughts or moods injected into the vulnerable relaxed minds of sleeping people. Bad-tasting milk? More likely this was merely the perceptions of the babies being affected. Mental attitude could change the perception of taste. To appreciate the effect, one had only to imagine that the pleasant pudding he was eating had been made of crushed grasshoppers.

Oops – some of that glop he had feasted on last night. The mead, for example. Primitives used natural sources of protein. Grasshopper juice? They would probably smack their lips and think it a great joke on the Imp. Ronald began to feel ill.

He forced the concept away. His question had been answered. Yes, telepathy was feasible. He should have thought of it before. The simple, literal projection of fear. Some minds were more receptive than others, and civilized education would be an excellent counterforce. Chief Speed, for all his protestations, was a knowledgeable, intelligent man; he was affected less than others of his tribe. Ronald was affected less yet – but not by much. So the story Speed had told him was true; only the interpretation made it sensible. Was there really much difference between telepathy and magic?

One element was missing: motive. What did Cerberus stand to gain by projecting fear into a general populace?

223

Fear could serve as a marvellous defence, but fear projected to creatures who were not attacking would be counterproductive. As now: Ronald was here to slay the monster, because of the superfluous fear it spread – so that fear had become a threat to the monster, rather than a benefit. The shame of being vulnerable to this emotion had abated, now that he had an honourable explanation for it, but the emotion itself remained.

Actually, he realized, the fear abated somewhat as he wrestled with this concept. If his attempt to comprehend Cerberus accomplished that much, success might complete the job. So he should keep thinking!

Nature did nothing gratuitously. It had to take some form of energy to project that fear – a lot of energy to cover the broad area of human habitation. Where did Cerberus get that energy? Any prey he hunted would flee him desperately; so as a hunting device it just didn't make sense.

Could the monster reverse the emotion, summoning prey for ready consumption? Chief Speed had made no reference to that; it was reasonable to assume that the projection was all negative. If people or their animals had been lured away to doom, Speed would certainly have told him.

So the mysteries remained: why did Cerberus do it, and how did he feed? If Ronald could figure out the answers, he might know how to prevail.

He pondered, but could not make sense of it. Things had been simpler when seen as magic. Magic did not need practical explanations. It did not need to make sense. It followed its own nonsensical rule.

Magic. Explore that again. The mythological Cerberus was the guardian of Hades. It was his purpose to permit only the doomed souls to cross the infernal river into the dread realms. And to prevent them from escaping. Fear

224

would certainly be useful there: the doomed souls had no choice about their route; all others would stay well clear.

Was this dismal dog guarding the gate to a local hell? Did Satan send fresh meat to feed the monster?

No, that could not be literal. But it could be figurative. The monster could be guarding something – something native, predating the arrival of the human colonists. Something aliens were not supposed to know about. So the three-headed dog constantly warned them away. If they could not kill Cerberus, they might have to vacate the colony – and that could be the purpose of this projection of fear.

Now Ronald was very curious about the nature of whatever it was the monster guarded. Incalculable wealth? Some planetary paradise? Or maybe even the richest treasure of all, an operative Ancient Site? Or something too alien for the human mind to comprehend?

His fear had diminished almost to nothing. Ronald strode forward, and the landscape passed rapidly aside. Soon he came to a clearing, where the ground turned dark and scorched. A volcanic region, perhaps? Such phenomena could assume diverse forms on alien planets. Faint wisps of steam issued from a narrow crevice.

There, beside the crevice, stood Cerberus. He was indeed vaguely canine, huge and fat, with three small, vicious heads. His skin hung in loose, leathery folds and was blotchy and thinly furred. The monster was hardly pretty, but he did not look vicious enough to represent a serious physical danger. The three heads were grotesque rather than formidable.

The monster spied him. First one head turned to stare balefully at him; the other two followed, as though advised by some internal channel. Each was 'normal', possessing two nostrils, two eyes, and a cruel mouth. Each eye was ringed by unhealthy red, as though it had

225

not slept recently. The baleful cynosure of the six was enervating.

You differ.

Ronald jumped. There was no question as to the source of the message; it had come from Cerberus. There was a curious triple quality to it, as if three mental colours or shades of meaning, emotion, and intensity had been superimposed for the projection, fashioning a rounded, whole, message. None of the grim mouths had moved; a thin drool of saliva descended from each. It had been telepathy.

Your mind complex.

Why should he be surprised? Ronald had already deduced that the monster must be telepathic. Perhaps three heads were better than one, each brain projecting a manageable portion of the thought, an aspect of it. Maybe ordinary thought could not be sent this way, but the components could, so the three signals were being received and recombined within Ronald's own brain like the sound and light components of a vidcast. Evidently the thing could also receive, the barrier of language being nullified by this mode of transmission. Language was, after all, merely the clothing put on thoughts.

'I'm civilized,' Ronald said, letting speech focus the thought. The human mind was so constituted that it could hardly formulate a cohesive thought without the aid of vocalization or subvocalization. Thus the clothing became the mind. Maybe this was because man had two brains, the left and right hemispheres, their natures discrete, which could not combine within themselves; they had to superimpose outside, the way the three brains of Cerberus did, and language was the mechanism of superimposition. Man was a creature of language; that had lifted him out of the jungle and plain.

You come kill me. There was neither fear nor challenge here, merely clarification.

226

'Yes. Because you frighten my people.'

This is how I live, the monster thought. There was a certain beauty in its triple mental articulation, as there was when three musical instruments played harmony.

'I know. It's a great nuisance to us. Why do you do it?'

How I live, Cerberus repeated with a shifting, almost viscous manipulation of emphasis and elements.

'I know enough of the how. Telepathy, a general broadcast of emotion, interpreted by each receiver-brain. I'm asking *why*. Why create this pointless discomfort for people?'

The creature tried again. Evidently there was confusion. The straight transmission of meaning did not preclude some misunderstandings. *Must. Need. Feed.*

'How does scaring people help you to feed?'

Feed on fear.

Then Ronald understood. 'You consume emotion!'

Feed on fear, the monster agreed.

'It's like priming the pump. You send out a little, and receive a lot more.'

Feed, Cerberus agreed again. He was evidently not extraordinarily bright. He hardly needed to be, with this system of sustenance.

'But why does it have to be negative? Why not broadcast love, and feed on happiness?' But as he spoke, he knew the answer. Fear was one of the strongest, least-reasoned emotions. There would be a greater percentage in fear, so Cerberus was tuned to that; probably he was unable to broadcast any other emotion. Maybe his distant ancestors had experimented with other emotions and natural selection had centred on this one.

That meant there was no peaceable way out. The monster was a menace to human society and had to be eliminated.

As Solarian Monsters were a menace to Band society . . .

But that was a thought from the underworld – that of the double ring. It did not belong here, however relevant it might be to his present situation. In this memory he had a purpose; for the sake of his pride, for the meaning of his life, he had to do what he had to do.

Yet even in the memory, he was not at ease. He did not really like destruction, and sought some other way. Violence, he remembered, was the last refuge of the incompetent. The primitive tribesmen saw no alternative except the killing of the monster; Ronald, more civilized, sought something better. Even Chief Speed remained primitive, highly informed though he might be about Spherical matters; at his gut level he sought revenge and victory over an enemy – a perceived enemy – rather than accommodation with a marvellously talented creature.

'You will not go away?' Ronald inquired. 'To some other part of the planet, where you will not make human beings afraid?' Maybe they could work this out.

For answer, Cerberus attacked. Not physically; mentally. The force of fear, which had been idle during their conversation, now intensified horrendously. The creature might seem clumsy dealing with dialogue-thoughts, but it was highly skilled in the manipulation of this emotion.

Ronald had never been so frightened in his life. Fear choked his throat, terror froze his body, and his mind was a storm. He had thought he had conquered the emotion by his logic, his civilized understanding – but he had not. The beast had merely held its power in abeyance. Perhaps that was the way with all the horrors of the human imagination; they were never truly conquered, but only restricted temporarily.

Vanity, vanity! He had thought that as a civilized man he could not be affected by magic. He had been wrong;

magic had turned out to be telepathy. Under that other name, it struck just as ferociously. He had thought he had conquered it through understanding; he had been wrong again. He had deluded himself; his faith in himself had been arrogance. In the end, emotion always dominated understanding; that was why people went to war. He remained paralyzed with terror.

Yet, oddly, despite the endless emotion and recrimination, he was not fleeing. The fear beat about him like a tempest, but something anchored him. A trace of morbid curiosity seeped through the tide of negative feeling: why?

Slowly, in the manner of a tree righting itself as the wind that almost broke or uprooted it subsides, he realized that his slender strength was stiffening. Though fear had overtaken him, even now it was not his most fundamental attribute. He could feel joy, anger, love, and fear, but he was not an animal to be completely governed by these emotions. There was something else in him that, when the final tally was made, preempted any of these.

It was pride. Ronald had few claims to exceptional status. His aura was high, but not truly remarkable in itself; it qualified him to be a routine Transfer agent, no more. He was, in his natural host, healthy and handsome – but again not to any really noteworthy extent. He was intelligent, but had encountered many people who dwarfed him in intellect. But Ronald had the ability to marshal all his capabilities, of whatever nature, large or small, to succeed to the maximum extent possible for him. He had a virtually perfect record: anything he really put his mind to, he accomplished. His private index of efficiency was high. Of course he did not tackle things foolishly; he always made sure he had a reasonable chance. A significant proportion of his success lay in his accurate judgement of what was and was not feasible. He knew his limits.

This time he was into considerably more challenge than he had bargained for. He had not had opportunity to assess the risks in advance. He had been sent unprepared into a situation of amorphous challenge. But this was the nature of Transfer duty: alien creatures were the ultimately unpredictable element. He had needed to discover whether he could survive when he had not been able to pick and choose carefully on the basis of information. If he wanted to hold this particular job, he could no longer play it safe. Instead he had to rise to the occasion, transcending his personal weaknesses.

This required a change in his philosophy. He had always played it safe while seeming to take risks. Now he had to take real risks, and perhaps suffer losses. He realized now that he had never thought through the nature of Transfer duty. He had been blinded by the delights of it, the novelty, the notoriety. Maybe it was not, after all, the proper employment for his type of personality. Surely his superiors, who had exquisitely detailed and cross-referenced computer printouts of all his qualities, were aware of his flaws. They had been uncertain whether he was suited to the job. So they had given him more than the routine break-in task he had asked for. They had deliberately placed him in a situation as challenging as an alien Transfer mission would be. First, the abrupt change in social values, such as the privacy of sexual relations, that he had navigated the night before. Second, this appalling terror. This was the crisis: could he handle it?

He could back down. He could admit that this was too much for him; that he was, after all, unsuited to this type of challenge. Far better that he do it now, than discover in alien host that he couldn't handle it! If he was not fated to be a Transfer agent, his sensible course was to recognize that now, take his lumps, and seek other employment. At least he would be alive.

But now that the crisis was upon him, Ronald discovered that his pride was greater than his practicality. He wanted, even more than success, to accomplish something meaningful in his life. Success came to many men; meaning to few. He could have success writing up routine reports in some planetside office, doing a job anyone else might do. But to have *meaning* – for that, he had to do a job no one else could do. Or one that no one else who had the capacity *would* do. A job like going native, bedding a buxom native girl in public on a banquet table, donning archaic and sweaty armour, and duelling a magic monster. Few, very few civilized people would or could unbend enough to make it with the girl, and few would be able to resist the terrible telepathy of the monster. Perhaps only he, Ronald, was in a position to do both.

Was this what he really wanted? And the answer was, he wasn't sure. His pride restrained him; he hardly dared desire what was beyond his capacity, because of his risk of pride. But if he could conquer here, then he could afford to desire more. He could enlarge his personal perimeter.

Terror still froze him in place. But it hadn't put him to flight, and it hadn't stopped his other thoughts. If he hadn't yet won, at least he had not yet lost. He simply could not yield that last portion of his dream: partly because the shame of failure would be worse for him than the release of fear; partly because the first step he took away from Cerberus would also be away from his dream of adventure on far planets, among completely alien creatures. He would rather, *yes he would rather*, die here, than survive stripped of his pride and his dream of the potential meaning in his existence.

The emotion abated. *You don't flee*, Cerberus thought, perplexed. *My power destroys you, yet you stay.*

Now the creature was uncertain. It, too, had encountered more than anticipated. It could comprehend resistance to its broadcast, but not this unresponsive susceptibility. A terrified individual always fled, yielding a rich harvest of delicious emotion. How could it be otherwise?

'I am civilized,' Ronald said weakly. It was all the explanation he could manage.

Again the terror tore at him, worse than before. But again the tree clung to its soil. Ronald now had a better understanding of his own motives, and that lent him strength. He had himself together now. Fear might kill him, but it would not make him flee.

The siege was shorter this time. Cerberus had thrown more energy into this effort, and received less back, and tired faster. He, too, had his limits. For the first time, Ronald sniffed the faint whiff of victory.

Now was the time. He took a step forward, his leg like lead. The monster hurled another surge of emotion, with a sharp cutting edge of despair. But it was the despair of Cerberus, not Ronald; the creature's power was weakening.

But conquest of fear was not enough. There was still the physical three-headed canine to deal with, and that was formidable enough. All those jaws . . .

Slowly Ronald drew his sword. His arm, too, was heavy with seeming fatigue and muscular reluctance. Fear inhibited the body. Step by step he advanced through a crumbling ruin of emotion that merged with the physical terrain. Volcanic fissures steamed and smoked in his mind as well as in the land. He did not like the notion of slaying a uniquely talented creature, but there was no other way unless the monster relented and retreated. And he would not, for his own pride and welfare were at stake. If Cerberus lost this battle by retreating from a terrified enemy, he was finished.

They were locked in a battle of pride, Ronald realized. There was no right or wrong to it; one force had to prevail over the other. In any event, it was not his place to make judgements of merit; he merely had to do his job – to help the Hurrians, and to prove that he could succeed as a Transfer agent.

Now he stood within sword range of the monster. Cerberus was evidently not accustomed to this sort of combat; his motions were awkward. Perhaps millennia ago, when his species was evolving, he had been a ferocious fighter with his three heads. But the efficiency of telepathy had made such combat unnecessary, and his body had atrophied much as the tail and appendix had in man. Use it or lose it: nature's law.

One head jerked forward. The jaws gaped wide.

Ronald's sword slashed. It was not a clean cut. He chopped the head in half, lengthwise. Blood poured out, and the head made half a scream.

The other two heads converged. One tried to bite him on the leg. The armour stopped it, and in a moment he had cut this head off, more cleanly, at its small neck. Then he whipped the sword backhand at the third, slicing on the bias, and the head fell to the ground, snapping at the dirt.

It was over. The fear was gone. A grotesque, flopping, gore-spouting hulk lay before him. Now all he felt was disgust fading into a dull lack of emotion. Had it been right to kill Cerberus? He couldn't say, emotionally, because that sort of feeling had been wiped out by the creature's death. Ronald couldn't *feel* remorse.

He braced one foot against the shuddering body and shoved. The corpse slid lumpily over the brink of the chasm and dropped out of sight. Ronald waited for the sound of its striking bottom.

Then a pinprick of apprehension stabbed at him. Ronald looked around. There, in a shallow crevice near the surface of the fissure, was a crude nest. In the nest was a tiny three-headed dog.

Ronald put his foot against the nest, about to shove it and its burden into the depths of the chasm. But he paused. This was a baby Cerberus, unable to terrify on a mass scale. It would be years, perhaps decades, before it grew to full size and power.

Ronald reached down his gauntleted hands and picked the creature out of the nest. It tried to bite his fingers, but recoiled in pain.

'Cerberus Junior,' Ronald said, trying to concentrate his thought so it could understand. 'You must forage alone.' The adult had been male; perhaps the mother had perished elsewhere, or maybe she was hiding, lacking in telepathic ability. So either the pup could survive without nursing, by scaring squirrels or whatever other small life lived here, or it had a remaining parent. 'Your father attacked a man, and was killed. You must never attack a man. Go, hide in the forest, survive. But stay away from this locale. Our fear is not for you.'

The baby whimpered, seeming to understand. Ronald set it carefully on the other side of the cleft and watched it scramble away. Yes, it had got the message.

And he, Ronald, had proven himself. He would be a Transfer agent.

CHAPTER 14

Maze

'What does it mean?' the Bands wondered.

'That is for you to decide,' Ronald replied. 'You evoked the memory.'

They tried. It was a moral puzzle. Had it been right to violate his social principles by copulating with the Hurrian female? If not, could his commitment to Cirl, to him an alien female, be justified? Had it been right to slay the fear-monster? This was a concept that would have been incomprehensible to the Band intellect prior to Rondl's training of Bands and the advent of the invasion of the Monsters. Now, since the slaying of the Kratch, they could to some extent appreciate his rationale.

'The fear-monster resembled the Kratch,' the thought circulated, picking up on that current. 'It sought to aggrandize itself at the expense of others. This was unsocial.'

'Yet destroying life is also unsocial,' Rondl argued, playing the advocate.

'To this extent we have become monsterized,' the Bands thought, and from the opposite circuit the emotion concurred. 'We now understand that sometimes evil must be met with evil. Yet never should evil be initiated.'

'Solarian Monsters initiate evil,' Rondl thought. 'It is their nature. It is *my* nature, for I am one of them. This memory merely shows the background of my actions among you. I was able to slay Cerberus and the Kratch because I was already tainted with evil myself. You Bands must remain untainted.'

'Without your leadership we revert to our nature,' they

agreed. The great majority of the participants of this circle were strangers, but a few had been part of Rondl's combat force, and these lent comprehension to the full circle. 'If what we participate in is evil, it is at your instigation. Yet we cannot condemn you, for now we comprehend your nature. This memory has shown us that. It has revealed your most basic motive.'

'You grasp me better than I grasp you,' Rondl flashed. 'Yet is that enough?'

'No. Now you must change circles.'

'How do I do that?'

'Cirl is before you. Rotate with her, exchanging glances and directions while we hold firm.'

Rondl was sorry he could not join Cirl in her own circle. But at least this way she would get to assimilate the conscious aspect of his memory, instead of the unconscious aspect. He rotated with her, exchanging places and circles. What an intricate device this double circle was!

Now the frame of the exploring Band hero opened out for him. He had flown to a strange planet, seeking something, and gone near the surface. The terrain had become strange indeed, a maze of surfaces and colours; of great mountains, deep valleys, and flat waters. Creatures had appeared, some seeming friendly, some hostile. That hostility was a new experience for Rondl the Band, an emotion he had thought alien. Of course his larger awareness advised him that this phenomenon related to emotion that generated from the other side of the circle, as a man approached a strange culture or a monster; but here the other experience translated into confusion and doubt. Yet there was a positive element, too. The friendly creatures thought he had come to help them eliminate the hostile ones, but he felt emotionally and physically ill-equipped. How could he, a visitor, do what the natives could not? *Should* he? Violence was not his nature.

236

No, violence was not necessary. Just assistance. If he could just converse with the hostile element, find out how the objection could be ameliorated, he might come to some understanding of its nature and discover a peaceful way to abate its animus.

Rondl realized that this Band approach differed from the Solarian approach to what might be a similar problem. The Solarians had never considered the view of the fear-monster; they had sought only to eliminate the creature. The Bands did not seek elimination, only accommodation. But perhaps that would be no easier than it had been for the Solarians.

Yet he had to try, for it was the Band way: to help one's neighbour. He agreed to seek the other party. Immediately he flew farther across the strange terrain, following the magnetic lines, finding his way to the region of the other.

He arrived, and discovered horrendously alien things. Alarmed, he veered away – and discovered himself captured.

The very notion of Band capture was alien, for Bands were completely free entities. Yet now there were a limited number of available lines, and across each of them was a globular, multiappendaged mass of creature. In the centre of each mass was a light-emitting disc. Each disc was flashing in a primitive emulation of communication.

Communication? Was it possible? Could these animals be sapient despite having no magnetic lenses?

This was, Rondl realized, a long time ago, before the Bands realized there were other intelligent species in the universe. All non-Band species they had known before were animals.

'Then who were the friendly creatures?' he inquired. 'I thought they were sapient aliens.'

'Not exactly,' the Bands of this side of the circle replied.

'They had lenses, but lacked civilization. This becomes complex to clarify.'

Without doubt. Rondl returned to the myth-memory, leaving the details of the order of discovery of sapient alien species for another occasion.

Experimentally, he flashed a beam of sunlight at one of the gross creatures. 'Meeting,' he said carefully.

'Meeng,' the thing replied, generating its own clumsy fluctuations. Yet this was a creditable effort. It was indeed trying to communicate!

With that confirmation, Rondl knew why he had come here. What the friendly creatures had taken to be animosity was in fact merely an effort to establish a dialogue. He, a civilized Band, had the intellect to appreciate this. He could meet the creatures on their own terms, perhaps to mutual benefit.

Rondl settled down for a sizeable portion of his life span and studied the language and customs of the Glowworms. When he had assimilated all he could, he disbanded.

That jolted Rondl out of his identification with the role. He wasn't ready to disband! 'But didn't he go home first?' he demanded.

'Why?' The Bands were perplexed.

'To report his discovery to others! To let all Bands know!'

'No, he disbanded without returning to System Band. There was no need.'

'But – then no one else knew. The greatest discovery of his time, that of alien sapient life, left unpresented. It was all pointless!'

'To the contrary. It was his ultimate realization.'

'To learn everything – then suicide without informing anyone?' Rondl still balked at this concept.

'He had fulfilled his mission of experience. He brought an unprecedented wealth of experience to the Viscous

Circle. That is why he became a legend, a figure of our mythology.'

'That remains a riddle to me!' Rondl flashed.

There was tolerant humour in the circle. 'Our other circle comprehends the adventure you shared with it. Perhaps in time you will assimilate our mythology.'

'Perhaps,' Rondl agreed dubiously. He suspected his problem related to his disbelief of the existence of the Viscous Circle. What was to the Bands the ultimate contribution was to him the ultimate waste.

'Can you provide the essence of that other experience? We felt its huge emotion.'

'It was an episode from my past, in which I ascertained the nature of my mission in life after being in doubt.'

'Then it is a true mirror of this experience! But if you did not disband on that occasion, what was the nature of that mission?'

'To come here and learn your philosophy. To help you defend against the Monsters.' For without that victory over Cerberus, he never would have been a successful Transfer agent. Of course, he had not set out on this particular mission with the intent to help the Bands resist the Solarians, but as he learned more of the situation, that had become his mission. The officials at home would call it treason; that did not matter. Monster definitions were now too narrow for him.

'That seems true,' the Bands agreed, comprehending. 'Once you understand us sufficiently, you can disband.'

Just when he thought comprehension was sufficient, he was reminded how far they all had yet to go to bridge the gulf between species! 'Without returning to my own kind to report,' he flashed wryly. He doubted his comprehension would ever be that complete. To master a subject, then suicide without leaving any record: that remained alien.

Then the double ring disbanded, having mastered its subject properly, and they were individuals again. Cirl rejoined him. 'You have farther to travel to reach us than we have to reach you,' she flashed cheerily. 'Now at last I perceive enough of your nature.'

'So it seems,' Rondl agreed. 'Yet I am glad you are able to accept me as I am.'

'Or as you can be,' she said. 'It is not easy for you or for me, but love and understanding can bridge the gulf between stars.'

That – and Transfer, he thought. What an experience that double circle had been! He would take a long time to assimilate all its revelations and implications, but he was sure that time would be worthwhile. Without comprehension, how could there be meaning to life?

But now he had more immediate, practical matters to attend to. He had been on his way to meet with the other Solarian Transferee, Tanya, if she really intended to be there, and if she had survived. Her host might have been lost while she was back among the Monsters. He and Cirl flew on, watching the other Bands spread in a dissipating cloud to other regions, following the lines out. Soon nothing remained of the fantastic circle except Rondl's memory, and Cirl's acceptance of him, Monster background and all. These things were, of course, enough.

They arrived in due course at Maze Mountain. This was an elevation with a number of projecting spikes, around which the magnetic lines wound. Bands were whirling merrily in and out, their colours flashing along with their joyous exclamations of light. The whole scene was very pretty, as Band congregations tended to be. To be a Band was to be peaceful, aesthetic, fun-loving, and happy – usually.

'It is a maze, you see,' Cirl said. 'You try to pass quickly

240

by every spire while making an aesthetic pattern. Or parties of people integrate patterns. It's fun.'

'I'm supposed to meet Tanya by the orange spire,' he said. It had not occurred to him that this region would be so crowded.

'Make a pattern till you encounter it,' Cirl suggested.

Rondl found a break in the traffic and flew in, Cirl behind him. The line was strong, providing plenty of power, and between spikes it intersected with other lines, so that it was easy to shift without losing momentum. Rondl spun by a blue spire, shifted lines, and passed a green one. Other Bands cut across, travelling their routes, flashing their colours. This was fun!

Suddenly he spied the orange spire – but his pattern was wrong, and he could not get to it. He saw it disappear behind him. He would have to loop around and hope to catch it on the next pass. This was more tricky than he had thought. Truly, it was a maze!

After several tries he found the right access line and swung into orbit about the orange spire. Cirl joined him.

He found himself still in a crowd. Bands of both sexes and every colour circled with him. Apparently this was a popular rendezvous point! But how could he know which one was Tanya, or even whether she was here? There were several orange females, and he had neglected to find out what her Band name was. They had set no specific time of meeting – though Bands were hardly aware of time anyway, and had no terms for specific hours. Even the normal day-night cycle was irrelevant, because Bands were not confined to the planet, and there was no such thing as day or night in space. Space was brightly lighted near a sun and dark between suns, so location counted more than time of planetary turnings.

Well, he was thinking like a Band, when he needed to think like a Monster. Monsters seldom suffered from

241

oversights of personal contact. They were practical. If they did not know where a person was, they put out a summons.

A summons. Would it work here? Not for a circle, but for an individual? He would try it. 'I am Rondl,' he flashed as well as he could to the others orbiting the spire. 'I seek a female who comes from afar, who may be named Tanya.' Only the name did not translate well to the Band flashes, and he garbled it.

There was no response. Rondl tried again, and again had none.

'She seems not to be here,' Cirl said after several failures. They had asked for an orange Band, and there were several, but none was the one.

'Maybe she has not yet arrived,' he said, though he feared she would never arrive. She could be dead; or she might have bounced in Transfer owing to a lost host; or she could simply have decided not to meet him – might never have intended to meet him. He did not know her intent, which was why he had to meet her. If she were more loyal to the Monster Sphere than he was –

He kept trying, unwilling to give up too readily. If Tanya was a Band again and differed from him in her attitude toward the Bands, he *had* to convince her to change. Otherwise she could undo everything he was trying to do and an entire species could be wiped out.

Every so often a newly arriving female would answer, inquiring whether there was anything she could do for him, and he explained that there was not. He had stopped asking for an orange Band; perhaps it was his Monster nature operating, but he decided he preferred to have a countercheck, to know when someone was trying to deceive him, even though he knew no Band would practice deception. Only a Monster would do that – and it was a Monster he was looking for. So he continued his solicitations, readily eliminating all who were not orange, and increasingly wondered whether this attempted rendezvous was worthwhile.

It was not anything positive, he realized. He had no interest in Tanya personally, though she was interesting enough in her Monster format. He just wanted to prevent her from completing the Monster mission. He had to know exactly how she felt about the Bands, then act accordingly.

What would he do if her loyalty remained firmly Monster? That was an ugly question! He did not like to think in terms of killing, and was not sure how one Band could deliberately disband another; it might not be possible at all. So it was better to look for other avenues.

But time was passing, and Rondl had his army to organize. Soon the Monsters would make another thrust, destroying more Bands. Rondl could not afford to wait here at Maze Mountain indefinitely. In fact, that could be a device of Tanya's: to keep him waiting while she performed mischief elsewhere.

'I distrust this,' he flashed covertly to Cirl. 'This female is a Monster, and her values may be Monster. I must see to the defence of the Band system.'

'I will wait here for her arrival,' Cirl offered. 'You can go about your business and I will bring her to you when she comes.'

Bless her! 'This is a fine favour,' he said gratefully. 'I will return here as soon as possible, so that you may also have relief.'

He wound his way out of the Maze and zoomed along the lines to the headquarters region of his forces. It was well he did so; his absence had been demoralizing, and the number of recruits had been shrinking. Now, reassured that he was present and able, his troops found their spirits ascending.

243

Rondl set up some new exercises and moved a sizeable contingent to the vicinity of System Band's next moon, Fair: the body the Monsters would most likely attack next. Then he convoked a circle and put the question: was there an Ancient Site in Band space? He described the concept as well as he could, since the Bands did not know about the Ancients.

He got, to his surprise, an immediate answer: there was such a construction – on Glow, the last moon overrun by the Monsters.

But why, then, were the Monsters gathering for an attack on the innermost moon, Fair? If they had already obtained their objective –

Further investigation provided the answer: the Site was of an atypical configuration, so that the Monster search pattern had failed to recognize it. Rondl himself had missed it, of course – but he had not had his memory at that time.

Failed to recognize it? The Solarians had sophisticated equipment and knew exactly what they were looking for. How *could* they miss it?

Gradually, with the aid of the circle, he worked it out. Most Ancient Sites were huge removals of planetary matter and had tremendous mounds or concavities, with extensive warrens beneath the surface. Some few had operative equipment; most had defunct equipment that could be studied for its secrets. This was what made the Sites so valuable; the species that exploited them usually gained considerable insight into an aspect of the advanced technology of Transfer or Mattermission. Such insight translated readily to power. Of course the archaeologists were interested, too; they always wanted to ponder the nature and history of this most mysterious Galaxy-spanning culture.

This particular Site, by design or accident, was diffe-

244

rent, and not merely in outer appearance. It matched the natural contour of the surface of Moon Glow, so that no photograph or sonic study showed it. The Ancient arte- facts were arrayed in the form of metallic lodes layered in the rock, interrupted by the geologic weathering of the surface. Moon Glow did have some token atmosphere and water, though its contours were really more pronounced than could be accounted for by such natural processes. The Ancients had sculptured it, for what purpose no one could say. The Monsters, with their narrow view of what an Ancient Site should be, had been fooled.

Could it be that the Ancients did not like Monsters? They could not have known, three million years ago, that these particular creatures would come questing for this particular Site. But perhaps they had known what type of creature would desire it, and had hidden it from that type. Just how prescient had the Ancients been? Not prescient enough to stave off their own extinction, obviously!

At any rate, there were pronounced magnetic effects about Glow, as the invaders had experienced. The Bands had been more sensitive to these, of course; in fact Rondl now learned that the Bands' advance to interstellar civili- zation had in large part been fostered by their fascination with the anomalies of Glow. They had realized that others besides themselves had used magnetic lines. They had not conceived of the Ancients per se, but had recognized the handiwork of prior intelligent creatures. Thus the site had become a kind of chapel, as well as a playground. Bands went there to improve themselves. They had not realized that much more was available, since Bands normally did not push hard. To be pacifistic, in this case, was to be without the cutting edge of scientific curiosity that the more aggressive creatures had. Why push the inanimate to its limits? That was not polite.

But Rondl, with his Solarian awareness and drive,

understood that the natural-seeming magnetic circuits represented a fantastic complex of potential. The Site was like a printed circuit board with microscopic detail, set on a planetary scale. Properly applied, it could yield secrets to transform the technology of this region of the Galaxy.

The Monsters already had possession of it – and didn't know it. Rondl was not about to inform them. Neither was Tanya, if he could ensure her silence.

It was time to get back to Maze Mountain. He *had* to intercept her – if she came there. If she had perished, he had no problem, but if she survived in Band form, he could not allow her to go free. Not unless she agreed with him.

He left instructions with his troops so that their organization for the coming encounter could continue, then flew back to Planet Band. He was not certain whether he hoped to find Tanya there or to have her never turn up.

Cirl remained dutifully on watch. Rondl relieved her, flashing his thanks for her effort, and set up orbit about the orange spire. She departed, going to consult with Proft about the theoretical salvation of Monsters. She wanted to get Rondl qualified for entry into the Viscous Circle.

The moment Cirl departed, an orange Band female flashed at Rondl. 'I am Tangt, the one you seek.'

He was surprised. 'I didn't see you arrive!'

'I arrived some time ago, but did not consider it proper to respond to the female. She is your Band mate?'

They were cruising on out of the Maze. 'True. She watched while I was busy elsewhere, so as not to miss you. I must find her now, to advise her that – '

'I need no trouble with her, as we agreed, just as you need no trouble with my mate. This is business they would not understand.'

So she had honoured their agreement not to tell their respective mates about the Monster spouses. 'I went ahead and told Cirl about my wife Helen. I thought it best. She understands.'

'I did not inform *my* mate. He would not understand. So let's keep the mates out of this.'

Maybe she was right. 'I need to know your position on – '

'In due course. Let us get to a private place.'

'But first I must at least notify Cirl where I shall be.'

'Our communication would then not be private. Let her go. This will not take long. We may be back before she returns from her errand.'

Ill at ease, Rondl did as bidden. He was, in a sense, deceiving Cirl. Yet how could one thread his way through a maze of loyalties without making errors along the way?

CHAPTER 15
Vicious Circle

They flew to a complex of caves Tangt knew of. These, like Maze Mountain, had been arranged for enjoyable Band access, with lines traversing them thickly. But this region was more extensive than the Maze and less frequented, so there was far greater privacy. She led the way down through a water-filled passage and up into a small air-filled pocket that had two artificial sources of illumination.

'I didn't know Bands had electric lights!' Rondl flashed, utilizing one.

'Bands do trade with other species, to a limited extent,' Tangt reminded him, using the other light. Obviously this cave had been deliberately crafted for exactly such private conversations. Because of the surrounding rock, their beams could not be intercepted by others, and the restricted access prevented any surprise intrusion. 'We have few needs, but light for nether regions is one of them. These are complete alien systems, powered from a central generator installed by the Bellatrixians, a species with mechanical dexterity.'

The Bellatrixians: of course. He knew about their enclave out in the orbit of Moon Dinge. This was one of the tangible evidences of their trade.

'So I see. Now let's complete our discussion started in System Sirius. I have other pressing business.' He also was uncertain why she had gone to such an extreme to keep their dialogue secret, even from Cirl. No one would snoop. It was the Monsters who needed to be fooled, not the Bands. If she had some dark design in mind –

'Other business?' she inquired, and her orange colour

seemed to brighten. Ronald remembered irrelevantly what an attractive female she had been in Monster form. Black hair fibres, slender yet full figure, aesthetic facial features; even her fluid-filled eyeballs had seemed harmonious, difficult as that was to imagine at the moment. It showed how Monster tastes differed from Band!

'Yes.' But he decided not to describe his Monster-combating project yet; not until he knew how she felt.

'Did you find me sexually appealing in human form?'

What was this? Was she reading his thoughts? 'As a matter of fact, I did. But that does not relate – '

'And I found you the same. We're both married there, so nothing could have been done openly!'

Now Rondl caught on. 'You thought I sought a romantic liaison?'

'Didn't you? This does represent a unique opportunity. I trust you approve the privacy I arranged. I feel this is an excellent place.'

'Tangt, I thought you understood. I'm married in this host, too!'

'Yes. So am I. Therefore it was necessary to be very careful. No one knows we are here.'

'That's why you did not answer Cirl's call? To set up a liaison between us without her knowledge?'

'Why else?'

Why else? Did he have a nymphomaniac here? 'Tangt, you misunderstood my signal. I have no wish to deceive my Solarian wife or my Band wife, and am certainly not seeking liaisons with business associates.' He had thought she understood, in their Solarian exchange; how could he have been so wrong?

'You don't desire me?'

Now he had to be careful. There was no sense in antagonizing her; she could betray him from spite. 'Were circumstances otherwise, I would be interested in you. You are certainly alluring, physically, in both human and

Band form. But I have become a creature of some scruple, and I have other commitments. Perhaps the males you have encountered before are otherwise. I had an entirely different purpose in coming here.'

'Then it seems I did not misread your signal,' she said.

'But you did! I seek no romantic liaison!'

'Neither do I,' she flashed.

'Now you have me thoroughly confused!'

'There were two interpretations to your manner when we conversed in Sphere Sol, assuming you were neither stupid nor crazy. Rather than betray myself needlessly, I was prepared to submit sexually. That would at least preserve my life.'

Rondl realized she had indulged in a rather neat ploy. Sex instead of treason – that was certainly safer! 'What is your alternative interpretation?'

'If I understood your signal correctly back in System Sirius, you have lost sympathy with the Solarian objectives.'

Now the treason was out in the open, at least between them. 'True. The Monster intrusion is decimating the Band population. I feel this is wrong.'

'I agree. But you understand that to take any action detrimental to the immediate objectives of our kind is to invite severe repercussion if it is discovered.'

Rondl felt relief, then renewed apprehension. She agreed with him – except that her like-mindedness could be a ruse. She could be trying to trap him into fully incriminating himself. How could he be sure she could be trusted?

He decided he simply had to take the risk. 'I understand that well. It is treason I contemplate, by the definition of my original species. But I no longer consider myself a Solarian; I identify with the Bands. There must be many Solarians whose conscience would agree with mine. It simply is not right to destroy one species, especially a sapient one, for the marginal benefit of another.'

'An Ancient Site is hardly marginal.'

'Compared to genocide, it is!' He drifted along his line a moment, then decided to tackle the issue forthrightly. 'My affinity, as I said, is with the Bands. My human conscience has been awakened, and I must and shall do what I feel is right. I realize that I cannot be sure of your own attitude, and I risk being betrayed by you. I hope your agreement with me is sincere, and that you will help me save the Bands. But I will try to help them regardless. The question is not which side I am on, but whether you are with me or against me.'

'You put it nicely,' she flashed. 'I am in a similar situation. I can't be sure of you; there is no honour among Monsters. But it is reasonable to assume you feel as I do. The Band society is very like the ideal that human beings have always professed to crave, but have never actually practiced. No Band criticizes another or lets another come to harm without trying to help. No Band wrongs another. There is no theft, no murder, no misrepresentation, no quarrelling. As I think you know, I found myself without memory in Band host. A male Band helped me, and I married him. I doubt I would have survived without him. In fact I think ten other agents succumbed because they failed to find such friends, though they could have had friends merely for the asking, had they but realized. Maybe their own distrust killed them, fittingly enough. I was happy. Then I suffered nightmares – '

'Me too!'

'And finally I was back in my own Solarian host body, and it was horrible. Not only the body – the society, too. That ingrained suspicion and narrow self-interest! I had leaped involuntarily from paradise to the gutter. I wanted to be a Band, but circumstance made me a Monster. I did not know what to do. So I played it safe by acting Solarian, and the stupid computer cleared me. But as time passed I did not settle into the Monster mode; the Band

251

system had the lure of some powerful drug, a good drug, bringing me back to it. Paradise is addictive!'

'My experience exactly!' Rondl agreed. 'I saw that if I did nothing, the Bands would be destroyed. The forces of Satan were invading Heaven itself, and how could I stand idly by? It is not that the Solarians mean to commit genocide; it is that they are hardly aware of what is happening, and hardly care. There might as well be buzzing gnats in their way, for all the consideration the Monsters give the Bands. By the time any protest could be lodged through channels, the Bands would be gone. So I had to act. When I learned there was only one other survivor – '

'Yes. Let's face it: either one of us can betray the other the moment we are again recalled to Sol hosts. Either one of us can give away the location of the Ancient Site.'

'You know where it is?'

'Not yet. But I'm sure I can find it by asking around, and so can you. Bands don't keep secrets. So neither of us has security in this respect.'

'Yet if you wanted to betray me, you could have done so without ever meeting me here,' Rondl pointed out.

'No. I might have misread your signals. Maybe you were just looking for a human mind in Band host to romance. There are ways and ways of getting sexual kicks.'

'So you explored that aspect first. That was intelligent. I never thought of it. But what would you have done, if – ?'

'As I said, I was prepared to carry through. I love my husbands, both of them, and I am not promiscuous. But I'm not suicidal either, and there just may be the biggest prize of the Galaxy on the line in the Ancient Site. If sex with you salvaged my life despite my treason, then it would have been a matter of necessity. But you would have had neither my love nor my respect.'

'The same for me. But the respect, I think, you are earning. I'm glad you arranged for such a private interview; it was certainly essential that we work out our confusions. We don't want or need the complication of any romantic involvement between us.'

'Agreed.' But there was something about the way she flashed it that made him wonder. She was beautiful in either form, and it might have been nice to –

No. He did not want to fall prey to the fickleness of the masculine urge.

'Now I think we'll have to plan a strategy if we are to help the Bands,' she said. 'We may not be able to stop the Monsters from discovering the Site eventually, but maybe we can lead them astray.'

'They have already missed it.'

'Already? But their search pattern is thorough!'

'The Site is on a moon. It looks like natural terrain. They'll never find it.' Some lingering vestige of caution caused him not to name the moon. He thought Tangt was all right, but there was no point in taking any unnecessary risk. She might find out anyway, of course.

'Then our problem is solved. We'll just report we couldn't find it.'

'And their continuing search will eradicate the entire Band society,' he said morosely.

'I fear you are correct. Then we'll have to give the Site to them after all.'

'Give it to them?'

'It is better to have the Monsters gain an Ancient Site than to have them commit incidental genocide in a vain search for it. Choice between evils.'

Rondl hadn't given serious thought to that course. 'I organized a Band army of sorts to repel the Monster advance. I prefer to drive the Monsters out of Band space entirely. Why should their violence be permitted to profit them?'

'You got Bands to fight? The ones I know would rather disband!'

'It takes special training. We do lose a number to disbanding. They don't even think of it as suicide; it's easy for them.'

'I know. I wonder how many human beings would suicide at some point in their lives, if it was as easy as thinking one thought and blinking out painlessly? Especially if they were assured of going instantly to heaven for eternal bliss.'

'Most of them. At some point, even if only briefly, we all want to die. It would certainly be better than struggling with progressive illness, or degeneration of faculties late in life.'

She spun thoughtfully. 'Their belief in the Viscous Circle is so firm! What survival value can there be in a species' belief in fantasy? It's almost as if someone inculcated this illusion to wipe them out.'

'That's the way I see it,' Rondl agreed. 'Yet their faith is consistent with their pacifism. Any aggressive, negative, emotionally off-balanced elements disappear, because it is the unstable individual that is most likely to suicide. What's left is the finest. It would be ideal for Band society to be isolated from the more aggressive Spheres – if only that were possible.'

'It was isolated until this Ancient Site showed up. I wish I could stay here forever.'

'But we can't. We must revert to Monster status, or have our auras slowly fade away to nothing. No Transfer is permanent.'

'Don't I know it! For us there is no Nirvana. But we must try to save it for the Bands.' She slid irresolutely along the line. 'I didn't know it was possible for Bands to fight. Do you really think they can drive the Monsters out?'

Rondl reconsidered soberly. 'No. Not alone. I have probably recruited the least stable of the Bands, the ones who are most willing to take risks and be unsocial. Even those are basically nice people, who would not partake of war as Monsters know it. We have to try for nonviolent ways to oppose the invasion, and that is difficult. We only delayed the siege of Moon Glow; we didn't halt it. We'll do better next time, but at best it's a holding action. And we have only one more moon to hold before they lay siege to Planet Band itself. We need more.'

'What we need,' she flashed brightly, 'is the use of that Ancient Site. There never was an Ancient Site in a decent state of preservation that didn't transform the situation of the discovering culture.'

'That's why Sol wants the Site,' Rondl agreed glumly. But the notion appealed to him. What could his group of trained Bands do if their powers were suddenly magnified by the technology of the Ancients? Bands were not atechnological; it only seemed that way because they had so few tangible artefacts. They could make complex electronic components merely by concentrating on the magnetic structure of metal objects. Bombs would be possible, perhaps, if a triggered release of intense magnetism were arranged; and super-powerful lasers. And devices no bigger than grains of sand might disrupt the computer circuitry of major ships. The possibilities were endless – with a little more technological information at their disposal.

'They might drive the Monsters right out of the System and preserve Sphere Band forever,' Tangt finished for him.

'If only we had the Site to draw on,' Rondl said. 'But we don't.'

'It's a vicious circle. You need the Site – to drive the Monsters *away* from the Site.'

'And if we don't get the Site, the Monsters will send all Bands to the Viscous Circle,' Rondl agreed.

'On the other hand, if we tell the Monsters where the Site is, we can probably save the Bands. The Monsters just don't really care about the Bands, one way or the other.'

'They just don't really care,' Rondl echoed.

'What moon is it on?'

Now was the test of his faith in her. It was insufficient. 'Dinge,' he lied. 'Moon Dinge, the smallest, farthest, faintest one.'

'Well, there's one moon remaining before they attack Planet Band itself,' she concluded. 'Let's try your way first. Try to fight them off, hold them back, save that moon.'

'Moon Fair, the closest, biggest, brightest, prettiest,' he agreed. 'If we could hold them off one moon, maybe we could push them off another, and finally win back the System.' Was this a foolish dream?

'And if we fail – if Moon Fair falls – then we shall report dutifully to our kind that the Ancient Site is on Moon Dinge,' she said.

'Yes,' he agreed, feeling guilty. Why did he keep reminding himself that he was a Monster? No Band could have lied like that – especially not to a friend. 'We'll report that, if we fail.'

'Then we are unified,' she flashed enthusiastically. 'Maybe we can break the vicious circle – and if we can't, at least we'll save the Bands.'

'One way or another,' he agreed.

'I'm almost sorry we came here on business. I think the other would not have been so bad.'

Now Rondl's guilt was two-edged: for the lie that helped make her amenable, and for his increasing desire for that amenability. She was magnetically attractive; among Bands, attraction was literal, though they also used the word figuratively. 'Let's get out of here,' he suggested, not wanting to be near her much longer – for both reasons.

CHAPTER 16

Moon Fair

Rondl and Tangt separated, he going to locate Cirl, she to rejoin her Band husband. If Rondl's army succeeded in driving the Monsters back, Tangt would help spread the news and rally more support for the continuing effort among the Bands. If Rondl failed, possibly getting disbanded himself, she would wait safely until recalled to her human host, then make her report. She would give the Ancient Site – or so she would think – to the Solarians, in the hope that they would spare the Bands.

Rondl hoped his lie to Tangt would not create more mischief than the worst application of the truth might have. He simply wasn't sure he had done the right thing, ethically or practically. Yet he was unwilling to correct the lie; that might be a worse mistake. So – he had better succeed in driving back the Monsters his way.

He made the rendezvous. Cirl was there. Suddenly he was doubly glad to see her. She was the one he wanted, not a Monster in Band guise – not even one like Tangt.

'When I returned to Maze Mountain, you were gone,' she flashed. 'Others reported you had left with an orange female, so I concluded she had arrived. What did you discuss?'

'She wants to give the Ancient Site to the Monsters, trusting that they will then leave us alone. But she agreed first to let me try to fight off the Monsters. We might make it work this time.'

'That was all she wanted?'

'That was all she got. She has gone back to her husband, to wait.'

Cirl seemed satisfied. 'I talked to Proft. He says he

knows of no precedent, but believes that an alien in Band host should be able to join the Viscous Circle if he disbands while in that host, and if he really wants to join the Circle.'

'If he has faith,' Rondl said regretfully.

'Yes. So you can join – if you really want to. Proft says he believes individual Bands have to find the way there, and the way can be found if the will is sufficient. So the only ones who get lost are those who do not want to join.'

Rondl had no response. Proft's reasoning was circular: failure meant the desire to fail, rather than any other theoretical reality. If no Bands reached Nirvana, it was because none wanted to. Rondl himself did want to achieve the Viscous Circle, but he did not believe in it. His capacity for self-delusion had been shrinking recently. It was best for him to let the matter be moot.

They got to work on the reorganization of their army. The partial success of the defence of Moon Glow had attracted wide attention; it had shown that it was possible to resist the devastating alien intrusion without violating the fundamental Band nature. Rondl's message had been spreading: the Monsters had to be stopped, or Band culture would disappear.

This time Rondl planned more ambitiously. He wanted not just to slow the Monster advance, but to roll it back – not merely to retain Moon Fair, but to recover Moon Glow. He did not inform them of the significance of Moon Glow, because the news might somehow leak to the Monsters. The Bands knew the Site was there, but did not realize that it was the Monsters' objective. So Rondl merely listed Moon Glow as the Band's own next major objective in the course of reversing the invasion.

They set up much as they had before. But this time the Bands were concentrated in an area that vaguely resembled a conventional Ancient Site. They carried metallic ores from elsewhere on the moon to this site, each Band drawing as much as he or she could carry magnetically and depositing it in the pattern Rondl indicated. They did not know why, and Rondl only told them that he believed this would attract the Monsters.

A giant circle formed, obviously artificial, suggestive of the surface aspect of a deep construction. In the centre the Bands formed a mound of similar ore, with passages leading into it, and cylindrical artefacts half buried in sand. Rondl hoped these cylinders would be taken for Ancient artefacts and transported to the command ships with incautious haste.

They were still at work, perfecting the trap, as the Monster fleet arrived. There were more ships this time, and they set up more carefully, evidently determined to prevent any repetition of the difficulties encountered in the conquest of Moon Glow. Monsters did not like to have their schedules interrupted.

Rondl tried to intercept one of the laser communication beams between ships, but this time the Monsters were using a multiple-band scrambler, with bits and pieces of messages being routed by lasers of several types and locations and intensities; there was no way for a single Band to intercept more than disconnected fragments. Some Monster technician had been very clever.

The search pattern proceeded smoothly; there were only token problems. Moon Fair was for the most part an uninteresting body, to Monsters. It had almost no atmosphere, and there was no evidence here of prior civilization (apart from the one just manufactured), nor was there current native life extant. It was just a barren world, covered with extinct volcanoes, evaporated seas, meteorite craters, mountains, anaemic dust storms, and thin films of ice. During its warm cycles the atmosphere thickened, which was when most of the slow weathering took place; in the cool cycles Moon Fair was virtually timeless. This happened to be a warm time; or perhaps the

Monsters had timed their occupation accordingly, since they preferred warmth and atmosphere.

Bands were able to traverse Moon Fair freely at any time, for it had a fine pattern of suitably magnetic lines and a number of naturally reflective surfaces that were convenient for conversation. It was called Fair because it was fair as seen from space; it had high albedo, and its reflected light was used for muted communication. All Bands found Moon Fair pretty, regardless; but its symbolism as the last property before Planet Band lent it special significance now. This was where the stand had to be made – and thousands of Bands understood this, though the term 'stand' itself was opaque to them. Bands never stood; they floated in place. But the stand had to be made the right way, for Rondl knew that the Bands would never be true warriors. Only he himself, a Monster in Band form, could truly fight.

The explosions were set off; now Rondl knew that this was not simple Monster mischief, but coordinated seismographic surveying and surface analysis. The high-flying debris from the blasts was spectroscopically analysed, the patterns of ground vibrations charted. Monsters could learn a great amount in the course of the destruction they wreaked. Yet, because of their too-narrow definitions, they had still managed to miss what they sought. Which was part of the irony of Monsterdom.

The tanks landed and cruised across the terrain, their sensors alert. They were taking soil and air samples and bouncing radar off the ground. On this mission, the Solarians' assimilation of a planet was informational rather than physical.

Then the tanks spotted the artificial circle – or perhaps the survey from space had located it and directed the tanks there. Messages radiated madly; Rondl could have intercepted one of these, but there was no point: there were hundreds – too many to change – and in any event, this time he wanted the Monsters' information to travel accurately. Tanks clustered like the flies Rondl remembered from Monsterland. The bait had been taken.

Larger ships landed. Monsters in Monster suits emerged, proceeding on their gross, fat, flesh-encased-bone limbs to the circle. More samples were taken, more visual, sonic, and electronic surveys made. Individuals proceeded semi-cautiously to the central mound, and entered the tunnels.

Soon they emerged, hauling the cylinders placed there for them. Their excitement was manifest: had they found genuine, precious Ancient artefacts?

Until this point the Bands had not interfered with the Monsters' activity. A few Bands had been taken aboard the ships, but they had lain quiescent, awaiting the signal. The Monsters had not discovered the extent of the Band resistance, but had realized that randomly caught Bands had played a role in the foul-ups of the occupation of Moon Glow. Perhaps they likened these Bands to insects in the machinery, causing short circuits merely by their presence. So now they guarded against such insect infestation, and were alert for the Ringers on this planet. But some Bands were camouflaged as metallic boulders, and others as slabs of metal; these had bypassed the Monsters' suspicions.

When the cylinders were securely aboard the command ships, Rondl gave final instructions, then flew toward the largest Monster vessel. Cirl had wanted to come with him, but he demurred. 'This may become unpleasant. I have Monster temperament; I will not disband under the pressures of the moment. But you would have trouble. Wait for me in space; guide the other Bands when the need arises. I love you.' And with that she had to be content.

He positioned himself as close to a shuttle as he could without being detected, and waited. The signal came on schedule. Bands flying all around the moon relayed the flash at the Monster vessels. Every visual aperture was bathed with the message; every Monster pickup transmitted it to the interior. *NOW*.

The Monsters noted the flash, but did not comprehend its significance. It was not blinding, not even particularly bright, to their orbs. It was merely a blink, a highlight, as from the facet of a diamond, passing quickly. But the Bands in the ships were alert for this flash and, having rehearsed for it, knew what to do now.

Bands exerted magnetic forces. Shuttles veered and missed their assignments. Onboard computers malfunctioned, sending out spurious information. Messages became garbled. All the mischief that had plagued the siege of Moon Glow now descended abruptly on this expedition. Before, the Bands' efforts had been largely experimental; now they knew what they were doing. Rondl had explained computers and drilled Bands on what circuits to locate and modify. From the Monsters' viewpoint, everything had suddenly gone wrong.

In the confusion, Rondl shot into the ship's opening receiver bay ahead of the shuttle. He exerted his magnetism on the control circuit of the interior airlock, and it admitted him. How much more he could do, now that he had his memory! He knew how Solarian ships operated; they were no longer mysteries to him. He knew that a little bit of magnetism applied to key places could work marvels: the unlocking of pressure hatches, the changing of control switches, the distortion of computer functioning. Soon he was in the pressurized interior, the residential and control part of the ship, joining the Bands who had been brought there as camouflaged specimens.

No Monster noticed what was happening to the precious Ancient-artefact cylinders. They shivered and fractured, falling apart. The individual slices were – more Bands. The Kratch-resistant tubes had now found service as Monster deceiving tubes. Hundreds of Bands now occupied the command ships – and they knew exactly what to do there.

They took up stations beside the life-support and emergency facility substations. Abruptly the lights went out. Monsters cried out in alarm, stumbling as the big ships gyrated erratically. The atmosphere within the ships thinned, causing the Monsters to gasp for oxygen. Messages appeared on communications screens: SURRENDER. The configuration was meaningless to the Bands, but Rondl had assured them it would have impact on Monsters.

Unfortunately, the Solarians did not heed the directive. They fought like the Monsters they were, appallingly physical. Some dived for the life-support controls, others for the emergency facilities. Most equipment had emergency manual override controls, and these came into play now. Magnetism could not affect these the way it could the small currents of computers.

The Bands, unprepared for the ferocity of the reaction, gave way. The lights came on again – and now the Monsters were alert. They saw the Bands hovering. 'Ringers!' one screamed; Rondl could not hear the sound, but knew it was present.

'Get out of reach!' Rondl flashed, using the convenient light. He had hoped to capture the ship in one swoop; now there would be a complicated fight – which was exactly why he had not wanted Cirl aboard. The unexpected had struck. 'Hide! But keep thinning the atmosphere, and interrupt the lights again.' For there were other places to interrupt the chains, places the Monsters had not yet covered.

They tried, but the Monsters were too quick and savage. The Solarians reached their awful bone-filled limbs out and smashed their digit-splintered hands into the Bands. Disbanding followed. Soon the number of

Bands in this ship had halved, and the survivors had little chance. Rondl was sure the Bands in the other ships were faring no better.

The communications screen flashed on. The top extremity of a Monster appeared thereon. Its atmosphere-imbibing orifice gaped, showing the white chew-teeth, the most salient characteristic of Monsterdom. The Trugd had teeth, and the Kratch had similar grinders. Whatever ship that image emanated from had surely been recovered by the Monsters.

Another Monster face appeared in the screen, with a different background image. That meant another ship lost. This effort of resistance, like the last, was failing; it was only inconveniencing the Monsters, not undoing their control. The brutes were all fighters, and could not be contained by the relatively delicate devices of the peaceful Bands. The effort to prevent the seizure of Moon Fair was not succeeding.

No! Maybe Bands could not do it, but Rondl was not a Band. He had the Monster fighting reflexes. He refused to let his major effort fail like this! The other ships might be lost, but *this* ship was going to pass into Band control! 'Avoid all Monsters!' he flashed. 'Fly erratically. Follow my directives!'

The surviving Bands responded. They no longer had to think for themselves – and such thinking was now dangerous. They were being chased by Monsters, and it was best to let the Monster Band think for them. That decision alleviated the pressure to disband.

'All green Bands join me,' Rondl flashed. 'All blue Bands concentrate on the communications apparatus. Foul it up, prevent meaningful signals from getting through.' Bands were coloured, but not colour-coded; he was using colour purely as an emergency convenience. 'But all Bands must stay clear of the Monsters. Do not allow them to touch you; take constant evasive action.'

The blue Bands clustered around the vision screen and its connections. The picture of the Monsters blanked out. This sort of equipment was especially vulnerable to magnetic influence, and no manual control could circumvent it. The ship could no longer receive orders from outside.

'Black Bands orient on the Alien life-support systems,' Rondl continued flashing. 'Trace their feeder circuits. Locate the inputs for sedating chemicals – sleepgas or similar.' But of course the Bands had no notion of such things; very few chemicals had any effect on Bands. 'At least identify any peculiarities of the system; I will examine what you find. Have no fear of actually hurting the aliens; sleepgas will merely make them passive.' Rondl knew that his recruits simply would not commit the ultimate violence of killing. They would thin the air to make the Monsters uncomfortable, that was as far as they could go. Otherwise it would have been possible to put this and all the other ships completely out of commission by opening the pressure-relief valves and letting all the air escape to space.

But the Monsters were already pressing them hard. The Bands needed to create distractions. 'Yellow Bands – play tag with the Monsters,' Rondl ordered. 'As with the Kratch. Swoop near, then away. Orbit their top extremities if you can. This will aggravate them. Do this as much as possible without getting so close they are able to touch you. It is a game; be alert and clever, not concerned.'

The yellow Bands commenced their grim game. They hovered near individual Monsters, retreating quickly when the creatures made clumsy swipes at them; it was soon apparent that Bands had better reflexes than Monsters did, at least in a situation like this. Yet the lines restricted them. Lines happened to be plentiful here, because of the metal of the ship, but there were gaps here and there. Some Bands were running off lines at crucial moments and getting caught and broken – forcibly disbanded. In time all would be lost.

'Red Bands, help the yellow Bands,' Rondl ordered. 'Remember, it's a game; we must show them that we are superior players.' If only they would respond to that!

A black Band was flashing to Rondl. Rondl flew across; for straight-line flying there was no problem at all. The machinery of the ship used so much power that it generated many lines on its own.

The black Band had located a unit connected to the atmosphere generation system. It seemed to be an oxygen activator – an artificial enzyme used to promote the effect of oxygen in the Monster system. In his Band form, Rondl found it hard to recognize the unit for certain, but he remembered it from his pre-Band experience. It was a backstop in case a ship in deep space ran short of oxygen, as could happen because of a meteoric holing, or as the result of enemy action. The enzyme enabled personnel to function on reduced oxygen, and could thus extend a limited supply by as much as fifty per cent.

No point in giving the Monsters any of this right now! He wanted them ineffective, not at peak efficiency despite the slight oxygen deprivation they were under.

But Rondl hesitated by the valve, his mind jogged by something elusive. There were a couple of contraindications to the use of this enzyme, he vaguely recalled. The Monster body's fundamental vitality tended to be depleted after extended operation with it, necessitating a convalescence of a similar period; that could be awkward for them in combat. And if it was used when the oxygen content of the ship's air was normal, the effect was cumulatively intoxicating. Usually this was not a serious complication, of course; but things could get awkward when discipline had to be maintained. There were stories –

Intoxicating! That gave Rondl an idea. Bands of course had no notion of the nature of Monster intoxication; Band minds were always clear. But changes of consciousness – yes, indeed!

Rondl flew close to the enzyme unit's trigger mechanism. He exerted his magnetism to reach down into the proper relay, and activated it. That sent the chemical into the air circulation system; soon, Rondl hoped, it would affect every Monster aboard.

'Allow the atmosphere to return to normal content,' Rondl flashed to the black Bands. 'But keep that valve open.'

He flew back to the main action. Now he had some new notions. This could become spectacular! 'Blue Bands, disrupt the food synthesizers.' Again he had to explain, for Bands used no food. So he revised his terms, describing the operation of the machines and encouraging the blue Bands to produce as much quantity and variety of substance as possible.

Soon solids and liquids and gels were pouring from the machine orifices, out over the floor, getting in the Monsters' way, squishing under bone-filled leg extremities. Angry as well as dizzy from the beginning effect of the enzyme, some of the Monsters picked up what Rondl recognized as pseudo skinless tomatoes and soft-shelled eggs and beverage bulbs and hurled them at the tormenting yellow Bands. Naturally they missed; Bands were excellent at dodging flying objects. Red and yellow gunk splattered across the ship's control mechanisms. Now *this* showed promise!

'Taunt the Monsters, positioning yourselves between them and equipment, or between one Monster and another,' Rondl directed.

They did so, getting into the spirit of this game. Sure enough, the tipsy Monsters began throwing food at the baiting Bands – and hitting each other instead. A Monster female got splattered on the back of the head by a cup of chocolate pudding; she whirled in outrage, swept up a meringue pie, and shoved it into the face part of the male Monster nearest her.

Now the Bands were able to withdraw and simply watch in growing amazement. The Monsters, true to their nature, were indulging in an orgy of food abuse. Ripe paper-shelled gourds bounced off the skull bones of standing Monsters; beverage bulbs exploded under trampling foot bones. Mock-lobster dishes clamped their decorative red claws on Monsters' stray finger bones. Bursting baked potatoes bombarded the posteriors of Monsters bending to pick up more ammunition; sausage links wrapped around limbs and necks. Well-sauced spaghetti slid down the front of a prim female Monster, outside and inside her uniform blouse; she let forth a scream that made the walls vibrate and began laying violently about her with a handful of carrots. Carbonated beverage fluid bubbled over the trouser section of the admiral who had once commanded this vessel, and fizzed into his underclothing. The admiral did a dance of discomfort, anger, and confusion, his mouth-orifice shaped into an O fully as round as a Band. Then he dived for a load of cream-filled eclairs just emerging from a machine, and commenced target practice of his own.

'They are distracted,' Rondl flashed, satisfied. 'Return to the ship-guidance mechanism. Direct the ship toward deep space, away from the Monster-controlled ships.'

The Bands went to work, experimenting with the unfamiliar mechanisms. They could affect the magnetic circuits – but control was quite different from disruption. It was far easier to prevent the Monsters from using the ship than it was to use it themselves. The ship lurched, seeming as drunken as the Monsters within it. But slowly it steadied and moved in the desired manner.

A Monster head appeared in the neglected communication screen, its orifices shaping into a scowl. 'Block that transmission!' Rondl flashed. Several Bands flew to the screen, and it blanked out again.

But Rondl felt insecure. The Monsters of this ship had

been nullified, but this effect was temporary; when they recovered sobriety, they would cause trouble. He was also uncertain what the other Monsters in the other ships would do. He needed to check on that.

Under Rondl's direction they got the incoming messages in laser form, bypassing the clumsy screen. They ignored the scrambled, multifrequency inputs and accepted only noncoded ones. Now they could intercept a certain percentage of messages without alerting the food-throwing Monsters.

The news was not good. '. . . final warning. Turn about and return to assigned orbit, or we shall open fire in nine minutes.'

Trouble! Individual Bands could avoid the explosive shells of the Monsters in space, but this ship could not. If the ship were destroyed, they would all be disbanded with it. They had to flee the ship immediately.

No! Again Rondl reacted like a Monster, not a Band. He had captured the ship; he would fight violently to hold it.

Except that his Bands would not fight in this fashion – and even if they would, they would not be able to handle the complex requirements of space combat. Only Monsters could fight Monster-fashion. Only Rondl himself could do it – and he could not do it alone.

Did he have to? Why not extend the disciplinary system he had set up for the training of Bands? The others did not have to fight, or to understand space mechanics; all they had to do was follow simple directions *Aim this tube* . . . *connect this circuit* . . . *now!* And a shell could be on its way to intersect another vessel. Only he, Rondl, would need to grasp the whole.

But he had very little time. The other ships were about to fire on this one. 'All available Bands proceed to defensive apparatus,' he flashed urgently. It was an anomaly of Monster nomenclature that the most aggressive and offensive paraphernalia were termed defensive. In this case, that fiction was useful.

The Bands flocked to the apparatus and began mastering its circuitry. They were not aware of the overall situation; each worked on a particular aspect, so that individual circuits would be responsive to Rondl's will.

In this manner Rondl got the weapons of the ship functional, and oriented on the pursuing vessels. When the firing commenced, Rondl fired back. His weapons did not have good aim, but at least the action put the Monsters on notice that they could not attack with impunity. Maybe they would desist, and he would succeed in absconding with this ship. What an advantage it would be to have a weapon equivalent to those of the Monsters! He could use the ship to fight, and to train Bands, and –

And convert the Bands into a technological, warring species like the Solarians? He always came up against that horror! What good would such a progression be? To win this war was to lose it!

Then an enemy shell exploded against the hull. The ship jolted. Air leaked out. Pressure dropped. This did not affect the Bands, but it touched the still-brawling Monsters immediately. Suddenly there was insufficient oxygen.

A repair robot slapped a brace on the hole and stopped the leak. New air was pumped in to restore pressure. But those moments of oxygen deprivation caused the enhancement enzyme to operate as it was supposed to. The Monsters were gasping – and suddenly sober.

Abruptly there was organization. Monsters brought out emergency space suits: standard operating procedure when under fire. Now they were not dependent on or vulnerable to the ship's air supply. They no longer imbibed the enzyme.

Suited Monsters were all over, assuming command of the equipment. The Bands could not restrain or distract them. The ship had been abruptly lost.

270

'Get out!' Rondl flashed. 'Concentrate on the space-disposal mechanism; make it eject us all!'

They clustered there. This move caught the Monsters by surprise; before they could act to prevent it, the Bands had had themselves ejected into space.

'Scatter!' Rondl flashed. 'Avoid their attack!'

The Monsters aboard all the ships tried to shoot down the Bands, but were not successful. Space was filled with futile laser beams and exploding shells. Soon all the Bands were out of range. They had escaped.

But Rondl knew the Bands had lost the battle – and the war. They had tried their best, and fooled the Monsters, and failed either to capture a Monster ship or to significantly impede the Monsters' progress toward Planet Band. Now, as the result of this effort, the Monsters knew what Bands were capable of, and would not be caught this way again.

Tangt, receiving news of this defeat, would proceed to try to save the Bands her way. It just might work – except that Rondl had given her the wrong information. And he wasn't sure he could locate her to correct the lie before they were both recalled to their Solarian hosts.

CHAPTER 17

The Lie

But by the time Rondl located Cirl, he had changed his mind. Too many Bands had been lost, and the cause of the Monsters was too wrong, to permit a simple hand-over of the Ancient Site. He almost preferred to risk the destruction of all the Bands than to give the gift of victory to the Monsters. Also, he lacked conviction that the Monsters would be magnanimous in victory. They might 'teach the Ringers a lesson' by exterminating them as a species.

This was Monster thinking he was doing, he knew – but the very notion of delivering benefit to the forces of wrong, merely to abate further wrongs, was repellent. Appeasement: it had a bad flavour in any framework. And if every species did that, the least scrupulous would inherit the Galaxy. A line had to be drawn somewhere.

Yet he had to be honest with the Bands. It was their species at stake.

Cirl met him gladly, and in that moment he knew he was doing it all for her. She had a right to her own type of existence, and her society had a right to the benefit of Ancient technology to protect that existence.

'Cirl, we must convoke a circle,' he flashed immediately. 'I have a pressing discussion to initiate.'

'Of course,' she agreed. 'The Monsters are drawing nigh our planet.'

They gathered all Rondl's recruits surviving the Monster engagement and formed a huge circle. 'Here is the situation,' Rondl flashed into it. 'We have tried to halt the invasion of the Monsters, and have failed. They will proceed to Planet Band and engage in their usual search schedule, incidentally extirpating the Band species, unless we take one of three courses.'

They were with him. They had fought the Monsters and suffered a fifty-per cent attrition. They knew that only Rondl had the capacity to help them.

'First I must inform all of you what some of you have known,' Rondl continued. 'I am not a true Band. I am a Monster in Band form.' A shock flowed around the circle, replete with viscous eddies and return shocks. Some Bands *had* known, but evidently they had respected his privacy and not bruited it about. Had he flashed this news to the Bands individually, some would have disbanded; but the power of the circle held them securely. Only a shock bad enough to destroy them all would destroy any; the circle unified them, providing the strength of mass.

'I did not know this when I commenced this resistance,' Rondl continued. 'I had amnesia. I thought I was a Band with a special talent for organization. I had nightmares about Monsters. Then I was recalled to Monster host, complete with bone-filled limbs and turgid eyeballs, and knew that I had been sent here to betray the Band species.' Again the shock; this was what the Monsters called strong medicine, delivered abruptly. But these Bands knew him; they had worked with him. They trusted him. Cirl was helping him, flashing a steady pulse of acceptance into the circle, making his ugly confession more acceptable. She loved him, despite what she knew. She made him seem better than he was. What would he do without her!

'But I had come to know the Band mode of life. It is better than the Monster mode. So although I knew myself to be a Monster, I tried to help the Bands. I am sorry that I had to employ Monster tactics of violence and confusion; it was the only way I could see to stop the invaders. And I am sorry it was not enough.'

They were all sorry; they had all failed.

The circle asked him: what were the three courses he saw to stop the Monsters?

'None of them is pleasant,' Rondl said. 'The first is to marshal an even larger force of Bands, and fight more violently than before.' A tremor went through the circle at the concept 'fight', so he hastily modified the thought to 'resist'. Then he continued: 'Last time we tried merely to disrupt Monster progress, and to take over their ships. This time we would have to try actually to destroy ships and kill Monsters. To cut off their life-support – ' But he had to halt; the reaction was so strong the whole circle was in danger of destruction. The Bands – his battle-hardened veterans – simply could not tolerate this sort of input.

'This is not acceptable,' Rondl flashed quickly. 'I describe it only to show the manner Monsters would act. Monsters are uncivilized; they believe the ends of conquest justify the means of extermination. At least some do; some Monsters are less uncivilized than others. They aren't all evil.' He thought of his Solarian wife, Helen, whose views he had only recently come to understand. 'If Bands were to adopt the tactics of the unethical Monsters, those Bands would be like me: Monsters in Band form. Because you are true Bands, you must reject this.' And the horror subsided. They *were* Bands, and they did reject it.

'The second course is to give the Monsters what they want,' Rondl flashed. 'There is an Ancient Site in the Band System, which we know as a pleasant retreat. It was constructed three million years ago by an unknown species who knew more about magnetism than any Galactic species does today. I believe the early Bands discovered this Site, and drew on its nature to shape the devices that channelize the lines on which we travel. Thus Band society became interplanetary and interstellar, with individuals travelling through space in a manner possible to no other species I know of. Without that Site, Bands might have been limited to primitive natural lines, mostly about Planet Band; you would have had to compete for limited living area and resources, becoming less pacifistic. Civilization as we know it now would not have been feasible. But we no longer need to have possession of the Site; we already have the technology from it that we needed to fashion the lines that give us freedom of space and conscience. If we give the Site to the Monsters – if we tell them where it is, so they will no longer need to search so destructively for it – they might take it over and ignore the Bands. We would be allowed to exist; since the Site is not on Planet Band, they should not go there.'

The circle considered that. There was no great shock of revulsion. This was the kind of action the Bands could accept, just as Tangt had thought.

'However, I am not certain this would work,' Rondl said. 'The Monsters could decide the site is too valuable to leave in the vicinity of an alien species. They might decide to clear us out anyway, or they might suspect that there were other Ancient Sites in this System, and search for them, destroying us anyway. The greed of Monsters has no known limit; they always want more than they possess, and build empires and still are not satisfied, being limited in the end only by force. So though this course is feasible, I do not trust it; it gambles on the goodwill of creatures who have little benevolence toward aliens.'

Again the circle considered. The Bands felt Rondl's reservation was well taken; this was a feasible course, but not an ideal one. They were ready to ponder the third course.

More Bands arrived. 'They cannot partake of this circle now,' Cirl flashed. 'They are not prepared for the magnitude and violence of these concepts. Release me, and I shall form a lesser circle with them to explain.'

'But I need you here,' Rondl protested. 'You have been stabilizing this circle.'

'I will go,' flashed Tembl, the blue philosopher. 'I can explain to them.'

There was a current of agreement. Tembl had been doing good work, helping to organize; she was competent. The circle abated its viscous current momentarily, allowing her to slide out without ill effect, then closed the gap she left. It would be devastating for a member of a circle to leave without warning, but when there was general agreement and preparation, it became possible. The currents of thought resumed, modified just slightly by Tembl's absence. Every circle, Rondl realized, was a little different from every other.

Rondl resumed his discussion. 'The third course is to find a way to repel the Monsters without killing them and without giving up the Site. To win without violence. For this we would need to possess technology greater than theirs. Perhaps tractor beams that would fasten to their ships, swing them about, and hurl them harmlessly back toward Sphere Sol, their home. Perhaps a way to make System Band repulsive to them, so that they flee it voluntarily. Or a way to change their auras so that they become more like those of Bands; then Monsters would not act the way they do now, and could coexist with Bands. The possibilities are endless – if we are only able to discover the necessary technology.'

Now the circle thrilled with agreement. This was the best course of all! Individual Bands were already racing ahead, working out what Rondl had worked out. 'The Ancient Site! It could have that technology!'

'It could,' Rondl agreed. 'That Site has never been fully explored; most of its secrets remain untouched. But such breakthroughs are the sort of thing that Ancient Sites are noted for. Certainly it seems worth the try. Unfortunately, we do not at present have possession of that Site. It is in the territory already overrun by the Monsters.'

The circle mulled that over, coming to grips with the

vicious circle that he and Tangt had encountered: how could they use the Site to prevail, when the enemy already had possession of it?

'We must recover that Site,' Rondl flashed firmly, and the circle agreed. 'Perhaps only for a short time – only long enough to find the technology that will enable us to prevail. We cannot do it violently; we have already eliminated that course. We must find another way.'

They were with him, their beams circling the circle with mounting conviction. 'What way?'

'We must cause the Monsters to temporarily vacate Moon Glow, where the Site is,' Rondl said. 'To depart voluntarily. Then we can move in, occupy it, study it, and perhaps comprehend its treasures in time to save Planet Band.'

Now there was doubt. How could the Monsters be persuaded to leave the Moon Glow?

'We shall have to deceive them,' Rondl said. 'To make them believe the Site is elsewhere. Then they will go there, deserting the other moons, and the Bands will be free to go to the real Site without difficulty.'

There was a rising disquiet. The circle was having difficulty assimilating this, deception being alien to Band nature. Rondl had to go over the principle again and again, trying to get across his concept of the lie.

At first there was tremendous resistance, as the concept eluded almost all the Band minds: deliberate misunderstanding? A contradiction in terms!

But finally a few Bands began to get it, aided by the great input of the circle. Their shocked revelation sent powerful pulses through the viscosity. Cirl laboured to keep the current manageable, though she herself was struggling with the concept.

These few contributed their comprehension to the whole, leaning on the full circle to maintain their equilibrium. Others, too, got it, and hung on similarly. There was a rising tide of excitement and dread as a larger percentage caught on. Finally it elevated into the most powerful current yet, a potent unified emotion of –

'Oh, Rondl!' Cirl's despairing flash came, discrete amid the torrent. 'Monster!' The emotion was pure anguish.

And he realized that with comprehension had come not acceptance, but total revulsion. The Bands had finally grasped the alien nature of his thought, and rejected it completely. Exactly as they had rejected the concept of war, before, and –

The circle disbanded. All its components disintegrated – not into component Bands, but into dust. The viscous circle was an entity itself, a temporary one, but possessed, while it existed, of the prerogatives of a living, sapient creature. Properly dismantled, with group acceptance, it reverted to the individuals who composed it; catastrophically sundered, as in this case, it died. When it died, so did its parts.

Only Rondl himself, an alien, managed to retain his personal cohesion. It was not his way to disband when faced with an appalling concept – and to him the concept was not appalling. Faced with several bad alternatives, he had chosen the least destructive one. A small sacrifice of honour for a tremendous gain in lives. He was practical – as the Bands were not.

He was also a Monster. His survival of the destruction of the circle proved it. Had he been a true Band, like Cirl, he would have perished, too. As it was, he was severely shaken, and still hung on to his cohesion with extreme difficulty.

The lie. It had started with the lie he had told Tangt, about the location of the Ancient Site. He had got away with that lie, and somehow assumed that he could do so with impunity in the Band culture. But Tangt was not a Band, but a Monster like himself. She would not disband when she learned about the lie, but any true Band would.

No, the lie had started further back – when he deceived Cirl by going unannounced with Tangt. That had been half a lie, for he had not really meant to do it. He had allowed the convenience of the moment to lead him into it. He should have declined to go with Tangt until he had informed Cirl. There was the half-step. Convenience had preempted truth, and after that the lie had become feasible. He had brought this mischief on himself, by failing to react at the outset in an ethical rather than a practical manner. He had chosen the Monster way, and now was paying the consequence.

'Rondl! Rondl!' someone was flashing at him persistently. 'What happened?'

It was Tembl. She had escaped disbanding, because she had joined the other circle before the lie.

What had he done? As he settled into some sort of equilibrium, he realized that not only had he lost all his trained Bands except one – he had lost Cirl. His love, his wife.

Again he experienced the terrible urge to disband, to suicide, to join her in oblivion. But he hung on, partly because suicide was not his way, and partly because he knew that only he stood a chance of saving all the remaining Bands from a similar fate. The threat to the species remained, regardless of his personal situation.

'Was it a bad concept?' Tembl persisted.

'It was a lie!' he flashed explosively at her, half expecting her to disband also. But the concept passed her by; she could not grasp it, so was not affected by it.

The species of Band would suffer extinction rather than fight; rather than be party to a lie. That was the way it should be, the way he should have known it would be. He had acted rashly; he should never have presented the concept to them. Now, too late to save his friends, his recruits, or his wife, he realized that.

Yet still there seemed to be no way to save the species

except that lie – now more than ever, for his trained troops were gone. Rondl was a Monster; he was able to lie. Only he could save the Bands – from both the Monsters and the Monster-concepts. He must use the lie – and use it by himself, without initiating any other Band to its awful secret. This burden was his alone to bear. And he would do it, honouring the memory of Cirl, whom he had loved. Whom he would always love. The Monsters were ultimately responsible for her death, for *they* had invaded; *they* had sent the likes of Ronald Snowden to interfere with her life. The Monsters would pay. Until they did, he could hardly afford the luxury of grief. That was part of his own punishment, richly deserved, for being what he was. A Monster.

'Let me help you,' Tembl said, hovering close.

He perceived her with the clarity of emotional distance. She was eager to take Cirl's place. She was attractive enough. She was competent, intelligent, and extremely adaptable for a Band. But she *was* a Band. Was he going to take her the route of Cirl, into comprehension of his true nature and thence into suicide? She deserved far better than that!

'Go away,' he flashed.

Hurt, uncomprehending, she departed. She had the strength not to disband. Rondl felt more like a Monster than ever. Everything he touched turned to dust. But this time, he believed, he had not taken the half-step of convenience – the convenience of allowing Tembl to cater to him, to please him, to share his burden. He had taken the hard step of rejection, and thereby freed her to live the life of a true Band.

Now he was alone. All his trained, hardened Bands were gone. It would take so long to train new ones that the Monsters would ravage the home planet first. And if he did train new Bands – what would prevent them from disbanding when faced with the necessity for effective action, as these had done? The plain fact was that Bands were not physically or socially constituted to fight. Why did he keep deluding himself that it wasn't so? Fighting was the prerogative of Monsters.

Rondl would have to do it alone, as he had already concluded. Yet what could a single Monster do by himself?

He had the answer to that: he could tell his lie. Not just a Monster-distracting lie, for that was no longer sufficient. A Monster-killing lie. Poetic justice: Monsters destroyed by a Monster who was the tool of Monsters. Because of who he was and what he was, he just might be able to pull it off.

Now he had purpose. He accelerated, going toward the planet. He needed to locate Tangt, to get his revised lie perfected.

He came to a thickly populated line. 'I seek Tangt,' he flashed in general. 'Can anyone direct me?'

No one here knew Tangt. It took only an instant to verify this; Band communications were very efficient when properly used. He flew to another well-travelled line and flashed again, again without success. He wished there were a better way to locate an individual, but knew there was not. That the society of Bands was anarchistic was part of its beauty – but at the moment it was frustrating.

He kept trying, surveying many hundreds of Bands randomly. And finally, from a purple individual, he got an answer: 'I encountered an orange Band of that name yesterday in the green plains region of the planet.'

'Thank you!' Rondl flashed. He zoomed toward the indicated region. To Monsters, a planetary surface was eighty per cent of awareness; to Bands only thirty per cent. A given Band could be anywhere in space near a moon or near a planet. What mattered was not matter, but the routing and strength of the magnetic lines. Yet a planet did offer a highly varied terrain, providing interest and diversion, and that was an attractive aspect. Many Band pleasure spots were on planetary surfaces. As was the case with other sapients, the Bands appreciated novelty.

Oh, Cirl – you were of this planet!

By his nature he had slain her, forcing her to self-destruction. But no: he could not afford to think about her. Not yet.

When the mountains flattened into a plain and local vegetation turned it green, Rondl began inquiring again. This time the responses were thicker. Soon he zeroed in on Tangt, who was hovering in the vicinity of an outcropping of grey rock. 'Tangt!' he flashed. 'This is Rondl!'

'Please depart,' she flashed. 'I am distracted.'

'I cannot. I need you to help save the Bands.'

'I cannot be concerned with that now.'

What was the matter with her? 'You must help,' he insisted. 'Otherwise the whole Band society will be lost, including your own Band husband!'

'My husband is dead,' she said.

'Dead?' He had not anticipated this.

'When I told him of my nature, thinking that if your wife could sustain it, perhaps after all so could he – he . . . he disbanded. Right here. I thought I loved him.'

'My wife also disbanded,' Rondl said, surprised at this parallel. 'When she learned more of my nature. I know I loved her.'

'He just wouldn't believe that disbanding is the end!' she flashed. 'He told me I could join him – '

'For what it's worth, Cirl consulted with an educated Band who felt it should be possible for Monsters in Band guise to join the Viscous Circle, if they believe in it – or perhaps even if they don't, so long as they really want to find it.'

'That is not worth much!' she flashed, then returned to her grief. 'Such a good person, but he clung to his superstition. "If you are more Band than Monster, follow me," he told me, and just like that he disbanded. And I can't follow.'

'They just don't believe in death, or in war, or in deceit,' Rondl agreed. 'It's a species-wide foible. Maybe that's what it takes to be truly pacifist – turn the other cheek, or whatever – because even if the enemy kills you, he hasn't really hurt you. We humans fight to the end because we don't believe in life after death, not really, no matter what beliefs we claim to hold or what our assorted religions specify. Our absolute horror of death gives it all the lie. All we have is this one life, so we refuse to give it up easily, even when the continuation is painful. We'll cheat, lie – ' He broke off his flash. He was setting up to lie to her now – again – and didn't want to give himself away. No honour among Monsters!

'They don't believe in death,' she agreed. 'Or in any other evil. They really don't believe. So why am I here, marking the gravesite of a mate who left no body? There is no grave! If I am right, he is beyond help or grief; if he is right, he is either laughing tolerantly at me or feeling sorry for my ignorance.'

'Exactly,' Rondl agreed, feeling his own suppressed grief lighten somewhat. 'The Bands die happy. To them it's like cutting losses by resigning early from a game. They don't understand grief. Only Monsters experience that.'

'Only Monsters deserve to!' She lifted away from the stone. 'Yes, it is fitting that we suffer. Why did you seek me?'

'My effort failed. All my army disbanded except one who escaped by coincidence. I sent her away rather than risk her following the same course.'

'Then it must be my way. We must tell the Monsters where the Site is.'

Now the lie. Rondl hated this, but steeled himself; it

was the only way. He had already paid the penalty for his lie; now he had to squeeze it for maximum advantage. He was fortunate, ironically, that Tangt's grief for her disbanded husband had prevented her from checking on the location of the Ancient Site. 'Yes. At Moon Dinge.'

'So you said. But we need to pinpoint it better than that, since they missed it before.'

'They had reason to miss it. Actually it's near Dinge, not right on it.' The lie loomed larger; could he get away with it?

'How can a Site be *near* a moon?' she demanded. 'You mean it's a satellite? They should have spotted that.'

'There's a planetoid in the same orbit. You know how populous this System is with debris, with rings and bands of material everywhere. This is just one of those anonymous chunks of rock, similar to the ones we use for Stations in System Sirius, not really near Dinge spatially, but it seems so because of the orbit. Similar designation – fourth orbit out from Planet Band. Not big enough to be considered either moon or subsatellite, but big enough for a Site. Really hidden out there, among thousands of similar chunks. But it's easy to travel back and forth, moon to Site, when the location is known.' He was making so much sense he was almost believing it himself.

'An Ancient Site – on a planetoid in moon orbit?' she demanded, seeming to balk at the concept. 'The Ancients usually built on solid land.'

'So the Monsters assumed, and missed the Site. What do we know about the Ancients? Most of what we see are their three-million-year surviving cellarholes. No wonder the Monster sweep overlooked this one, and perhaps countless others elsewhere in the Galaxy. No one thought to check planetoids.'

'Small wonder!' But she seemed to be accepting the idea. After all, the Monsters *had* missed the Site, so an explanation was needed. 'Well, there'll be no trouble locating it now. Do you think it's a live Site?'

'A fair chance. You never can tell about the Ancients.'

'That's certain!' She whirled about, riding a line upward. 'We must not tell the Bands about this,' she flashed back.

'Agreed.' Actually, the Bands would not care about the Site itself; in fact they would gladly give it up to make peace. He knew; he had surveyed them. He had been the one to doubt the efficacy of that strategy, fearing the continuing greed and ignorance of the Monsters. But if the Bands knew the truth now, they could flash to Tangt the correct information about the Ancient Site, and that would destroy Rondl's lie. So Tangt's own furtive nature was her undoing; she was protecting the lie that deceived her.

'You're the only one who understands,' she flashed.

'It takes a Monster to understand a Monster.' Again he felt attracted to her. It was not love of the sort he had held for Cirl; that was dammed back for the moment, so that he could do what he had to do. With Tangt the attraction was plain understanding.

'This is crazy,' she said in a flash tinted with romantic invitation. 'But shall we – ?'

And he thought, why not? This was not Sphere Sol, and their Band mates existed no more.

Yet Rondl had a misgiving. First, his loss of Cirl did not automatically free him to love another; he still loved Cirl. She, at least, had been true to her belief; her pattern of life. Certainly he had a kind of camaraderie with Tangt. But it was an affinity of the Monster aspects of their nature, rather than of the sublime. Oh, they both wanted to save the Bands; that was a sublime motive. But that did not mean they needed to make love to one another. Tangt was no better than he was, except that she was not duping him into participation in a lie.

That made him pause. She was his kind, capable of violence and cheating and all the other crimes of Monsterdom. How could he be sure she *wasn't* duping him?

Yet in what way could she do it? They had agreed to give the Ancient Site to Sphere Sol; that was his lie. They had each lost their Band mates, and she now turned to him for comfort and understanding; where was the problem there?

The question showed the answer. Female Monsters did not operate that way. They were seldom genuinely giving; they sold their sex for some sort of advantage, small or great. His Monster wife Helen always did. She talked of love, but what she wanted was a suitable environment for her offspring. It was a commendable objective – but she had given him short conjugal shrift for years until recently deciding it was all right. And had it never occurred to her that he also might want a suitable environment for his offspring? That he might care for his child as much as she, and not require any bribery to do what was right? Women who sold their bodies openly were termed harlots; those who sold them covertly were considered decent. Both wronged their men and themselves by their contempt for the male mystique. Monsters, all!

So what was Tangt buying? Surely not his green colour or forthright personality! Not even his camaraderie; she had not missed him until he located her, just now. So this interest was an on-the-spot thing, as it had been before. Now why should she have no interest in him when they were apart, and want to make love when they were together?

Because, perhaps, she had her own report to make, not necessarily the one they had agreed on. His absence could have meant he was dead, therefore no worry. His presence meant he had survived; therefore she needed to take action. So she was doing so. But what did she really intend?

'You seem pensive,' Tangt flashed. 'Don't you like me?'

She was definitely up to something! How should he handle this? Was there a way to kill a Band in the guise of making love, perhaps by means of some horrible thought that would force reflexive disbanding, and was that what she planned to do? Or was she trying merely to compromise him, using the act as a lever against him to endorse her story to the Monsters? She might fear he would change his mind later and try to prevent her from reporting on the location of the Ancient Site; he would be less likely to change if he had a more personal commitment to her. Thus she could be using sex purely as a standard precaution, a device to help ensure his loyalty.

Yet if he turned her down, she would know he suspected her motive.

Best to stall, until he had a better notion what she intended. 'I find you most attractive, Tangt. But I loved my wife, Cirl.'

'Before she died. Of course. And I loved Fomt. Yet now, with each gone – '

What recently widowed female who had loved her husband would within hours be soliciting sex from another male? That decided him. 'I cannot at the moment love another Band. The memory is too fresh.' And that was no lie.

'Well, we shall soon be recalled to our natural hosts.'

To make their reports. But that would happen regardless. How could romance – or sex – affect it? This really bothered him; he did not want to fall into the twin traps of taking Tangt at face value or affronting her and making an enemy unnecessarily. To be a Monster was to have Monster problems! To struggle with lie against possible lie, never being truly sure of oneself or of one's companions. How much better the Band way was! 'Maybe we should talk again. As Monsters. Privately.'

'Privately,' she agreed, after a pause during which, no doubt, she considered the ramifications of this counter-offer. She knew she was unusually attractive in Monster host, so a male might very well prefer to have her that way. 'Before making our reports?'

'That could be awkward, since the computer will get at us first. Perhaps before making the reports final.'

'Before finalizing them,' she agreed. She was surely suspicious now – yet so was he. What kind of game were they playing with each other? Who was author of the most fundamental lie?

They located a line loop, a place where they could safely leave their Band hosts. A host could survive for a time without an aura, if kept in an environment reasonably secure from dangers. Since Bands did not need anything more than a line for sustenance, there would be no problem about nourishment.

They set themselves up in miniature orbit about a rocky outcropping, and chatted innocently while waiting for the Transfer recall of their auras. 'I'm glad these are not the bad old days when a Transferee had to reach an alien Transfer unit in order to return to his natural host,' she flashed.

'That was why the early agents, like Flint of Outworld, had to have auras in the range of 200,' Rondl agreed. 'Not only did they suffer a much more rapid attrition of aura in Transfer, they had to supervise the construction of a Transfer unit to send them back. It took real courage to travel to a foreign host then! But this new system remains uncertain. Some of the losses in this mission may have been mis-Transfers.'

'Yes,' she agreed. 'The old – '

CHAPTER 18

Triangle

He found himself back in Monster host. It was a shock, no easier to accept the second time. This body revolted him!

Revolted him? It was his own, natural host! He was a man, not a Band! How could he be revolted by his own body?

Because, he realized, he now identified utterly with the Band host. He had been corrupted by the Band form and the Band culture. It seemed the more time he spent in Band host, the stronger the effect was.

Was it something physical? It couldn't be, because all that travelled was his aura. So it had to be something mental or emotional.

That was it. He had seen Heaven. In comparison the human state was Hell, his own trafficking in it hellish. He wished he could simply cut away and slough off the Monster attributes of his personality. He was telling the big lie to save the Bands, a thing they could and would not do to save themselves. It might be the only way, but it was also his shame. How could one of Satan's minions join the company of Heaven, however much he might want to?

I will never see the Viscous Circle, he thought, and grief welled up in him. So corrupt was he, he couldn't even believe it existed.

When the computer interviewed him, he gave the lie. Using mental and emotional devices he was trained for, he almost convinced himself it was the truth, so that the computer could not detect the falsity of it. Computers thought they were infallible; it was a machine illusion. They were fashioned by Monsters, with Monster flaws, and in any event the human will remained more complex than the machine programming. Any Monster with his experience and motive could deceive the essentially naïve computer.

Yet not entirely. 'There is an element missing here,' the machine said.

Rondl suppressed a reaction of fear, knowing that could give him away faster than any words might. He converted it to righteous ire at the challenge. 'You can verify my report against that of the other Transfer agent,' he pointed out, contemplating his bone-filled extremities with his paired liquid-inflated eye orbs. There was so much to dislike about this body!

'Hers also has a missing element.'

This was falling into place almost too neatly. 'Perhaps the two of us should consult again.'

'That seems inadvisable at this stage.'

Did the authorities suspect? He would have to let it go, at least for now. 'As you wish. It's your show now.' But he hoped to be back in Band host before the occupation of the supposed Site proceeded. Monster hell would become indeed hellish once his lie became known. Court-martial would be just the beginning. And he had business in the Band region. Without his further input, the Bands would still be wiped out.

They let him go home. He might be under suspicion, but he had delivered the goods, and they had no tangible evidence against him. They could not interfere without obvious cause; other agents would grow wary if normal practice started getting set aside. Some oddities were to be expected in returning agents, after all.

He wended his way along the free-fall passage, no longer thrilled by the weightlessness. The foreboding was growing: he had betrayed his kind, and lost his Band wife too. The Solarian authorities surely ought to know, unless they were totally out of touch. His future was fast becoming a dead end. Betrayal of one's species was a baleful matter, for internal as well as legal reasons.

Helen was waiting for him. She was garbed in a most fetching cling cloth outfit, her hair puffed out artfully by static electricity, her eyes brightened by luminescent eyedrops. Disgusting artifices.

She realized at once that they were not working. 'Your Ringer femme is that important now?'

She knew such terminology grated against his sensitivities; why did she employ it? 'My Band wife is dead. I am careening toward a blank wall.'

Helen was not stupid. 'Then I'd better take you out for a spin in space. Few walls there.'

What was she up to? Ronald had no stomach for connivings. In fact, he wished he had no literal stomach, for that was an especially disgusting aspect of Monsterdom. 'I think our plans need revision.'

'Oh come on! A spin will do you good. Get that post-Transfer depression out of your system.' She bullied him out of the yard and along the road to a nether exit. They stepped on the platform, and it slid down and along under their weight, carrying them to the very rim of the barrel that was the residential section. Here the private spacecraft were suspended like lifeboats – which is what they would be if the Station ever suffered serious breakdown. Every resident family was required to maintain its craft in spaceworthy condition, and to use it often enough to keep personal piloting skills sharp. It was also military policy to keep a certain percentage of the ships in space at all times, so that in the event of attack, some of the Solarians here would survive. This percentage varied according to the high command's estimate of the interstellar situation; usually it was low enough so that voluntary excursions filled it. At present it was elevated, because of the System Band 'action'. Officially there was no war, but the Station was on a war alert. Ronald, as a participant on leave, was not required to put his craft into space, but could if he chose to. That would relieve one conscript of the obligation.

There was no problem about departure clearance; Helen was efficient about such details.

They buckled in and snapped the craft loose from its mooring. It dropped into the exit chute as its engine took hold, spiralling out smoothly into space. The auto-pilot took care of this portion; manoeuvring in-Station was too important to be left in the uncertain hands of the operator. Ronald was content to watch the bell of the chute expand like some gross musical instrument, until the ship shot out over the ragged, rocky terrain of the planetoid. Now it was as if they were a light-year from civilization, out in the wilds-beyond-the-wilds.

Then the forest of antennae and vent snouts and scope optics came around the close horizon, and brutal civilization was back. A planetoid did not sport much surface.

If aliens were to bomb this Station, how would the Monsters react? Like hornets emerging from a shaken nest. There was a lot of hostility and aggressive force packed into this planetoid, as there was in any military base or trading enclave. Monsters of any Sphere always had their weapons with them.

Then out on the tangent into suddenly deep space, the sun Sirius blazing. But it wasn't like being in Band host, flying free on the lines in the light of twin suns. Ronald felt enclosed, limited and stifled. 'All we need is to get drunk on enzyme,' he muttered.

'Drunk in space?' Helen asked. 'Not while I'm along.'

'Not us. It happened in System Band.'

'Bands get drunk?'

'Not exactly. This was a Solarian Space Admiral, with fizz in his breeches and a food-flinging war in his cabin. You should have seen the lieutenant who got sauced spaghetti down into her blouse.'

After setting a destination, Helen left the controls on auto and turned to him. 'Now what is this? You were going to save the Bands, and the news is you're not doing it. Something's up, and I think I have a right to know.'

'I suppose you do.' He knew she had got him out here so that they could not be overheard. The ship radio kept in touch with the Station, but did not pick up the pilot's conversation for broadcast unless activated for that. There was no sense in wasting power that might be needed for propulsion.

Helen was in some respects a problematical woman, but she would not betray him. 'I loved Cirl, my Band wife, and wanted to stay with her. I fought hard to balk the Monsters' invasion, using semipacifistic means, because the Bands really can't be violent. We tried to take over a command ship by getting the crew drunk on oxy-enzyme, but we didn't quite make it. So I'm trying to save the Bands now by using a lie. But when a group of Bands understood this, they disbanded – all that knew the notion – and Cirl went with them.'

'Oh, I'm sorry! She had such a good effect on you,' Helen said, and he knew she meant it. Helen felt sympathy for all lesser creatures, and she regarded the Bands as being in that category. She had told him she was not concerned about Cirl as a rival, and she would not have said that insincerely.

'I'm still working on the lie,' he continued. 'It's an abomination, and I never want to lie again after this is over, however it ends, but I have to carry it through now. I told it to Tangt – Tanya, the other surviving Transfer agent. She believes it – I think – though she's trying to help the Bands, too. I just couldn't risk her way – '

'Her way?'

'She wants to give the Monsters the Ancient Site outright, hoping they will then leave the Bands alone. But I don't trust that.'

'I should think not! Remember Pizarro and the Incas.'
She grimaced. 'The Indians gave him a tremendous
ransom in gold – but he destroyed them anyway. Time and
again, those who trusted to the mercy of conquerors have
regretted it.'

'But now I have committed overt treason against my
species. When they find out – I'm finished here, Helen.
I've got to get back into Band host; at least I'll die happy
there. I'm sorry to mess up your plans, but that's the way
it is.'

She considered soberly. She seemed less like a Monster
now; it seemed that her agreement with his views rendered her more attractive physically. What a tremendous
difference the subjective element made! 'I suppose I did
wait too long. But I haven't lost you yet. It's the very thing
that makes you a traitor that also makes you worthwhile
as a man, ironically. Our kind just happens to be wrong
this time. Now you understand about my causes. It is not
treason to try to correct the abuses that come from an
erroneous philosophy; it is patriotism. History will in due
course correct the record. Meanwhile we must seek to
help and protect the lesser species.'

'There are no lesser species,' Ronald said curtly.

'Exactly. Only species with power, and species with less
power. Might does not necessarily make right.'

'Yet it was my association with Cirl that showed me
this, not my life with you.'

'She must have had something I don't.' Helen shrugged.
'Maybe I am after all a Monster, necessarily imperfect, as
are we all in this System. I suppose any of us would be
corrupted by Heaven if we actually visited there. Anyone
would fall in love with a genuine angel.'

'You are most understanding.' But he remained cold.

'The same thing happened to Tanya Coombs?'

'The same. She loved a Band male, and when she told
him her real nature, he disbanded.'

294

'So it probably would have happened to me, had I been there. I wish I had been.'

'You could put in for Transfer.'

'No, I have business here.' She turned to face him squarely. 'Ron, I'll make a deal with you. I'll help you get back to Band host for another tour, and I'll help you beat the treason rap when you come back. In return, you're mine thereafter.'

'That's very generous, Helen. But I don't think I love you anymore.'

'Well, after things settle down – '

'I doubt I'll ever return to being the man you knew before. I am no longer one of your causes. I have achieved my final orientation. You'd do better to give me up.'

'When I've just found you? Not likely! I can live without your love, just as you lived without mine. You aren't going to be loving any Solarian for some time, I think, but you can do a lot of good for me in the interim. And maybe in time you'll come to love me again. We have a much better base to build on now. I understand you better than any other Monster does.'

'Except perhaps for Tangt. She's been through the same change I have. She has trafficked with the angels, too.'

'The other agent? Interesting conversion of names. Just how close were you two, over there?'

'She tried to seduce me.'

'She must have wanted something from you. Oh, not that you're unattractive; it's just that she's a calculating military female. I know the type. I looked up her record while you were gone. She isn't much moved by love.'

So Ronald had concluded on his own. Tangt had surely cared for her Band husband, but had reverted to her normal mode of cynical manipulation the moment he was gone. 'One calculating female taking the measure of another?'

'Your grasp of the essentials is improving. But what would she want? I thought you were deceiving her.'

'Yes. She may be suspicious, though. The computer is, I'm pretty sure, but because her story corroborates mine, the machine can't come to a conclusion yet.'

'That would do it. If you loved her, you wouldn't lie to her. Or at least you would be less likely to. Love is overrated as a device to promote truth, but she might consider it worthwhile to increase the auspices. To protect herself. If you're a traitor, she's a traitor, too, right now. She has no intention of being dragged down by your male foolishness.'

'That thought had passed my mind. Few women offer love for the sake of love.'

She laughed. 'Don't try to bait me! If men ever insisted that love have something to do with love, they would be much harder to deceive.'

'She was foolish herself,' Rondl said. 'Instead of verifying my information, she stayed to mourn her lost Band love.'

'That must be some society! So she really has been converted too?'

'It *is* some society. It's everything ours is not. You try to protect alien cultures, but you have not actually experienced them. You're objective about them, and therefore you miss the essence. It's like trying to define the concept of love itself objectively. You'll never get there. Tangt – you're right about that, there is a conversion in Transfer of names – really does want to save the Bands, her way.'

'Or so she tells you. She could be trying to learn your plan so she can spike it.'

'She could have turned me in anyway, without any trouble. Why would she support my story if she's not with me?'

'Why shouldn't she? The authorities want the Ancient Site. She wants to give it to them. She has no conflict –

296

and her apparent agreement with you keeps you from trying to put her out of the picture.'

It was a revelation. 'Of course! She let me do the dangerous work, keeping herself safe, in "mourning". But why didn't she check my information?'

'How do you know she didn't?'

'But she substantiated my report!'

'Openly, yes. What did she say in secret?'

Ronald was stricken. 'My God! I've been a fool!'

'Men are, especially with women. Most particularly with women who look like her.'

'I spent so much time wondering whether to let her seduce me, I never realized that that was what she *wanted* me to do. To wonder. To be distracted by her, instead of figuring things out logically.' He sighed. 'You're right. I've been outfoxed by a woman. But why haven't they arrested me?'

'They're waiting until they've gleaned all they can from you. You're a highly capable agent, and much of what you have done and thought, you haven't told anyone. You could be working some sort of double-double cross, feeding them true information in the guise of a lie, so that they will penetrate the "lie" and be truly deceived. You were the one who conquered the telepathic dog, way back when, remember; you know how to deal with people and machines who can read your mind, or who think they can. Even if they have fathomed the right information, based on what Tanya has given them, there could be wrinkles. They don't know yet who your accomplices may be. They don't know whether I'm in on it, and if so, on what basis – or whether you have connections elsewhere in the System. They can arrest you any time; there's nothing to be gained by rushing it. You don't get rid of a weed by yanking off the part that shows; you ease it out root and all. The same with the cancer of ideological treason. The longer they give you, the more you may show them. You should know that.'

'I *do* know that,' Ronald agreed, disgusted with himself. 'I allowed myself to forget. As a Band I think a lot like a Monster; as a Monster, I think a lot like a Band.'

'On the other hand, this could be a simple, routine snafu, a miscoordination between machines and departments. Never underestimate the idiocy of the bureaucracy! History is rife with examples of gross errors based on stupidly simple failures of communication.'

'There is that,' Ronald agreed wanly. 'Shall we call my chances fifty-fifty?'

'It means there is hope for you. You should know how to thread through this mess, maximizing your chances whichever turns out to be the case. It's your area of expertise.'

'By playing them along while they're playing me along. Sure. All I need is to get back into Band host, take out Tangt – ' He shook his head. 'Helen, the trap I've set for the Monsters, if it works – and the chance now seems miserably slight – will guarantee they won't let me off, ever. I'll never be able to return to human form. I can't make that bargain with you.'

'Well, at least you're doing what *I* can't do: saving the Bands. That's half of it. And if things do happen to work out, on the off-chance we've misjudged Tanya and she hasn't turned you in – and that is possible, since the motives of women are complex – '

'You're indulging in foolish hope yourself, Helen. They'll still know me for a traitor, once that trap springs. I'll be better off dying in Band host.'

'Not necessarily. They might arrest you, throw the book at you – but meanwhile the word will spread exactly what they have been doing in System Band. Those creatures are sapient, and they're organized in their fashion; it just doesn't happen to be an authoritarian organization. They may be classed as a common-law Sphere despite their seeming lack of qualification. If the Sphere Sol authorities not only invade and destroy that Sphere, but also prosecute the person who tried to prevent them from committing this crime, there could be a stink of Galactic proportion. It could become a cause of more than incidental scope.'

'And you know how to promote a cause,' Rondl said, smiling somewhat grimly.

'I do know how. You just might come out of this looking like a hero.'

'Or a martyr.'

'They may not care to take the risk. Appearance is often more important than substance. They might buy you off with an advantageous assignment and a promotion – '

'Or might arrange to have me "accidentally" liquidated, so that I'd be no embarrassment to them at all.'

'There is that. Monsters are Monsters. So we'll fight to save you, but in case we fail, there are two things you can do, and I'll be satisfied. Not happy, you understand – I like you a lot better now that it may be too late, and I'd love to keep you another term – maybe I should say I'd keep you to love you – but satisfied that I've got as much of you as you can give.'

'I don't understand. What two things?'

'Second, you're going to have to seduce Tanya.'

'What?'

'In Monster form. To ensure she believes she has you secured. If she is in doubt – if she hasn't made her private report yet – this will lull her until you get her into Band host. You've got to seem to be overwhelmed by her charms. That should not be too much of an effort.'

'I can't believe my wife is saying this! Sending me to another woman, setting up a triangle – '

'I love you, Ronald. I want to save you. I want to inherit your loyalty if you survive this. I'm the truest friend you've got among the Monsters. We don't have time or occasion for narrow jealousies.'

299

'That must be true,' he agreed, dazed. 'I wish I'd understood you better, years ago.'

'Crisis brings things out. You never know how strong a tree is until it survives a hurricane.'

'That's the way I felt when I faced Cerberus, before I married you. I was a small tree, a sapling, bent almost to the ground by the force of that monster's mind – its three minds – by the terrible fear it projected. But then I began to strengthen, to rebound. I hadn't known I had that reserve until it manifested.'

'I knew you had it. But you never showed it, when you were not in crisis. Now you face a crisis of a different kind, and that strength of character is manifesting again. It confirms my decision.'

Her decision to marry him? 'You told the second thing I can do, which still amazes me. What was the first?'

She played with the control panel, resetting the course. The ship commenced a curving acceleration. 'We are now on our way to Tanya Coomb's Station. It will take a while. So there's time.'

'Time?'

'For you to seduce me.'

'I'm not sure – '

'I want your baby, Ronald. If you're dead, I'll still have it, if I get it now. And I can get it now.'

'The neutralizers – '

'You've been off the sterilizer for the duration of your mission. I'll bet you're fertile now. And I started taking null-contraceptives last week. And a conception aligner, tuned for today. I'm ready right now. Chances are two to one it will take.'

Ronald had to laugh. 'You certainly plan ahead!'

'I certainly do – when I have reason. I've been waiting four years for this alignment, and I don't propose to miss it. Now let's not waste time. This hour may be all we have.'

'Let me see if I have this quite straight. You want me to seduce you now, and Tanya an hour from now – if "seduction" is not a misnomer in both cases. Did it occur to you there might be certain practical difficulties?'

'Practical difficulties?' she inquired with mock innocence. 'I really can't think of any. I'm sure you'll rise to the occasion. She's one pretty woman, and there's always the thrill of new conquest.'

'Within one hour? When she's a Monster? I'll hardly get the fun of it that might otherwise – '

'Yes, you may not enjoy it at all,' she agreed smugly. 'But it's a necessary chore.'

How neatly she had planned it! She had disposed her cards so that she obtained maximum advantage from a very difficult situation. She would have made an excellent Transfer agent. And she was doing it all to salvage as much as she could – of him.

Suddenly Ronald found himself flaming with passion for her. It wasn't love; love was what he felt for Cirl, pointless as that was now. But it wasn't merely sex, either; sex was what he would use against Tanya, reversing her own ploy. It was fascination. The emotion that could, when conditions were right, convert into love. Fascination was a house built on sand. If he survived this mission, that sand might very well stabilize into rock and he would love her again. Helen was a lot more woman than he had realized. But right now –

In moments they had the seats converted to full recline. She turned to him, and her liquid and bone-filled aspects became, subjectively, attractive, and it began.

301

CHAPTER 19

Trap

Their Band hosts had survived. 'So we talked them into sending us here one more time, to warn the Bands away from the Site,' Tangt flashed. 'I admit to being gratified. I'd like to stay here for life, even without my Band mate.'

'So would I,' Rondl agreed. 'But it cannot be.'

'I don't think there's much we can do here to forward the mission or the fortune of the Bands. We can convoke circles to explain things, but they don't congregate much in the orbit of Moon Dinge anyway. I just had to be here again, somehow. That's why I went along with you. I'd have gone along with anything to rejoin this host, if only for an hour.'

'That was the only reason you came on to me? To get back here?' For she had turned out to be eminently seduceable in the Monster state, and Ronald had enjoyed the experience more than Helen would have thought was fitting.

'No. I was afraid you'd pull some crazy male ploy and jeopardize the welfare of the Bands. So I wanted to be on the scene to make sure the Bands survive. Just in case.'

Ronald distrusted that. She was correct in her suspicion of his 'crazy male ploy', but there would be little she could do to stop it in Band form. She might like her Band host, but why would the Solarian authorities care about her preferences? They must have had more compelling reason to accede to this unnecessary third Transfer; they would hardly care if any Bands got wiped out near the Site. That most likely meant they were still using her to explore the extent of his treason.

'That's all?' he asked. 'You don't care about the Monsters? Whether they get the Ancient Site?'

'As a professional, I care. That's my mission. But as a person, I'd rather see the Site in the possession of the Bands. I'm sorry your programme of resistance didn't succeed.'

Could he have misjudged her motive? It was becoming more important to know. 'I need to acquaint more Bands with the situation. All my prior recruits except one are gone. There is a shrine on Moon Glow where educated Bands congregate – '

'I'll go with you,' she flashed. 'After what has happened, they need explanation and reassurance. And of course the warning to stay clear of Moon Dinge and its orbit. I hate to have the Monsters permanently preempting any part of the Band System, but it's a lesser evil than the extinction of the Band society.'

They set off for Moon Glow. 'I thought you might be more interested in promoting the Solarian cause,' Rondl flashed, still fishing for her true motive.

'Like you, I was converted to the Band cause. I really hoped your programme to turn the Monsters back would work. Perhaps I dawdled deliberately, praying that no other action would be necessary.'

Rondl felt increasingly guilty about his lie to her. She certainly seemed to be playing it straight with him. Yet he hesitated to tell her the truth even now. She might be bait for a trap, getting him to confess in time for the Monsters to correct their thrust and nail the real Ancient Site.

In due course they arrived at Moon Glow. The Monsters were departing; the big, clumsy ships were accelerating outward toward the orbit of Dinge. The moon was not directly out from Glow; that happened only rarely. But the location of the Ancient Site he had provided was fairly convenient. The ships thrust outward while allowing orbi-

303

tal inertia to carry them forward. With proper coordination of vectors, they would swing into the vicinity of the Ancient Site without great waste of momentum. The manoeuvre seemed ponderous, because of the seeming anomalies of orbiting that affected the massive ships.

'It's working,' Tangt flashed. 'The Monsters are vacating the other moons!'

So it seemed. But would it have continued working, had he provided the real location of the Site? Rondl had assumed that the Monsters would not long be content with the genuine Site; that they would sooner or later clear the System of Bands, as if the Bands were so many annoying insects. So appeasement was not the long-range answer. Yet Rondl was not sure – and if he was wrong –

As they homed in on Moon Glow, there were distant flashes in space. 'What is that?' Tangt asked. 'This host is far better at visual perception than the jelly-fluid eyes of the Monsters are, but I can't tell – '

Now at last he had to reveal it. 'The trap has sprung,' Rondl replied. 'The Solarians attacked a Bellatrixian enclave. That has prompted Bellatrixian measures of defence.'

'Bellatrixian?' she flashed blankly.

'Remember the aliens who made the cave-lighting system? Huge sapient grasshoppers with manual dexterity? They are not pacifists.'

'Of course I know who they are! But why should Solarians attack them?'

She really did not seem to know. 'They might be considered rivals for possession and exploitation of the Ancient Site.'

'If the Bellatrixians had wanted the Site, they could have taken it centuries ago! They were content to trade peacefully here, however aggressive they may be elsewhere. They don't believe in appropriating the resources of peaceful Spheres.'

304

'All this is true. But I suspect the Solarians have foolishly provoked the Bellatrixians to armed reprisal.'

'This makes no sense at all!' she flashed. 'The Solarians want the Site, not inter-Sphere war.'

'I fear I will have to explain,' Rondl flashed back. Oh, she was not going to like this at all! 'The location of the Ancient Site we gave the Monsters was actually the location of the Bellatrix enclave. Too bad the Monsters were so eager to move in that they did not cross-check coordinates.'

'The Bellatrix enclave! But if Solarian ships converge on it in force – '

'And perform their initial bombardment of survey detonations – ' Rondl added.

'And start landing ships and disgorging tanks – why, that would cause an explosive reaction!'

'That was my assessment of the situation. I fear we have an inter-Sphere space battle in present progress.'

'But how could you make a mistake like that? You said you knew where the Site was!'

'I do know. It was no mistake.'

'No mistake! You mean the Bellatrixians already possess the Site? They built their enclave on it?'

'No, the Site is elsewhere.'

'You deliberately – '

'I felt the Bellatrixians might do the job the Bands could not: drive out the Monsters.'

'Then you lied to me! And caused me to lie to the Solarians!'

'So it seems.' She certainly seemed to be surprised and chagrined by events, which suggested that she had not been playing a double game with him. The snafu theory of the bureaucracy's failure to act must be correct. He had been lucky there. Too bad he felt so guilty!

'Why?' she demanded, distracted.

'Because I do not believe appeasement is effective

against Monsters. The only way the Bands can be saved is if they use the resources of the Ancient Site to drive off the Solarians.'

'But they can't, because the Monsters already control the location of the Site. The Bands need the Site to win control of the Site. It's that vicious circle we discussed before.'

'The Monsters just vacated that region. The Bands can now move in.'

'Where is the Site?' she demanded.

'Here on Moon Glow.'

She flew flashless, mulling that over. Now the lie was out, and it was too late for her to correct it. The trap had sprung; Monster blood had been shed.

'You realize that now we can never go back?' she demanded after a time.

'Did you want to?'

'Certainly – for a while. To wrap up my affairs.'

'We'll go back on schedule, when our auras are recalled. We have no choice, since we cannot remain indefinitely in alien hosts.' Actually, Rondl was contemplating exactly that: to allow his aura slowly to fade out, until he became his host and had no further recollection of his origin. It was as peaceful a way to expire as existed.

'We'll go back to mind-destroying interrogation and imprisonment and possible aura-wipe so that our vacant bodies can be used as hosts for others, for more loyal visitors or alien Transfers. You have doomed us!'

'Doomed *me*. Not you. You were innocent; interrogation will reveal that.'

'No. I conspired against the Monsters too. I just happened to compromise more than you did. I tried to buy off the Monsters rather than fight them. I failed to be properly suspicious of your motives, so I am culpable too. Now the fight is on.'

'But you did want the Monsters to have the Site. That's worth something.'

'Not much. I felt that giving them the Site would be the least injurious course. That's not the same as liking it. I like your way.'

'You like getting lied to?'

'That, no, though I should be used to it by now, from men. I thought we had an accord. I thought you trusted me as I trusted you. I see now I was foolish.'

Not half as foolish as Rondl had been, he thought. He had mistrusted the motive of Speed, the Hurrian Chief, during the episode of the telepathic dog. Speed had been honest. Now he had done the same with Tangt, again wronging an honest person. What mischief lay in such unfounded suspicion! 'If I had been sure of your motive, I would not have lied to you. Now I'm sorry I did.'

'And our liaison in Solarian host – that, too, a lie?'

'My Solarian wife sent me.'

'Beware of dealing with Monsters!' she exclaimed. Then: 'Your *wife* sent you?'

'She suspected your motive, so felt I should allow myself to seem smitten by you. To give you false security. So I played along.'

Another facet registered. 'You were so slow responding. Before you came to me, did she – ?'

'Yes. She wants my child.'

'And I thought I was losing my touch!' She dimmed, the Band equivalent of a half-rueful head-shake. 'I wonder what I could have done with you, given a fair chance.'

'Considerable,' Rondl admitted. 'Yet even as it was, it was quite – '

'It never occurred to either of you that I might actually be attracted to you? That I might like you for yourself?'

'You're married – '

'One term, not to be renewed. No present significance. I assumed it was the same with you. It's the time for explorations, and considering the unique experience we shared – ' She dimmed more abruptly, the equivalent of a shrug.

'You are a trained Transfer agent,' Rondl continued defensively. 'You should be in control of your emotions. Most agents are. I assumed you were using me.'

'I was certainly a fool. Normally I don't get involved with associates. You seemed to be the one person who understood the lure of the Band society. That made you special. I suppose I just wanted to believe in you.'

Rondl felt worse and worse. Had he sprung a trap upon himself? 'I wanted to save the Bands above all else. I may have been blinded by that. I misjudged you, and I'm sincerely sorry. You were less important than the Bands.'

She relaxed, her flight becoming smoother. 'I understand. It's the same with me. If you had not supported the Bands so firmly, I would not have been interested in you. But if only you had trusted me, it would have been so much better.'

So his lie had ruined what could have been a good relationship – more than good! Yet what else could he have done? He could not even now trust her completely. After all, what would she have stood to gain, under present circumstances, by berating him? Her best course, if she was not in agreement with him, would be to win his trust now, in case the opportunity should arrive to reverse the disaster he had fashioned. He wasn't sure what she could do at this stage, for surely the Solarian ships were being destroyed by the fire-power of the Bellatrix enclave, but he remained wary. How sad that suspicion should so interfere with interpersonal relations! Yet this, too, was a cross that Monsters necessarily bore.

Bad as it was, this was not the whole of it. 'This may not be a consolation,' Rondl flashed, 'but I do – did – love my Band mate, Cirl, and may love my Solarian wife, Helen. Even if I trusted you completely, I could not love you at this time.'

'I understand,' she flashed tightly. Either she was expert at mimicking subtly hurt feeling, or –

They had arrived at the Site. There were no Bands present. The Monsters had vacated the moon too recently. 'This looks like natural landscape, and the magnetic patterns are not like those of ordinary machines,' Rondl explained. 'But this is the Ancient Site, where the Bands first mastered the technology of artificial magnetic lines and became an interstellar species.'

'Without Galactic recognition,' she commented. 'Maybe that's the route we should have gone. Petition for Sphere status for the Bands, seeking an injunction against alien interference until the issue was decided, so their territory could not be raided. A long shot, I admit, yet – '

'The Bands have no government and no interest in Galactic status,' he reminded her. 'And a petition on their behalf from a non-Band, such as either of us, would not be accepted by Galactic authorities.'

'But if you had trained your recruits in the mechanics of token government, instead of in token warfare – '

'True,' Rondl agreed, mulling it over. He had not considered all the options. 'Yet the Galactic wheels do turn slowly. Sometimes they set up committees whose wheels don't turn at all. Long before Sphere status could be granted, the Bands could be illegally extinct. The Monsters would not have honoured any injunction; they would have sent in a covert party to secure the Site regardless, and if challenged would claim the raiders were outlaws.'

'Yes, that is the way Monsters operate,' she agreed regretfully. 'Their actions are even uglier than their appearance. So now it's up to the Site. This was not the route I intended, but now I have to hope that it works. Let's pray the Site has what we need.'

They entered the obscure passage to the shrine. The line wound through a series of naturalistic caverns until it looped about within a subterranean river excavation wherein stalagmites joined with stalactites above them to form ornate columns. But these formations were not completely natural; the core of each was of Ancient construction, with specially layered metals imbued with intricate magnetic patterns.

The columns were physically beautiful, in many pastel colours and designs, but it was the internal patterning that was compelling. Rondl and Tangt, as Bands, could detect what the Monster sensors had missed: the exquisitely intricate artifice of each individual column, and a suggestion of the way the larger pattern of columns interacted. This whole cave was the control unit of the larger Site – and it was almost all in operating condition. A Monster shell had interrupted a portion of it; but the Ancient device had already compensated by routing its network around the gap, without changing anything physically. This was, apparently, that most precious of rarities in the Galaxy – an operative Ancient Site.

'I am awed,' Tangt flashed. Artificial Bellatrixian illumination had been installed to facilitate flash communication. 'As a Band, I can feel the splendour, though it is faint, very faint. Nothing like this exists elsewhere, I'm sure.'

'The ultimate art form of magnetism,' Rondl agreed. 'There has never been anything to match the achievements of the Ancients.'

'But why didn't the Bands draw on this to develop their powers further?' she asked plaintively. 'The data are freely available to Band perception! They could have used this information to become the dominant power in this region of the Galaxy!'

'Except that the Bands are utterly anarchistic as well as pacifistic,' he said. 'They would never abuse power. In fact, they won't even use it. They drew on this technology to fashion lines that extended their reach to neighbouring

Spheres, such as Bellatrix – and no farther. They arranged only to make alien contact, not alien conquest. To facilitate the freeness of their society. That is their nature.'

'That is their nature,' she agreed faintly. 'The very species that most deserves power, refuses to take it. And you know, now that I realize this, I wouldn't change it. The Bands are unique; they must be preserved just as they are.'

'Just as they are,' he repeated. 'A model for all other cultures. One problem I had was that by trying to make the Bands fight to save themselves, I was trying to make them resemble Monsters. Had I succeeded, they would have lost what makes them worthwhile.'

'Yet surely some compromise – if the alternative is to suffer extinction – '

'Those are the jaws of the trap. Either way, paradise is lost. Unless the potential of this Site can provide a fast, appropriate, miraculous salvation.'

'You have gambled the survival of the species on this hope,' Tangt said. 'I hope you win.'

'I hope so, too. Now let's analyse this Site. If the key is here, we need to know it before the Monsters catch on, make truce with the Bellatrixians, and resume their conquest.'

'I'm not trained in electronics or magnetics,' Tangt protested. 'As a Band I can sense the circuitry all about us here, and revel in its artistic complexity, but I can't truly grasp it. My speciality is social engineering. That discipline is largely wasted on this mission.'

'I can handle it.' Rondl moved close to a column, letting his Solarian training integrate with his Band perception. Like a Monster using a scalpel to cut open an interesting carcass, he felt inward through the complex magnetic fields. It was like performing microsurgery on a whale. The inherent Band sensitivity to magnetism was finely attuned; no Monster perception or Monster machine

311

could match it. This Ancient construction was a marvel of intricacy and efficiency; Rondl had never imagined such eloquence in concept or application.

The essence was here. This was not actually a 'live' Site, he now realized. The better part of its active function had been lost, and he could not fathom what that might have been. Only a small fraction of its circuitry operated as intended by the constructors. But he could read the inert circuitry, much as a tourist might gaze at the ruins of the Parthenon, and be awestruck at its grandeur even in ruins. What an education this was!

It should be possible, he perceived, for Bands using amplified magnetic impulses to master a form of Mattermission. There seemed to be an inherent limit of scale here, but the Band mass was, perhaps by no coincidence, just within its upper extremity. Instead of riding the lines, the Bands could jump them, passing virtually instantaneously from one point to another within the framework. One-step travel of several light-minutes, with little energy wasted. Nothing like this existed within the scientific horizons of the Monsters; it would be hard for any Monster not in Band form to comprehend or accept it. But it was true. With this ability, Bands could avoid the Monsters entirely.

'Mattermission?' Tangt asked as he flashed her his finding. 'That's true, that would help – but how long would it take the Bands to develop it?'

'No longer than twenty Solarian years; the technology is pretty clear, but there'd be some complex initial construction involved. The Bellatrixians could – '

'Anything that takes longer than twenty *days* won't do them much good. The Monsters will overrun the planet and wipe them out.'

He had been considering the technical aspects rather than the practical ones. 'You're right!' he flashed, chagrined. 'And even Mattermission won't save them if the enhancement of the lines required for it comes from equipment set up here or on Planet Band. The Monsters will simply destroy the equipment. It's no answer at all.'

'What's needed is something that can really stop the Monsters – like a huge magnetic field that bollixes up all Monster equipment.'

'Nothing like that here,' Rondl said regretfully. 'This technology can't affect Monster equipment at all. Only small-mass, magnetic-sensitive creatures like the Bands can use it. Monsters would require centuries to gear to this refinement, and even then they could never use it to transport anything Monster-size. Mail service is about its best Monster application.'

'You mean Monsters can't actually use this Site?' she asked, amazed.

'Not to enhance Monster power. This is strictly a small-mass technology, like the magnetic lines the Bands have already derived. For Bands it's wonderful, and scientifically it's as sophisticated as anything we know of; for Monsters it just doesn't work.'

'Because they're Monsters,' she said.

'Because they're Monsters. Fittingly.'

'But then the Monsters have no reason to take this Site! This whole invasion is wasted effort for them.'

'Ironic, but true. The Monsters will destroy a superior species, commit sapienocide, for something they can't even use. If only they had known it at the outset!' He paused, reflecting. 'That must be why the Bellatrixians weren't interested. They surely had located this Site in the course of their dealings with the Bands. They installed these lights, after all. They knew the Site was useless to their kind – to the kind of creature who needs heavy spaceships to travel between planets. That includes the great majority of all sapient species. Any of them who investigated in past centuries or millennia would have discovered this. Only the Solarians bulled ahead without

313

reconnoitering to be certain the Site would be worth their own possible bloodshed.'

'So all we need to do is tell the Monsters, and they'll go home. Not because they care for the preservation of the Bands, but because they never spend energy without promise of immediate material gain.'

'I think so!' he agreed, realizing. 'We should have done it your way at the outset. All this mischief with Sphere Bellatrix, all the slaughter of Bands could have been avoided.'

'You'd better inform the Monsters now,' Tangt said.

'No good. I have ruined my credibility by lying to my employer. You will have to tell them the truth; you never knowingly deceived them. Their interrogation will exonorate you, and so they will believe you.'

'Perhaps so,' she flashed after a pause. 'But they will suspect what I suspect. You lied to me before; why should I believe you now?'

'Because I'm telling the truth now!'

'How convenient. If this Site were a bonanza for Monsters, would you tell me that? Do you expect me to shill for you a second time? You know the truth, whatever it is. Only a direct interrogation of you will convince them – or me.' Her flashes had an adamantine sparkle of anger.

He had ruined his credibility with her, too. He had, in effect, scorned her, though their objective was the same, and he knew females could react very strongly to this sort of thing. If only he had been sure of her before! 'At this stage, seeing the Site useless to the Bands in the existing circumstance, I'd have to turn it over to the Monsters regardless. But, as it happens – '

'I trusted you before, and was deceived. I can't afford to trust you again. You must be up to something, and I'm afraid whatever it is will cost the Bands a lot more than the truth.'

What infernal mischief his original lie was making!

Rondl heartily wished he had stayed with the truth. 'What could I be up to?'

'I'm working on that. You want me to tell the Monsters something that will bring them right here in force. You refuse to go to them yourself, despite the fact that they could have the truth from you as readily as from me, using special interrogatory techniques. Now why should that be? What could I do that you could not?'

'You could bring them here to see for themselves much faster than I could! Deep interrogation takes time. You –'

'Since you obviously think in terms of traps, and the nature of the trap is in your mind, not mine –'

'It's no trap!' Rondl protested. 'I just want the Monsters to see that there's nothing for them in System Band, so they'll leave the Bands alone.'

'So you say. Now suppose this Site has the capacity, as some Ancient Sites do, to explode like a nova, destroying all creatures in its vicinity, and the entire Monster contingent is within range –'

'It has no such capacity! These magnetic circuits are physically very weak. They can hardly even be detected by –'

'Or a more subtle radiation, that wipes out all local auras –'

'How can I convince you?' he flashed desperately. 'I'm telling you the truth this time! I deeply regret the lie I told before, and I renounce my Monster nature that led me to it. I only want to save the Bands by showing the Monsters that they have no use for this Site!'

'After the way you deceived me before –'

'I should never have done that! I will never deceive anyone again! It's an abomination on my conscience!'

'And let me seduce you,' she continued furiously. 'Or was it vice versa? You performed at the behest of your wife, of all things! How can I ever trust you again?'

'But we share the will to preserve the Bands –'

'Do we? I have been trying all along to save the Bands, and I thought you were, too. But now I must wonder – '

Rondl saw that he had hopelessly alienated her, and he could hardly blame her. The situation had passed beyond the redemption of apology. The suspicion of her that had caused him, for what he had deemed at the time to be sufficient reason – ah, the arrogance of ends and means! – to lie to Tangt – that suspicion now clouded his own credibility. There was nothing he could say that would convince her of his sincerity. She was angry; she did not want to be convinced. She had been doubly deceived, and was determined not to let it happen again. In her position, he would feel the same.

Yet what would happen to the Bands if news of the Site's specific location and nature did not reach the Monsters soon – news from someone the Monsters were prepared to trust? The Monsters would proceed to Planet Band, perhaps doubling their ferocity in reaction to the recent deception. For the diversion of the Bellatrixian incident would not last long; the two Spheres would already be getting in touch with each other through Galactic diplomatic channels and negotiating a truce. So there would be no further bar to the destruction of the Bands.

Could Rondl go to the Monsters himself, and allow them to destroy him with deep-probe interrogation? Yes, that would do it – but such a procedure took time, many days or weeks, as layer beneath layer of the subject's consciousness was peeled away and analysed. The sapient mind was horrendously complex! Meanwhile the invasion of System Band would proceed, since the Monsters would suspect that his proffering of interrogation was merely a ruse to give the Bands time. By the time they verified the truth from his mind, the Bands would be gone. Tangt could convince them much faster, because she never had intentionally deceived them; her conscience was clean, and her probing could be accomplished in hours, perhaps minutes – in time for the Monsters to go to the Site and ascertain that it was exactly as Tangt said, before they proceeded to the destruction of the artefacts of the Planet.

He *had* to convince Tangt! Yet how?

Then it came to him. The Bands had an answer, for those capable of assimilating it. 'You and I are Monsters,' he told Tangt. 'We envy the values of the Bands, but do not share them. We dream of peace in life, and fulfilment in death, but never actually grasp those dreams. Because we are what we are. A swine cannot wear a pearl; a Monster cannot be perfect. For us there is no peace, no fabulous realization of afterlife – '

'And no truth,' she agreed bitterly.

'Very little truth. We believe in self-interest, not in truth. Our ethical framework has all the aesthetic appeal of an eyeball fairly bursting with fluid. Only when we are ready to die for a cause can we truly be believed.'

'Perhaps so. The Bands die for their beliefs.'

'I am ready to die to save the Bands. I admit I don't have much future anyway, yet life is as precious to me as to any Monster. So my sacrifice will be genuine.'

'You're not the suicidal type,' she flashed. 'You aren't going to convince me of anything by bluffing about something like that.'

'Just bring the Monsters to this Site,' he said. 'Believe me about just this much: it is not a trap. Tell them to transfer an electronics expert to another Band host to verify what I have told you about the Site. Explain how I lied to you before. I think they'll let you off.'

'Stop this nonsense! I have no intention of – '

'And tell my Solarian wife, Helen, that I'm sorry about her, too. I want her to remarry, to provide a good home for our child.'

'You are only annoying me with this blather – '

317

'For that too, I apologize. You are a better creature than I have been. Farewell.'

'Now where are you – '

Rondl willed himself to the proper state, finding it surprisingly easy. His magnetic pattern reversed.

He disbanded.

CHAPTER 20

Reality

Rondl discovered that consciousness remained. Had his aura somehow taken another host, or returned to his Monster body?

No – he had no familiar perceptions. He could not detect magnetism in the manner of a Band, could not hear in the manner of a Monster, and could neither see nor feel, physically. Yet he was aware of the gravity waves of a large mass, and the diffuse aura of another person.

'Tangt?' he inquired. But no flash issued from him. He seemed to have no lens, neither magnetic nor physical. It was as though he was disembodied.

Or disbanded. He *had* disbanded! Yet how then could there be consciousness?

Rondl mulled that over as he checked and rechecked his situation. He was definitely conscious and definitely massless. He was able to perceive planets and stars and auras indirectly, or perhaps it was directly, without senses; but he perceived little else. He was unaffected by solidity and energy. He could – he did – travel right through the matter of Moon Glow without impediment, noting merely a slight change in his environment. He believed he could move similarly through the centre of a star, barely aware of the heat. So: he was indeed disembodied, a ghost – a disbanded aura.

This meant that the mythology of the Bands had, after all, some basis. The aura did survive the loss of the host, at least for a while.

Yet he was not a Band. He did not believe in any of this. How could it affect him?

Well, Cirl had said an alien aura could join the Viscous

Circle, if the alien disbanded in Band host and really wanted to join. So the philosophical basis seemed to be there, for what it was worth.

Still . . .

This could be a dream, a vision. Maybe he had tried to disband, had not succeeded, and now lay inert on the floor of the Ancient Site, inhabiting another nightmare world. If so, he would either wake in due course, or click finally into oblivion. That set of possibilities seemed the more likely.

Tangt's aura remained near. He tried again to communicate with her, but could not. Her aura remained bound to its host, chained to mass, and in that form it could not communicate freely with other auras. It was largely contained, restricted, dependent on the host, as a person became dependent on his spaceship when travelling between planets. That was a different universe.

There was nothing for him here. Even if this was merely a dream taking place while his body died, probably his essence would dissipate soon and he would pass painlessly into nothingness. Yet two things concerned him, even in this state. First, had he succeeded in convincing Tangt and saving the Bands? Second, in what state was Cirl? For in life or death, he wanted the Band society to survive – and he loved Cirl.

Was it possible that for her the rest of the myth had some validity? That she really had found a group soul? What a marvellous thing that would be!

Rondl extended himself, travelling without effort out into deep space. In this dream he made his own rules! He became aware of the Monsters, each of their auras crammed into its gross physical confinement, clustering around the rocky orbit of Moon Dinge like angry hornets. The battle with the Bellatrixians seemed to be abating; he had known that ploy was no more than a temporary diversion.

320

Then he travelled forward in time, suddenly discovering that he had neither spatial nor temporal limits, and noted how the Monsters abruptly focused on Moon Glow and then vacated the System. Tangt had done it! She had told the Monsters, and they had verified her story and given up this invasion. The Bands were saved!

Now he could expire. His mission had been accomplished. The ideal species would continue. His sacrifice had not been in vain.

Yet he remained. Why? Could – ?

He spread out across light-minutes, spatially, searching for what he hardly dared hope for. After all, he was not a believer. The moons and planets of System Band became as pebbles within the immensity of his nonsubstance, tiny interruptions of little account. Size was a physical concept, hardly relating to his present state.

The universe was diffuse, the stars small and far apart. It no longer interested him. Nothing interested him except his quest for Cirl. If she had dissipated, then he had no reason to retain awareness. He could truly extinguish himself; he now realized that he had this ability, too.

The universe was large. The distances between the planets of one system were minuscule compared to the distances between individual stars, and there were billions of stars. He stretched into light-years, finding nothing. The tiny, confined auras of individual living creatures, clustered like maggots on their several little planets, no longer registered. Space went on and on.

Then he sensed something. It was neither a spatial nor a temporal thing; it existed greater than such minor definitions, in a kind of dimension other than whatever he had known – at right angles, as it were, to his universe. It was an encompassing quality vaguely like a sphere, a tremendous and significant something.

It was nonphysical, yet tangible to his present perception. Without vision there was no colour, yet there was

321

psychic colour. The thing spanned the universe in its fashion, grandly turning, currents within it causing it to shift aspects even as he oriented on it.

Slowly he recognized it. This was a composite of human souls. This was Nirvana, by whatever designation.

So it was true. There was an afterlife.

Rondl found himself being drawn into the mass. This seemed to be where he belonged. Yet there was something missing –

Abruptly he reacted, flinging himself out and away, rejecting this resting-place. He searched for a different something. Through the continuums he went, orienting on –

He found it, with a convection of hope, a radiation of joy: another soul-mass, this one in the general spatial/temporal form of a torus. Its currents evoked its lovely viscosity.

Rondl! Rondl! You found us!

It was the aura of Cirl, jumping toward him, welcoming him – formless, yet recognizable, because she was herself.

Now at last he believed. He knew it was all true, all of what he had taken as mythology. Human Nirvana was real, for those who chose it; the aural afterlife of other species was similarly valid; and the Viscous Circle of the Bands was exactly as represented. They really did have an afterlife, or rather a larger existence, of which the individual life was only a fragment, no more than a planet of the universe – a single aspect amid the infinite variety of the totality.

Cirl had held herself discrete for him, not yet joining the encompassing mass, and now they were together. She had forgiven him his Monster blemishes and trusted in his perfectability. She had waited because she loved him – and he loved her.

Together they floated toward the joy of the ultimate mergence, the unity of the Viscous Circle.

Epilogue

As Rondl had seen, the ploy was effective; the Monsters departed System Band. The unique Band culture survived. Rondl and Cirl themselves merged into the ultimate viscosity of the Viscous Circle, sharing their wealths of experience with all the other auras of this group, giving it a better awareness of the nature of alien creatures. In time – though the Circle was essentially timeless – parts of the aura substance that had been theirs were infused into newly conceived Bands, continuing the natural cycle; and these new Bands, though remaining true to the pacifism of their kind, did have a slightly improved tolerance for the nature of Monsters. Future incursions by other sapients into Band space would be handled more realistically, with fewer automatic disbandings. The Bands did finally petition for Galactic recognition as a Sphere, so that future intrusions into their space were less likely. So the fate of Rondl and Cirl was as satisfactory as exists in these continuums.

The fate of the Monsters called Solarians was not as sanguine. Much energy had been expended in the futile quest for the priceless technology of an Ancient Site, and the government of Sphere Sol was now deeply in debt. As a result, the Solarians running the Sphere were at a disadvantage, and political and economic power shifted more rapidly to the Solarian/Polarian combine of Planet Outworld in System Etamin. Within a century Etamin was the dominant force within this Sphere, and the discredited authorities who had sponsored the raid on System Band no longer had power. In this incidental way, the Band episode helped shape the development of an empire.

However, it was not an event that the Solarians cared to dignify in their history texts, and its significance was not widely appreciated among them until many centuries had elapsed and new standards of scholarship obtained. The names Ronald and Tanya did not become legend, and the names Rondl, Tangt, and Cirl were unknown.

Ronald's widow, Helen, in due course bore a son. She undertook a new term marriage, which was reputed to be more satisfactory than her first. The boy grew up to be involved in liaison work with non-Solarian sapient species and had a good reputation for competence, integrity, and empathy.

Tanya had brief notoriety for breaking the scandal of Ronald's betrayal, but when the Ancient Site turned out to be useless, she became anonymous. She retained an interest in the culture of the Bands and retired from Transfer service to labour on the Bands' behalf, eventually succeeding in getting their petition recognized, qualifying them as a legal Sphere.

The Polarian chaplain, Smly, returned to his native System of Etamin and counselled many of the important creatures whose influence was increasing. They called him 'Smelly', in the fashion of Monsters, and said there was a good odour to his advice. Perhaps he influenced the decision to treat the Bands more graciously.

Thus the Bands survived, despite their mythology. Therefore the Viscous Circle survived, too, and this was perhaps the most important and least appreciated thing of all.

Author's Note

On May 8, 1980, I started writing the first draft of *Viscous Circle*. I had sold it the year before on the basis of a summary, and now it was time to get to it. I was running on a tight schedule, because my agent had got me contracts for five novels, more or less on top of each other; I had completed three and this was the fourth. Fortunately I am one of the most disciplined writers extant; I allow nothing to interfere with my work.

Well, almost nothing. I have two little girls and one big girl – daughters and wife – and a number of animals and neighbours and fans and similar ilk, and all of them seem to have better things for me to do than write my novels. So I try to isolate myself in my study, which is a twelve- by twenty-four-foot wooden cabin two hundred feet from the house, in the pasture with the horses and the squirrels. It has no electricity, and in the summer afternoons, even with all windows open, the temperature rises to 102°F. My glasses slide off my sweaty nose and I leave sweat-prints on my manuscript, but I do work. The ilk let me have about six working hours a day, seven days a week. I do sneak in reading at odd moments, such as while eating and watching TV and waiting in lines; and I have learned to write novels on a clipboard in pencil anywhere, such as when riding in a car, visiting relatives, babysitting horses, waiting for the dentist to proceed with his next torture, and similar occasions of otherwise wasted time.

You see, I am strange: I actually like to write. Most writers prefer to make money, have best-sellers, win awards, and get drunk. They don't really enjoy the lonely chore of writing, and are glad of any opportunity to escape from it. I, in contrast, escape *to* writing, for my personal life is hopelessly pedestrian. I have never been drunk or drugged in my life, and I have never been to a science fiction convention, where I understand the action is. I have been told that stories circulate about what an ogre I have made of myself at such conventions; would it were true, for I do like ogres, but apart from the fiction of my attendance, the fact is I get along personally with everyone I meet, even those who aren't ogres. I realize this confession could have an adverse effect on the success of my novels, especially among ogres. Anyway, once I get into the safety of my study, nothing interferes with the progress of a novel like *Viscous Circle*.

Except . . . I happen to be a puzzle freak. Intellectual and practical puzzles fascinate me, as well as convolutions of numbers and words, as may be apparent in my novels. We had recently obtained a puzzle-cube, with nice squares of colour on each side: the trick is to scramble the 54 colour-squares by rotating the axes this way and that, then put them back together so that each face of the cube is a single colour. Easy – hah! The manufacturer claims there are three billion combinations. That confounded cube tied me up for two hours, interrupting the novel, so that all I wrote on May 8 was 600 words on *Viscous* and 450 on another novel, *Juxtaposition*. It was not a phenomenally efficient writing day, and those who may have felt doubts about my claim to being well disciplined may now be permitted a knowing smirk. But it does take time for the mind to orient and the subject to properly coalesce. The first day of *anything* is not efficient, except perhaps for World War Three.

The next day, May 9, started even worse. It was a cloudy, rainy morning, so I got wet as I ran our dogs on the leashes on the half-mile path we use. The TV radar showed no precipitation at our location, which is a typical example of the weather bureau's fiction. Then I fed our horses, and found that Blue, my favourite, who is featured on the cover of another novel of mine, was not eating well. Twenty-two years is old for a horse; in fact the average horse dies around that age in these parts, so I began to get that uncomfortable feeling that is best not bruited about. Then I went down to feed our neighbour's horses – we have this deal whereby we may ride one of them if we feed him – and the neighbour's cat had had kittens recently and was desperate for food, so I fed her too. I don't like cats, but cats like me. I am a vegetarian, because I don't like to have animals suffer or die in untimely fashion, so I am an easy touch even for cats, and they know it. So I gave her what there was: a handful of dog food. But the neighbour's dogs would not permit any cat to get a mouthful – which was one reason this cat was hungry – so I had to put the food on the feedshed roof, shoo away the predatory chickens – everyone is hungry at seven in the morning! – and lift the cat up to it. She was so eager to get at the food that she scrambled from my hand, scratching me on the left wrist in the process. Then, finding the food wet from the rain, she jumped down, intending to sneak into the feedshed for something dry. I'd been that route before; once the animals get into the feedshed, it's a federal case to get them out again, and my neighbour would hardly be pleased if I let his animals clean out his week's supply of feed in an hour. So I sent the cat off. I had precious little thanks for my attempted kindness, which of course is one reason I don't like cats. My scratch was stinging, at the base of my hand near the wrist. But after the forty minutes the morning chores take me, I finally got to settle down to make and eat my own breakfast, which got disrupted by assorted thises and thats, delaying the start of my working day.

Naturally something really bad was developing; the omens were plain enough. I don't believe in omens, which is why they plague me. Something sure enough did happen, and it made national headlines – but it was not right at our place, and I must take a moment to make the context plain. This is the sort of task writers are supposed to do, after all. To wit:

I used to live in the Tampa Bay region of Florida, not far from the famed Skyway Bridge. This bridge, according to the covenant under which it was financed, was to be paid off by tolls, then not refinanced. Once paid for, it was destined to be forever free. It did so well that the tolls were reduced, and still the bridge paid off ahead of schedule and was in imminent danger of achieving that reprieve. But the local politicians, typical of their breed, violated the covenant and refinanced it to build a second span. The Skyway was just too good a money-maker to let go of. Now, instead of one free bridge, there were two toll bridges.

Well, God got them for that. On this particular morning the storm was most intense around the bridge, and the wind blew a freighter into a support-pylon and knocked it out. The guilty new span of the Skyway Bridge came tumbling down. Cars plunged merrily into the bay, as did a bus, and a section of the roadway landed on the deck of the ship along with a pickup truck. It was said to be the worst bridge disaster in the history of America. So it seemed that my cat-scratch was merely a fringe effect of the Act of God that punished the machination of the unfreed Skyway span, eighty miles to the south, on May 9, 1980. What kind of a scratch would I have got had I not moved out of the centre of that vortex? It gets scary, especially for someone who does not believe in Acts of God. Nevertheless, in the afternoon I did buckle down and write a thousand words of *Viscous*.

So it went. On the tenth I wrote 1200 words, and next day 1300, nudging gradually up to my normal stint of 2000 words per day. My motor had finally warmed up, and no Act of God had touched me, I thought in my innocence.

But this novel was not moving as well as it should; I was satisfied with neither the quantity nor the quality. Was I losing my touch? Writing is never a chore for me; could something be the matter?

Well, let's consider the puzzle from another angle. One reason I do not suffer from the dread ailment Writer's Block is my health. I am something of a physical fitness freak and health-diet nut. It pays; I am perhaps the healthiest middle-aged diabetic bad-kneed vegetarian science fiction writer in the world. At this time I was routinely doing 19 or 20 chins on my study rafter. I was doing Japanese pushups too, and had recently set my personal record of 50, nonpause. But my main pride was running.

In the city, dogs and cars and ignorant neighbours had prevented me from distance-jogging, but in the forest I measured a one-mile loop cross-country and in the course of three years had built up to a regular 2·5-mile run that I did three times a week. This summer I had cracked the eight-minute-per-mile barrier. That is, I consistently ran the distance in 20 minutes or less. Now I know that Olympic runners break the four-minute mile, and that marathoners maintain the five-minute mile indefinitely, and a healthy young man can do a mile in six minutes. But for a 45-year-old science fiction writer, running at noon through loose sand, over tree roots, uphill and down, keeping a wary eye out for snakes and wild dogs while he swats at stinging deerflies and avoids sandspurs, eight minute miles are just fine. It is the same velocity certain American presidents have been known to run, after all. It's hard work; I weighed myself before and after, and discovered that I sweated off an even two pounds per run. And I was still gaining. First run in June, with the outdoor temperature 90 degrees, I completed the course in 17:37, just seven seconds over a seven-minute-per-mile average. Few middle-aged, diabetic, etc. people could match that, I think. I was at my very peak of physical fitness, and proud of it.

Ah, but has it not been said that pride goeth before a fall? Believe it! Partly at the behest of my worrying wife, who feared I would keel over and die from heatstroke – she tends to concern herself with such nonessentials – I extended my run to three full miles and slowed the pace, making the workout easier. But instead the runs became more difficult, even when the heat was down on cloudy days. I maintained my eight-minute miles, but raggedly. Yet I was not sick. Well, I had a little sore on my left wrist that was sensitive to the touch, but that was probably an embedded splinter. Then my left arm, near the inside shoulder, began to hurt as if I had pulled a small muscle – but the twinge didn't go away. My chins became awkward, and my pushups sent a streak of pain through my arm. But these bruises happen.

Then the fever began. Now, I am wary of fevers. I take vitamin C to stop colds, and it works. Once upon a time my nose dripped into my typewriter, which was annoying – one can imagine the grumbling editor shaking out a damp page of manuscript – but that doesn't happen any more. One gram of C per hour stops the faucet, and after a while the cold gives up in disgust and departs, no doubt seeking some idiot who doesn't believe in C. But, for me, C does nothing for a fever – and this one shot up to 102°F. So I stopped the exercises, which was a relief at this stage, and saw my doctor. Turned out to be a lymph infection, travelling down my arm from that wrist-lump to my armpit, aggravating the lymph nodes along the way. Nothing serious. Some pills and rest, and in a week I was ready to resume typing. For by this time, mid-July, I had completed my plodding first pencilled draft of *Viscous* and was well into the typed second draft, proceeding more or less on schedule.

My fever dropped, and I resumed exercises, at a

cautious half-level – for one day. My fever shot up again. The lump in my left armpit swelled to what seemed like half-tennis-ball size (though my fevered imagination probably exaggerated it), and I could hardly use that arm at all. At night I was unable to turn over, and changing clothing was pain. The doctor gave me much more powerful pills, costing seventy-five cents each, and I had to take eight a day. No effect; the fever kept coming, rising as high as 101 degrees, and the swelling persisted. So he upped the ante, prescribing one-dollar pills. Nothing worked. My family had to take over the chores I had done, while I slept and fevered.

Finally, in desperation, the doctor put me in the hospital. For three days I lay with an IV hooked to my left hand, dripping sugarwater and penicillin (it burns!) and garamycin into my throbbing vein, while nurses measured my every fluctuation of fever, appetite, and drop of urine. Still no effect; my fever came and went at will, mocking the entire modern medical establishment, and my swelling remained adamant.

I had, of course, a science fiction illness, undiagnosable, odd; and commonplace medications like dollar pills and antibiotic fluids can hardly be expected to work on that. Now if they'd had something futuristic, like Venusian orb-grackle juice . . .

Actually the hospital was not a bad place. They allowed my children to visit me, and found me a roommate with a vaguely similar ailment – his was blood poisoning from a thorn – and the personnel were competent and friendly. They did not wake me up to give me a sleeping pill. I passed out copies of my novels. My vegetarian and low-sugar diet brought the head dietician to my bedside, so that I was able to explain all my foibles: no coffee, tea, cola, sweets, etc. I'm a man of few vices; I don't smoke or otherwise debilitate myself, which seemed to surprise some personnel. They X-rayed me, EKG'd me, blood-pressured me, took blood samples (ouch!) for tissue cultures to find the bug in my system: nothing. I was completely healthy, except that my system was waging a raging battle with an invisible enemy. There was simply no handle on this illness.

I think the doctor's hair was thinning: he was tugging out handfuls in frustration? He wasn't used to dealing with science-fiction illnesses. 'Do you have cats?' he asked irrelevantly, betraying how greatly his mind had deteriorated out of strain. I replied gently that we had two horses, five dogs, twelve chickens, two children, and no cats. 'Then you couldn't have been scratched by a cat,' he grumbled.

Oh? As it happened, two and a half months ago when God punished the Skyway Bridge . . .

And so the diagnosis was reached at last: I had contracted cat scratch disease, normally a rare childhood malady. It is unresponsive to medication, shows no bacteria in cultures, and simply has to run its ornery month-long course. It's not too serious, it just takes time – a bit like a writer working on a novel, or a woman shopping for a hat.

So here I was: my exercise programme destroyed at its height, my once-proud muscles melting into glop, my novel halted dead in space – for the first time in forty novels, I was destined to be late on a contract deadline – medical bills piling on (I carry no medical insurance – this is not lack of foresight so much as ire over the time they tried to rider me for mental disease), my wife wearing down to a frazzle – all because I fed one hungry cat on the morning an Act of God was scheduled.

And do you want to know what happened to that cat? That cat died. No, I know you're thinking of Goldsmith's poem *An Elegy On the Death of a Mad Dog*, wherein the dog bit the saintly man and the dog died. It wasn't like that. My blood may be potent, but not poisonous. What happened was the cat got into an altercation with a larger cat and got chomped and gave up its ninth life. (Then again: you don't suppose that my blood *could* have made that cat crazy enough to pick that fight?)

The hospital let me go, still with my fever and swelling and mad science-fiction brain; there was nothing they could do for me. Freed of all this attention and medication, I began to improve. I finally turned the corner in early August, on my forty-sixth birthday: my month-long fever stayed down. But the swelling persisted, so a few days later the doctor stuck a brute needle into it and drew out a vial of mudwater. Viscous ugh, of course. He called this 'aspiration' – a fancy term for a hellishly painful process. But it reduced the swelling to half-golf-ball size and freed my arm somewhat, and my armpit began to reappear. A few days later the puncture started leaking chocolate syrup on to my T-shirt: messy, but a relief, since it meant I would not have to suffer that dread needle again. Things continued to improve. In late August I resumed cautious exercise, my performance down to roughly a third what it had been, but improving rapidly.

My writing never came to a complete standstill, for I am, as claimed, a disciplined cuss. I did a great deal of research reading on World War Two, and in the hospital started writing the first chapters of *Volk*, my projected WWII novel. Thus I actually got a head start on a new project, thanks to my pencil-and-clipboard technique. Now I resumed typing on a limited basis, though it did somewhat aggravate the swelling. I completed the second draft of the novel in the middle of August, typing in the mornings and resting, often sleeping, in the hot afternoon. I also typed second draft on my WWII chapters, since I had them on hand. Then I typed the submission draft on *Volk*, extending my limits on the fifty-page small project before tackling the three-hundred-fifty-page big one, just in case. All seemed well. Gradually I worked back up to a full schedule, typing twenty or more pages a day, and completed the submission draft of *Viscous Circle* on September 20, just two days after the doctor cleared me as cured.

So the novel was done almost entirely in the gradual course of the illness. If it seems sick, blame it on that cat. My clean living, wholesome diet, avoidance of vices, and vigorous exercise, a supposedly sure formula for health, did not preserve me from this experience. Perhaps I will never know the meaning of it, if there is one. But still there lurks the hope that, in some devious way, this ordeal does have meaning. For a while there was one hope: when they drew the sludge out of my swelling and made a culture to grow some of the whatevers that cause this mysterious disease, I thought my case might be the first to reveal the agent of that disease. If so, it would be a significant medical breakthrough, a mystery of decades solved, sparing others a good deal of misery. But no; my cultures came up as sterile as space samples, as is typical for this disease. That medical breakthrough awaits some other cat.

Maybe this narration will help some reader who would otherwise suffer an unknown malady, the hint 'cat scratch' putting his doctor on the track. Remember, this particular illness always gets better on its own. It is not nearly as serious as it seems.

When you're sick it's a great time to do research, because you can read in bed. During this period I read Frankl's *Man's Search for Meaning* as part of my research for the WWII project. The thesis of this book is that man truly wants to live a life that is meaningful. Certainly he has strong drives to protect, feed, and reproduce himself, and whole philosophies of psychology have been constructed on the assumption that one or the other of these drives is paramount. But all other animals act according to these same drives, too often with greater enthusiasm and success than man. If man is really the highest of the animals, it is not because of his various physical appetites. Man's quest for meaning may be his truly distinguishing mark. This makes sense to me, and that notion is reflected in *Viscous Circle*.

What, then, of my own quest for meaning? I have plumbed the depths of this illness in tedious detail and found no meaning therein. It cost me a thousand dollars in medical expenses, and perhaps more than that in lost time. I'd hate to have it count for nothing. Yet this does happen to be, coincidentally, a time of transition in my career, and this is the reason for this long Author's Note. Perhaps I can squeeze out a certain amount of Significance after all.

I have written a lot of science fiction, and it has been well received. I am becoming one of the most successful of contemporary genre writers. I get fan letters at the rate of about one a week, and I answer them. Many people seem to enjoy my science fiction and fantasy, and that's nice. I love this genre; it gave me reason to live when I was in doubt, long ago, whether life was worthwhile, and it has been good to me since. But *Viscous Circle* was difficult when it should have been easy, and may lack that spark of wonder that is the essence of this type of writing. Maybe my sickness spoiled my objectivity – but maybe also it cost me some of the necessary magic. I never want to be a hack writer, turning out adventure merely for the money. Perhaps I need some sort of break, to sort it out.

I'm not swearing off science fiction, but I expect to do less of it for a while. This has nothing to do with disenchantment with the field: the field is strong. It's not money either; I am well paid for this writing. It is no onus against this particular publisher, who has the science fiction option on Anthony; Avon has been consistently kind to me, even while other publishers were blacklisting me, and I am grateful. I just don't know exactly where to find meaning in writing.

I'll be trying fantasy and horror and World War Two and general mainstream writing, and anything else that takes my fancy, exploring my parameters, to discover where my true direction lies. I'm not young any more; I don't have forever to experiment. Illness has heightened my awareness of that, once again bringing home to me my own mortality, and that may have been the purpose of this particular Act of God. Perhaps I'll find that there is nothing better for me beyond this genre. Certainly science fiction was my first true love, and that passion will never be forgotten.

But I hope my horizons do expand, and that my readers will approve. Meanwhile, I'm having my study electrified at last, so that I can run a fan on those hot summer afternoons and keep my glasses on my nose. Awareness of mortality tends to enhance the value of the minor creature comforts, such as a breath of breeze at a hundred degrees.